MIKE EVANS

THE
CANDIDATE

Published by TimeWorthy Books
P. O. Box 30000
Phoenix, AZ 85046

The Candidate

Copyright 2012 by TimeWorthy Books
P. O. Box 30000
Phoenix, AZ 85046

Design: Lookout Design, Inc.

USA: 978-0-935199-47-5
Canada: 978-0-935199-51-2
Hardcover: 978-0-935199-46-8

This book is dedicated to

my mentor and Israel's sixth prime minister,

Menachem Begin,

to whom I owe a deep debt of gratitude.

He was, in my opinion,

Israel's greatest prime minister.

He endorsed my first book,

and when I warned him against it,

he laughed and said, "I am a short prime minister.

If they criticize me, I will stand on the newspapers

and be much taller. Besides, today's news

is just a wrapper for tomorrow's fish."

Menachem Begin was my hero then and still is today.

Over thirty years ago, he inspired me

to build a bridge based on mutual respect between

Christians and Jews—a bridge that now

has tens of millions of supporters—a bridge of love.

CAST OF CHARACTERS

ESTHER ROSENBERG— a Jewish attorney in Washington, D.C. Her husband, Ephraim, worked for Mossad, Israel's primary intelligence agency. He was killed by a car bomb while on assignment in Jerusalem. Esther is now dating Paul Bryson, whom she met at a fund-raiser for the Ben-Gurion Institute. She works as a consultant to Mossad.

PAUL BRYSON— a former congressman from Texas who now works as a consultant. His wife, Linda, was killed in the September 11 attack on the Pentagon. While in Congress he became interested in issues affecting Israel. He is a Christian and deeply committed to his relationship with the Lord. His attraction to Esther has caused him to grapple with many of the things he knows and believes about Jesus and salvation.

REUBEN BRODY— Esther's contact within the Israeli intelligence community.

LISTON COOK— a former congressman from Chicago and candidate for the Republican nomination for president of the United States. As the story begins, he trails all candidates in the race.

CHRISTOPHER WILSON— Democratic candidate for the presidential nomination.

PHILIP LIVINGSTON— Cook's chief of staff.

DAVID MCNEIL— governor of Virginia and leading candidate for the Republican nomination for president of the United States.

CARTER HEWES— Chief of staff for David McNeil.

HENRY CALDWELL— wealthy Republican Party operative and McNeil's mentor.

TAYLOR RUTLEDGE— FBI agent assigned to investigate a break-in at Liston Cook's campaign headquarters.

BRIAN CULPEPPER— a private investigator hired by Liston Cook to investigate the break-in at his office.

OREN COHEN— director of Mossad's operations center at Beersheba, Israel.

THE ORDER OF MALTA— originally formed to protect crusaders traveling to the Holy Land during the Middle Ages. Later focused on eliminating a supposed worldwide Jewish conspiracy. Although many of its members are ordained clergymen, the Order is a landless sovereignty and is not directly accountable to any ecclesiastical organization other than itself. Known simply as the Order.

SIERRA RESOURCES— major defense services contractor. Engaged in special operations, assassinations, renditions, and aggressive interrogation. Secretly owned by the Order.

DR. WALCOTT— a physician who works for Sierra Resources, where he specializes in the use of bio-implant technology and personality modification for warfare applications.

IGNACIO SPOLETO— Grand Master of the Order of Malta.

CARMINE RUSSO— at the beginning of the story, assistant to Spoleto.

JAVIER ROLDAN— an assassin, formerly of Spain.

PHILIPPE JOBERT— an assassin living in Washington, D.C.

FATHER PENALTA— a priest from the Order of Malta. As the story begins, he has traveled to Zurich to meet church authorities.

ANGELO BARBERINI— Penalta's assistant.

PREFACE

At its core, *The Protocols of the Learned Elders of Zion* purports to document a late nineteenth-century meeting at which Jewish leaders discuss their goal of global Jewish hegemony. According to the book, Jews plan to accomplish that goal by subverting the morals of Gentiles, by gaining worldwide control of the media, and by dominating the global economy. It is a classic case of inventing a lie so huge, so satanic, and so twisted that in time it becomes accepted as fact.

Originally written in Paris, and later altered and published in Russia in 1903, it contains numerous elements typical of what is known in literature as a "false document"—a document that is deliberately written to fool the reader into believing that what is written is truthful and accurate even though, in actuality, it is not. Numerous scholars have proven it to be fictional in its entirety, yet the book has been translated into multiple languages, distributed around the world, and remains in print today.

As incredible as it may sound, American automaker Henry Ford accepted it as truth and in the 1920s funded the printing of half a million copies for distribution. Adolf Hitler was a major proponent of the work and ordered that it be studied, as if factual, in German classrooms following the Nazis' rise to power in 1933. To this very day, Muslim students are taught from this writing as though it were the truth. And these are just a few of the many who have joined together over more than a century to subscribe to and pass down the twisted concepts contained in *The Protocols of the Learned Elders of Zion*.

CHAPTER 1
ZURICH, SWITZERLAND

FATHER PENALTA SHIFTED POSITIONS in the chair and glanced around the room. Before him was a heavy oak desk, the top of it clean and spotless. A lamp sat to the left. Its amber glow sent shadows dancing across smooth paneled walls that had been burnished to a deep, rich luster from centuries of meticulous care. Beneath Penalta's feet lay a stone floor, worn smooth by the footsteps of faithful penitents. Saint Anton's Cathedral, the oldest Catholic parish in Zurich, had been around since before Charlemagne, dispensing grace and mercy to the contrite committed to its care. Seeing it now, with its paneled walls and stone floor, reminded Penalta of the lives that had been entrusted to him and the secrets he'd come to betray.

As a young man, Penalta had entered the priesthood from his home parish in Formia, a city of modest size on the western coast of the Italian peninsula, halfway between Napoli and Rome. After seminary, he was assigned to a church in Tivoli. The following year, he petitioned for admission as a novitiate in the Order of the Knights of Malta.

A blend of political influence, military might, and ecclesiastical dogma, the Order had been formed in the Middle Ages to provide security for Christians making the pilgrimage from Europe to the Holy Land. With the help of Spain, its members fought valiantly but even they could not stem the tide of history. As the region came under Islamic control, the Order retreated, first to Malta, then to the island of Rhodes. Yet, though cloistered behind the walls of Knights Castle, change found its way inside. Slowly, spiritual discipline gave way to political expression and in a perversion only pride and power could create, the Order turned from defending the faithful to the all-consuming task of extracting revenge on the Jewish race for the death of Christ. It was that unholy purpose that brought Father Penalta to Zurich and the meeting at Saint Anton's Cathedral.

Seated across from Penalta behind the oak desk was Serafino Rampolla. As secretary to the Congregation for the Doctrine of the Faith, Rampolla was the first stop for all accusations of heresy, the gatekeeper for all challenges to the doctrinal propriety of the religious orders subject to the Pope's authority and jurisdiction. He flipped through the handful of documents that lay before him and looked over at Penalta. "You have more?"

"Yes," Penalta nodded. "Much more."

Penalta had come there that day to present evidence that the Order of Malta no longer conformed to the tenets of the Christian faith— that its practices had moved beyond the bounds of orthodoxy, and that it operated for no purpose other than the attainment of its own glory. In short, it had succumbed to heresy. It was a bold statement, even for one with the reputation and experience of Father Penalta, urging the Pope to exercise his authority over the Order and bring its operations to an end. In support of his claims he spent the afternoon with Rampolla outlining the Order's most grievous breach, the formation of Sierra Resources and the nature of its unholy agenda.

An American corporation, Sierra Resources had been formed for the sole purpose of conducting business with the United States military and intelligence community. Using the Order's vast resources and its far-flung network of relationships, Sierra won initial contracts to provide guards for military and intelligence detention facilities operated by the CIA at locations around the world. Later, the company expanded to the rendition of detainees, seizing and transporting suspected terrorists to secret facilities in countries where lax criminal justice systems incorporated torture as standard procedure. When the White House finally cracked down on the use of aggressive interrogation techniques, Sierra Resources took over that role, establishing its own facilities in remote areas of central Africa and northern Mexico, where it conducted prisoner evaluations without the limitations placed on government agencies. That program proved successful, yielding information that curtailed attacks by insurgents in Iraq, put the Taliban on the run in Afghanistan, and revealed previously unknown threats in Yemen, Bahrain, and Syria.

As Sierra's success continued, it expanded into special operations and experimental warfare employing mind-altering psychological techniques. At first designed to assist in the recovery of soldiers suffering from stress disorder, the program quickly shifted to focus on capability enhancement. Its most recent efforts included a plan to retrain captured terrorists using implants and electronic chips, then send them back to infiltrate their own terrorist cells. It was an incredible tale, one Penalta was sure would be met with skepticism, but he had come to the conclusion there was no other way, especially now, after all that had happened in—

Rampolla cleared his throat. "And you are certain the additional documents you have will verify these accusations?"

"Yes," Penalta nodded. "I am certain."

"It seems a little far-fetched." Rampolla laid the documents on the desk and leaned back in his chair. "A religious order in the defense contracting business. Interrogating prisoners. Implanting terrorists with computer chips." His forehead wrinkled in a troubled frown. "Controlling their minds and sending them back to their own people."

"I know." Penalta nodded in agreement. "It is far beyond what one would expect, which is why I am here."

"You think the Order is aware of this?"

"Aware of Sierra Resources?"

"Aware of what the company is doing."

"It was their idea," Penalta replied. "It is part of their plan." He leaned forward, his hands resting on the edge of the desk. "Their ultimate plan is to use these programs to gain control of an American president."

Rampolla struggled to maintain his composure. "An American president?"

"Why do you find that so hard to believe?"

"We are talking about a religious order."

"A military order. One whose sovereign is recognized by the nations of the world."

"And why would they want to control an American president?"

"To exterminate the Jews in America and remake the American government into an entity of the Order."

"Really?" Rampolla's eyes darted away. He ran his hand over his chin to hide the amused smile that turned up the corners of his mouth.

Penalta knew he had lost the moment, but he'd come too far to stop now. Instead of retreating, he plunged headlong into an explanation. "They already have implemented enough changes in American law to allow this to happen. Their Patriot Act and newly enacted state immigration laws have given their government unprecedented power and authority at every level. Sierra Resources will provide them with a private army accountable to no one. All they need is a president who is willing and able to put the Order's plan in motion."

Rampolla turned back to face Penalta once more. "But a candidate. Really." He tossed his hand aside in a dismissive gesture. "That would require someone willing ... gullible. Not even the Americans are that oblivious."

"The Order has already found its candidate and he is well on his way to gaining office. That is why I decided to come to you."

"And who might this candidate be?"

"David McNeil. Governor of Virginia and the Republican front-runner in the current presidential election."

"Well ... I don't know. This matter is far beyond the scope of my purview. And well beyond the authority of our office."

"I have documents to prove what I am saying."

"What sort of documents?"

"Bank statements. Ledgers. Correspondence."

"That can directly link the Order to Sierra Resources?"

"Oh my, yes," Penalta sighed. "That's what I have been telling you. The Order created Sierra. The Order funds Sierra. The Order controls Sierra. The Order owns Sierra Resources."

"You know this for a fact?"

"I was there when we voted to do it."

"You voted for it?"

"That is beside the point. And the documents go further."

"Further? How much further?"

"There were political contributions from the Order, through Sierra Resources, to several political action committees. Those committees in turn transferred the money to Governor McNeil's campaign accounts. All of which is contrary to the laws of the United States."

Rampolla's face turned serious and he glanced again at the documents on his desk. After a moment, he scooted back his chair and stood. "Well," he said, smiling politely. "I will need time to look over what you have presented." He came from behind the desk. By then, Father Penalta was standing and Rampolla guided him toward the door. "If you will send me those additional documents, I will look at them, as well. But this will take some time."

Penalta glanced up. "You understand the sensitive nature of this, do you not?"

"Certainly." Rampolla reached around Penalta and opened the door. "We shall treat our discussion today as confessional in nature."

"Good," Penalta sighed. He stepped from the office to the hallway. "I would not want—"

"I will be in touch," Rampolla interrupted. He stepped back, moving inside the office, and closed the door without waiting for a reply.

As the door closed behind him, Penalta turned away and started across the hall. Seated along the wall was his assistant, Angelo Barberini. He'd been waiting since they'd arrived more than three hours earlier.

Like Penalta, Barberini came to the Order as a novitiate early in his career as a priest. Italian by birth, Barberini was from Cagliari, Sardinia. He became a candidate for ordination during high school but, unlike others in the Order, he took his ordination vows in the Greek Orthodox Church and came to the Order upon the recommendation of the abbot at Saint Catherine's Monastery on Mount Sinai. Though an Italian citizen by birth, his membership in the Greek Church touched deep-seated prejudices that reached back almost as far in the life of the Order as its hatred of the Jews.

Barberini rose from his chair as Penalta approached. "Did all go well?"

Penalta brushed aside the question with a wave of his hand. "Come," he grumbled and started down the hall. "We have wasted too much time here already."

"Did he not listen?"

"Whether he listened is only important if he acts."

"Surely he will act on what you have shown him."

"There are powerful people who do not want us to succeed."

"Yes. I understand, but surely Rampolla is not one of them."

"One can only hope."

On the sidewalk outside, Barberini hailed a taxi. They climbed in back and rode in silence for several blocks. Finally Penalta spoke. "Powerful men in the Church secretly want the Order to succeed in eliminating the Jews."

"You are worried he is one of them?"

"Rampolla is not a powerful man."

"But he can help us."

"If he will. Every man holds in his hands the power to do good or evil." Penalta gave a heavy sigh. "Perhaps we should have taken this to someone else."

Twenty minutes later they arrived at an apartment building in Wiedikon, a neighborhood along the western edge of the city. As the taxi came to a stop, Barberini reached for the door handle. "Perhaps we should eat dinner out tonight, before we retire for the evening. It will do you good to take a break."

"No," Penalta said, shaking his head. "There is no time for that." He stepped from the car to the curb. "Go to the café on the corner and get something for us to eat. Bring it back to the apartment." He turned toward the entrance to the building. "We have work to do."

CHAPTER 2
ZURICH, SWITZERLAND

ACROSS THE STREET from the apartment building, Philippe Jobert sat behind the steering wheel of an Audi sedan. Dressed in gray slacks and a white shirt, he wore a brown leather jacket and dark sunglasses with a leather tam pulled low over his brow. He held a copy of the latest edition of *Blick*, one of Switzerland's most popular daily tabloids. He slowly leafed through the pages as he glanced out the window. His eyes followed Penalta as he came from the taxi and moved inside the building. As Penalta disappeared beyond the door, Jobert looked up the street and focused on Barberini, who was just then reaching the corner. When Barberini made the turn and vanished from sight, Jobert laid aside the newspaper and opened the car door.

With the grace of a gentleman, he swung his legs from the seat and climbed from the car. He pushed the door shut, tugged his leather jacket in place over his waist, and stepped with quick but measured strides across the street. The door to the apartment building was closed, but as he approached the curb a young man appeared on the sidewalk. He entered a code on a touch pad near the doorframe and pulled open the door. Jobert caught the door before it closed and followed him inside.

Moving quickly up the steps, Jobert arrived at Penalta's apartment just as Penalta unlocked the door. Jobert approached from behind and slipped his hand over Penalta's mouth. Clamping it tightly in place, he muscled his way forward, shoving the old man through the doorway while making certain to avoid a commotion.

A short hallway led from the door past a tiny kitchen to a living room. Jobert used his foot to push the door closed behind them and guided Penalta up the hallway. With his hand pressed even tighter, he shoved Penalta against the wall, pinning him in place. Penalta squirmed and wiggled in an effort to twist free. When that proved futile, he reached out with his hands and clutched at Jobert's hair and eyes.

For his part, Jobert hardly seemed to notice as he reached with his free hand inside the pocket of his jacket. After a moment, he took out a syringe and, with a flick of his thumb, flipped the cover off the needle. With a single jab, he buried the needle in Penalta's thigh, moved his thumb over the plunger, and pressed it all the way down.

Penalta's eyes were wild with fright but Jobert paid them no attention. He held Penalta tightly in place as the old man's flailing arms grew weak. Finally, his eyes rolled back in his head, his arms fell limp to his side, and he slumped forward. His weight rested against Jobert's shoulder.

Jobert eased the body to the floor and stood there, staring down at him, waiting to make certain he really was dead. When Penalta did not move, Jobert knelt beside him and pressed his fingertips against his neck to check for a pulse. Satisfied he was no longer alive, Jobert withdrew the syringe from Penalta's thigh, replaced the cap over the needle, and tucked the syringe inside the pocket of his jacket.

With little time to waste, Jobert hurried to the bedroom. A bed sat along the wall to the left. Beyond it was a small writing desk near a window. A laptop computer lay there next to a notepad and three pens. He moved behind the desk and opened its lone drawer. There he found a file folder stuffed with documents. A smile spread across his face as he thumbed through the contents. Assured that he had what he needed, he tucked the file beneath his arm, picked up the laptop, and started from the room.

CHAPTER 3
ISLAND OF RHODES

IGNACIO SPOLETO MADE HIS WAY down the main corridor of the Knights Castle. As he passed the doorway to the Hall of Saints, he glanced inside and caught a glimpse of the massive table that occupied the center of the room.

Located near the eastern tip of the island, the castle sat atop a hill that overlooked the sea on one side and the surrounding countryside on the other. It had been home to the Order of the Knights of Malta since they first occupied the island in 1309. Constructed of stone quarried from northern Greece, its walls were thicker than the length of a man's arm and had withstood the attacks of Arabs, pirates, Ottomans, and modern armies. Though the island had been ceded from nation to nation, the Order retained ownership of the Castle as it maintained its independence, becoming the world's only landless sovereignty.

Since the day they arrived there, the table in the Halls of Saints had been the site around which members of the historic Order had found the courage to press forward, sometimes against great odds. Now they were about to achieve the goal for which their predecessors gave their lives— the ability to impose their will upon the entire world— and he, Ignacio Spoleto, would be remembered as their leader when that day finally arrived.

Like most of the members, Spoleto had come to the Order following service in the parish priesthood and a stint at one of the church's missions to the needy. His introduction had come in India where he worked with refugees from Bangladesh at a mission near Kolkata. Under the tutelage of Giuseppe Cantarini, he learned the dark teachings of an unnamed sect, a loose confederation of priests that for centuries had gone undetected by church authorities. Dedicated to preserving the belief that the Jews were responsible for Christ's death, that secret alliance sought to bring the Jews to repentance, by force if necessary, and if they would not repent, then they must be destroyed. As part of his instruction, Cantarini gave Spoleto a copy of *The Protocols of the Learned Elders of Zion* and insisted that he commit long passages to memory.

Fabricated in 1897 as a Russian propaganda tool, *The Protocols* had been the crowning achievement of Sergei Nilus, a struggling writer from Moscow. Weaving a tale from myths and legends— that Jews used Christian blood to celebrate the Passover, offered human sacrifice, and sought global domination— unleashed a campaign of violence upon Jews that led to deaths at an alarming rate. Long after the Russian pogroms subsided, the book's influence spread the message of hate, finding a ready home in Hitler's Nazi Germany and later with the radical Muslims of the Middle East.

That message found a home in Spoleto, too. Day and night he meditated on teachings from the book and let them sink deep into his soul. With Cantarini's help he came to believe that many of the world's important institutions— banking, media, and entertainment— already were under the Jewish spell. Exposing and destroying that evil conspiracy became the chief aim of Spoleto's life, even if it meant eradicating the Jews entirely.

When he came to the Castle, Spoleto's superior intellect and decisive character set him on a meteoric rise to the Legislative Council, the supreme body that set policy for the Order. He was elected to the Military Vicariate from which, following the untimely death of Carlo Busca, he was elevated to the post of Grand Master and head of the Order. Rising to the

Order's highest position had been his lifelong dream, but now, with the reins of power firmly in his grasp, Spoleto found holding that position as elusive as it had been for Busca. *Things are always just beyond our reach. Always with something new to—*

The sound of hurried footsteps caught his attention. He turned to see his assistant, Carmine Russo, coming toward him. He waited for Russo to catch up, then turned to him with a smile. "We have news?"

"Yes," Russo answered confidently.

"Good news, I hope."

Russo took an iPhone from beneath his robe and read from the screen, "Message delivered. Package acquired."

"Good," Spoleto sighed. "And the documents?"

"He has them."

"Where is the laptop now?"

"On its way to us."

"We must have someone analyze it as soon as it arrives."

"Yes," Russo nodded. "Of course."

"I do not have to tell you what would have happened if those documents had been delivered."

"We have discussed it many times."

"Penalta was a traitor."

"A Judas," Russo agreed.

"He knew everything, and he was ready to sell us out to protect those stupid Jews."

"But not now."

"What about the Greek?"

"There is no news of him."

"I thought he was to get them both."

"Yes," Russo nodded. "He was."

"He has failed us."

"Perhaps he will make it right."

"Has he ever failed before?"

"Not that I know."

"The Greek is as important as Penalta. He could know everything."

"Do you think Penalta told him?"

"I think we should have observed our long-standing practice and never allowed Greeks to join the Order."

CHAPTER 4
ZURICH, SWITZERLAND

THREE BLOCKS AWAY, Barberini stood inside the Café Uetli while the wait staff gathered his order from the kitchen. To the right, through a window, he watched a group of diners seated at a table beneath the canopy along the sidewalk. Loud and boisterous, their voices filtered in from outside. On the street behind them, evening traffic crawled by as commuters made their way home, and in the steady stream of cars and trucks, a bus eased along. Its blue and white colors seemed bright and alive against the backdrop of suburban sprawl. Barberini loved the city. Life at the Castle deprived him of many things, and of all those things he'd forsaken, the bustle of city life was the thing he missed most. People. Voices. The blare of horns. Even the smell of diesel fumes. It all made his senses come alive with energy. Contrary to most in the Order, his brain seemed more focused, his mind more clear, in the midst of a crowd. Most days at the Castle, with its solitude and quiet, he found it difficult to stay awake.

In a few minutes, a waitress appeared with a sack. She smiled as she handed it to him. He stared at her, wanting to say something, but in the end he simply smiled in reply and turned toward the door. There was no time to engage in pleasant conversation. Penalta enjoyed eating and he liked his food hot, but he did not like to eat out. Which meant Barberini was always tramping out to a café at mealtime, then rushing back to the apartment, hoping to arrive before the food got cold. He stepped out to the sidewalk and hurried away.

Two blocks up the street, Barberini turned right and retraced his steps toward the apartment. Before long, the building came into view. He shifted the sack to his left hand and repeated the numbers for the entry code, making certain he had them correct. Two days before, he had forgotten the code and had to call Penalta on his cell phone. Penalta detested cell phones more than cafés. It was not a pleasant experience.

When he reached the door, Barberini entered the code on the keypad. The electric lock clicked. He pushed open the door, stepped inside, and started up the stairs. Moments later, he reached the apartment. With his free hand he took the key from his pocket, then unlocked the door and stepped inside. As he pushed the door closed behind him, he came to an abrupt halt.

Just beyond the entrance, Penalta lay motionless on the floor, his feet pointed toward the door, his head resting on the carpet. Barberini dropped the sack and knelt beside him. "Father," he whispered, but already he was certain Penalta was dead. He pressed his finger against Penalta's wrist and felt nothing. Then he tried the neck. When that proved fruitless, he leaned close, pressing his ear near Penalta's nose, but heard no sound of breathing.

For an instant, he thought of calling the police. Then he noticed a tiny mark on the leg of Penalta's trouser. He touched it with the tip of his finger and realized it was blood. All at once, fear stabbed his chest. His eyes darted around the room and came to scuff marks on the wall. They hadn't been there before. He was certain of it. He stood and ran his fingers over them. Images of a fight filled his mind, Penalta struggling against a nameless, faceless foe.

Barberini pushed the images aside, stepped over Penalta's body, and hurried toward the bedroom. From the doorway, his eyes fell on the bare desktop where the laptop had been. That it was gone told him all he needed to know. They had come for Penalta and for the secrets he bore, just as

Penalta had suggested many times before. They had killed him, hoping to seal inside his lifeless body the knowledge of their evil schemes. But he wouldn't let that happen. No one but Penalta would have the last word. Ornery, cantankerous Penalta would speak from the grave and condemn them all. He would see to that.

With only a moment's hesitation, Barberini stepped from the doorway and moved behind the desk. There he saw the open drawer and realized the file was missing. He grasped the drawer on either side and pulled it from the desk, then turned it upside down, dumping the contents on the floor. A flash drive was taped to the back. He pulled it loose, checked to make certain it was unharmed, and shoved it in his pocket.

Then he heard again Penalta's words as they rode from the cathedral earlier that afternoon. *Perhaps we should have taken this to someone else.*

"Perhaps we shall," Barberini mumbled in reply. "Perhaps we shall."

He crossed the room to the closet and took out a heavy coat. The musky scent of wool enshrouded him as he slipped it on. He shrugged it in place across his shoulders and started back toward the front door. When he reached the hallway by the kitchen he paused over Penalta's body. "I do not know if I shall succeed, Don Penalta. But I shall try." He buttoned the coat. "For both our sakes, I hope I find someone to listen." Then he eased open the door, stepped quietly into the hall, and hurried down the steps to the street.

CHAPTER 5
ZURICH, SWITZERLAND

ACROSS THE STREET from the apartment building, Rami Gadot, a Mossad agent, watched from a window on the third floor of a townhouse. Using a telephoto lens mounted to a camera, he followed Barberini through the apartment windows as he disappeared from the bedroom, crossed the living room, and entered the front hallway. As Barberini appeared in the windows, Gadot pressed the shutter button and held it down. The camera clicked in quick succession as it reeled off dozens of pictures, first in the bedroom and then in the living room. When Barberini crossed the room toward the hall, Gadot trained the camera on a window in the kitchen and waited to see Barberini move by. Seconds passed but still he did not appear.

"Come on," he whispered. "Where are you?"

Finally, Barberini's head appeared from the bottom of the frame, as if he'd bent over and only now stood up. Gadot snapped a series of photographs with Barberini in a solemn pose, hands folded at his waist, head bowed. From a distance, looking down the lens of the camera through the kitchen window, the sight of it seemed oddly out of place. Then Gadot saw Barberini's lips moving.

"I do believe he's praying," Gadot whispered to himself. "But what could he be praying for?"

After a moment, Barberini opened his eyes, made the sign of the cross on his chest, and stepped toward the door. In less than a minute, he emerged from the building and walked to the corner. He paused at the curb and glanced up and down the street, a searching look on his face. Before long, a taxi appeared. Barberini stepped from the sidewalk into the street and raised his hand to wave. The taxi came to a stop beside him and he got inside.

As the taxi drove away, Gadot slipped on his jacket, came from the townhouse, and calmly crossed the street. He paused to let a young couple move by on the sidewalk, then stepped to the doorway and entered the code on the keypad. When the lock clicked, he opened the door and made his way to the steps.

On the second floor, he found the door to Penalta's apartment was closed. Gadot gave the knob a twist but it was locked. He glanced around warily, checking to see if anyone was watching, then took a pick from his jacket and slipped it into the keyhole. With a delicate touch, he manipulated the tumblers and felt the familiar twitch as they moved aside. When the last one was in place, he twisted the knob and slipped inside.

A few feet beyond the door, Penalta's body lay facedown on the hall floor. Gadot snapped a picture of it and moved on. He had no need to check the condition of the body. He had followed Jobert for the last three days and had seen what happened earlier. Penalta had been marked for death since before he left the Castle.

At the kitchen doorway, he paused to take another photograph. The counter was clean, the sink dry. A kettle set on the stove with a teapot close by. Doubtless, the kitchen had been used sparingly. He took another picture, then moved to the living room.

A sofa sat along the far wall, with an overstuffed chair at a right angle next to it. Between them was a coffee table. Two magazines lay on top. Nothing seemed out of place. Gadot took three pictures, then moved on to the bedroom.

From the doorway, he looked inside. A bed sat neatly against the wall to the left. The spread, wrinkle free and smooth, was tucked tightly over the sheets. To the right, the closet door was closed. Beyond the bed was a desk. Behind it, a chair sat near a window that looked out on the street below. The end of a power cord rested precariously near the edge of the desktop. Gadot followed the cord to the floor with his eyes and found a power supply lying near a leg of the desk. An HP emblem was visible on the side. No doubt, the cord had been connected to a laptop computer. He raised the camera and took more photographs, then stepped into the room.

In four steps, he came to the end of the desk and moved around the corner. There he found a drawer lying upside down on the floor. A piece of clear tape attached to the bottom reflected the overhead light. Sticking out from beneath the drawer was a single sheet of paper. Gadot stooped over and picked it up. He stood there a moment and studied it.

Written on letterhead from the Knights of Malta, the paper contained a memo from one Fr. Galena of the Military Vicariate, to Tony Floyd, president of Sierra Resources. It had been signed by Galena. A note scribbled at the top read, "Approved," followed by the initials, "I.S." Gadot let his eyes scan over the page and saw that it was a directive to Floyd concerning a "special operations program." He wasn't sure what it meant but the fact that it was from the Order left him confident it was important.

Gadot spread the document on the desktop and trained the camera on it, making sure to get as close as possible while keeping the print in focus. He propped his elbows against his chest to steady the camera and took the picture. Then he took a cell phone from his hip pocket and sent a text message. "Subject terminated. Items missing. Assistant fled on foot."

Without waiting for a response, he took a cord from the pocket of his jacket and connected the camera to the phone. Seconds later, he uploaded the photos to a server at a Mossad operations center. A text response indicated the transmission had been received.

CHAPTER 6
ZURICH, SWITZERLAND

BARBERINI SPENT THE NIGHT in a youth hostel on the opposite side of the city. The following morning, he took a taxi to Minjan Wollishofen, a synagogue near the lake, about twenty blocks east of the apartment building where he stayed with Penalta. He'd seen it a few days before, when they were going to another of Penalta's meetings. The building was a nondescript, gray concrete structure, but the wooden doors caught his eye. They were large and heavy, made of blonde teak in four panels with a Star of David carved on each. Above it, a much larger Star of David was molded into the concrete wall. Barberini came from the cab and walked to the entrance.

The doors opened to a foyer, where light filtered through a narrow window on the wall to the left. Barberini waited a moment for his eyes to adjust. Directly opposite the entrance was a doorway into the sanctuary. A hall led to the right. Voices seemed to echo from that direction and Barberini walked toward them. Slightly brighter than the foyer, the hall led past several classrooms to an office. The door was open and through it he saw a woman seated behind a metal desk cluttered with papers and files. A telephone sat to one side. A computer sat on a table behind her. She glanced up as he appeared in the doorway and spoke to him in Hebrew, but when he didn't respond she tried English.

"May I help you?"

"Could I see the rabbi?"

"Is he expecting—"

Just then, a man emerged from a doorway behind her desk. His sudden appearance interrupted the woman and she glanced in his direction. Almost six feet tall, he had dark, curly hair and a full, thick beard. His eyes were intense, but with a hint of kindness. He looked Barberini in the eye as he spoke. "What may I do for you?"

Barberini nodded politely. "Are you the rabbi?"

"Yes. Mendel Levy. And who are you?"

Barberini glanced nervously at the woman, then back to Levy. "May we talk in private?"

"Yes," Levy replied slowly. "I suppose so." He turned away and motioned for Barberini to follow. "Back here."

Barberini followed Levy into an office. A desk sat opposite the door. Bookcases, stuffed with books, lined the walls around it. Levy moved behind the desk and took a seat. He pointed to a chair nearby. "Please, sit." Barberini pulled the chair closer and sat down. Levy looked over at him. "Now, what is this all about?"

"My name is Angelo Barberini. I need your help."

For the next twenty minutes, he explained to Levy the tale of Father Penalta— how he'd come to the Order of Malta full of passion for the care of others, but as he learned the Order's secrets he grew troubled and uncomfortable. Lately he had become disenchanted. He explained all the activities in which the Order was engaged— Sierra Resources, an attempt to influence an election in the United States, and the plot to ultimately eliminate the Jews in America. Hearing the words roll from his lips left Barberini astounded at how incredible and unbelievable the tale must be to one not privy to the details of life at the Castle. From the expressionless reaction of Rabbi Levy, he was certain that was just how he was being received.

"And so," Barberini continued, "we came here. To Zurich for a meeting with Serafino Rampolla, secretary to the Congregation for the Doctrine of the Faith."

"For the Catholic Church."

"Yes. You know him?"

"I know of him. Why did you come to see him?"

"In the hope that he would hear Father Penalta's evidence and proceed with a charge of heresy against the Order."

"That was an ambitious purpose on your part. Were you successful?"

"No."

"What happened?"

"He listened politely. And then they killed Father Penalta."

"They what?"

"He listened politely all afternoon as Father Penalta made his case. Not his entire case. He would never give them everything in a single meeting. For one thing, he had too much. And for another ..." Barberini caught himself. "Forgive me. I tend to ramble."

"That is quite all right."

"Well, anyway, Father Penalta met with Rampolla and did his best to show him that he had convincing evidence. Then we went back to our apartment in Wiedikon. I walked to a café up the street to get something for our supper and when I returned I found Father Penalta lying on the floor. Dead."

"Did you report it?"

"No. The bedroom had been searched. The laptop was gone. A file we had in the desk drawer was missing. I knew what was happening. So I left as quickly as I could. And now I am bringing this to you." He leaned forward, took the flash drive from his pocket, and laid it on the desk.

Levy stared at it a moment, then looked over at Barberini. "What is this?"

"That is a memory stick. A flash drive. Plug it into your computer and you can see all the documents Father Penalta collected. Bank records. Notes and minutes of meetings. It's all there and it will prove everything I have told you." Barberini stood. "I know the history between the Church and the Jews. I assure you, this is not a setup." He backed away. "Powerful people were opposed to Father Penalta. That is why he is dead. I will be too if they ever find me." Then he turned toward the door and was gone.

CHAPTER 7
BEERSHEBA, ISRAEL

OREN COHEN SAT IN THE MOSSAD operations center and stared up at an image on the television mounted on the wall. At sixty-one, Cohen had enjoyed a long and distinguished career, both as an officer in the Israeli Defense Force and later with Mossad. With a brilliant mind and an uncanny intuition, he had risen quickly to become Director.

Like operations centers at the White House and Pentagon, the one at Beersheba had large flat screens that covered the walls. On a typical day, they showed images from key locations throughout Israel. During special operations, they relayed footage from the ground, allowing staff to review events as they happened. That day, the screens on the back wall of the room held images uploaded by Gadot from inside the apartment in Zurich.

Cohen studied the pictures a moment, his eyes darting back and forth, searching for discrepancies, something out of place, something they hadn't noticed before. Finally he turned to an operator seated at a console near the center of the room. "Do we still have the security camera video from the apartment building?"

"Yes, sir," she replied, then pressed a button on the console. Images from security cameras mounted outside the apartment building appeared on a screen to the left. Video from the camera in the hall appeared on a screen to the right. As the video played, people came and went. A man and woman passed by, their arms locked together, his face pressed against her neck. Moments later, a mother and young child hurried by, then a man walking alone, and finally Penalta, who walked with a halting gait. Not far behind him came the man with the leather jacket.

Cohen pointed. "That is him? The guy they are talking about?"

"Yes, sir. The one with the leather jacket."

"Tighten up on him." The operator's keyboard clicked as she entered a command. A box appeared around the man on the screen, then magnified that portion of the picture. Cohen glanced over his shoulder. "Is that as close as you can get?"

"We will lose focus."

"Enhance it." After a moment or two, an image of a man's head filled the screen. Cohen stared at it, trying to notice every detail. "I think that is our man."

"Perhaps, but who is he?"

"What did Gadot say?"

"He did not get a good look at the face. His back was to the window."

Cohen pointed to the screen. "Can we run that picture through a face-recognition program?"

"Yes, but it will take a while. This video does not give us much to go on."

"It might be enough. Get moving on it." Cohen turned away from the screen. "Any more information on Barberini?"

"None."

"Well, he did not just disappear. Tell our people to find him."

CHAPTER 8
ZURICH, SWITZERLAND

LEE ZELMAN SAT ATOP a low concrete wall behind Minjan Wollishofen and watched as two young boys dribbled a basketball. "Make it bounce evenly," he called. "The same height every time." He held his hand out to his side, near his waist, to demonstrate. "Let the ball come to your hand."

Recently graduated from George Washington University, Zelman struggled with two desires— one to enter the rabbinical ministry, the other to live and work in Europe. He came to the synagogue in Zurich as an intern with the hope of settling both questions at the same time. Though Europe had proven to be very different from America— even more so than he'd expected— he was making friends and settling in to the local culture.

While the boys on the court continued to bounce the ball, a door to the building opened and Rabbi Levy appeared. Zelman glanced in his direction, then pointed back to the boys. "I'm not sure they've ever seen a basketball before."

"Maybe not," Levy replied. "But you should put the ball on their toes. Then you would see their true talent."

"Soccer?"

"Football," Levy smiled. "The way it was meant to be played."

Zelman kept his eyes on the court. "I hear you had a strange visitor in your office this morning."

"You saw him?"

"Edita told me. She seemed a little nervous about it."

"Yes. Well," Levy sighed. "Edita should learn to keep things to herself."

"Trouble?"

"I do not know." Levy shrugged. He reached into his pocket and took out the flash drive. "He gave me this," holding it for Zelman to see.

"A flash drive. What's on it?"

"I do not know." Levy paused a moment. "Not sure I want to know."

Zelman smiled. "Would you like for me to take a look at it?"

"So nice of you to ask." Levy placed the flash drive in Zelman's palm. "That way, when you download a virus to the system and all our computers blow up, I can blame it on our resident American."

Zelman slid from the wall. "That's what I am here for." He started toward the door, then remembered the boys on the basketball court. "Keep dribbling," he called over his shoulder. "Waist high. Every time."

Inside the building, Zelman made his way up the main corridor toward the front. Halfway there, he turned right into a narrow hallway that led toward the furnace room. A few feet from the steam pipe stack, he came to his office.

Not much larger than a broom closet, it had a small desk with two chairs. A bookcase stood along the wall to the left. A single light bulb hung from the ceiling. Zelman took a seat behind the desk and lifted the screen of a laptop. When the operating system was ready, he slipped the flash drive into a USB port and opened the first file. In it, he found bank statements for an account in the name of Sierra Resources along with pages of records documenting the large transfers to and from that account. Confusing at first, Zelman took a notepad from the desk drawer and made notes while he read. Slowly, a chain of transactions began to emerge. Most of them started with accounts in Greece and followed a circuitous route through various financial institutions before finally arriving at three political action committees— Policy Institute of America, Think Pac, and Environmental Policy Center— all of them in the United States. In turn, those committees made corresponding contributions to the campaign committee of David McNeil, the Republican governor of Virginia and a candidate for president of the United States.

Though living now in Switzerland, Zelman continued to stay abreast of political developments in the United States, some through the daily *International Herald Tribune*, but most from the Internet.

That year, as Robert Marich neared the end of his second term as U.S. president, a crowded field from both political parties stepped forward to take his place. The first round of caucuses and primaries narrowed both groups but still left four candidates on either side. For the Democrats, Christopher Wilson established himself as the frontrunner, though he had been unable to deliver a knockout blow to his strongest contenders. Among them, Benjamin Rush, a physician and former governor from Pennsylvania, presented the most credible challenge.

For the Republicans, David McNeil fared somewhat better. Flush with a seemingly endless reserve of money, he ran well in every state and dominated the national conservative debates, so much so that most newscasters referred to him as the presumptive nominee. As the late-winter primaries gave way to the spring contests in larger states, it seemed their confidence in McNeil might actually prove correct. He looked to finish strong and wrap up the nomination well ahead of the convention. And though the remaining Republican candidates— John Franklin and Liston Cook— seemed unlikely to drop out, they had little hope of mounting a challenge that would allow them to influence the Party platform. Their refusal to bow out gracefully left McNeil forced to campaign in the final state, spending cash he would have rather used in the general election. That Liston Cook remained in the race, ranking in polls even below the Democratic candidates, was particularly troubling.

Unlike the others, Cook was almost twenty years older than any of the candidates from either party. He had served eight terms in Congress before receiving an appointment to the State Department as Deputy Secretary for

Asian Affairs under Ronald Reagan. He'd gone on to serve every Republican president since, including eight years as National Security Advisor under Robert Marich. His underfunded and understaffed campaign battled like David against Goliath and, while professional political operatives were certain he would fail, Cook proved to be resourceful and resilient.

All of this swirled through Zelman's head as he read the documents on the flash drive and did his best to make sense of what he learned. After what seemed like only a few minutes, he leaned back from his desk and rubbed his eyes. He glanced at his watch and saw it was almost two in the afternoon. He'd been sitting at his desk for three hours. "This could take—" All at once he remembered the two boys he left on the basketball court. "Oh no," he gasped. "I was supposed to be working with them." He rushed from behind the desk and ran down the hall to the back door. As he stepped outside, he found the court empty and deserted. Two basketballs sat on the ground at the base of the wall where he'd been sitting before.

"They left," a voice said.

Zelman wheeled around to see Edita standing behind him. A cigarette dangled from her left hand. She raised it to her lips and took a long, slow drag. "They got tired of waiting for you." She paused to exhale a cloud of smoke. "I sent them home."

"Sorry," he said sheepishly. "I got absorbed in what I was doing."

"I cannot imagine what that would be." She gave him a knowing look.

"Did I get you in trouble for my comment to Rabbi Levy?"

"Nah," she said, dismissing him with a wave of her hand. "It would take more than that."

"Did you talk to him?"

"Rabbi?"

"No. The visitor."

"Not really. Just to ask him what he wanted. Like I told you already. Did you find something on that flash drive?"

"Just documents."

"And those documents support what he said to Rabbi Levy."

"How do you know what he said?"

"No way," she said, shaking her head.

Zelman had a guilty grin. "What?"

"I am not telling you what I know," Edita said warily. "You will just run tell Rabbi."

"I guess I deserve that."

"I think so." She took another drag on the cigarette. "You have finished with the documents?"

"Not quite. Still a few more pages to read."

"Rabbi was asking about it earlier. I think he is curious about why it is taking you so long." She smiled. "Just to let you know."

"Thanks."

"Do not mention it." She dropped the cigarette on the pavement and ground it out with the toe of her shoe, then turned toward the door.

When she was gone, Zelman took a seat on the wall and thought about what the documents on the flash drive meant and what he should do with them. Levy's strange morning visitor had given them evidence of a foreign organization's donations to an American presidential candidate. Carefully hidden, and no doubt certain to remain undetected by U.S. officials, Zelman was positive that sort of activity was illegal. And if, as the visitor said, that organization was the Knights of Malta, it could mean yet one more plot to vent their hatred for Jews everywhere.

Zelman picked up one of the basketballs and gave it a bounce as he considered the options. He could forward the documents to the FBI, but it would take months for them to realize what they meant and even then they would never piece it all together. Or, he could send them to federal election officials in Washington. *They might be interested, but it would take them even longer than the FBI. I need another option. Someone familiar enough with elections and investigations to know what the documents meant and someone with an incentive to see that they actually received the attention they needed.* "A political candidate." He stopped himself. "No. Not a candidate," he corrected. "They would never take the risk." But a candidate's friend might do it. Or someone who worked on a campaign— a political operative or a campaign assistant— and then he thought of Richard Stockton.

Stockton was a staunch Republican from Maryland who came to school at George Washington University as a history major, but that was just a cover to keep his parents happy. All he really wanted was to work at the center of a red-hot, issue-oriented political campaign. Zelman met him in a freshman history course and, though they came from different political perspectives, he quickly learned that Stockton was an avid supporter of all things Israel. They spent hours in the lounge at the Marvin Center locked in heated debate about healthcare reform, tax policy, and how to shape the federal budget. But they never disagreed about Israel, its stance against Palestinian terrorists, or its opposition to the land for peace initiative.

After graduation, Stockton went to work for Liston Cook as a member of his campaign staff. Not exactly the dynamic candidate he'd hoped for, but the campaign was desperate for help and Stockton was willing to work for little pay. And he was dating Cook's niece.

"Stockton would know what to do with the documents. In fact," Zelman chuckled to himself, "he would love it. This is just the kind of thing he'd get into."

Zelman slid from the wall and started toward his office. If he could find Stockton's email address, he would upload the files right then, before he changed his mind.

CHAPTER 9
FORT STEWART, GEORGIA

DEEP INSIDE AN NSA LISTENING POST located at Fort Stewart, Georgia, a NORIC-835 computer monitoring Internet traffic flagged keywords from the email sent from Lee Zelman to Richard Stockton. The message, along with all attachments, was copied to a server housed in a secure facility at Toms River, New Jersey. At the same time, an alert message was transmitted to NSA headquarters at Fort Meade, Maryland. Seconds later, a Level One Priority notice flashed on a monitor at the desk of Travis Hyatt. He opened the file and scanned through the contents, noting the name of the sender and the person to whom it was sent.

Using a MemNor program, he quickly located the IP address of both and learned the message originated from a computer in Zurich, Switzerland, and was sent to one in Washington, D.C. With the help of a data mining program developed by WebLive Systems, Hyatt obtained the name and physical address associated with both Web addresses— Lee Zelman in Zurich and Richard Stockton in Washington. By then he knew he was dealing with an email sent between two U.S. citizens. To confirm his suspicion, he ran the names through a government database that included information from State, Treasury, and Justice Departments. Both men had FBI files. Stockton had been cleared twice by the Secret Service Protective Division. When Hyatt saw that, he picked up the telephone and called his supervisor, George Warden. "We have a problem. You got a minute to talk?"

"If you hurry."

Hyatt rose from his chair and walked down the hallway to Warden's office. Warden spoke without looking up. "Make it quick. I have a meeting."

"The computer at Toms River sent me an email for review."

"What kind of email?"

"Level One."

"What is it?"

"A message from an American in Zurich emailing someone at a computer in D.C."

"Do you have a physical address?"

"The one in D.C. is an apartment in Georgetown."

"And you're concerned because ...?"

"It's a message from a U.S. citizen to a U.S. citizen."

"I've told you before, that isn't your concern. If the message originated outside the U.S., we're good. If it's a problem, we have seventy-two hours to get a warrant. That gives you plenty of time to figure out whether it's important. Who lives in the apartment?"

"Someone named Richard Stockton."

"Never heard of him. Who is he?"

"I don't know yet, but the Secret Service cleared him— twice."

"Protection?"

"Yeah."

Warden leaned back in his chair, a thoughtful look on his face. "What flagged the message?"

"The attachments. From what I can see, they're huge files of financial records. Some of it relates to David McNeil."

Warden's eyes narrowed. "*The* David McNeil?"

"I suppose. I don't know. When I saw the Protective Division cleared Stockton, I knew it was political. So I stopped looking and called you."

"Okay." Warden glanced at his watch and stood. "Keep looking. We need to know exactly what we're dealing with. Go through the whole thing and see what you can find." He took his jacket from a coatrack in the corner. "I have a meeting, but I'll be back in an hour. Keep me informed." He moved past Hyatt, then paused at the door. "We'll keep this between us for now. We have three days before we have to notify anyone about what we're doing. See what you can find out. If there's anything to it, we'll alert someone then." And with that, he disappeared up the hallway.

CHAPTER 10
OAK PARK, ILLINOIS

BRIEFCASE IN HAND and a garment bag slung over his shoulder, Richard Stockton trudged up the steps to his second-floor apartment. His day had begun at four a.m. in Denver, Colorado, followed by briefings in Las Vegas, then a quick trip to Houston. Now, at two a.m., he was finally home, where he had time for a shower and a few hours of sleep before heading off to another event— this one, a gathering at the Cook family farm outside Rochelle, Illinois. But that was later. Right then, all he wanted was a shower and the bed.

Stockton grew up on Tilghman Island, a remote area on the eastern shore of Chesapeake Bay. His father was a fisherman. His mother was clerk at the county courthouse in Easton. Both came from staunchly Republican families. While a student at George Washington University, Stockton became active in the campus Young Republicans. During a rally at the Lincoln Memorial, he met Emma Hopkins, a student at American University. They became friends and soon began dating. They'd been seeing each other for several months before he learned her uncle was Liston Cook. When Cook announced his candidacy for the Republican Party presidential nomination, Richard and Emma joined his campaign.

Underfunded and battling a crowded field, the work was challenging right from the start. With little money for salaries, attrition among the staff was high. After only two months on the job, Stockton found himself in a senior advisory position with responsibility for Cook's entire advance team. The job kept him on the campaign's cutting edge but constantly on the road, which meant he was almost never with Emma. Lately, he'd begun to wonder if that wasn't by design.

Stockton shoved open the door and stepped inside the apartment. He tossed his garment bag over the back of the sofa and walked into the bedroom. A desk sat directly opposite the door. He set his briefcase beside it, took out his laptop, and connected it to the power supply, then headed to the shower.

Four hours later, the alarm on his cell phone rang, jarring him from a dreamless sleep. He groped for the phone and knocked it to the floor. When the alarm continued to ring, he leaned over the edge of the bed to pick it up and tumbled headfirst onto the carpet.

Awake now, he stumbled across the room to the desk and flopped down on the chair. He propped his chin on his hand and lifted the screen on the laptop. While the operating system loaded, he closed his eyes and dreamed of being back in bed. The sheets were warm and the pillow soft against his head. He could—

The computer beeped. Stockton opened his eyes, logged on to the Internet, and checked his email. His in-box was jammed with messages and he scrolled through them, checking the sender address in an attempt to read the most important ones first. Partway down the screen he came to the message from Zelman. The sight of his name brought a smile to Stockton's tired face. He opened the message and was immediately absorbed in the documents, but almost as quickly his cell phone rang and the daily stream of campaign questions began. He dodged most of the calls until one came from Emma.

"I thought you were picking me up," she said, doing little to hide the frustration in her voice.

"I am," Stockton replied. "What time is it?"

"Almost ten."

"Oh no." He glanced at his watch. "I'm running a little late. I'll be there in a minute."

"Are you ready?"

"Yeah. Sure," he replied as he headed toward the bathroom. "Just need a minute to finish up a couple of details."

"Right." Her voice took a playful tone. "You haven't even had a shower yet, have you?"

"I'll be there in fifteen minutes," he countered.

"Okay," she said. "We don't want to be late."

Three hours later, Stockton and Emma arrived at the Cook family farm, a rambling two-story house set amidst sprawling oaks and surrounded by cornfields. He turned the car into the driveway and brought it to a stop in the shade on the east side of the house. Emma sat waiting while he came around the car and opened the door. As she stepped out, she kissed him lightly on the lips. "I think we should—"

Just then, Philip Livingston appeared from the opposite side of the car. "You two finally decided to arrive."

"Philip," Stockton said with a nod. "Good to see you."

"Good to see you. I get your emails, but we don't seem to cross paths much."

Livingston was Cook's chief of staff and one of the few people who came to the campaign from the Security Advisor's office. He'd worked for Cook since his first term as congressman. "I thought since you're here maybe we could find time to go over the schedule for the next few weeks. Do it in person. See if we can iron out some of the wrinkles. Advance work was a little sloppy at a couple of the stops."

Emma stepped between them. "You can have him when I'm done." She smiled at Philip. "Today he's all mine."

"Okay," Livingston smiled. His eyes met Stockton's. "But see me before you leave. We need to talk about a couple of things."

Emma steered him across the lawn toward a long table that served as a wet bar. "What was that all about?"

"A little trouble in Pennsylvania, I think."

"Anything serious?"

"Not really."

"Good." She locked her arm in his. "Let's enjoy the afternoon."

"Okay," Stockton grinned. That part would be easy.

The late-winter air was crisp and fresh. Overhead, the sky was clear and blue. Everyone who was anyone in Republican politics was there. They wandered across the yard, shaking hands and talking, and enjoying an afternoon together, even if they had to share it with several hundred guests.

Finally, near the middle of the afternoon, Stockton managed to get Liston Cook alone for a few minutes on the side porch of the house. "I received some information we may need to review," he began.

"Okay," Cook replied. "Philip was looking for you."

"I'll see him in a minute. We need to talk first."

"Okay," Cook nodded slowly. "What kind of information are we talking about?"

"Financial information."

Cook had a quizzical look. "I thought our last fund-raiser gave us some breathing room."

"It did. This is about David McNeil."

"You have financials from McNeil's campaign?" Cook looked troubled and he gestured with the glass he held in his hand. "You know I don't care for this sort of campaign 'espionage.'"

"It's not that. I received some documents. From a friend. He doesn't have anything to do with anyone's campaign."

"You are certain of that?"

"He's a rabbinical student serving an internship at a synagogue in Zurich."

Cook frowned. "Are you making that up?"

"We were friends in college. Emma knows him."

Cook's frown turned to a worried look. "Has she seen the documents?"

"No." Stockton shook his head. "I haven't mentioned them to anyone."

"What do they show?"

"Foreign influence."

"Talk to me about it tomorrow. We're in Indianapolis for the morning?"

"Yes."

"See me after that."

CHAPTER 11
WASHINGTON, D.C.

THE FOLLOWING MORNING, Esther Rosenberg stood in line at a Starbucks café not far from her townhouse in the Georgetown section of the city. She glanced at her watch to check the time and grew increasingly impatient. By now she should have been at the office, seated at her desk, diligently working through a hundred details that awaited her. She took a deep breath and forced herself to relax. She was a partner, she reminded herself, and she produced more than her share of the law firm's income. No one would complain if she stopped for coffee.

As she stood there thinking about what she ought to be doing, she heard a voice from the left. She turned to see a young man, about college age, seated at a table along the wall. Across from him was a young woman who seemed to hang on his every word. Seeing them together made her think of Ephraim.

They had met while attending law school. She was the disciplined student. He was the perennial PhD candidate, a free-spirited intellectual who spent most of his time on a bench outside the library discussing politics with anyone who would stop to listen. They began dating their second year and, in spite of their differences, quickly became inseparable. Over late-night dinners and morning coffee she helped him take charge of his life and make progress on his dissertation. In return, he opened her eyes to the political realities of a world where turmoil was the norm. They married shortly after graduation.

That was a long time ago. Much had happened since then. She had spent five years at the Ben-Gurion Institute, many more than that practicing law. And then the chaos after the car bomb ended Ephraim's life. Yet even now, after all that had happened, she could still feel the tingle of his touch.

While Esther inched forward in line for her morning coffee, the door opened and Reuben Brody entered. Brody worked from an office at the Israeli Embassy in the northwest part of the city. Officially, he was listed as an assistant to the director of cultural affairs. In reality, he was an agent with Mossad accountable only to Oren Cohen.

Brody took a place in line behind Esther. "We need to talk," he said quietly.

"Good morning, Reuben," she replied.

"Don't use my first name," he said, tersely.

She smiled at him over her shoulder. "Do you really think anyone in here cares what your name is?"

Brody's eyes darted around the room. "I don't know if they do or not. But I do."

In a few minutes they were seated at a table in the corner. Esther took a sip of coffee and waited. "Okay," she said, finally. "No one can hear us. What did you want?"

"Five days ago," Brody began, "a priest named Penalta traveled from Rhodes to Zurich where he met with Serafino Rampolla, a fellow priest in the Catholic Church."

"Rhodes? He was with the Order? The Knights of Malta?"

"Yes," Brody nodded. "He was traveling with an assistant, Angelo Barberini. They hoped to convince Rampolla to prefer charges against the Order."

"Ecclesiastical charges?"

"Yes. Rampolla has something to do with the doctrine of the church."

"The Congregation for the Doctrine of the Faith?"

"Yeah," Brody shrugged. "That sounds like it. I guess dating Paul isn't so bad after all."

"Paul isn't Catholic. And you already know that."

"Catholic, Protestant," Brody rolled his shoulder in a deferential manner. "They're all Christian."

"Whatever." Sometimes Esther found it useless to explain the subtleties to him. "Go ahead. Tell me about Penalta."

"He thought he could convince Rampolla that the Order had crossed the line into heresy."

"What brought that on?"

"That part isn't so clear. Penalta had a number of documents that were incriminating, but I'm not certain the church would have seen it as evidence of heresy."

"So, what happened?"

"Penalta met with Rampolla and presented his evidence, but when he returned to his apartment he was killed."

"Any idea who killed him?"

"We're working on it." Brody glanced over the edge of his cup and surveyed the room. "Our agent checked the apartment before the police arrived. The files and documents Penalta supposedly brought with him were missing. His assistant, Barberini, was gone, too."

"Anyone know where he went?"

"Not exactly."

"So, why are you telling me this?"

"A source with connections to the Order tells us the documents Penalta was using indicate a link between the Order and a company called Sierra Resources."

Esther frowned. "The defense contractor?"

"Yes." Brody seemed surprised. "You know about them?"

"Don't waste my time. You know Paul consults for them." She shook her head in disgust. "That's why you came to me."

"Cohen thinks this could be big."

"I don't care what he thinks. Don't patronize me by acting like you don't know what's going on."

"All right," he said, changing his tone. "But we need your help. Sierra is into rendition, assassination … any number of black operations. Everything Congress has outlawed for the U.S. intelligence community, everything the president has publicly ordered to stop— Sierra is doing it for them under secret contract arrangements."

"This can't be good."

"Cohen is worried that the Order is using Sierra to create its own private army. Equipped and sponsored by the U.S. government."

"We have a source still?"

"Not inside. On the mainland in Athens." Brody took a sip of coffee. "And it gets worse. Apparently, the Order has been funneling large sums of money through Sierra to American political campaigns and committees in an attempt to influence U.S. elections."

"Which committees?"

"I do not know for certain. But rumors suggest most of their money has made its way into David McNeil's campaign."

"So, what does Cohen want from me?"

"He wants you to find out if the Order has actually been doing that— sending money to McNeil's campaign."

"How am I supposed to do that?" Brody gave her a knowing look. She shook her head. "I told you after the last time, I don't want to involve Paul in this kind of thing."

"But he wants to help," Brody argued. "You said so yourself."

"Maybe he does, but I lived through this once already with Ephraim. I don't want to live like that with Paul."

"Well, Cohen wants you to find out if any of this is true." He looked over at her. "Shall I tell him you have refused?"

"No," she sighed. "I'll take care of it."

CHAPTER 12
INDIANAPOLIS

THE NEXT DAY, LISTON COOK appeared for a breakfast gathering of the annual Firemen's Association convention at Conseco Fieldhouse in Indianapolis. He spoke for thirty minutes, then worked the crowd for almost an hour. As he was leaving the building, Richard Stockton pulled him aside to a conference room. When they were alone, Stockton showed Cook a sample of the documents he received from Zelman— bank records and transaction reports detailing the flow of money from offshore accounts, through Sierra Resources, to the political action committees and into McNeil's campaign. Cook studied them a moment. "The amounts match up, but there is still a question about whether McNeil or anyone with his campaign knew where the money came from."

"Right."

"Are you certain these documents are authentic?"

"All I know is that they came from a man who had accompanied a priest to Zurich. He intended to use these documents as evidence for charges against something called the Knights of Malta."

"Charges?" A skeptical look wrinkled Cook's forehead. "Under canon law?"

"Yes," Stockton nodded. "The priest— I think his name was Penalta— wanted to bring charges with the Church authorities."

"Did he do it? Did the Church agree to look into it?"

"I don't know. The priest was murdered shortly after attempting to present his claims."

"So," Cook gestured with the papers in his hand, "how did these get to you?"

"A man accompanied the priest. He left a flash drive containing the documents at the synagogue, hoping someone would know what to do with them."

"Have you confirmed that the priest is dead?"

"Yes," Stockton nodded. "He's dead."

"I don't know." Cook stared down at the documents a moment. "What do you think?"

"Assuming these documents are accurate, McNeil's campaign could have broken the law."

"Assuming," Cook grumbled. "That's quite an assumption for us to make." He looked up at Stockton. "Think they're a plant?"

"A plant?"

"To get us to do something that would cause a problem for us."

"I don't think so. We're running an insurgency campaign. We're third in a three-man race. No one has any reason to muscle us out."

"John Franklin might. If we're out, it's a lot easier for him to raise money."

"I don't think Franklin's people are smart enough to do this."

"To get McNeil's records or to make them up?"

"To think of sending them to me, then masking an email address to make it appear it came from a Jewish rabbinical intern living in Zurich."

"You may be right about that," Cook grinned. "So, what do we do?"

"Take the flash drive to the Federal Election Commission. If we're lucky, they'll launch an investigation into McNeil's campaign, the *Washington Post* will pick it up, and the race will get a lot tighter."

"Could be risky. They'll want to talk to us, too. And someone will find out we gave them the documents."

"They're going to find out sooner or later anyway. Something always happens. And when they do, we'll be the ones who sat on the information."

Just then, Stockton looked up to see Donnie Read standing in the hallway outside the room. From the look on Read's face, he'd been listening for quite a while. Stockton walked to the door and pushed it closed. "Whatever we do," he continued, "we have to keep this close." He gestured with his index finger. "Just between you and me. No press releases. No announcements. We simply give them the documents and let them do what they think is appropriate."

"You're right." Cook handed the documents to Stockton. "Take care of it and let me know what they say." He opened the door and stepped out to the hall.

CHAPTER 13
WASHINGTON, D.C.

ESTHER SPENT MOST OF THE MORNING searching the Federal Election Commission website for financial disclosure reports from the McNeil campaign. She found plenty of donor records— his campaign had amassed far more contributions than any of the other Republican candidates— but none of them connected McNeil to Sierra Resources. Two hours later, and still no closer to the information, she picked up the phone and called Amy Goodwin, an attorney who worked for the Commission. The two had met while appearing at an election law seminar for congressional candidates. They had remained friends, occasionally crossing paths at House hearings and Washington social functions. When her call to Amy was routed to voice mail, Esther gave up and assigned the project to an associate, then turned to the files that cluttered her desk. For the remainder of the morning she did her best to focus on billable work. Still, the conversation she'd had with Brody played in her mind. The suggestion that she ask Paul to help left her troubled.

Like Esther, Paul Bryson had enjoyed a long and full career. Born and reared in Texas, he grew up on a ranch that had been owned by his family for six generations. After graduating from Texas A&M, he went to work as a sales representative for a chemical company. He married Linda McAdory, his college sweetheart, and settled near Longview. But by the early 1980s, he and Linda were bored. In search of something new, he began dabbling in local politics. Linda went back to school, pursuing a graduate degree in history at LeTourneau University. Not long after that the congressional seat for their district came open. Paul made a run for it and won.

For eight terms he served the people of East Texas in the U.S. Congress. Linda remained in Longview until the children were out of high school, then joined him in Washington. While there, she attended Georgetown University, obtained a second master's degree, and landed a job at the Pentagon. She was at her office on September 11, when an Arab terrorist flew a 737 jet airliner through her window.

Linda's death left Paul devastated. He was reelected to his congressional seat that year but he was no longer interested in electoral politics. At the end of the term he left Congress and returned to Texas to pick up the pieces of his life. The following year he returned to Washington, opened a consultancy office in Georgetown, and began searching for clients. Several former campaign donors hired him immediately and business took off. Before long, he was busier than he'd expected to be. One of his clients was the David Ben-Gurion Institute. A few months later, Paul attended a conference at the Institute, and that's where he met Esther. By then, she was a partner with Litton, Lyle, and Levine, one of Washington's premier law firms. They were attracted to each other immediately.

Sierra Resources was one of Paul's largest accounts. The company's CEO, Edgar Logan, had been an early donor to Paul's first congressional campaign. Back then Logan worked for AIT Systems, a manufacturer of guidance controls for cruise missiles. He used his clout in the industry to steer thousands of dollars in corporate donations to Paul's campaign. By the time Paul opened his office as a lobbyist, Logan was working for upstart Sierra Resources. The company was one of Paul's first clients.

Esther was certain Brody knew about Paul's relationship with Logan, and she was sure that was the reason Brody came to her with the request. "Cohen told him," she whispered to herself. Cohen knew everything about everyone. As head of Mossad it was his business to know things about people. Lots of things. Very little in Washington or anywhere else escaped their notice.

They even knew I would be reluctant to drag Paul into this. Which was all the more reason to ask me to do it. And then she remembered what happened the last time— the scene with Paul at the end of the alley, his body bloodied and bruised, lying on a stretcher as they loaded him in the ambulance. Tears came to her eyes. "It was all because of me," she whispered. If she'd just left him out of it. If she'd broken things off between them when … She wiped her eyes. That was impossible now. She wasn't going to push him away— living without him was unthinkable— but she wasn't going to lose him to the demons Brody chased, either. If anyone was going to change, it would be her. She could do that. She could tell Brody to find someone else and then she and Paul could slip off to Texas and spend their days sitting in the swing on the front porch, sipping coffee, and watching the breeze blow through the tall grass in the field beyond the driveway.

She wiped her eyes again. "Who am I kidding?" she sighed. That would last until the first cup of coffee was gone. Then they'd both be looking for something to do.

But how was she supposed to get him involved? What was she supposed to say? "We think one of your major clients is a front." She spoke out loud with a mocking tone. "A front for an anti-Semitic organization that's funneling millions of dollars into the presidential campaign of an anti-Semitic candidate. Will you ask them if that is true?" She slapped a notepad on the desktop. "This is crazy!"

Suddenly a voice spoke from across the room. "Is something wrong?" Esther glanced up to see an assistant standing in the doorway. He stared at her with a perplexed look on his face.

"No," she sighed. "Just frustrated. Did you need something?"

"There's a man out front. Said he was supposed to take you to lunch."

"Oh." Esther glanced at her watch. "I didn't realize it was that late." She scooted back her chair from the desk. "Tell him I'll be right out."

A few minutes later, Paul escorted Esther from the building. As they came through the lobby, he turned to the right to walk up the street. She tugged on his arm. "Let's go to the mall."

He gave her a puzzled look. "The mall?"

"Yeah." She smiled playfully and gestured to the left. "The National Mall."

"I thought we were going to Antoine's."

"I need to talk to you about something," she replied, her face turning serious. "Let's go for a walk."

"Okay. But can't we talk in the café?"

"Not about this."

Two blocks from the building, they crossed Constitution Avenue and made their way onto the lawn of the Mall. When they were well beyond the sidewalk, he glanced over at her. "Okay, what's this about?"

"A few days ago, a priest traveled from Rhodes to Zurich with information about the Knights of Malta. He went there to talk to an official of the Catholic Church in hopes the church would consider a charge of heresy against the Order and shut them down."

"And now he's dead."

She gave him a startled look. "You know about this?"

"No, but I've seen enough of the Order to know how the story ends."

"The priest *was* killed, but that's not the end of the story."

"What happened?"

"According to a source, the priest's documents showed that the Order has been secretly funneling money through a U.S. corporation into David McNeil's campaign."

"That would violate a few laws."

"Yes. Several."

"How did they get it to the campaign?"

"Political action committees."

"Makes sense, I suppose. If you're going to break campaign finance law, that's the easiest way to do it with the least risk of getting caught."

"Well," she began slowly, "you may be right about that. But the PACs aren't the problem."

"What's the problem?"

Esther pulled him close and leaned near his ear. "The corporation they've been using is Sierra Resources."

Paul leaned away and stared at her, a questioning look in his eye. She nodded her head. "Impossible." His voice was almost inaudible.

"Maybe, but that's what the source is saying."

"I've known Edgar Logan a long time. I can't imagine he would let something like this happen."

"What do you know about Sierra Resources?"

"They're a defense contractor. What are you asking about?"

"Who owns the company?"

"Sierra Investment Group. Private investors in California. About a dozen people."

"Brody says that's just a front."

"For what?"

"He thinks the company was formed by the Order and that they really own it."

"I don't know," Paul said, skeptically. "That seems a little far-fetched to me. Sierra is a huge company. Defense contractors who work on classified projects are closely scrutinized. It would be pretty tough to get something like that past DoD."

Esther took his arm and continued walking. "Think you could find out?"

"I suppose. But wouldn't that breach my relationship with them as a client?"

"I'm not asking you to tell me what you find. In fact, don't tell me. Just look into it and see if there's something you've missed."

His forehead wrinkled. "You want me to—"

"Look," she interrupted him. "There's a cart." She pointed to a hotdog vendor on the opposite side of the mall. "We can have lunch over there."

"I was looking forward to crab cakes and bisque at Antoine's."

"A hotdog would be better," she said, playfully. "We can sit on the bench and eat."

They bought a hotdog from the vendor and took a seat on a park bench down the way. After a moment, Esther picked up the conversation. "Are you okay with this?"

He gave her a playful smile. "A hotdog for lunch?"

"No, silly," she nudged him. "What we were talking about earlier."

"I'm fine with looking. Checking around to see if they're really who they claim to be." He looked over at her. "Just promise me one thing."

"What?"

"That you will always be honest with me."

"I promise," she replied softly.

CHAPTER 14
WASHINGTON, D.C.

MEANWHILE, TRAVIS HYATT continued to work through NSA's intercepted copy of the email and attachments sent to Stockton by Zelman. In less than seventy-two hours he concluded that there was more than enough evidence to warrant a criminal investigation. He reported his findings to George Warden, who forwarded the matter up the NSA chain of command.

After a quick review, the case was transferred to the FBI where the file was assigned to Taylor Rutledge, an agent with a Counterterrorism Unit in Washington, D.C. A message flashed on Rutledge's monitor to let him know the file had arrived.

"Great," he grumbled.

Elizabeth Caffery, seated at a desk across from him, turned in his direction. "I thought you loved your job."

"I do, but it's late." He pointed to the monitor. "And they just sent me a Priority file."

"Want some help?"

"Nah," he said with a smile. "No sense in ruining both our evenings."

Tall, lean, and ruggedly handsome, Rutledge had come to the FBI after graduating from law school at Vanderbilt University. Exceptionally bright, he could have landed any job he sought. Yet he declined lucrative offers from major law firms and ignored suggestions that he pursue a life in academia. Instead, he chose the FBI, partly from a desire to serve but mostly because he liked being at the center of breaking events. After he completed training at the FBI Academy in Quantico, he applied for a position in Counterterrorism. He had expected to be assigned to glamorous work that took him deep into the heart of sensational conspiracies and major threats to national security. What he found was the mundane work of a new agent, which for him began with reading files. Though the job turned out to be different from what he'd expected, he applied himself to the assigned tasks. Gradually he developed an expertise for complex financial transactions and paper-intensive cases.

With a fresh cup of coffee in hand, Rutledge opened the original email and quickly read through the contents. In the NSA file that accompanied it, he noted the details already obtained by Hyatt's initial work. That gave him the physical name and location of the parties. A check of their names in the FBI system confirmed their identities. A quick read of information available from Stockton's Secret Service history informed him that Stockton worked for Liston Cook, that he had no criminal record, and had been cleared "Yankee White" for access to the president. Then he opened the attached files and began sorting through the documents.

At a first read, he was skeptical that the documents purporting to be from the Knights of Malta were actually authentic. Some of the copies were scans but many were digital photographs. Some of the most crucial documents were photographs made on film that had been digitized. The quality was poor, but even more, the accuracy of what they purported to show seemed suspicious.

As he sorted through the documents, Rutledge checked the FBI electronic archives for files and information about the Order of the Knights of Malta. Those files showed that while the FBI had investigated allegations of nefarious plots supposedly orchestrated by the Order, it had failed to uncover evidence that explicitly linked the Order to any criminal conduct. Files for one of those cases— allegations that the Order was behind a plot to bomb key synagogues— was code-word classified beyond Rutledge's access authority. He prepared a memo requesting a briefing on the case, then returned to the transaction documents included with Zelman's email.

Late that evening, Rutledge came to the Sierra Resources documents. His eyes were tired and his neck stiff from staring at the monitor. He should have quit for the day and resumed work the following morning, but Sierra Resources was a major defense contractor, and the suggestion that it might be linked to the Order piqued his interest.

For the next three hours, Rutledge followed the paper trail through FBI files on Sierra Resources. Finally, he came to a report that mentioned something known as "Operation Livewire." When he tried to access files for it, he was blocked by the security system. He leaned back from the desk and checked his watch. He should have been home hours ago. Still, there was something about this case that seemed out of place. A Jewish rabbinical student, files about an obscure religious order, and a congressman's underfunded campaign all intersecting at Sierra Resources— a defense contractor with protected FBI files. "Something's not right about this," he whispered.

"Yeah," a voice replied from behind him. He turned to see Elizabeth standing near his desk. "Sorry," she smiled. "Didn't mean to scare you."

"That's all right," he sighed.

"You've been up here all this time?"

"Yeah." He pushed back from the desk and stood. "And you?"

"Came back to pick up my car. Saw yours was still here. Came to see about you." She gestured toward the notepad on his desk. "Interesting case?"

"Yeah," he nodded. "The further I read, the more interesting it gets."

"Want to tell me about it over breakfast?"

"I don't know. It's really late."

"No," she said, shaking her head slowly. "It's really early now." She took him by the arm. "Come on. I'll drive. You can buy."

CHAPTER 15
ZURICH, SWITZERLAND

WHEN LEE ZELMAN FINISHED reviewing the documents on the flash drive, he removed it from the USB port of his laptop and stuck it in his pocket. Then he rose from the chair behind his desk and walked up the hall to Rabbi Levy's office. Levy was standing near the window with a book open and resting on his palm. He glanced over his shoulder as Zelman entered the room. "Lee," he said with a smile. "Something wrong?"

"No." Zelman shook his head. "Just wanted to tell you I finished with the documents."

Levy had a perplexed look on his face. "The documents?"

"From the flash drive."

"Oh, good. What did you find?" Levy set the book aside. "Did it actually have the documents he told me about?"

"Yes."

"But are they authentic?"

"I don't know," Zelman shrugged. "They look real to me. Bank statements. Transaction records. Rather convincing."

"And what do they mean?"

"I think they mean what that man said they mean. There's a money trail from several accounts in Greece, through Sierra Resources, to a political campaign committee in the United States. I don't know if the accounts are owned by the Knights of Malta, but the trail is just like he said."

"So, what do we do with them?"

Guilt stabbed at Zelman's heart. He'd already done something with them by sending them to Stockton. "I think we should give them to someone," he replied with a straight face. "I mean, wasn't that the point? Isn't that why he brought them to you?"

"Yes." Levy nodded. "That's what he said."

"So, you want me to take them to the U.S. Embassy? I could probably find someone there who would take a look at them."

"No," Levy replied, shaking his head. "Give me the flash drive." He held out his hand. "I think I know someone."

Zelman handed him the drive. "You want me to go with you?"

"I don't think so," Levy demurred. "I'll be fine by myself."

*   *   *

Late in the afternoon, Levy took a taxi from the synagogue and rode across town to a high-rise building on Schulstrasse, across from the Swissotel. A brass nameplate on a column out front identified it as the offices of the World Jewish Congress. Levy stepped from the taxi and made his way through the front entrance. A young woman at a reception desk near the center of the lobby greeted him with a smile. "May I help you?"

"I would like to see Oscar Pemper."

"Is he expecting you?"

"No," Levy said, shaking his head. "I do not have an appointment."

"You must have an appointment," she replied. "Perhaps you should have called first."

Levy was undeterred. "Would you ask him if he has time to see me? Mendel Levy."

"I do not think—"

"You ask him. Mendel Levy. That is my name." He pointed to a bench across the lobby near the elevators. "I'll wait over here. Tell him Mendel Levy would like to speak with him. It will only take a moment." He took a seat on the bench and watched as the receptionist placed a phone call.

In a few minutes, an elevator door opened and Oscar Pemper appeared. He was a tall man with curly gray hair, an angular chin, and steel blue eyes. His face lit up when his eyes met Levy. "Mendel!" he exclaimed. "Why didn't you call me? I would have been here waiting for you." He grasped Levy across the shoulder and pulled him close in a friendly embrace. "I would have arranged for a building pass. You could have come right up."

"I only thought to come at the last minute," Levy explained.

Pemper's face turned serious. "Has something happened?"

"Sort of."

"Do you need to talk?"

"Only for a minute."

Pemper gestured toward the door. "We could go for a walk."

"No, I just need to give you something." He took the flash drive from his pocket and placed it in Pemper's free hand.

Pemper's forehead wrinkled in a frown. "What is this?"

"A man came to see me today." Levy lowered his voice. "Said he had evidence about the Knights of Malta." Levy closed Pemper's fingers around the flash drive. "This is what he gave me." His voice became a whisper. "There are documents on here that I think you will find interesting."

Pemper slipped his arm away from Levy's shoulder. "Does this man have a name?"

"Angelo Barberini."

Pemper's eyes opened wide. "The Catholic?"

"You know him?"

"We have files on all the Knights of Malta." Pemper slipped the flash drive into the pocket of his jacket. He gave Levy a serious look. "You know, Mendel, men have died for things that could be on that drive. You are aware of this?"

"He told me."

"Yet, still you came to me with it."

"It seemed important. You are my friend. I knew you would know what to do."

Pemper slipped an arm across Levy's shoulder once more. "I do not deserve such trust."

"I would trust you with my life."

Pemper gave his shoulder a squeeze. "Mendel, my friend, this is precisely what you may have just done." He looked away a moment, then picked up the conversation once more. "Where is Angelo Barberini now?"

"I do not know," Levy shrugged. "He told me his story, gave me the flash drive, and then he left."

"Has anyone else seen the contents?"

"My intern."

"Mmm," Pemper groaned. "That is all? Just you and your intern?"

"Just the intern," Levy said, correcting. "I didn't review the documents. My intern told me what was on the drive."

"Good." Pemper turned to the right and guided Levy toward the door. "You must speak of this to no one. Go about your business as if none of this happened." They reached the door. "In fact, put it completely from your mind as if it never happened." Pemper grasped Levy's hand. "I will take care of everything."

"Yes," Levy replied. "I am certain you will. That is why I came to you. I knew you would know what to do."

CHAPTER 16
WASHINGTON, D.C.

THE FOLLOWING DAY PAUL was on Capitol Hill until the after-noon assisting executives from Winfield Construction at a congressional hearing. Winfield was an old, well-established company with expertise in building secure underground facilities. It also had a reputation for expensive cost overruns that often brought its executives before congressional committees to explain the need for additional money.

When the hearing concluded, he drove toward his office at the Watergate Building. As he steered the car along Pennsylvania Avenue, his mind returned to Edgar Logan, Sierra Resources, and the conversation he had with Esther the day before. He and Logan had known each other a long time and he'd never heard a single word from him that hinted of anything like what Esther had suggested— nothing about the Order or prejudice against the Jews or even a comment about the Middle East. He'd been to Logan's home in Texas, and more recently to the one in California— a large house in Malibu overlooking the ocean— and he'd ridden on Sierra's jet, which Logan seemed to enjoy immensely, but they'd never talked politics other than to discuss the opinions and attitudes of particular congressmen and senators. No late-night discussions about how to make the world a safe place, the need for regulatory reform, or the evils of the federal tax code. None of the usual political banter ... and now that seemed odd.

As a defense contractor, Sierra Resources operated in a highly charged political environment. The fate of its business rose or fell on the whims of congressmen, all of whom were driven by the political nuance of even the smallest issues. Despite that, Logan never once mentioned his own personal political views.

No one could be that removed from what happens in the world. By the time he reached the office, Paul was beginning to wonder if he'd missed something in his relationship with Logan. Perhaps Esther was correct. Maybe there was more to Sierra Resources than he'd been led to believe, but getting access to detailed information about the company would be a problem.

Contractors who performed work for the Department of Defense on classified projects were certified by the Defense Security Service. Housed in the Pentagon, DSS was responsible for maintaining the integrity of each classified project. Part of its work included employee background investigations on personnel who actually worked on the project. It also investigated company executives and members of the board of directors. If there was any evidence connecting Sierra to the Order, it would show up in the DSS files. Paul had sufficient clearance to read the material, but access required more than just clearance. It also required the "need to know," a legitimate reason to review the Pentagon's information.

At the office, Paul moved to the chair behind his desk and logged on to his laptop. In the course of lobbying for Sierra and guiding them through the defense procurement process, he'd collected hundreds of electronic files that contained thousands of pages of contracts, supporting documents, and related correspondence addressing company business. *Perhaps if I looked through the pages of documents in my own files I might find a hint of what Sierra was really doing. Not an explicit reference, but maybe a note or comment that would point me toward something I've missed. And I know right where to begin.*

A year earlier, as part of its normal review process, agents from DSS re-investigated Sierra's board members. Paul assisted company attorneys in preparing responses to the agency's questions. In the course of that work, he came to know details of their lives, things not known to the public and about which he couldn't talk but nevertheless made him all the more certain that Esther's source was wrong. As the afternoon grew late and darkness descended over the city, Paul came to a report on Edgar Logan.

While investigating Logan, DSS conducted interviews of company employees. Their efforts focused on personnel who interacted with him on a regular basis— mostly office assistants and building staff— but at least three interviews were directed toward the pilots who flew the company jet. As part of those interviews, the agency requested copies of the aircraft logs. Using information from the logs, they created a schedule of Logan's travel for the past two years. Then they conducted on-sight interviews in each location to confirm he was actually there. Five of his trips were to locations outside the U.S. Three of those international trips were to Athens, Greece. When asked about it, Logan said he was staying with Manos Dianellos, a friend with an address on Achilleos Avenue, not far from the U.S. Embassy. That explanation seemed plausible at the time and nothing more was said about the issue, but now, seeing the address again in light of the questions Esther raised, he wasn't so certain the explanation was accurate. He couldn't say how or why, it just didn't seem right— taking a company jet three times in a single year to spend a few days with a friend. He took a piece of paper from the drawer and scribbled down the address. Then he picked up the phone and called Esther.

"Have you eaten dinner yet?"

"No," she replied cheerfully. "I was hoping you'd call."

"Good. We need to talk. I'll be over in a few minutes."

CHAPTER 17
TALLAHASSEE, FLORIDA

PHILIP LIVINGSTON SAT AT A TABLE near the kitchen in Mockingbird Café. He ate a grilled chicken salad while he reviewed a copy of the weekly itinerary. As Liston Cook's chief of staff, he was responsible for allocating the candidate's time. Every event, press interview, telephone call, or meeting— anyone who wanted five minutes of exclusive time with Cook— had to come through him. Enforcing that limitation turned out to be much harder than he first thought.

While he scanned down the last page of the itinerary, Donnie Read slid onto a chair across from him. Livingston barely looked up. "Okay," he sighed. "You wanted to see me. What's it about?"

"What?" Read had a look of mocking dismay. "No 'Hello, Donnie. How are you doing?'"

"I just saw you ten minutes ago at the hotel. You said it was important." Livingston glanced at his watch. "Start talking."

"You remember the stop we made at Indianapolis?"

"Yeah, Donnie." There was a note of sarcasm in Livingston's voice. "I remember it. What about it?"

"I was the last guy out of the stage area. Checking to make sure we didn't leave anything behind."

"Glad you were doing your job."

"As I left, I walked down the hall toward the back entrance to get on the bus. I saw Stockton and the congressman in a room. Talking about something."

"And you're telling me this because …?"

Read leaned closer. "I stood outside the door where they couldn't see me." A smile flickered across his face. "And listened."

A frown wrinkled Livingston's brow. "You eavesdropped on Liston Cook?"

"I didn't eavesdrop," Read protested. "The door was wide open."

"If they'd wanted everyone to hear, they wouldn't have been standing in a private room."

"I'm not everyone."

Livingston reached for his water glass and took a drink. He swallowed it slowly and set the glass on the table. "What were they talking about?"

"Something about the FEC, the U.S. Attorney's office, and David McNeil." Read paused to catch Livingston's eye. "Is something about to break?"

"Like what?"

"I don't know. Something big."

Livingston looked away. "Not that I know of."

"Really?"

"Really." Livingston glared at Read. "You think I'm lying?"

Read had a calloused look. "I think I've been the last person on this campaign to know anything. And I don't want to be the one left holding the bag."

"No one's cutting you out."

"Yeah," Read said, nodding his head slowly. "They are. And if you don't know what they were talking about, they're cutting you out, too."

"What do you mean?"

"I mean Stockton knows more about what's going on than either of us."

"I doubt it."

"No." Read wagged his index finger. "I'm telling you, the guy is bad news. I see him going around you all the time, playing the Emma card every day."

Once more, a frown wrinkled Livingston's forehead. "The Emma card?"

"Emma," Read explained. "Cook's niece."

"Congressman Cook," Livingston corrected. "Or Ambassador Cook. Or Mr. Cook to you. And don't talk about her like that."

"Like what?"

"With a tone that implies she's less than honest."

"Look, all I know is I see these two in there talking. It's serious. They're talking about David McNeil, the FEC, and the U.S. Attorney. That means either McNeil's campaign is about to implode, or we're all about to be out of a job. Now, if I'm going to be unemployed, I need to know about it before it happens."

A condescending look came over Livingston. "Got a line on a new job?"

"No." Read leaned away from the table. "But there are very few slots left on anyone's campaign and I want first shot at the ones that are still out there. So I want to know, are we in trouble?"

Once again, Livingston's eyes darted away. "I don't know."

"Come on," Read blurted. "We've been friends longer than this. You're the candidate's chief of staff. I know how you operate. Nothing gets to him without coming by you first. So, I'll ask again. Are we in trouble?"

"I don't know!" Livingston shouted. As soon as the words left his mouth he knew they were too loud. He glanced around to see who was watching, then lowered his voice and leaned over the table. "I don't know," he said, quietly but earnestly. "Believe me. I really don't know. But I'll find out what's going on." He sighed and slumped backward. "I'll find out."

After dinner, Livingston returned to the hotel and rode the elevator upstairs to Cook's suite. He arrived to find two advance men preparing Cook for an evening fund-raiser. "Which one is Wyckoff?"

"Tall guy. Broad shoulders. Looks like a football player."

Livingston moved past them and flopped onto the sofa. Cook straightened his tie and continued with the advance men. "Wyckoff. Have I met him?"

"Yes. But it was last year."

Cook slipped on a jacket. "Anyone else?"

"Linda Goddard. Telephone executive."

"Anything I need to know?"

"Her husband is on the board of St. Joe Paper Company. They're big in the state party."

"Paper company?"

"Largest landowner in western Florida."

"Okay." Cook straightened the lapels of his jacket and glanced over at Livingston. "Aren't you coming?"

"I'll be down in a few minutes." Livingston took his iPhone from his jacket. "Just need to return a couple of emails."

"Don't forget about us," Cook cautioned. "We need to squeeze every dime out of this crowd."

"I'll be right there." Livingston propped his feet on the coffee table and continued to review his email account. When Cook and the advance men were gone, he tossed the iPhone aside and walked into the bedroom.

A briefcase sat on a table near the window. Livingston opened it and flipped through a stack of papers that lay inside. Speech ideas, the week's itinerary, a campaign finance report, staff evaluations. Near the bottom he came to a plain manila file folder. He slipped it from the stack and opened it.

Inside he found a memo written on Sierra Resources letterhead, a bank account statement from an account in Greece showing a long list of transactions, another statement from a bank in California, and a page showing contributions to Think Pac— a political action committee developed by the Franklin Foundation, a conservative research and policy organization. The final page was from a David McNeil campaign financial report.

Livingston pondered his discovery. *This is what Cook and Stockton were talking about. They have the records. But why is Cook discussing them with Stockton? Something like this would change the nature of the campaign. And not just the Republican campaign but the entire presidential election cycle. This is big stuff. So, why didn't Cook talk to me about it? Why was he talking to Stockton? Maybe Read is right for once. Maybe Stockton is bad news.*

He pushed the briefcase aside and laid the documents on the table, side by side. Using the camera from his iPhone, he snapped a picture of them, then checked the photo to make certain the heading on each of the documents was visible. Satisfied the documents could be clearly seen, he slid the phone into the pocket of his jacket and returned the papers to the briefcase. Then he positioned the case exactly as it had been before on the tabletop.

As he came from the room, he typed a simple email message on his phone. "They have the documents." At the elevator, he paused and attached the photo to the message. He located the telephone number for Carmine Russo in his contacts list and pressed a button to send the message.

CHAPTER 18
WASHINGTON, D.C.

LATER THAT EVENING, Paul arrived at Esther's townhouse. She met him at the door and he escorted her to the car. From there they drove across town to Clyde's, a popular Georgetown restaurant. It was almost nine when they arrived. After a brief wait at the door, a waiter led them to a table near the wall on the far side of the dining room.

When they were alone, Esther looked over at Paul. "How did the hearing go today?"

"As well as could be expected."

"I heard they were rough on your guys."

"Gossip travels fast in this town."

"Think they'll still get the contract?"

"I don't think they have much choice," Paul shrugged. "Winfield's already two years into the project. Would cost more to replace them than it would to finish the project."

A waiter appeared at the table to take their order. When he was gone, Paul glanced over at Esther. "You asked me the other day about Sierra."

"Yes," Esther nodded. "And you didn't think there was anything to it."

"And I'm still not sure there is."

She gave him a knowing look. "But?"

"I found something that might be interesting." He slipped his hand into his pocket and took out the slip of paper with the address he'd scribbled down earlier. "Have someone check this address." He laid the paper on the table and pushed it toward her.

Esther rested her hand on his. "You don't have to do this."

"It's an address." He pushed the paper closer. "That's all."

She covered it with her hand. "It's still a line."

"I'm crossing it with you, aren't I?"

"Yes."

A smile curled up the corners of his mouth. "Then I don't mind."

CHAPTER 19
RHODES

LATE IN THE EVENING, Carmine Russo was awakened by the ding of a message alarm from his cell phone. He rolled on his side and took the phone from the nightstand by the bed. The glare of the light from the screen made him squint as he scrolled down the email list and clicked on the new message. The one-line statement from Livingston made him sit up in bed. "They have the documents." He rubbed his face with his hand and forced his mind to think. Who? Who had what documents, and why was he getting this message? Slowly, the haze of sleep lifted and he realized what the message was about. His fingers typed in a reply. "Who has them?"

The reply came almost immediately. "Cook."

Russo continued. "Others?"

And the response came without delay. "More than likely."

Russo's heart sank at the thought of what that meant.

After Father Penalta had left on his trip to Switzerland, a routine security audit of the Order's computer files revealed the presence of a large encrypted file that was not included on the authorized log. Cracking the encryption took considerable effort, but once access had been obtained they found a cache of financial records and internal memos. Electronic footprints from those files led to a laptop computer assigned to Angelo Barberini. They had recovered the computer, but analysis of the hard drive was not yet complete. If copies of the files were in Liston Cook's possession, they could be in any number of other locations as well.

Russo threw back the covers and climbed from the bed. He took a robe from a chair near the door and slipped it on. A pair of slippers sat near the bed. He slid his feet into them, grabbed the cell phone, and started from his room.

Minutes later he reached the door to Spoleto's suite. He tapped on it softly, then eased it open and went inside. The room was dark, but a nightlight from the kitchen guided him down the narrow hall to the bedroom where Spoleto lay fast asleep. Russo stood at the foot of the bed and gently shook Spoleto's foot.

"Sir," he said, barely above a whisper. "Sir."

"Huh," Spoleto mumbled.

Russo shook his foot again. "Sir."

Spoleto's eyes opened and he sat up in bed. "What? What is it?"

"I received a text message from the United States."

A lamp sat on a table beside the bed. Spoleto switched it on. He ran his hands over his face and rubbed his eyes. "What time is it?"

"About one, sir. In the morning."

"What happened?"

"I received a text message. From our contact with Liston Cook's campaign."

"What did it say?"

"'They have the documents.'"

"What documents?"

"The ones Father Penalta took with him."

Spoleto stared at Russo, his eyes fixed and unmoving. "Well," he said finally. "That changes things."

"Yes, sir."

"You must find Father Galena at once and tell him to convene the Military Vicariate."

"Shouldn't we handle this ourselves?"

Spoleto looked him in the eye. "Have you forgotten what happened to Carlo Busca?"

"Father Busca?" Russo frowned. "He died of a heart attack. How does that have anything to do with us or this?"

Spoleto dismissed him with a wave of the hand. "Don't be naïve. There was no heart attack."

"No heart attack?" Russo looked bewildered. "I don't understand."

"You understand. And if you don't, it's because you do not want to. Handling things himself is precisely the kind of decision that led to his downfall. Contact Father Galena." Spoleto switched off the lamp and slid down in bed. "Tell him everything you told me. He will know what to do." Spoleto pulled the covers over his shoulders. "Make certain you close the door when you leave."

CHAPTER 20
WASHINGTON, D.C.

THE FOLLOWING MORNING, Taylor Rutledge arrived at his desk later than usual. Elizabeth was already there. She gave him a knowing look as he passed by. He responded with a smile. "I see you made it home okay?"

"Yes," she replied. "Made it home without falling asleep." She pushed her chair away from the desk and turned toward him. "The guard at the parking garage called up here a few minutes ago. He wanted to know why your car was in there overnight."

"What did you tell him?"

"That you were on a last-minute assignment."

"Yeah," he grinned. "An assignment. Thanks."

"Anytime."

Rutledge took a seat at his desk and logged on to the computer system. Then he opened the files he'd been working with the night before. He glanced through them, seeing at first little more than words and numbers on the pages, but after a few sips of coffee he remembered where he'd left off in reviewing the documents. Before long, he was immersed in bank records.

Tracking each transaction with painstaking precision, he followed a trail of money from an account in Greece through banks in Switzerland,

Luxembourg, and Andorra, then to Sierra Resources accounts in California. From there, corresponding contributions were sent to three political action committees— Policy Institute of America, Think Pac, and the Environmental Policy Center. Each of those committees made contributions to the campaign committee of David McNeil and to a committee he formed under state law during his last gubernatorial campaign.

Committee to committee transfers. Money from foreign entities making its way to a U.S. presidential campaign. "This can't be legal," Rutledge said to himself.

Robert Brenner, who sat at a desk nearby, glanced in his direction. "What's that?"

"Transfers of money from one political action committee to another. Is that legal?"

"I'm not sure."

"What about as a channel for foreign contributions to a U.S. political campaign?"

"No," Brenner said, emphatically. "That I know is not allowed."

"I wonder if the FEC knows about this."

"If they know about the law?" Brenner frowned.

"No. This right here." Rutledge pointed to the monitor. "The situation I'm looking at. I wonder if they know about it."

"They don't actively audit campaigns. I mean, most of the illegal activity they know about comes from something someone reported. I have a friend over there. Catherine Olsen. Works in enforcement. You could give her a call."

"Yeah," Rutledge nodded. "I will."

"She's not bad looking either," Brenner added.

"Then I should call her now," Rutledge quipped.

After a brief conversation, Olsen agreed to meet him at her office. Rutledge rose from his chair and slipped on his jacket. Elizabeth looked over at him. "Going someplace?"

"Federal Election Commission," Rutledge replied. "Want to come?"

"Can't," she said, pointing to a file on her desk. "Setting up a sting on an art dealer in Alexandria."

"Sounds interesting. Need some help?"

"Nope," she smiled. "Got it covered." She pointed toward the door. "You have to get to the FEC."

"Yeah," he groused. "Election returns and mountains of paper. Just the kind of terrorism fight I signed up for."

On the opposite side of the building, Rutledge found Susan Dey, a research assistant, and gave her copies of the bank transactions involving the account in Greece. "I need to know who owns the account and where the money comes and goes."

"Okay. When do you need it?"

"By the end of the day."

"You don't ask for much, do you?"

"I need it," Rutledge repeated as he turned away. "By the end of the day."

From there, he made his way down to the lobby on the first floor. A door near the elevator led to the parking garage in back of the building. He crossed the garage and continued to the sidewalk on E Street. The Federal Election Commission was housed in an office near the corner. Inside the building, a guard directed him to the elevator. He rode up to the fourth floor and found Olsen at her desk.

Almost six feet tall, she had long legs, a slender waist and was every bit as attractive as Brenner had suggested, but she wasted little time with introductions and went straight to business. "You said you had something important to discuss. What's this about?"

"Two days ago, NSA flagged an email from Zurich. It was referred to our office because the destination was associated with a physical address here in D.C."

She leaned back and rested her hands in her lap. "This email involves American citizens?"

"Apparently."

She arched an eyebrow. "Emailing each other?"

"Yes."

"NSA's still trapping domestic emails?"

"I don't know what they're doing," Rutledge said, trying to avoid a legal argument over jurisdiction and authority. "I just know what they sent me."

Olsen stared at him. "And what was that?"

"Attachments to the email included bank records from several foreign accounts. As best I can tell, money was routed from a foreign source through a company called Sierra Resources and into several political action committees formed under U.S. law and physically located in the United States. Once the money reached those PACs, it was forwarded in what appear to be corresponding amounts to David McNeil's campaign committee."

"David McNeil." She took a sardonic tone. "The presumptive Republican presidential nominee?"

"I don't think he's been declared the winner yet. But yes. That David McNeil. And I suppose by your reaction I should assume the FEC isn't actively investigating him for any campaign violations."

"Not that I know of. You guys looking to make a criminal case out of this?"

"I don't know," Rutledge shrugged. "Not sure what we're looking at yet."

Olsen leaned forward. "We have exclusive jurisdiction on civil fines."

Once again, Rutledge ignored the interagency territorial argument. "Do you think your office would be interested in checking into it?"

"Maybe," she nodded. "We would be glad to look at whatever information you would like to share with us." Her eyes narrowed. "But if you think you can use us as a cover for your criminal investigation, that isn't happening."

"I just thought we could work together. Your expertise with campaign law. Our investigative resources."

"I don't know," she sighed. "These things always get messy. Justice Department pursues the criminal cases. Maybe you should talk to them."

"I prefer to work this one a different way."

"Why?"

"I'm with the Counterterrorism Unit. We received this because of the NSA intercept. When lawyers from Justice see it, they'll start tripping all over themselves with questions about jurisdiction and authority. Criminal case versus intelligence inquiry. Just like you did when I mentioned the email."

"You don't like following the law?"

"I love following the law," Rutledge countered. "But they'll spend a month trying to decide what the law is, and by then this case will be cold. My job is to interdict terrorist activity. That means catching the bad guys before they act. I don't have time to argue with Justice about it." He paused and took a deep breath. "So, do you want in on it, or not?"

"Like I said." Olsen rose from her chair. "I'll take a look at whatever you want to send me. But I'm not doing your investigation for you."

"Good." Rutledge stood. "I'll email the files to you as soon as I get back to my desk."

CHAPTER 21
BEERSHEBA, ISRAEL

OREN COHEN SAT HUNCHED over the polished oak desk that filled his office. Head down, he bent low over a photograph that lay flat on the desktop. Holding a loupe gently between his fingertips, he slowly worked his way across a still photo captured from the video taken by Rami Gadot at Father Penalta's apartment in Zurich.

As director of Mossad, he didn't need to analyze photographs himself. Indeed, the task already had been assigned to highly skilled technicians who employed the latest analytical tools to tease every scrap of information from photographs just like the ones Cohen so assiduously studied. But there was something about the situation in that apartment that left him with nagging questions, and he was certain the answers lay in the details of the photo before him. As he moved slowly over the image, there was a knock at the door.

"Yes," he called without looking up.

The door opened and Mara Moss, a young assistant, entered. "This came for you."

Cohen glanced up to see she was holding a padded envelope. "Who is it from?"

"Oscar Pemper," she replied, reading from the packing label. "World Jewish Congress. Looks like it was sent from Zurich."

Cohen set the loupe aside and reached across the desk toward her. "Give it to me." She placed the envelope in his outstretched hand and turned toward the door. When she was gone, he tore back the flap and glanced inside. A small flash drive lay at the bottom fold of the envelope. He dumped it onto the palm of his hand.

"Oscar," he whispered. "What are you up to now?"

Born in Vienna shortly before World War II, Oscar Pemper was detained by the Nazis and sent as a young boy to Mauthausen-Gusen, a German concentration camp, where he was forced to work long hours under miserable conditions in the camp quarry. Three hundred boys arrived with him, but when the camp was liberated only four of them were still alive. Many of those who died met their death at the hands of Aribert Heim, a physician assigned to the camp by the SS to conduct experiments on the prisoners. Pemper escaped Heim's scalpel long enough to develop expertise in setting charges with the quarry blasting crew, an ability that helped him avoid some of the more inhumane Nazi practices. After the war, Pemper formed an organization known as Kristallnacht, which was devoted to tracking down and bringing to justice those Germans who worked at the camp. Much of that effort focused on Heim. After several years of intense effort, Pemper located him living on the coast of Mexico, just south of the U.S. border. Pemper notified Israeli authorities, and Mossad organized a secret team to seize Heim and bring him to Jerusalem. Members of the team were selected from the Israeli Army's special forces. Cohen was one of those chosen for the mission. He and Pemper worked together closely to make the effort a success and became good friends. In the years that followed, they collaborated on many clandestine operations.

Cohen tossed the envelope aside and turned to a laptop computer that sat on the credenza behind the desk. He slid the flash drive into the USB port and opened the first file. In it he found records from a bank account in Greece. The second file contained internal memos from the Knights of Malta. Without reading further, he reached for the telephone and pressed a button. In a moment, the door opened and the same young assistant entered his office. "Yes, sir," she said with a matter-of-fact tone.

Cohen took the flash drive from the port on the computer and handed it to her. "Take this to Yaron Klarsfeld. He's one of the analysts upstairs."

"Yes, sir," she replied and turned toward the door.

"And Mara," he paused to catch her eye. "Guard it with your life."

"I will take it to him now. Any instructions for him?"

"No." Cohen picked up the loupe and bent over the photograph once more. "He will know what to do without being told."

CHAPTER 22
RHODES

DEEP INSIDE KNIGHTS CASTLE, three floors beneath the Hall of Saints, was a room known to the Order as The Dungeon. Once used to hold prisoners, it had been converted to a secure meeting room not unlike those at government buildings in Washington, D.C., and capitals around the world. With the castle towering above and thick stone walls forming the outside perimeter, it was virtually impregnable to eavesdropping technology.

A long, slender conference table occupied the center of the room. Made of oak, its smooth top was polished to a glossy shine. Around it sat thirteen high-backed leather chairs perfectly positioned an equal distance apart. Overhead, small spotlights shined down on each of the chairs, giving the occupants an eerie luminescence.

Alipius Galena sat at the end of the table near the door. Gathered around him were the twelve prelates of the Military Vicariate, a group of men designated by Rule to implement the Order's military policy. Each of the twelve had been appointed to the Vicariate by the Grand Master but they all served at the discretion of Galena. Not even the Grand Master could question how they executed policy.

When they were all gathered, Galena rose from his place at the head of the table and spoke in a clear, strong voice. "Gentlemen, we are gathered here at this hour because a grave situation has developed concerning our former brother Penalta." He paused a moment to make certain he had their attention. "As you are aware, five days ago Penalta left the Castle in the company of his assistant, Angelo Barberini, allegedly for the purpose of attending a conference in Zurich. Almost as soon as they were gone, we learned the real point of the trip was to meet with Serafino Rampolla, secretary to the Congregation for the Doctrine of the Faith. Penalta scheduled that meeting to present evidence he hoped would incite the Congregation to pursue charges of heresy and apostasy against the Order. Once these matters were fully known, Jobert was assigned the task of interdicting Penalta's efforts."

From the left side of the table, Father Caruso interrupted. "We were under the impression he was successful."

"He succeeded with Penalta," Galena replied. "And he retrieved the laptop on which Barberini had loaded the files he stole from our system. But we have since learned that the documents in those files are now in the possession of an American politician named Liston Cook— a candidate for president in the Republican Party."

Father Ameche spoke up. "We are certain he has the documents?"

"Yes. Some of them have been seen in his possession."

"How is this possible?"

"They are electronic files. Easily duplicated and easily disseminated."

"What does he plan to do with them?"

"No one is certain." Galena glanced around the table. "Cook's assistant, Richard Stockton, has hard copies in his possession. He has reviewed them with Cook, but as of now nothing has happened with them."

Father Armetta leaned forward. "I still would like an answer to Father Ameche's question. How did someone from Cook's campaign obtain the documents?"

"We are still pursuing that issue," Galena demurred.

"You don't know?"

"No." Galena shook his head. "We do not."

"Does McNeil know about this?"

"No."

"Should we not tell him? The matter poses as much risk to him as it does to us."

"We can address that in a moment."

Father Caruso spoke up again. "Where is Barberini?"

"No one has seen him since Penalta died."

"Jobert did not take care of him?"

"Jobert's order was only for Penalta."

"At the time, it did not appear necessary." Ameche turned in Caruso's direction. "We thought Barberini was with us."

"We should have terminated them both," Caruso groused. "We have been victimized by a Jew-lover and a Greek." He threw up his hands in frustration. "How did we come to this?"

Galena's eyes darted around the room, gauging the reaction of the others at the mention of Barberini. Then he turned the conversation back to the question at hand. "For now, we must deal with the matter of Liston Cook and the documents. We cannot afford to let this go any further. Those documents could jeopardize everything we have worked to accomplish."

"We must not be too hasty. We need to verify exactly which documents they have so we can act from a position of confidence." Father Armetta tapped his finger on the table for emphasis. "Right now, I sense we are uncertain. Acting from a position of uncertainty will only compound our problem."

Someone else spoke up. "How many teams can Sierra Resources deploy?"

"Many." Romano Vignola, seated at the opposite end of the table, raised his voice in a defiant tone. "They have as many as we need."

Others nodded in agreement around the table. Ameche turned to Galena. "Then we should have them check every office, every computer, every file cabinet, every desk. As long as we have the men at our disposal, we should use them."

"Yes," Caruso added. "And they must act quickly. Before the East Coast media finds out about it."

"I am not so sure." Father Brancato raised his hand for attention. "I am not so sure this is wise." He slid back his chair and stood. "The measures you propose are thorough and would result in a search of every conceivable location. But that strategy bears considerable risk. So many men in so many places bring the likelihood that one of them will be caught." He looked at the men around the table. "Is it not better to have Livingston look for them alone? After all, he is already there, with Cook. He can search for them himself without raising any suspicion."

"He can check only one location," Caruso argued. "And even then, he would have a difficult time explaining how or why he had access to someone's laptop. Better to use Sierra for this. They are skilled in locating items of this nature. We must retrieve the documents before they attempt to use them."

"I agree," another added. "Using only Livingston would take much too long. Besides, he is an amateur at these things. Sierra has teams trained for this."

Vignola spoke up once more. "I move that we inform Sierra and McNeil of what has happened and authorize them to take all action necessary and appropriate to remedy the situation."

Galena stood. "Very well, gentlemen. We have a proposal on the table. Contact Tony Floyd at Sierra Resources, and Henry Caldwell on behalf of the campaign. Tell them what has happened and to retrieve the documents at all costs. Are we in agreement?" Galena let his eyes roam the table, looking at each man until his gaze fell on Brancato. The old man nodded ever so slightly.

Then the twelve all stood and replied in unison, "So be it."

Galena rapped the table. "I will deliver the decision."

CHAPTER 23
WASHINGTON, D.C.

NEAR THE MIDDLE OF THE MORNING, a courier appeared at Esther's office with an envelope addressed to her. Inside was a simple handwritten message. "Vietnam Memorial. Ten minutes." From the handwriting she knew the note was from Brody. She laid it aside and continued working.

Twenty minutes later she left the office and walked down the street to the National Mall. Brody was waiting at the memorial.

"You're late," he snapped.

"Why don't you just call or send a text message?"

"Too traceable."

"Whatever," Esther said with a sarcastic tone. "If you want to go through the cloak-and-dagger routine, I'll play along. What did you want?"

"We have a new development in Zurich."

"With the dead priest?"

"Yes," Brody nodded. "Father Penalta. He was traveling with an assistant, Barberini. He disappeared when Penalta was killed. A few days later he appeared at a Zurich synagogue. He told the rabbi about their trip to Zurich and something about the Knights of Malta working to influence a U.S. presidential campaign. He gave the rabbi a flash drive that supposedly held copies of the documents that supported their claims."

"Tell me we have the flash drive."

"We have it, but there's a little more to it than that." Brody glanced around nervously, then lowered his voice. "The rabbi didn't believe Barberini but had someone check out the flash drive."

"Who did he give it to?"

"An American intern working at the synagogue."

Esther shook her head. "If you made this stuff up, no one would believe you. What happened next?"

"The American read through the documents, then sent the files to a friend who works for Liston Cook."

"The congressman?"

"Former congressman. Now he's a candidate for president."

"Penalta thought the Order was trying to influence Liston Cook?"

"No. The documents don't have anything to do with Cook."

"What about the flash drive? Where is it?"

"The intern gave it back to the rabbi, who took it to someone at the World Jewish Congress. They sent it to Beersheba."

"What does Oren say about it?"

"They're still analyzing data, but a preliminary reading suggests the documents on the drive link the Order to Sierra Resources, just as our source told us before."

"Well," Esther said as she stretched out her hand. "Add this to the analysis." She pressed her palm against his and gave him the slip of paper she'd received from Paul. "Have someone check this address."

Brody took it from her and slid his hand into his pocket. His eyes darted around, once more checking the faces nearby. "You are certain the information is good?"

"Brody," Esther said with a lilt. "It's an address. Have someone check it out." And with that she walked away.

CHAPTER 24

RHODES

THE SOUND OF FATHER GALENA'S footsteps on the stone floor echoed through the hall as he made his way toward Spoleto's apartment. He arrived at the door and rapped on it. Russo answered and gestured for him to enter.

"Come in," he said quietly. "Father Spoleto has been expecting you."

The door opened to a small living room. Spoleto was seated in a chair near the corner. He gestured to a chair at his right. "Alipius, have a seat." Galena slumped onto the chair. Spoleto patted the back of his hand. "You look tired, my friend."

"I am tired."

Spoleto glanced up at Russo. "A cup of tea for us, please." Russo acknowledged him with a nod and disappeared around the corner into the kitchen. Spoleto crossed his legs. "The meeting went well?"

"Yes," Galena nodded. "It went well."

"And you reached a decision?"

"They have instructed teams from Sierra Resources to search all of Liston Cook's campaign locations to find the documents. And they want to inform McNeil of the documents."

"So, they think they can contain the situation."

"Yes," Galena nodded. "They would like to try."

"I do not think that will be possible."

"If the teams from Sierra are as good as they claim, I think we can."

"But the documents are contained in electronic files."

"Cook was approached by one of his workers with a hard copy. Someone has printed at least part of the documents."

"Hmm," Spoleto mused. "That is not good."

Just then, Russo arrived with a tray holding a pot of tea and two cups. He set it on a table to Spoleto's left. When the tea was poured, he moved back to the kitchen.

Spoleto picked up the conversation. "They will send teams to search Cook's offices?"

"Yes. I assume so. Those were my instructions."

Spoleto grinned. "You do what you and the Vicariate think you must. I would never attempt to interfere."

They talked for a while longer, then Galena excused himself. When he was gone, Russo came from the kitchen. Spoleto glanced up at him from the chair. "You will notice he mentioned nothing of Barberini."

"Barberini?" Russo frowned. "What about him?"

"He has disappeared and no one has a clue where he has gone."

"You are searching for him?"

"He was Penalta's assistant. He knows everything Penalta knew."

"They are not pursuing him?"

"No," Spoleto said, shaking his head. "I am sure they are not."

"Why? Why would they not?"

"When Barberini was a young man, Galena visited the churches of Sardinia. Barberini was Greek Orthodox but attended mass at one of the services where Galena celebrated Holy Communion. The two became acquainted and Galena took him under his wing."

"A Catholic and an Orthodox? Yet they are both Italian."

Spoleto smiled. "Penalta's mother was Greek."

Russo arched an eyebrow. "This is widely known?"

"No." Spoleto shook his head. "And it must not be told."

"I should think not. Most of the members here think the Orthodox are traitors."

"A sentiment I hope you do not share."

"I serve you, my lord," Russo replied.

"Good." Spoleto continued, "Barberini is one of only three men who followed Galena into the priesthood, albeit Greek Orthodox. Galena thinks of him as his son. That is how Barberini came to be here among us. Galena prevailed upon me to intercede for his admission, when Father Busca was Grand Master. I did it as a favor to Galena."

"You think now it was a mistake?"

"No. I did not think so then, and I do not think so now. Things were different then. People were different then."

"So, what do we do now?"

"You must find Barberini."

"Me?" Russo exclaimed.

"Yes. You."

"Is this not what you were trying to avoid when you turned the matter over to the Vicariate?"

"They had their chance and they did not finish the job. Now I must."

"And you want me to find Barberini and finish the job for you?"

"I do not mean for you to do the work. I mean for you to have someone find him and have him do it."

"Who?"

"That, you must determine on your own." Spoleto stood. "My name must never be associated with it."

CHAPTER 25
ARLINGTON, VIRGINIA

SATURDAY AFTERNOON, Paul drove across the Potomac River to Arlington Community Church. Located on Wilson Boulevard, he had attended services there since arriving in Washington as a freshman congressman. The pastor, Stuart Palmer, grew up in Lake Jackson, Texas. He and Paul were friends. That friendship, and the support of the congregation, got Paul through some tough times in the aftermath of Linda's death. Since then, he'd found it difficult to get moving on Sundays in time to make the morning service, but the Saturday evening service suited him very well.

By the time Paul entered the sanctuary, the praise band— complete with guitars, drums, horns, and electronic keyboard— had the congregation on its feet. He slipped into a vacant space on a pew near the back and took a seat. Dancing down the aisle of the church, as some in the congregation occasionally did, wasn't something that appealed to him, but he found the energy of the freewheeling service stimulated his spirit and he encountered God in a way not readily available to him at other times. As he sat there with his eyes closed and his head bowed, his foot began to tap in time with the music. Before long, he was on his feet and singing.

When the service concluded, Paul lingered near the pew as the crowd slowly made its way from the building. In a few minutes, the sanctuary was empty. Paul sat there, staring at the cross that sat on the altar table down front. As he stared at it, he thought of Jesus and what it might have been like for Him, knowing He was about to be crucified by the Romans— not the theoretical knowing, but the personal, emotional, fully-human knowing that came with an awareness that death was at hand. How was He able to do it? What was it like, having the power to choose another course of events but refusing to take any other option?

Just then, a hand touched Paul's shoulder. He glanced up to see Stuart standing in the aisle beside him. "Scoot over," Stuart said with a nudge. Paul slid aside and made room for him. "Good to see you."

"Good to be here."

Stuart glanced in Paul's direction. "Thought you were going to bring Esther."

"I don't think she's ready for this."

"Is she not ready," Stuart needled, "or is it you?"

"Yeah," Paul smiled. "That, too."

"I enjoyed spending a little time with her the other night over at Benny's house."

"Yes," Paul nodded. "We enjoyed that. Benny and Sarah are great hosts."

"You know, if this is going to work between the two of you, you'll both have to find a way to include each other in every aspect of your lives."

"I know."

"You'll have to get comfortable with her being Jewish. And she'll have to get comfortable with you being a Christian."

"I just don't want her to feel like I'm trying to convert her."

"Are you trying to convert her?"

"No, but sometimes I think I'm supposed to be."

"You're supposed to love and worship God and let Him sort out the issues from there."

"That's not as easy as it sounds."

"Are you embarrassed by what we do here?"

"Not at all," Paul replied with a shake of his head. "This is my life.

I'm alive today because of what we do here ... because of what God has done in me."

Stuart cut his eyes at Paul. "But ..."

"You know," Paul shrugged. "It's ... intimate. I mean, the service is public but what really happens is personal. My relationship with Him is personal. I trust Him with my life."

"A relationship is about trust. You have to trust Esther with this part of your life."

"What if she can't respect it?"

"Give me a break," Stuart chided. "We're talking about Esther. Do you really think 'respect' will be a problem?"

"I don't know."

"What are you afraid of?"

"I'm not afraid," Paul replied lamely.

"Yes you are," Stuart prodded. "What is it?"

"Rejection, I guess."

"That's right. Rejection. If she knows who I *really* am, she won't like me."

Paul looked over at Stuart. "I've lost one woman already. I don't want to lose Esther."

"I know." Stuart gave him a friendly tap on the arm. "But I don't think this will be a problem for her. I mean, I don't know her as well as you do, but I think she'll see us— this congregation, the way we do church— for what it is— a part of your life. And she'll treat it the same way she treats other things that are important to you."

"I hope so," Paul sighed.

Stuart grinned. "You really like her, don't you?"

"I really do." Paul felt his cheeks blush. "I really do."

"I think God knows that, and I think that's why He brought the two of you together."

"You think He brought us together?"

"I do," Stuart smiled. "I really do."

CHAPTER 26
CHICAGO, ILLINOIS

SUNDAY EVENING, A VAN ROLLED slowly down Polk Street. It came to a stop near Harrison Street at an alley that ran behind the old Grand Central Station. Once the main passenger terminal for the Baltimore and Ohio Railroad, it had been a bustling destination for passengers arriving in Chicago to seek their fortunes in the factories of the 1890s. But with the rise of air travel in the 1960s, passenger trains faded from the tracks. Even in a city the size of Chicago, the building saw declining traffic and finally was closed. It remained empty and unused for the next forty years. Developers suggested razing it to make way for modern high-rise office buildings, but neighborhood groups protested and city officials balked at approving plans that required the building's removal. Now its cavernous halls and endless rooms housed the national headquarters of Liston Cook's presidential campaign, and once again there was talk of developing the block on which it sat, this time with a plan that included the building's renovation. But that Sunday night, those plans were only a dream and the old red brick building stood on the corner shrouded in mystery as thick and dark as the shadows that lurked along the lee of its towering walls.

As the van came to a stop, the side door slid open and four men stepped quickly into the shadows. They made their way behind the building to a loading dock that once was the platform for departing passengers.

Mike Thomas led the way. Tall and broad-shouldered, he was a former Green Beret. A few steps behind him were Jeff Carlisle and Spencer Adams, both former Navy SEALs. Bill Sisson brought up the rear. Lean and muscular, with intelligent eyes and a disarming smile, he was the one about whom the least was known. His company file indicated he'd spent time in Beirut, but his age made him much too young for deployment with the Marines in the 1980s. His service record showed he'd spent time in Baghdad and Kabul, but he was discharged from service before U.S. forces were deployed to either region.

Moving quickly but quietly, the four men climbed onto the loading dock and took up positions on either side of the rear doors. A card reader was mounted near the doorframe. Thomas glanced at Sisson and motioned for him to move. Sisson stepped up to the door, took an access card from his pocket, and swiped it through the reader. A magnetic lock on the door clicked. Thomas pushed it open and led the way inside. The others followed close behind.

From the rear entrance, they made their way up a long, wide hall to the central lobby. A guard sat at a security console in what had once been a large, circular information kiosk. While the men climbed a winding staircase that led to the second floor, Sisson walked to the guard's station. The guard stood as he approached.

"May I help you?"

"Just came back to check on a few things in the office," Sisson replied.

"Yes, sir," the guard replied. "You'll need to sign in." He gestured to a logbook on the counter and handed Sisson a pen.

Sisson avoided the guard's gaze as he grasped the pen but he could feel him watching to see the name he used on the book. "I don't think I've seen you here before," Sisson said as he signed on the open page. "This your first night?" Making small talk was a risk, but he was certain the guard was suspicious.

"No," the guard replied tersely. "I've been here since the building reopened."

"Guess I've just missed you." Sisson turned away. "Glad to have you on board." And he started toward the stairs.

By the time he reached the second floor, the others were already in the office at the end of the hall, a bullpen reserved for advance teams when they came in from the road. From the railing, Sisson could see down to the lobby below. The guard held the telephone receiver in his right hand. With his left he held the building logbook. Sisson's mind raced as he moved down the hall. He'd signed the book as Allen McLean. That was the name they said to use. Donnie Read had given it to them. He assured them it was a name no one would question. Had he used the wrong name? Was McLean no longer with the campaign? When he reached the opposite corner, he glanced down at the lobby once more. The guard station was empty. Sisson opened the office door and joined the others in the advance office.

"We better hurry."

Thomas looked concerned. "Something happen?"

"I think the guard is suspicious."

"Why?"

"The way he looked at me. And when I came up I saw him talking on the phone. He had the building logbook in his hand."

"What did you say to him?" Thomas growled.

"Nothing. I didn't say anything."

"Did you use the name?"

"Yeah. Allen McLean. Just like they said."

"Get moving," Thomas hissed. "We have to get out of here."

CHAPTER 27
TUCSON, ARIZONA

FROM A COMMAND CENTER in a nondescript single-story building on Valencia Road on the southern edge of the city, Sierra Resources employees monitored teams assigned to fifteen Cook campaign sites. Jeremy Bartlett, Sierra's director of special operations, stood in the center of the room and scanned images as they appeared on thirty screens that lined the walls. Live video and audio streamed into the center from each of the teams.

Born and reared in Tyler, Texas, Bartlett had grown up with a love of country and deep sense of patriotic duty. His father, an Army veteran who served three tours in Vietnam, drove a truck for an oil services company. His mother was secretary at the Baptist church. His ancestors had served in the American military since the Revolution and he had relatives on both sides of the Civil War. Convinced from an early age that service was every citizen's obligation, he enlisted in the Army the day after he graduated from high school. His mother had tried her best to dissuade him and cried at the news of his commitment, but his father and three of his Army buddies took Bartlett out for a night-long celebration.

In spite of his mother's misgivings, Army life served Bartlett well. After basic training, he was stationed at Fort Leonard Wood, Missouri. That fall, he enrolled at nearby Drury University from which he earned a degree in history. From there he went to Fort Bragg, North Carolina, where he completed special warfare school. He was recruited by Sierra Resources following his fourth deployment to Afghanistan.

While Bartlett studied the screens, an assistant appeared at his side. "Sir, we've picked up a telephone call from the site in Chicago. I think you ought to hear this."

"What is it?"

The assistant snapped his fingers and gestured to an operator on the far side of the room. A voice came from a speaker mounted near one of the screens on the wall to the left.

"Sir," the first voice said, "this is Brasher at the front desk." It was a man's voice, but he sounded young and nervous. "We may have a problem, sir."

"Okay." The second voice was older, confident, and unfazed. "What's up?"

"A man just now signed in to the building using the name Allen McLean."

"Yeah," the second voice replied. "He's in town. Just came in this afternoon. We have a meeting in the morning. It's not on the schedule."

"Sir, a different man signed in under that same name with Mr. Stockton a few hours earlier."

"What time did the second man enter the building?"

"Eleven fifty-one, sir. He came in through the rear entrance. Used a swipe card."

"Whose card?"

"It's registered to McLean, sir. But this is not the man who signed in under that name earlier with Mr. Stockton."

"You're sure about that?" The older voice was growing tense. "This wasn't the Allen McLean you saw earlier?"

"No, sir. This was not the same Allen McLean who came in with Mr. Stockton earlier this evening. I've never seen this man before."

"Okay, call the police. I'm on my way."

Bartlett turned to a woman seated at a console to his right. "Alert the team in Chicago. Get them out of the building. Now!"

CHAPTER 28
CHICAGO

WHILE THOMAS AND THE OTHERS rifled through desks in the campaign office, Sisson worked his way to a row of filing cabinets on the opposite side of the room. He opened one and flipped through the files. He stared down at the papers before him, but his ears were attuned to the hallway, listening for the slightest sound. After a few moments, he closed the drawer and opened the next. There was nothing inside except a handful of blank notepads and three cell phones. He pushed the drawer closed and reached for the next. As he grasped the handle to open it, he heard a sound from the hallway. His eyes darted across the room to the space at the bottom of the door. A flash of light reflected through the narrow sliver, then disappeared.

Sisson eased the drawer closed and moved to the left, working his way along the row of cabinets until he reached the corner. He crouched there and scanned the room for a way out. Windows lined the wall to the right, but multiple coats of paint sealed every crack. He was certain they would never open. Already he was frustrated with himself for not reviewing the floor plan more closely. He glanced over his shoulder and saw a closet door a few feet away. *That's a trap. Anyone searching the room will check in there and when they do I'll be caught.*

Movement in the hallway reflected through the space beneath the door. They were coming. The guard. The police. Any moment now they would burst through the doorway, flip on the lights, and it would all be over. Sisson's eyes darted around the room once more and then back to the closet door. There was no other option. He ducked around the corner of the filing cabinet, opened the closet door, and slipped inside.

Only a little wider than his shoulders, the closet was musty. With the door closed, the stale air tickled his nose. He pinched his nostrils and stifled the urge to sneeze. By then his eyes had adjusted to the light. Above him, the closet rose into a dark expanse. If he could get up there, perhaps the darkness would hold when the door was opened and no one would notice him.

Sisson pressed his back against one wall and put his right foot against the wall on the opposite side. Using his leg as a wedge, he held himself in place while he lifted his left foot from the floor and moved it to a spot a little higher on the wall. By alternating the effort, he steadied himself with his elbows and slowly worked his way up the closet wall. As he climbed into the darkness, the faint outline of an access panel appeared in the center of the ceiling. When he neared the top, he pushed the panel aside and grabbed the edge of the opening with both hands.

Then from down below, he heard the sound of loud and angry voices.

"Hands in the air!" someone shouted.

"Up against the wall," someone else commanded.

Sisson relaxed his leg muscles and let his body swing free. He dangled a moment in mid-air, then slowly hoisted himself through the access hole and into the crawl space above the ceiling. He wiggled through to safety, then turned back to replace the access panel. As he pushed it in place, the closet door opened.

CHAPTER 29
TUCSON, ARIZONA

BACK AT THE SIERRA RESOURCES command center, Bartlett stared up at the screen, watching images from the Cook campaign offices in Chicago. Three men— Mike Thomas, Jeff Carlisle, and Spencer Adams— stood with their hands raised in the air as security guards and police flooded the room.

Bartlett called out to no one in particular, "Where's the other one?" When no one replied immediately, he called over his shoulder in a loud voice, "Who's the fourth man in Chicago? What's his name?"

"Sisson," someone answered. "Bill Sisson."

"I don't see him in the office." Bartlett turned back to the video screens. "Anyone see him on the live feed?"

"He was standing by the filing cabinets just before the police arrived."

"Play back the tape," Bartlett ordered.

"Sir?"

"Play back the video here." Bartlett pointed. "Put it up here. On this screen." A moment later, images recorded earlier in the office appeared on a flat screen. Bartlett watched intently, then pointed with an outstretched finger. "There's Thomas."

An aide moved closer. "I see Carlisle and Adams."

"Where's Sisson?"

"He didn't come in with them," someone offered.

Bartlett frowned. "Why not?"

"He was signing the building logbook at the desk downstairs," the aide explained.

An analyst joined them. "Should have been there by now."

On the screen, the office door opened and Sisson squeezed inside. He approached Thomas, and the two could be seen talking.

Bartlett's aide turned to an operator. "Can we get the audio on this?"

"No," Bartlett said, cutting them off. "Let's watch it like this for now. The voices will be a distraction." They watched as Thomas gestured toward Sisson, then turned to a nearby desk and opened a drawer. Sisson, visible over Thomas' shoulder, walked to the filing cabinet. Bartlett continued to watch as the video played. Then he pointed to the screen again. "There," he blurted out. "Right there." He jabbed with his finger. "Back it up." The video stopped, then played in reverse. "Okay," Bartlett said, his eyes focused on the screen. "There," he pointed again. "Run it from there."

The video paused, then started forward showing Sisson as he opened a file drawer. His back was to the camera but from the motion of his hands and arms, he appeared to be looking through the files in the cabinet. Suddenly his head jerked to the right.

"Stop!" Bartlett exclaimed. "Right there." He pointed once more to the screen. "Something caught his eye. What is he looking at?"

"Something to his right."

"But what?"

"Nothing over there but the door."

"The door," an analyst said, her eyes wide in a look of realization. "He saw something at the door."

"Run it from there," Bartlett said. "Slowly."

As the video began to play, moving frame by frame, Sisson dropped to a crouching position and moved toward the corner of the filing cabinets. He paused there, glanced around warily, then crawled around the corner and disappeared.

Bartlett turned to the aide who stood at his side. "What's back there where he's going?"

She opened a notebook and flipped through the pages to an office diagram. "A closet. Nothing but a closet."

"That's a trap," Bartlett observed. "Why would he go in there?"

"Desperate," someone suggested. "No other choice."

"Are we sure that's all?"

"Maybe not," the aide said, pointing to the diagram in the notebook. "There's an access panel in the closet ceiling. It leads to a utility crawl space between the floors."

Bartlett looked over her shoulder at the notebook. "Where does it go?"

"It's open across the entire floor." The aide traced the diagram with her finger. "Electrical wires, cables, telephone lines. It's a space about three feet high that runs over the top of all the offices. He could crawl through there and drop down anywhere on the floor he wanted."

"Or sit tight and wait for the building to clear."

"Did he know about it beforehand?"

"They had the drawing," the aide replied. "Each team had drawings for each site. I don't know if Sisson reviewed it." She looked up at Bartlett. "But he had the diagram in his packet."

"But if he heard something in the hall, why didn't he warn the others?"

"Good question." The aide closed the notebook. "You want to review his file?"

"Not right now," Bartlett said, shaking his head. "We don't have time to second-guess him yet. Find out where he went and alert the pick-up unit. We find him and get him in first, then we can figure out what happened."

CHAPTER 30
WASHINGTON, D.C.

TAYLOR RUTLEDGE STOOD in the Filene Center, an outdoor concert venue at Wolf Trap National Park, just beyond the Beltway, not far from downtown Washington. Elizabeth Caffery was next to him, her arm wrapped in his. They'd been there most of the evening listening to a concert by the Doobie Brothers, a band made famous in the 1970s and still performing. As the band concluded its third encore and the crowd moved toward the exits, Rutledge felt the phone in his pocket vibrate. He took it out and glanced at the screen. The call was from the office.

The evening was cool, almost uncomfortably so, but the music was exhilarating and he looked forward to spending the evening with Elizabeth. The last thing he wanted was an interruption. But the bureau had a policy. When the office called, no one refused to answer. Reluctantly, he pressed a button on the phone and raised it to his ear. The call was from the overnight desk. "We have a development in Chicago. The New York office routed it to you. They want you to look into it."

"Now?"

"Yes. This is a priority matter. Don Harper is here. He's waiting to see you."

"What could possibly happen in Chicago that needs my attention now?"

"Come to the office."

Rutledge ended the call and returned the phone to his pocket. Elizabeth pulled her coat tighter around her chest. "You have to go."

"Yeah," he sighed. "I'll drop you at your apartment."

Two hours later, Rutledge arrived at the office to find Don Harper, the assistant agent in charge, standing at his desk. Harper glanced at his watch. "Took you long enough."

"I was at Wolf Trap, at a concert."

"If you want to move up in the bureau, you'll learn to move faster."

"Yes, sir."

"A few hours ago, a four-man team broke into the Chicago headquarters of Liston Cook's campaign."

Rutledge gave him an ironic smile. "Watergate."

"Let's hope not. New York wants you to investigate."

"What about the Chicago office?"

"You're already working on a lead from NSA that involves Cook. They want you to handle it."

"Okay." Rutledge rubbed his eyes. "I can get out there first thing in the morning."

"Negative," Harper snapped. "There's a plane waiting at Dulles. You can go now." Rutledge glanced at his watch. Harper backed away from the desk. "Get your things. A car will take you to the airport. You can sleep during the flight."

CHAPTER 31
CHICAGO

BILL SISSON MOVED QUIETLY through the crawl space above the second floor at the Cook campaign headquarters offices. He heard the muffled sound of voices but he paid them little attention. He was more concerned with what might be lurking in the darkness that surrounded him. Cables and wires snaked across the floor. Air-conditioning ducts, a later addition to the building, added another dimension to an already treacherous maze, forcing him to move cautiously in order to avoid banging into them.

After what seemed like hours, he finally reached the wall on the Wells Street side of the building and felt his way toward what he thought was the front of the building. A few minutes later, he came to an opening that seemed to be a window, but it was small and no light came through it. He ran his fingers lightly over a wooden frame until he found what felt like the handle of a latch. He slid his thumb against one end and gripped the other with his fingers, then gave it a twist. To his surprise, the handle moved freely. He turned the latch to a vertical position and tugged on it. Cold air rushed in from outside. He bent his head closer and saw that he had indeed opened a small window that looked out on a narrow ledge. Shadows from a clock tower that stood near the corner shielded the ledge from view and kept it almost as dark as the crawl space. He pushed his head through the opening and checked to see if his shoulders would clear the window frame. Then a noise behind him caught his attention. He turned to see a shaft of light illuminating the crawl space from the access hole in the closet where he'd been hiding. *They're searching for me. The guard must have told them I wasn't among the men they caught.*

Sisson reached through the opening and pressed the palms of his hands against the outside wall. With a heave, he pushed himself head-first through the window. Just as his body tipped forward, threatening to plunge him headfirst to the ground, he reached back and grabbed the bottom edge of the window frame. Holding tightly with his fingers, he let his legs swing down until his feet touched the ledge below. Then he let go of the grip on the frame and worked his fingers into the mortar joints between the bricks on the exterior wall. Carefully, he inched along until he came to a copper downspout. He grasped it with both hands and placed his legs on either side. Squeezing tightly with his legs, he worked his way down to the ground.

Light flashed from a dozen police cars parked out front. Two cars were parked in the alley behind the building. Sisson glanced in that direction, then darted across the street. With every step he was certain someone would shout for him to stop, but no one seemed to notice. A few minutes later, he reached the corner at the opposite end of the block. He pulled the collar of his jacket tight around his neck and walked quickly up the street.

An hour later, he reached the rendezvous point, a house on South Vincennes Street that had been converted to an apartment. If they became separated, they were to meet back there. Sisson approached the house from the far side of the street. A construction dumpster sat at the curb three houses away. He paused there and studied the neighborhood. Cars and trucks that lined the street appeared as usual. The guy next door had a Buick that had seen better days. Next to it was a blue Ford pickup with a green door. A young kid drove— Nick or Andrew or something like that. The door had been hit by the street sweeper and the kid replaced it with one from a junkyard out in Elmhurst. Sisson scanned the street once more but saw nothing that made him suspicious. After a few minutes, he made his way toward the house and walked around to the stairs in back.

As he neared the corner, a car stopped out front. He ducked out of sight and waited for the sound of the car door. When he heard nothing, he peered around the corner. Two men sat in the front seat of the car. One of them held a cell phone and appeared to be engaged in an animated conversation. Sisson crouched low to the ground and made his way up the side of the house to an overgrown wax bush that stood near the front corner. He tucked himself behind it, squeezing in between the bush and the house.

Seconds later, the doors opened and the two men started toward the house. Sisson listened as they approached. "I don't think he'll be here," the first one said in low voice. "But be careful."

"You really think he's here?"

"This was the plan. Come here if they got separated. They're sending someone to his apartment."

"Can't the command center track him?"

"They said something's wrong with the chip. Having a problem with it." The first man took a pistol from the waistband of his jeans and nodded to the left. "Go around back. Make sure he doesn't run."

"And if he does?"

"Do what you have to do."

"Shoot him?"

"We can't have him on the loose."

Sisson sat motionless behind the shrub and waited for the second man to pass. When the man disappeared around the corner of the house, Sisson crawled from his hiding place and hurried to the street.

CHAPTER 32

RHODES

THE CELL PHONE ON Carmine Russo's desk vibrated, creating a buzzing sound as it hummed against the desktop. He picked it up and glanced at the screen. A text message read simply, "Email."

Russo logged on to the Internet and went to a Google email account. In the draft file he found a new entry and opened it. His eyes skimmed over it quickly. "Fourteen teams successful. Chicago three in custody. One unaccounted." As he read the words, he felt his stomach tighten. This was bad news. He pushed back his chair from the desk. Spoleto insisted on hearing bad news immediately. Russo stood and walked toward the office. He tapped lightly on the door and waited.

"Enter," a voice called from inside. Russo pushed open the door and stepped into the office. Spoleto's eyes met his. "You look troubled."

"We have news from America."

Spoleto leaned back in his chair. "What happened?"

"On orders from Father Galena and the Military Vicariate," Russo began, "Sierra deployed fifteen teams to search the campaign offices of Liston Cook."

"Fifteen teams?"

"Yes."

"How many in each team?"

"Four."

Spoleto had a questioning look. "He has fifteen separate offices?"

"Yes."

"I thought they had money problems."

"They do," Russo nodded. "But they still have multiple sites."

"What did they find?"

"I do not know yet what they found. But that is not the problem."

"What is the problem?"

"The team in Chicago was captured."

"Captured?" Spoleto leaned forward. "How is that possible? What happened?"

"I don't have details. My contact only told me three of them were arrested. One is missing."

Spoleto leaned back once more, his hand to his chin, his mind lost in thought. "Yes," he said finally. "You have your phone?"

"Right here." Russo held it up for him to see.

"Send a message to this number. Five—"

"Who is this to?"

"You do not need to know that," Spoleto said, dismissing Russo's look of concern with a wave of the hand. "Just do as I say." He took a plain white card from his desk drawer and turned it so Russo could see. On it was a telephone number. "This number." Spoleto tapped the card with his finger. "Say only, 'Confirm Chicago result.'"

"That is it?"

"Yes. Do it now." Spoleto rocked the chair gently while Russo entered the message. "This will be bad for us," he continued. "I do not like it."

Russo sighed. "The message is sent. How long before we—" The phone interrupted him with a message alert. He glanced at the screen. "Three in custody at Cook County Jail," he read. "One still missing."

Spoleto nodded. "Leave me the phone." He held out his hand. Russo placed the iPhone in his palm. "Find Galena. Unless he objects, we shall convene the Legislative Council without delay." Russo hesitated. Spoleto scowled at him. "Go now. Call them to the meeting. And close the door behind you."

Russo crossed the room to the door and caught hold of the knob to close it. As he glanced over his shoulder, he saw Spoleto texting a message on his phone.

CHAPTER 33
CHICAGO

THE GULFSTREAM JET with Rutledge aboard touched down in Chicago a few hours after midnight. By then he'd had a nap and been briefed on the case. According to the earliest reports, a security guard at the building became suspicious and called his supervisor. The police were alerted and responded within minutes. Three men were apprehended in an upstairs office. The guard was certain a fourth man he'd seen earlier that evening was part of the break-in team, but that man had not been found. The three men arrested by the police were being held in the Cook County Jail.

The plane taxied to a stop near a hangar on the far side of the runway. Out the window, Rutledge saw a black SUV parked on the tarmac. As the jet engines whined to a stop, the door of the SUV opened and Matthew Davis, an agent from the Chicago office, stepped out. Rutledge came down the steps from the plane and walked toward him. They met beside the wing of the plane.

"Hope you had a pleasant flight," Davis offered.

"Could have used a few more hours of sleep."

"It'll have to wait." Davis motioned toward the SUV. "We have to get down to the jail as soon as possible."

"What's the rush?"

"The men you want to see are in Cook County custody. We need to get down there before they get lawyered up."

"No one else from the office was available to question them?"

"Once D.C. said you were on the way, no one wanted to intervene."

"Great," Rutledge scowled. "We've lost a lot of time."

Thirty minutes later, they arrived at the jail. Davis parked near the rear entrance and the two went inside. As they came into the booking area, a deputy caught Davis' eye. "Too late," he growled. "They already asked for their lawyer."

Rutledge spoke up. "Did you interview them?"

"Strickland did." The deputy gestured over his shoulder. "He's down the hall."

Rutledge moved around Davis and started in that direction. He made his way down the hall, glancing in each office as he moved along. Finally he came to one with desk and chair. A man seated there looked up. "Can I help you?"

"I'm looking for someone named Strickland. Interviewed some of the guys who were arrested a while ago inside Liston Cook's offices."

"Who are you?"

"Taylor Rutledge. FBI." Rutledge flashed his badge.

"You new to the office? I know most of the guys down there and I don't recall anyone named Rutledge."

Davis appeared in the doorway. "He just got off the plane from D.C."

Strickland stood and reached across the desk to shake Davis' hand. "Called in some reinforcements for you?"

"Rutledge was already working on a related investigation." Davis closed the office door. The three men took their seats. "He flew out here as soon as he heard about the arrests."

Strickland looked over at Rutledge. "Not much to tell that you don't already know. Security guard became suspicious. Called his supervisor, then the police. Found three men in a second-floor office."

"What made the guard suspicious?"

"A man came in around eleven. Signed in at the desk with the name

'Allen McLean.' But the guard had already encountered a man earlier that day using the same name. Came in that afternoon with someone the guard knew. He wondered why two men were using the same name, so he called it in."

"Is there a real Allen McLean?"

"Yeah. One of the advance men. Works out of Los Angeles. Almost never comes to Chicago." Strickland leaned forward. "Did they give you a copy of the arrest reports?"

"No," Davis replied. "Think we could get one?"

Strickland opened a drawer and took out several sheets of paper. "You can have mine. I'll get another."

Rutledge scanned the report while Davis continued. "I understand they've requested a lawyer."

"Already called them. Says they're on the way."

Rutledge pointed to the page. "Down here, in the narrative section, there's a note about the contents of this man's pockets." He looked up to the top lines of the report. "Says he gave the name of Smith."

"He's not Smith," Strickland smiled. "He's Jeff Carlisle. We ran their prints. For once, your famous FBI laboratory gave us a quick result."

"Know anything else about him?"

"No. But he had a scrap of paper in his pocket with a number on it." He handed Rutledge a piece of paper with the number on it. "Looks like a phone number."

"Did you call it?"

"Just get a voice mail. It's a cell phone number. We're running it down now. Takes a little while for us to get it." Strickland glanced over at Rutledge with a smirk. "Since you're from the D.C. office maybe you can get it a little faster."

"Yeah." Rutledge nodded. "Maybe so." He gestured with the pages of the reports. "You gave me three. Someone said something about a fourth man."

"The guard." Strickland leaned back in his chair. "He says the man who signed in at the desk that night wasn't with the men they found in the office."

"Is anyone looking for this missing fourth man?"

"We have a description of him. Put the guard with a sketch artist." Strickland took a copy of a drawing from his desk drawer. "That's what they came up with." He looked over at Davis. "We sent all of this to your office."

"Good. And I think your team conducted a search of the building?"

"Yes. Went through it from top to bottom."

Davis leaned over to Rutledge. "The offices are in an old train depot."

"Lots of dark corners in there," Strickland continued. "But they assure me we looked in them all."

CHAPTER 34
CHICAGO

ON THE OPPOSITE SIDE of the jail, Jack Lea approached the security checkpoint at the lobby entrance. An attorney with a downtown defense firm, Lea had spent most of his career defending white-collar criminals. He was well-known in Chicago and had a reputation for being thorough, persistent, and difficult to handle. With him were Ruffie Naylor and Brad Sowell, two associates.

After clearing the security check, a deputy led them down a long, dimly lit hallway. As they neared the end, the deputy paused and gestured to a doorway on the right. "Mr. Carlisle is in here. The others are on the end."

Naylor took Carlisle. Sowell entered a room to debrief Adams. Lea reserved Thomas, the team leader, for himself. They sat across from each other at a table in a tiny interview room and waited while the deputy locked the door behind them. When she was gone, Lea took out a legal pad and looked over at Thomas.

"You were arrested inside Liston Cook's campaign offices?"

Thomas gave him a skeptical frown. "Who are you?"

"I'm Jack Lea. You called for a lawyer. Sierra Resources sent me."

"I've never met you before."

"And I've never met you," Lea quipped. "Time is of the essence, Mr.

Thomas. We need to get to work." He looked Thomas in the eye and repeated the question. "You were arrested inside Liston Cook's campaign office?"

"Yeah."

"Did the arresting officer inform you of your rights?"

"Yes. I think so," Thomas shrugged. "I can't remember exactly. Somebody was saying something about it."

"You entered the office. Did whatever you did. Then you were arrested. Tell me how that happened."

"We were in there. Doing what we do. And the door opened. A guy came in and said, 'Hands in the air.'"

"He actually said 'Hands in the air'?"

"I think so," Thomas grinned. "It was a little strange. But we did what he said."

"Who said that? Who said, 'Hands in the air'?"

"I think he was the building guard. It wasn't the cops. They usually want you on the floor. But the guard was a little more … into it."

"Anyone with him?"

"Yeah. Half a dozen police officers. They pushed their way past the guard and rounded us up. Shoved us against the wall. Handcuffed us. Led us from the room."

"Have you made any statements to anyone since the moment the officers entered that room?"

"No," Thomas said, shaking his head. "Not really."

"What do you mean by 'not really'?"

"They asked me my name."

"And you answered them?"

"Yes."

"What name did you give them?"

"Kent Robinson."

"You gave them a false name."

"Sort of."

"What does that mean?"

"It means Kent Robinson is a name with a record. A file. I don't think they know who I really am."

"Yes, they do."

"You sure?" Thomas frowned. "How?"

"Fingerprints."

"That fast?"

"Apparently, the FBI was already working an investigation on this. How did you get into the office?"

Thomas leaned away from the table. "You really want to know?"

"Walk me through it. How did you get in?"

"One of our guys— Bill Sisson— had a pass card."

"You've worked with Sisson before?"

"Once or twice."

"So, he had a pass card. A swipe card?"

"Yeah. He had a source inside the campaign. I'm not sure who. The card was in the name of one of the campaign people. That was Sisson's responsibility. I don't know whether the name was real or fake. We got to the back door. He swiped the card. The lock opened."

"Then what happened?"

"Sisson went to the desk in the lobby to sign in to the building. While he did that, we started upstairs."

"Which stairway?"

"The main one. Some of us had been in the building the week before and we knew—"

"You used the card before tonight?"

"No. We went in a few days ago. As deliverymen. Scouted the location."

"And what did that tell you?"

"Not that much. Just helped us work out the details of getting in and out of the building. We planned to enter with the card through the rear entrance. That would give us the best chance of not being seen. But the only way to get upstairs from the back hall is to go out to the lobby and take the main staircase. While we were in there earlier, we figured out we could get to the staircase without being seen if we stayed right up against the wall and slid around the corner of the banister. The corner of the building cuts off the angle from the lobby. No one can see you and there's a blind spot in the security camera's range. Worked perfectly."

"So, you got upstairs. And Sisson signed in at the desk."

"Right. We were already in the office and working when Sisson came in."

"Did he say anything?"

"He said the guard was curious."

"Anything else?"

"I think he tried to chat up the guard."

"Chat up?"

"Small talk. He wasn't supposed to do that. But I think he did."

"Why do you think that?"

"I asked him about it. He gave me a lame answer."

"Then what happened?"

"I told everyone to work fast. We'd have to cut it short."

"What did Sisson do?"

"He started looking through the filing cabinets."

"There's a closet around the corner from the filing cabinets. What's in there?"

"Nothing. Why do you ask?"

"The video shows Sisson moving in that direction right before the police arrived."

"You saw the video?"

"Yes."

"There's an access hole," Thomas explained. "Leads up to the crawl space between the floors."

"That's where Sisson went?"

"I assume so. It was one of our alternate exit routes."

They continued to talk as Lea probed for details and Thomas grudgingly conceded information. An hour later, Lea was certain he'd obtained all the information Thomas had to give. He left the room to find Naylor and Sowell waiting for him. He motioned for them to follow and led them outside. When they were well away from the building, he glanced at them. "Did either of your men give a statement?"

"No," Naylor replied. "He gave them a name, but that's all."

"Not his real name?"

"No," Naylor said, shaking his head.

Lea looked over at Sowell. "How about your guy. Did he talk?"

"Just a name."

"Either of them have any idea where the fourth man might be?"

Naylor spoke up. "Carlisle saw him climb into the closet. Just like we saw on the video."

"What did he think?"

"He thought Sisson knew more than he was telling. Sisson came into the office after everyone else was already in there. He and Thomas got into a discussion about what he'd been doing. Sisson seemed nervous. Like he was waiting for something he knew was going to happen."

Lea looked back at Sowell. "Did your guy see Sisson?"

"He saw him when he came into the office, but my guy was on the opposite side of the room. He couldn't see Sisson, even when he was talking to Thomas. He heard them, but he couldn't see them."

"All right," Lea said with a nod of his head. "Let's get to the car."

As they walked, he typed a simple sentence on his Blackberry. "They're clean." Then he scrolled down his contacts list and sent the text message to Jeremy Bartlett at Sierra Resources.

CHAPTER 35
RICHMOND, VIRGINIA

AS MONDAY DAWNED, David McNeil sat in the breakfast nook on the second floor of the governor's mansion. He spread cream cheese on a bagel and took a huge bite while he read the morning paper.

Born into a liberal family— his father spent the 1960s mobilizing campus demonstrations, his mother was an artist who spent the same decade in a California commune— McNeil had chosen a more traditional life. He attended Washington and Lee University, where he majored in history. During his junior year he caught the eye of a professor who introduced him to Henry Caldwell.

Many years McNeil's senior, Caldwell was a native Virginian and lifelong Republican. He also was a lay member of the Knights of Malta and a serious student of *The Protocols of the Learned Elders of Zion*. Through him, McNeil gained access to old money, old connections, and even older prejudices. With the money and connections diverting his attention, he never noticed the prejudices as they burrowed deep into his soul. All the while, Caldwell used their relationship to tutor McNeil in a toxic mix of traditional American conservatism, radical nationalism, and ultraconservative Christianity.

After graduation, and with Caldwell's help, McNeil landed a job as an aide to Senator Robert Gerry, a member of the powerful Senate Armed

Services Committee. There McNeil learned the inner workings of government from a firsthand view. The following year, he enrolled in the University of Virginia law school. Upon graduation he went to work for a Richmond law firm where he learned complex litigation while defending the interests of tobacco companies. At a reception that year he met Nikki Leigh Haley, who would become his wife. Their relationship was arranged conveniently by Caldwell. Her father and Caldwell were friends.

A few years later, at Caldwell's prompting, McNeil entered politics in a race for the Virginia legislature. With money supplied through Caldwell, and the help of key tobacco industry investors, McNeil won. In the legislature he worked hard to understand the state's issues and became an advocate for education reform. One of his first proposals was a measure that diverted public money to charter schools. The plan was touted as cutting-edge and progressive. In fact, it bifurcated public schools— creating an elite educational environment for the academically successful and relegating everyone else to vocational training. He also made sure to repay his supporters with liberal tax breaks and lax regulations for large corporations.

Having found success in the legislature, McNeil considered a run for lieutenant governor but, once again, Caldwell's influence held sway. With only two terms as a legislator, and just a few months after his thirty-fifth birthday, he entered the race for governor. Political pundits gave him little chance and viewed his campaign as merely a learning exercise for future efforts. But they didn't know about McNeil's connections or the money that supported him.

As governor, he quickly perfected the education reform he'd begun while in the legislature. His efforts imposed a battery of tests administered to elementary students that were used to separate college-track students from everyone else. At the same time, he poured billions of state dollars into new facilities, most of them for charter schools. Over the next four years, Virginia's public school system became the institution of choice among the state's wealthiest families, while the poor and minorities were shunted to the vocational system.

At the same time, McNeil led the fight to transform Virginia's tax structure to make it more business friendly, changed state usury laws to create a banking haven, and courted foreign business at every opportunity. National and local media focused on what appeared to be a glittering success story— a state education system that actually worked, paid for with income from a pro-business environment— and before long people began to wonder whether he might be able to do the same thing for the nation. Following reelection to a second term, it took little effort for Caldwell to coax him into establishing a presidential campaign exploratory committee. Soon after that, McNeil was the frontrunner for the Republican presidential nomination.

The months that followed were a whirlwind, taking him from state to state in the run-up to the primary elections that had just begun. That morning, sitting in the breakfast nook with a bagel and the morning paper, was one of the rare moments he spent at home. He took another bite of bagel and pointed to an article on the front page. "Did you see this?"

Nikki glanced across the table with a frown. "See what?"

"Someone broke into Liston Cook's Chicago campaign headquarters."

"Why would they waste their time with him?"

"Liston's a good man," he countered.

"He's a loser," she said, with an arrogant tone.

"Not a loser," McNeil sighed. "Just behind in the polls."

"That makes him a loser." She picked up her coffee cup from the table and stood. "You better get moving."

"I haven't finished the paper." He looked up at her with a smile. "I want to enjoy the morning while I can."

"You can enjoy it while you get ready."

He had a puzzled look. "Get ready for what?"

"You have a meeting with Morris Wythe."

"Oh," McNeil said with a start. "I forgot."

"Don't they give you a schedule?"

"I left it in the bedroom." He pulled her close and kissed her. "Does that mean I can ignore it?"

Nikki ran her hand over his shoulder. "I wish we could. But we can't." She tousled his hair as she pulled away. "Get moving. Don't want to keep the good reverend waiting."

As pastor of the New Vine Community Church, a mega church located in Nashville, Tennessee, Morris Wythe had a huge audience at his command. On most Sundays he preached at three services to a packed house. The main church sanctuary comfortably seated twenty thousand, and the service was transmitted by a satellite link to four auxiliary campuses in the Nashville area. The following week the service was broadcast on three separate cable channels. He had written a number of books, most of them best sellers, and had an array of teaching series on DVD— all of them available through multiple retail outlets and venues. The television and media operation alone was a far-flung, multimillion-dollar enterprise with a reach no politician could ignore.

McNeil laid aside the newspaper and stood. "I guess you're right," he said with a long stretch. "But I'd like to just stay right here."

Nikki moved past him and swatted him on the bottom. "Get moving. We can win this election if you don't quit on me."

Just then, the phone rang. McNeil bristled at the interruption. "Who's calling here?"

"Probably one of your loyal staffers," Nikki replied. She stopped in the hallway to take the call. "It's Carter," she said in a loud voice. "He says it's time to get moving."

"Carter Hewes," McNeil grumbled as he rose from his chair and started toward the phone. "That boy should get a life."

Nikki returned to the room and handed him the phone. "I think being your chief of staff is his life."

CHAPTER 36
CHICAGO

THROUGH THE NIGHT, Bill Sisson made his way from the apartment, keeping to side streets and alleys, and came out at Ninety-Ninth Street. Sometime before sunup he found an empty building and forced open the back door. The interior was swept clean and sheets of wallboard leaned against a column to the left. A worktable stood to the right. He found a rag and wiped off the table, then lay down and went to sleep.

A few hours later, he was awakened by the sound of a truck door as it slammed shut. He opened his eyes to see workmen on the sidewalk out front. Sisson rolled off the table, crouched low to keep out of sight, and made his way to the back door. He slipped out to the alley behind the building just as the workmen entered.

At the corner, Sisson turned right and walked back to Ninety-Ninth Street. Half a block later he came to the Blue Moon Café. He paused to check his appearance in the reflection of a nearby shop window, then opened the door and went inside. A waiter greeted him with a smile and guided him to a table near the kitchen. Before he was seated, a young woman came by and set a cup on the table. "Coffee?" she asked with a smile.

"Sure."

She filled the cup and moved on to the next table. A few minutes later, she returned with cream, sugar, and a plastic stirrer. Made with vivid shades of blue and yellow, it had a decorative half-moon on the handle. "Yours to keep," she said playfully as she set it beside the cup.

While he sipped coffee and ate a breakfast of eggs and toast, Sisson thought about what had transpired the night before. The plan had been wrong from the beginning. They should have simply bypassed the security system and crawled inside the same way he got out. Using the swipe card was too risky. "I knew it would never work," he mumbled to himself. Bob Casper, his contact in the Cook Campaign, had assured him Allen McLean never went near the Chicago office. *"They keep him on the road all the time,"* Casper insisted. *"He's out there doing the work of five men. They can't afford to bring him in."* It didn't sound right at the time, and now he wondered if he'd been set up all along.

As he continued to eat, he recounted the conversation he overheard when he returned to the apartment. The men who came looking for him were people he'd never seen before. Everyone else associated with the Cook assignment were men he'd worked with in the past. Why the new faces? How did they know so much about him? And why did they think the command center in Arizona could track him? One of them mentioned a chip. What chip?

Suddenly a memory flashed through his mind. A room with tiled walls. Water dripping. A voice from behind him speaking in an easy, steady tone. *"Are you ready?"* He tried to protest but the words wouldn't form in his mouth. *"Are you ready to leave that world behind?"* the voice continued. There was a burning sensation on his left arm. His fingers tingled, then his hands went numb. *"I'll ask you once more,"* the voice said again, *"are you ready?"* He nodded his head, slumped forward, and the room went black.

"Sir," a voice said.

Sisson glanced up to see a young woman, coffeepot in hand, standing near the table. Not more than twenty years old, she wore a red T-shirt with the Blue Moon Café logo on the front. Her eyes stared down at him with a confused look.

"Sorry," he said, forcing a smile. "Got lost in thought."

"That's okay," she gestured with the pot. "Would you like some more coffee?"

"Sure," he nodded. "Coffee would be good."

She moved the cup to the opposite side of the table, filled it, then slid it back to him. "Can I get you anything else?"

"No," he shook his head. "I'm fine." But he wasn't, and he was sure the waitress knew it. He kept his head bent low, as if focused on the plate in front of him, but his eyes darted around the room. A man near the window was staring at him. Two women at a table across the room seemed to be looking straight at him. And then a workman appeared on the side- walk in front— he was one of the workmen from the building up the street where he'd slept the night before.

Suddenly it seemed as if the walls were closing in, moving closer and closer. Sisson felt his chest grow tight. Breath came in short, quick gasps. He fumbled in his pocket, pulled out a twenty and tossed it on the table. *That's too much.* But by then he was up from his chair and moving toward the side door. He gave it a shove and stumbled outside.

On the sidewalk, the morning air was cool and crisp against his skin. He ran his hands over his face and took a deep breath, filling his lungs until it seemed they would burst. Then he slowly exhaled, only to take another long, deep breath. After a moment, his heart rate slowed. The throbbing pulse in his neck subsided. The sounds of the street returned.

Still suspicious of the workman he'd seen earlier, Sisson made the block by circling behind the café and came around to the cross street on the opposite side. As he walked back to Ninety-Ninth Street, a city bus approached. He flagged it to a stop at the corner and rode downtown to Wacker Drive. A World Gym stood on the corner at West Monroe. He pushed open the door and went inside. An attendant acknowledged him with a nod— Sisson had been there before. The morning crowd was gone by then, only a few people remained. No one else paid him any attention as he moved past the treadmills and free weights and made his way to the dressing room.

Inside the room, rows of lockers lined the space between the door and the showers. He walked to a locker on the back row, gave the dial on the lock a twist to the correct numbers, and jerked open the door. Sneakers and a backpack sat on the bottom. Workout shorts and T-shirt hung from a hook attached to a shelf at the top. On the shelf was a bar of soap, a shaving kit, and a towel. He took them out and headed to the showers.

Fifteen minutes later, he stood at a sink and dried off. In the mirror, his face looked tired and older. He leaned closer, inspecting his stubbly beard and the bags beneath his eyes. Then, in the harsh light of the locker room, he noticed a bump on his left shoulder. It was long and slender, with a dark streak just beneath the skin. He had never noticed it before and traced along the top with the tip of his index finger. From the way it felt, there was something hard buried beneath the skin.

He opened the shaving kit and found a pair of nail clippers with a metal file on one side. He unfolded the file to a straight position and pressed the edge of it against the lump. Now he was certain something was in there and he pressed it harder and harder until the point of the file broke the skin. Blood spurted against his neck, but he kept pressing harder until finally a shiny gray object popped free. It tumbled from his shoulder, bounced off his foot, and struck the floor. He stooped over, picked it up and held it between his thumb and index finger.

This is what they were talking about. This is a microchip. An electronic tracking chip.

Suddenly the images returned to his mind. A hospital ... an examination room. He was seated on a table, his feet dangled just above the floor. A man stood to his right, out of sight. He grasped Sisson's arm above the bicep. *"This will sting a little."* Then a searing-hot pain shot through his shoulder.

"Won't be long before there's snow," a voice to his left said.

Sisson jerked in that direction to see the gym attendant standing near the door. In his hand he held a towel. A pail half full of water sat on the floor beside his foot. The man seemed not to notice the blood on Sisson's shoulder.

"Felt it in the air this morning," the attendant continued. "Wind coming off the lake was different. It'll be cold for sure in a few days."

"Yeah," Sisson replied. He draped the towel over his shoulder to hide the wound. "I think you're right." He turned away and gathered his things, then moved toward the doorway.

At the locker, he dressed quickly and tucked the microchip in the pocket of his jeans. He unzipped the front panel of the backpack and took out an envelope filled with cash. He slipped some in his pocket and tucked the rest in the corner of the pack, then zipped it closed. When he was ready, he slung the backpack over his shoulder, closed the locker door, and headed toward the exit.

Outside the gym, he waved to flag down a taxi. The car came to a stop at the curb and Sisson slid into the back seat. "Where to?" the driver called.

"Bus station." Sisson pulled the door closed with a bang.

As the car rattled down the street, Sisson took the tracking chip from his pocket. He slid his hand over to the edge of the seat and tucked the chip into a crease in the upholstery.

A few minutes later, the taxi came to a stop outside the station. Sisson paid the driver and went inside to the ticket counter. An hour later, he boarded a bus for Indianapolis.

CHAPTER 37
CHICAGO

LATER THAT MORNING, Taylor Rutledge rode with Matthew Davis to the Chicago FBI office. Located on Roosevelt Road, it wasn't far from Liston Cook's headquarters. By the time they arrived, a report on the break-in suspects was ready and waiting. There were also FBI records for several individuals identified as probable matches for the sketch of a fourth suspect that had been prepared by Strickland's artist.

Rutledge took a seat at an empty desk, leaned back in the chair, and closed his eyes. "What about the phone number?"

Davis turned to Michelle Weaver, another agent. "Did you run that number I gave you?"

"It's a cell phone. Belongs to Ron McGuire."

"Do we have a file on him?"

"We do." She laid a file on the desk. "And so does the Secret Service." She dropped a manila envelope alongside the file.

Rutledge opened his eyes. "Why the Secret Service?"

"McGuire works for Christopher Wilson."

He had a puzzled frown. "The Democrat?"

"Yes," she nodded.

"Why would anyone from Wilson's campaign be connected to a break-in at Cook's office?"

"I don't know," she shrugged. "Politics makes some people do strange things."

"Well, that makes no sense." Rutledge leaned back again and once more closed his eyes. "Why would Wilson take a risk like that? He's a senator with impeccable credentials. He outpolls all the Republican candidates. And unless something crazy happens, he's going to win the nomination and run against McNeil in the general election anyway. Liston Cook has no chance of winning anything."

Davis spoke up. "Think the phone number's a plant?"

"Could be," Rutledge mused. "Somebody puts the number in his pocket to make it look like he works for Wilson. That way, when the news gets out, Wilson is all anyone is talking about."

"But," Weaver spoke up, "is McNeil crazy enough to pull a stunt like that just for the effect?"

"No," Davis replied. "But Liston Cook might be."

Rutledge opened his eyes. "Now, that's an interesting idea. Cook stages a break-in at his own headquarters and plants the Democratic frontrunner's phone number in the pocket of one of the burglars. Then when the news breaks, his campaign is instantly identified as a threat to the Democratic frontrunner." Rutledge's eyes were alive with the intrigue. "That would be a brilliant plan and revives my confidence in the electoral system." He leaned back once more and closed his eyes. "But I doubt anyone on either side of this election would ever think of it and if they did they wouldn't have the intestinal fortitude to do it. We better have a talk with McGuire."

Davis leaned against the desk. "What about the video from the building? Can we run that through a face-recognition program?"

"Already doing it. Takes a little while to get the results, but hopefully we'll get a match that looks something like that sketch."

Rutledge opened his eyes again and pointed to Weaver. "Good work."

CHAPTER 38
RICHMOND, VIRGINIA

LATER THAT MORNING, David McNeil rode downtown to meet Morris Wythe. He found Wythe ensconced in a four-bedroom suite at the Omni Richmond Hotel.

"Great to see you," Wythe began. He held the door open while McNeil stepped inside, then ushered him to a sofa in the living room. "I sent everyone out so we could have our weekly meeting alone."

"Good," McNeil nodded.

"That way," Wythe continued without missing a beat, "we can share whatever needs to be shared without you worrying about someone over-hearing it and getting it in the papers."

They'd been meeting like this for the past two years, and every meeting began the same way— with Wythe assuring him they were alone. McNeil was equally certain someone was always listening.

"So," Wythe continued as he moved to a chair near the end of the sofa. "Anything interesting happen since we last met?"

"Nothing you haven't already seen on CNN."

Wythe scoffed. "I don't watch CNN. Way too liberal for me. That stuff's not even news, and that's the problem we have today. Lots of people on television giving their opinions and passing them off as news stories.

I'm strictly a talk show man myself. Rarely listen to those so-called news reports."

From there Wythe launched into the stream of topics that had become typical for their meetings— God, country, the Founding Fathers, a need for lower taxes, less government regulation, strong national defense, and immigration reform. On that topic, he digressed into a long dissertation about how pastors and theologians in the South during the Civil War argued that Scripture authorized separation of the races, a view with which he was inclined to agree. McNeil nodded at appropriate moments but mostly kept quiet and listened.

Forty-five minutes later Wythe began to wind down and concluded by praying for McNeil. When he finished, he rose from the chair and crossed the room to a table near the window. "You care for some coffee?"

"Sure." McNeil joined Wythe at the table. "I've enjoyed our meetings, but when do I get to see your church?"

"Now, that's a great idea." Wythe handed him a cup of coffee. "You need to come down to Nashville and speak at our services." He led the way back toward the sofa and chair where they'd been sitting. "Better yet, we could do a two-day conference. Make a weekend of it. Do some seminars about how America has strayed far from the values around which the country was established, the need for minimal government. Maybe a session or two on immigration and the church." His face wrinkled in a disapproving scowl and he shook his head from side to side. "We can't keep accommodating people who come here illegally."

"I'm not sure I could give you an entire weekend. Time is rather precious right now."

"We wouldn't need you there for the entire weekend," Wythe countered. "Just come in on Sunday to speak. Maybe bring your wife down for the Saturday night event."

"She'd love that," McNeil nodded. "I'm sure she'd be glad to speak."

"This could work out real well," Wythe grinned. "Broadcast it on our cable network. Reach a lot of people." He paused to take a sip of coffee, then continued brainstorming. "Produce a set of DVDs. We have the equipment and editing suites to produce DVDs while the events are still in progress. Sell them the same day."

McNeil was skeptical. "The same day?"

"Yeah," Wythe beamed. "By the time the second event is over, they'll have DVDs from the first one in the lobby." He took another sip. "We'll sell a bunch."

"But will it get us any votes?"

"That part's easy. They're already committed." Wythe reached over and slapped McNeil on the back. "Just waiting on Election Day."

"Okay," McNeil grinned. "I'll have Carter Hewes call you about some dates."

"Good. I'll get my people working on it."

CHAPTER 39
WASHINGTON, D.C.

EARLY THAT SAME MORNING, Esther was jarred awake by the ringing of her cell phone. She groped for it on the nightstand and pressed a button to answer. The call was from Brody.

"Have you read the morning paper?"

"What time is it?" she groaned.

"Four. Have you read the paper? A team of burglars broke into Liston Cook's campaign headquarters in Chicago."

"Why are you calling me about this at four in the morning?"

"Meet me at the corner." Brody ended the call without waiting for a response. Esther rested her head against the pillow and closed her eyes. A few minutes later the phone rang again. Brody sounded concerned. "Where are you?"

"I'm asleep," she growled.

His voice became insistent. "You're supposed to meet me on the corner."

"I'm sleeping."

"We need to talk."

"Liston Cook is as inconsequential as a candidate could possibly be," she mumbled. "I have to be at the office in three hours and I need to be awake when I get there. Call me later." She switched off the phone and pulled the covers over her head.

Sometime later she was awakened by a knock at her front door, followed by the ring of the doorbell. She opened her eyes to find sunlight streaming through the bedroom window. She threw aside the covers, took the phone from beneath the pillow, and glanced at the screen to check the time. It was six already. She climbed from bed, pulled on a robe, and walked through the house to the front door.

With her eye pressed against the peephole she saw Brody on the steps out front. Esther opened the door and glared at him. "What are you doing?"

"We need to talk."

"About what?"

Brody pushed past her and stepped inside. "A team hit Cook's office in Chicago."

"You told me that already."

"We think they also hit a couple of other sites as well."

"This is ridiculous," she grumbled as she closed the door behind him.

"The break-ins?"

"No. Your obsession with them."

"Cohen thinks it has something to do with the documents from Penalta's flash drive."

"Why does he think that?"

"Because of the—"

Esther cut him off with a wave of her hand. "I remember," she frowned. "The intern." She stepped away from the door and started toward the kitchen. "I need some coffee."

Brody continued talking as he followed after her. "Look, Esther. I know this is way beyond what you do at the law firm, but Cohen wants to know if you have any contacts inside Cook's campaign."

She knew of one really good contact but she wasn't about to tell Brody. Instead she took a container of coffee from the cabinet, set it on the counter, and reached back on the shelf for a filter. "I'll have to think about it when I'm alert."

"How long will that take?"

"Judging from the way I feel right now, about three cups."

"They want us to move quickly."

Esther filled the coffee basket with ground coffee, poured water in the coffee maker, and turned on the switch. "I'm sure they want an answer quickly," she said, finally, "but just what do they expect me to find?"

"They want to know if the people who broke into Cook's office were looking for those documents."

"I don't see how."

"Why not?"

"Think about it, Brody." She gave him a perplexed scowl. "The documents were transmitted as an attachment to an email. They're in an electronic file. With the touch of a button, the click of a mouse, they could be in a thousand different places by now. Who do they think conducted this break-in?"

"No one knows yet. Three men were arrested. They're being held in Chicago."

"I thought you said there were four."

"The fourth man got away."

"And no one knows who these men are?"

"They know who they said they are, but no one knows yet who sent them." He leaned against the door facing. "Look, I don't know many details. I'm just telling you what they tell me."

"Well," Esther sighed and ran her fingers through her hair, "tell them I'll look into it."

"Work fast." Brody turned toward the hallway.

"Hey," Esther called after him. "Did you find anything about that address I gave you?"

"Not yet. But we're still working on it."

"Don't you want some coffee?"

"No," Brody called as he opened the front door. "I've had your coffee before. I'll get mine at the shop on the corner."

*   *   *

Later that morning, Esther met Paul for breakfast at Moynihan's, a café on K Street. They sat at a table near the window. Esther got to the point quickly. "Did you hear about Liston Cook?"

"The break-in?"

"Yes."

"Couldn't miss it. Made the front section of the newspaper. All the morning shows are talking about it."

"Brody came to see me."

"Already? This morning?"

"Woke me up. He wants to know if there's a connection between the break-in and the documents."

"The documents?"

She leaned closer. "The ones the priest took to Zurich."

"Why does he think there's a connection?"

"Penalta's assistant had a flash drive with the documents on it. He took them to a rabbi in Zurich. The rabbi gave the flash drive to an American intern working at the synagogue. The American read the documents and emailed them to a friend who works for Liston Cook."

Paul grinned at her. "Sometimes I think Brody stays up late at night making this stuff up."

"I know." She looked amused. "It's a little convoluted, even for Brody."

"If he emailed the documents," Paul continued, "they could be in a dozen places by now. What good would a break-in do?"

"That was my response, too."

"What did Brody say?"

"He says he's just the messenger. The center at Beersheba wants to know if the break-ins are related."

"And Brody asked you to ask me because he knows I'm friends with Liston."

"No," Esther said, shaking her head. "He doesn't know you're friends with Liston."

Their eyes met. Paul put down his fork. "You're asking me?"

"I think we have a choice. Either we do this together, or we go to Texas and forget the world."

"We've discussed this before. I want to help you. Why do you keep bringing it up?"

Her eyes widened. "This is dangerous. It's not a movie or a television show. People actually die doing this."

He reached across the table and took her hand. "If I die helping you, then I die happy."

"I don't want to lose you."

"You won't lose me." He squeezed her hand tighter. "But you can't live in fear of what might happen, either."

Tears rolled down her cheeks. "I've lost one to this cause already."

"You didn't lose him. Ephraim is with you every day. And so am I."

She smiled at him. "How did I find you?"

"You didn't find me. I found you." He lifted her hand to his lips and kissed it, then let her fingers slip from his. "Okay," he took a deep breath. "I think Liston is back in Pennsylvania this week. I'll see what I can do." He checked his watch. "We better get moving. The morning is almost gone."

CHAPTER 40
RHODES

SPOLETO GATHERED WITH THE Legislative Council in the Hall of Saints. As he entered the room, the Council, known simply as the Twenty-Four, took their seats around a long conference table that occupied the center of the room. Spoleto made his way to a chair at the opposite end of the table. Father Galena took a seat to his left. When everyone was in place, Spoleto rapped his knuckles on the table and began.

"As you are aware, several days ago Father Penalta traveled with Barberini to Zurich for the purpose of bringing charges against us. He carried with him certain documents stolen from our files which he thought would lend credence to his claims. While he was making his case, Penalta met a most unfortunate end and Barberini is now missing."

Someone to the right spoke up. "Was Barberini involved?"

"One may assume so. An agent acting on orders of the Military Vicariate entered the apartment where Penalta and Barberini were staying and made a thorough search of the premises. He secured the laptop on which the documents were stored and assured us no copies remained. However, it subsequently came to the attention of my office that other copies of the documents did, in fact, exist. I informed Father Galena of these circumstances and referred the matter to him." Spoleto gestured in

Galena's direction. "He will now report to you on the matters that have transpired since."

Galena rose from his seat at the table. "Three days ago," he began, his voice wavering and unsteady, "an informant working with the Cook political campaign notified us that the documents Penalta took to Zurich had been transferred to a member of the Cook advance team. A review of the matter showed this information to be accurate and—"

A hand went up at the far end of the table. "How? How were they transferred?"

"By email."

"Have countermeasures been taken?"

"That is why we are here now. Please allow me to continue." He nodded politely, then began again. "In an effort to protect the Order from the consequences of Penalta's tragic mistake, the Military Vicariate authorized Sierra Resources to attempt a recovery of the documents. Teams were dispatched for the purpose of ascertaining whether the documents existed on Cook's computer system and, if so, to facilitate their removal."

Someone seated to the left spoke up. "This was the work of Barberini." He shook his head in a disapproving manner. "He manipulated Penalta into doing it. I have known Penalta a long time. He would never do something like this on his own. That Greek convinced him to do it."

"Why was Barberini not taken out with Penalta?"

"We met with Barberini before the trip," Galena explained, "and understood he was with us in our effort to bring the matter with Penalta to an amicable conclusion. Instead, he turned out to be a traitor."

Others spoke out in rapid succession. "Judas helping Judas."

"We should have never admitted a Greek to the Order."

"Yes," someone added. "The Ancients were right. The Orthodox are too orthodox. They are worse than the Jews."

"Sardinia comes under the Italian government. He was an Italian citizen."

"Yes, but he was Greek Orthodox by faith and that blinded his heart. They believe the lies told by those American Jews."

"Please," Galena interrupted. "Allow me to continue." He paused a moment for the Council to come to order. "As I was saying, in an effort to contain the matter, the Vicariate called on Sierra Resources to deploy multiple teams to retrieve the files."

Father Molina spoke up. "How many teams?"

"Fifteen teams, four men in each."

"Fifteen teams?" Molina looked concerned. "Deployed at fifteen different locations?"

"Yes." The men seated at the table exchanged looks of incredulity. Galena ignored them and continued. "Fourteen of the missions were completed without incident." Council members grimaced at what was coming next. "One of the teams was caught and arrested."

"Where?" Molina asked. "Where were they arrested?"

"Chicago."

"Where, specifically?"

"Inside Liston Cook's official headquarters."

A murmur rose from the table. Molina gestured for quiet. "How many were caught?"

"Three for certain. Perhaps a fourth. The reports are still not clear."

"I think it unlikely that they were simply caught," Molina replied. "These are specially trained teams. They practice all the time for this sort of thing."

Someone across the table looked over at Molina. "Could the authorities have been helped by someone on the inside?"

Molina shook his head. "I do not think so. An inside informant seems even more unlikely than that the team was simply captured. These men are loyal beyond question." He turned to Galena. "What was their cover story?"

Galena's shoulders relaxed. He was thankful to finally have a question for which he was certain he had a good response. "They were carrying enough information to make it appear that they worked for Christopher Wilson."

"The Democrat?" Molina's voice was sharp and abrasive.

"Yes," Galena replied, his shoulders suddenly tense once more. "He is of no concern to us."

"Yes, but a cover like that is dangerous. The story is not believable."

"Christopher Wilson outpolls all of our candidates," someone explained. "He would not waste a moment on Liston Cook."

"But we do want Wilson out of the race," another insisted.

"If this gets to the press, he will have to spend valuable time defending it."

"But if he defends it vigorously, Sierra's cover story will fall apart."

Spoleto tapped his knuckles lightly against the table. The room grew quiet. He caught Galena's eye. "Who approved such a thing?"

Galena looked nervous. "The Military Vicariate approved the operation."

"No," Spoleto said, correcting him. "Not the operation, the cover story. The story was a detail arranged by someone in charge of the actual operation. Who coordinated the operation on the ground?"

"Jeremy Bartlett, Henry Caldwell, Jim Nash."

Spoleto turned to the Council. "This story— giving the men information that implicates another politician— sounds like something Caldwell would think of."

Others at the table picked up the suggestion and turned the discussion away from the Vicariate. Galena gave Spoleto a look of relief.

"Sounds like Tony Floyd and Ed Logan," someone suggested. "Using this to try out their latest ideas."

"Or Dr. Walcott."

"At the expense of our candidate."

"I thought Logan's people were better than this. They are supposed to be shaping the election. We do not want to run against Wilson."

"Can we really shape an election to that extent?"

"We need Jacob Rush to win the Democratic primary. McNeil can beat him in the general election."

"I do not think Rush can win, even with our help. He is as far behind on the Democrat side as Liston Cook is on the Republican."

"Well, regardless, we need Christopher Wilson out and this sounds like an attempt to do just that."

A face leaned out from the chairs that lined the table to Spoleto's right. "In light of these new developments, are we certain McNeil can really do the job?"

"This was not McNeil," Spoleto replied, then he rose and addressed the Council. "The fact remains, the Cook campaign has copies of documents that can destroy our candidate and put at risk all we've accomplished. We've worked long and hard to get to this point— the Patriot Act, anti-terrorism laws that give the central government broad powers, states passing their own immigration laws empowering local police to round up illegals. Law enforcement is fully authorized at both the state and federal levels. They have all the authority they need to carry out our Grand Strategy to once and for all eliminate the Jewish stronghold in America."

"And," someone added, "the churches are too theologically ignorant to recognize what's happening. This is an opportunity of a lifetime."

"We planned that, too," another chimed in. Laugher rippled across the room, then someone else spoke up. "All we need is a president willing to act. Round up the Mexicans first and then the Jews are next."

"We can have that president with McNeil," Spoleto added. "And it will be the end of the Jews and their attempts to rule the world."

"We still have a problem in the U.S.," Father Molina interjected. "This story about the break-in will never hold. Someone will talk and I'm afraid they will very quickly discover the connection. Not to us but to Logan and the others, and that will lead them to McNeil."

"That must never happen."

"They have to clean this up right away." Everyone nodded in agreement.

"Should we replace Caldwell?"

"No," Spoleto replied. "I think that would be a little too disruptive for the candidate right now. He relies on Caldwell too much to remove him. We do, too."

"Should we bring him in for direct talks?"

"No," Spoleto said once more. "That would be far too risky for us."

"We could send a delegation to meet him in Athens."

Molina threw his hands in the air. "That is as risky as the strategy they just tried."

"Very well, gentlemen," Spoleto said, interrupting the discussion. "I think we have reached a consensus. I suggest we have our contact in America meet with Caldwell and instruct him to clean up this situation and to redouble efforts to locate the missing documents and files but in a less overt manner." Around the table the men nodded in agreement. Spoleto continued. "You will signify your agreement in the usual manner." In unison, the delegates pushed back their chairs from the table and stood. "Any opposed?" The room fell silent. Spoleto let his gaze roam the table, looking every man in the eye. When he had gone all the way around, he rapped the table with his fist. "So be it."

Then, as if on cue, the delegates responded, "In the name of the Father, and of the Son, and of the Holy Spirit. Amen." And with that, the meeting adjourned.

After they were gone, Spoleto turned to Galena. "You must do better."

"I cannot always guide them to where you want them to go."

"Perhaps not, but fifteen was too aggressive. And it has been noticed you did not go after Barberini."

"Go after him?" Galena bristled at the comment. "You want to blame this on the Greeks?"

"No. I am just saying, people have noticed."

"I sponsored him. You did, too. This is as much your issue as it is mine."

"Yes," Spoleto nodded. "I know. You and I are in this together, but you have to hold the Vicariate in check."

"I am doing my best," Galena lamented.

"You cannot let them run off with ideas like this."

"I know," Galena sighed. He bowed his head. "I am in your debt."

"Very well." Spoleto extended his hand. "We will work this out." Galena took Spoleto's hand in his and kissed Spoleto's ring. Then, without saying more, he turned aside and walked away.

When the room was empty, Russo appeared at the doorway. Spoleto motioned for him to come nearer. "I want you to get a message to Wallace Jordan," Spoleto said in a hushed tone.

"You mean Edgar Logan. He is in charge of Sierra Resources."

"No," Spoleto said, wagging his finger. "Wallace Jordan."

"What shall I tell him?"

"Tell him I expect him to be the janitor."

"The janitor?"

"He will know what to do. And see that this mess is cleaned up."

"I should tell him that?"

"No." Spoleto tapped Russo on the chest. "I am telling you."

Russo was taken aback. "You want me to clean up the trouble Sierra has created?"

"I want you to see that it gets done."

"Sir, you have already given me this same order regarding Barberini." Russo looked perplexed. "You wish to involve us directly in everything?"

"No," Spoleto said with a smile. "I want to involve you."

"Me?"

"If we are to salvage anything from McNeil's campaign, it will require our most direct involvement."

"But that places the Order at risk. We cannot do that. It is beyond the authority of the Council. The Military Vicariate would be free to—"

Spoleto cut him off with a smile. "I am not placing the Order at risk." He rested his hand on Russo's shoulder. "I am placing you at risk. From now on, you will be the control point."

Russo's eyes were wide. "Me?"

"This is the obligation of your office." Spoleto's voice took a serious tone. The expression on his face turned solemn. "It is your service to the Order and an act of allegiance to me." He looked Russo in the eye. "You will accept it?"

"Yes," Russo nodded, reluctantly. "I accept."

CHAPTER 41
TUCSON, ARIZONA

JEREMY BARTLETT STOOD in the Sierra command center and stared at the screens that lined the walls. He squinted against the glare of the light and rubbed his eyes with his fingertips. It had been two days since he last slept. He'd been living on coffee and doughnuts, working around the clock to contain the problem in Chicago, and still he could not locate Bill Sisson. "How long before we reestablish contact with the chip?"

Donna Preston called from across the room, "Tech is working on it."

"That's what you said last time I asked."

She rose from her desk and came to his side. "Everyone is working as hard as they can," she said quietly. "Maybe you should take a break. Sleep a little. Actually eat a decent meal instead of all those doughnuts."

"I can't sleep until we find him."

"Technical support is doing all they can. We knew this chip had problems. That's why we changed the others. They'll get it straightened out, but it takes time."

"We don't have time."

Just then, Angela Thornton called from a desk behind them, "We've got it now. Tech has the chip working."

"Great," Bartlett replied. "Put up a map on the screen and show me Sisson's current location."

A map of the United States appeared on a screen to the left. As Bartlett watched, the image switched to a map of Illinois, then narrowed to Chicago, and finally to a grid of the streets inside The Loop. A red dot blinked near Wacker Drive. Bartlett pointed to it. "Is that him?"

"Yes, sir," Thornton called. "That's his current position."

"We're certain?"

"The code number from the chip is the one assigned to him."

"Okay," Bartlett said to no one in particular. "Let's get a team down there to bring him in." He turned away from the screen and started toward the operator's desk in the center of the room. "We need a rendition …"

"Sir," Thornton shouted. "Sisson is on the move."

Bartlett turned back to the screen and watched as the red indicator moved steadily down Wacker Drive. "He's moving fast. Must be in a car."

"Where did he get a car?"

"Maybe he stole it."

"Let's hope not. That would be one more complication we don't need."

"Taxi," Preston suggested. "He's got to be riding in a taxi."

"Or a bus."

"We have a team on the move now," Thornton offered. "Video on screen three."

Images appeared on a screen to the right, giving a view out the front windshield of a van as it moved through Chicago traffic. Bartlett stared at it a moment, then pointed. "Do we have audio on this?"

Moments later, a voice came from the speaker mounted on the wall in the corner of the room. "Are you sure that's the one?"

"Yes," a second voice replied. "I'm reading the signal off the chip. That's him."

"I don't see anyone inside except the driver."

"Pull him over."

"How?"

"There's a traffic light at the next corner. It just turned red. He'll have to stop for it. Sam can get out and jump in the back seat."

"Sam, are you ready?"

"I'm ready," a third voice replied. "Just tell me when."

"Okay, we're coming up on them now." The taxi stopped for the traffic light. The van came to a halt just behind it. There was the sound of a van door sliding open, then Sam appeared on the screen as he came from the van, opened the rear door of the taxi, and crawled inside.

Through the rear window the driver could be seen gesturing with his hands in an animated conversation. Sam leaned over the seat as the heated exchange continued. Moments later, the taxi started forward, lurched through the intersection, and came to a stop at the curb to the right. The van followed and parked at an angle with the rear bumper hanging out in the street. The front doors of the van flew open and two men emerged. One of them ran to the rear door of the taxi. The other approached from the driver's side and leaned through the front window.

Then the man at the rear door of the taxi stepped back from the car and turned toward the van to face the camera. "Command, this is Mobile Three. We have a problem."

Bartlett turned to the operator. "Find out what he's talking about."

"State the nature of your problem."

"We found the chip. It was tucked into the upholstery of the rear seat."

"Can the driver confirm Sisson was a passenger?"

"Jimmy is talking to the driver now."

Bartlett struck the wall with his fist in a gesture of frustration.

CHAPTER 42
WASHINGTON, D.C.

LATER THAT DAY, Esther left her office and walked up the street toward the federal courthouse. The afternoon was cool, sunny and bright. As she made her way along the sidewalk her mind wandered over the conversation she'd had with Brody and the one she had earlier with Paul over breakfast. With her attention diverted, she didn't notice someone approaching from behind until she heard a voice. "A couple of your associates were in our office yesterday."

The sound of the voice startled Esther. She turned to see Amy Goodwin walking beside her. Esther gave her a smile. "Did they find what they were looking for?"

"That depends."

"On what?"

"On why you sent them over there." Amy took her by the arm and steered her aside. "They were asking about David McNeil's campaign and looking for records of political contributions from Sierra Resources. If you sent them to actually see the records then no, they failed. But if you wanted to stir things up, I think you succeeded royally."

"So, the records exist?"

"I can't acknowledge that we have records on McNeil, other than the ones accessible through the website."

"So, what's the problem? Were they rude to someone?"

"No. They were cordial enough. That's never been a problem with lawyers from your office. But there's something you should know." Amy drew Esther closer, steered her farther away from pedestrian foot traffic, and lowered her voice. "The agency received information from at least two sources raising questions about donations to McNeil's campaign. We've launched an active investigation and we're taking a serious look at his connections to Sierra Resources."

Esther arched an eyebrow. "That's interesting."

"Why?"

"You can't acknowledge records we both know you have, but you can tell me about an active investigation of the Republican frontrunner in the current presidential election."

"Look, I'm telling you this as a friend. Everyone in the office is wondering why, just days after we launch an investigation into two high-profile targets— one a major candidate and the other an influential defense contractor— your attorneys show up asking about the very same thing."

"I guess I'm just an influential attorney with influential clients."

"Esther."

"You know I can't tell you what I'm doing."

"Okay. But this is big. Really big."

"You're the second person who's told me that."

"Well, maybe you should listen. The FBI is investigating with us and if this blows up, you could get dragged into a long investigation."

"Criminal?"

"Criminal on their side. Civil on ours."

"I'm not worried."

"Okay," Amy replied. "But don't say I didn't warn you."

CHAPTER 43
CHICAGO

RUTLEDGE SPENT THE MORNING at the FBI office, then went to a nearby hotel and took a nap. Later, after a shower and change of clothes, he returned to find Davis at Weaver's desk.

"We got the report," Davis grinned.

"What report?"

"From the face-recognition software. We ran the security video against it and got a hit."

Weaver handed Rutledge a photograph. "That's your fourth man. Bill Sisson. Former Marine."

"Now works for Sierra Resources."

Rutledge shot him a look. "Sierra Resources?"

"Yes."

"What about the other three? Do they work for Sierra?"

"Don't know. Still checking."

"Any chance the break-in was a Sierra job?"

"Can't say yet. No one at Sierra is talking right now."

"Yeah," Rutledge nodded. "I can imagine."

"Could be Sisson was simply moonlighting on his own."

"I suppose."

"Sierra is a huge company. Makes most of its money on defense contracts."

"Trains people for all kinds of classified programs," Weaver offered. "It wouldn't make much sense for them to risk it all on breaking into an office like this."

Rutledge glanced in her direction. "An office like this?"

"Cook's barely hanging on," she said flatly. "A few more weeks and he would have been out of money."

"Would have been?"

"Publicity from the break-in sent donations through the roof," Davis explained. "He's got more money now than ever before."

Weaver smiled at Rutledge. "You might want to rethink that idea of yours."

"Which one was that?"

"The one about Cook orchestrating the break-in just for the publicity." Weaver folded her arms across her chest and leaned back in her chair. "So, what was the investigation you were already doing about Cook?"

"Investigation?" Rutledge forced a puzzled look. He wasn't sure he wanted to get into it right then.

"Yeah, they said they were sending you out here because you were already investigating Cook. Told us to help you, but that you had the lead."

"I don't know if I should ..."

"We aren't going to be much use to you unless you tell us."

Rutledge hesitated a moment. In the few years he'd been with the FBI he'd learned that maintaining control of an investigation was a touchy matter. Assignments for agents of his rank were handed down from supervisors. The younger agents were expected to work the initial aspects of a case— interview witnesses, collect evidence, conduct research. At that point, no one else cared to get involved because they all had their own cases to worry about and the work was rather routine. But as a case unfolded, especially one with high-profile targets, and as word of it spread around the office, everyone wanted in on the act. Younger agents who had worked the case and developed the leads were sometimes pushed aside in the latter stages, just as the case became public.

Telling Davis and Weaver about what he'd been doing would widen the scope of agency participation, which in turn would dilute his control of the case. He'd be going back to D.C. in a day or two, but Davis and Weaver would continue to work the case from Chicago. Telling them details about Cook and the NSA intercept would pique their interest, draw them deeper into the investigation, and broaden their sense of authority to work on their own after he was gone. No telling what they would do in his absence. Still, he needed their help.

Reluctantly, Rutledge closed the office door and turned to face them. "A few days ago … I think it's been days, maybe a week. I'm operating from memory and very little sleep…. A priest from a religious order known as the Knights of Malta traveled to Zurich with an assistant. They brought documents they claimed would support charges of heresy against the Order. They presented the charges and the documents to a church official. Before they could return home, the priest was killed."

"You mean murdered?"

"Yes," Rutledge nodded. "A few days later his assistant showed up at a synagogue with a flash drive that contained the documents they presented to the church."

Weaver had a puzzled look. "Why a synagogue?"

"The priest claimed the Order was secretly promoting an anti-Semitic agenda."

"So," Davis began, "what's that have to do with Liston Cook and his presidential campaign?"

"Here," Rutledge smiled, "the story gets interesting. According to the priest, the Order has been working to influence the U.S. presidential election by controlling one of the candidates."

Weaver had a skeptical frown. "Cook?"

"No." Rutledge shook his head. "McNeil."

"A secret anti-Semitic order controls David McNeil?"

"I know." Rutledge gestured with his hands. "It sounds crazy. But if you saw the documents on the flash drive, you might not be so quick to dismiss the idea."

"They actually documented what they were doing?"

"Not about the Jews, but the documents show a money trail from foreign banks into the McNeil campaign."

"So, how does that connect to Cook?" Davis asked.

"An American working in Zurich emailed the documents to a friend who works for Cook."

"Okay," Weaver nodded. "That tells us about Cook. But what's the connection with Sierra Resources? I mean, assuming this break-in was a Sierra job, why do they care?"

"The money from the Order," Rutledge explained, "passed through Sierra's bank account before it ended up in McNeil's campaign accounts."

"Has anyone talked to Cook?"

"We're working on it from the Washington office." Rutledge glanced down at Sisson's picture. "He looks familiar."

"Think you've seen him?"

"Maybe." Rutledge stared at the photo a moment longer, then looked over at Weaver. "Where does he live?"

"Has an apartment in Alexandria, Virginia."

"Okay," Rutledge sighed. "Get me that address and I'll have someone get over there right away."

"Already alerted them. Your office has a team there now."

It was the right thing to do, but Rutledge could feel the case slipping from his control. "Who did they send?"

"Brenner and Caffery."

"Good." Rutledge forced a smile. "They'll do a good job." He handed the photograph to Davis. "Make sure we get this photo out to the local police departments. Flag all his known aliases."

"Want to alert the media?"

"No," Rutledge replied. "Not yet. Let's let him think he got away clean. Make it a lot easier to find him."

CHAPTER 44
CHICAGO

A FEW BLOCKS AWAY, Henry Caldwell turned the car into a parking lot at Lincoln Park. He brought the car to a stop near the fountain and got out. Caldwell, always with his finger on the pulse of McNeil's campaign, maintained a far-reaching network of contacts and friends. He received a call as soon as Chicago police responded to the break-in at Cook's headquarters. Before the arrests were made, he boarded a private plane in Virginia and headed to Chicago. He didn't need a message from Spoleto to tell him what to do. He knew what to do without being told and he had the personal resources to react without waiting for others to authorize a response.

Caldwell quickly surveyed the area, checking to see if anyone was watching. When he was satisfied, he crossed the parking lot and started down a narrow footpath that led to the back side of a large fountain. There he found Jim Nash seated on a concrete bench beneath the low-hanging branches of an oak tree. Caldwell took a seat beside him.

"You have the lawyers in place?"

Nash smiled confidently. "They told me you would come."

"You have the lawyers in place?" Caldwell repeated. "For the three who were arrested?"

"Yes, everything is under control."

"No one talked?"

"No." Nash shook his head.

"You have to make sure of it."

"I am certain."

"You have to—"

"Tell me something," Nash said, interrupting. "Is it really true that you once convinced the Democratic Party in Virginia to support your guy for the Republican nomination?"

"Did it several times," Caldwell said, curtly. "You have to—"

"Why would they do that?"

"Do what?"

"Kick their own candidate to the curb and support a candidate from the opposing party?"

"I showed them how it was in their best interest to do so." Caldwell's patience was wearing thin. He pressed forward once more. "We need to—"

"You're that good?"

"I'm that convincing," he said, sternly. "And if you keep ignoring me, you'll find out what that means. Now, I want you to be sure they haven't talked already, and that they do not talk in the future. We can contain this, but they have to keep quiet. No matter what happens."

"I'm on top of it," Nash assured him.

"Have you located the fourth man?"

"We're on his trail."

"But so far, he has eluded you."

"He was trained to be elusive," Nash countered.

"Any estimate of when you will locate him?"

"Like I said, we're working on it."

"Okay. Here's how we're going to do this. If you have any problems, you deal with me." Caldwell made a definitive gesture with his hand. "No one from the campaign. No one from the governor's office. You deal with me. Got it?"

"We've done this before, Mr. Caldwell. I know what to do."

Caldwell's eyes were ablaze. "This isn't a drill or an exercise, son." His voice was tense, his words clipped and rapid. "When I ask if you have it, I mean to get an answer. Lives and futures are on the line and I don't have time for your attitude. You got it?"

"Yes, sir," Nash replied with a nod. "I got it."

"Don't contact anyone else about this except me. Got it?"

"Yes."

"And you're certain they didn't talk?"

"As soon as the police started asking questions, the men all asked for lawyers. No one talked. The lawyers got there quickly. We're good."

"You deal with me and only me on this," Caldwell repeated again. "Got it?"

"I got it." Nash gestured with his thumb. "Make your call."

"What?"

"Make your call."

Caldwell took a cell phone from the pocket of his jacket and placed a call.

CHAPTER 45
DETROIT

LATE IN THE AFTERNOON, Rutledge boarded a plane and flew to Detroit, Michigan, to catch up with the Wilson campaign. That evening, he met Wilson and his campaign chairman, Pat Waters, in a hotel room.

"Okay," Wilson said after a brief introduction. "What's this all about?"

"I need to talk with you about a sensitive topic," Rutledge began. "And I prefer to speak with you alone."

"No way," Waters replied. "He's not speaking to anyone without me being present."

"You're his lawyer, too?"

"This is a presidential campaign, Mr. Rutledge. We've worked long and hard for this opportunity."

Rutledge looked over at Wilson. "What I'm going to ask you about hasn't yet reached the media. I need your assurance that it won't come from you."

Wilson glanced at Waters. "Wait outside."

"What?"

"It's okay, Pat. Wait outside."

Waters stepped from the room and closed the door. When he was gone, Wilson looked over at Rutledge. "Okay. What's so important?"

"As I'm sure you are aware, there was a break-in at Liston Cook's campaign headquarters in Chicago late Sunday night."

"I read about it in the paper."

"Three men were arrested in the building. When they were booked at the jail, the police found a scrap of paper in the pocket of one of the suspects. That paper had Ron McGuire's cell phone number on it."

Wilson seemed amused. "Let me ask you something, Mr. Rutledge. I see polling data almost every day, same as every other candidate. I outpoll every candidate in this race, from either party. So why would I care about what Liston Cook has in that old train station?" He leaned over and took a soft drink from the minibar. "I like Liston. Everybody likes Liston. But he's not going to get his party's nomination. I'm running against Democrats right now." He opened the drink and took a sip. "And in November I'll be running against McNeil."

"Do you know Ron McGuire?"

"The name seems vaguely familiar. We have hundreds of people working for us right now." He took another sip and shrugged. "Maybe thousands. You want to talk to him?"

"Yes."

Wilson opened the door and leaned out to the hallway. Waters was standing a few feet away. Wilson motioned for him. Waters stepped into the room.

"Rutledge needs to talk to someone named Ron McGuire. Is he with us?"

"He coordinates local volunteers. I saw him in the lobby when we came up."

"Get him up here. Rutledge needs to talk to him." Waters took an iPhone from his pocket and placed a call. While he talked to McGuire, Wilson glanced at Rutledge. "You finished with me?"

"For now. But we may need to talk again."

"Sure thing," Wilson nodded. "I'll help in any way I can." Then he opened the door and disappeared up the hallway.

In a few minutes, the hotel room door opened and a slender young man appeared. Waters pointed to a chair near a table by the window. "Have a seat." The young man did as he was told. Waters sat on the bed. "This is Mr. Rutledge. He's from the FBI. He wants to ask you some questions. Whatever he asks, you have to tell the truth."

"Yes, sir."

"But you can't tell anyone else what we talk about."

"Okay."

Waters nodded to Rutledge. "Go ahead."

"Are you Ron McGuire?"

"Yes."

A leather satchel sat on the dresser near the television. Rutledge reached inside it, took out a single sheet of paper, and handed it to McGuire. "There's a number on that page. Recognize it?"

McGuire glanced at it and nodded. "Yes. That's my cell phone number."

Rutledge returned the page to the satchel and took out three photographs. He handed them to McGuire. "Recognize any of those men?"

"I don't think so."

"These men were arrested Sunday night. One of them was carrying a scrap of paper with your cell phone number on it. Any idea how they got it?"

"No." McGuire looked over at Waters. "What's this about?"

"Just answer the questions."

"Are you familiar with a man named Bill Sisson?"

"No. I don't know anyone by that name."

"Ever have any contact with a company called Sierra Resources?"

"Not that I can recall."

"When were you last in Chicago?"

"Last week, I think. The days kind of run together. We were there for a rally. Spent the night. I work with the advance team to make sure we have plenty of local participation."

"Has anyone on the campaign recently quit?"

"We have people coming and going all the time."

"Any of them work with you?"

"No … I don't think so."

Waters glanced at his watch. "Are we about done?"

"Just about. Mr. McGuire, do you know anyone who works for the Cook campaign?"

"No. Not really."

"What does that mean?"

"I see their people sometimes. I recognize their faces as being people with Cook, but I don't know them."

"Okay." Rutledge looked over at Waters. "I will need to talk with him again as we go forward. You'll make sure I can find him easily."

"Of course," Waters smiled. "Always glad to help the FBI."

CHAPTER 46
CHICAGO

THE FOLLOWING DAY, Harry Giles, an assistant from the U.S. Marshal's Service, steered a Ford Econoline van to a stop at the security gate outside the Cook County Jail. A guard stepped to the driver's door.

"You picking up today?"

"Yeah," Giles replied. "I have an order for three."

"Where's Allen? He usually makes the run for the Marshal's office."

"I don't know. They told me to come down here. So I came."

The guard stepped to the guardhouse and returned with a clipboard. "I don't see you on the list."

Giles took an envelope from the dash and handed it to the guard. The guard opened it and glanced at the papers inside. "Okay," he said after a moment. "Must be an add-on." He handed Giles the envelope and gestured with a sweep of his arm. "You can go on through."

Giles guided the van behind the building and backed it into a spot at a loading dock. He stuffed the envelope into the pocket of his jacket, then climbed from the driver's seat and entered the building from the rear. A deputy met him in the booking section.

"You're from the Marshal's office?"

"Yeah," Giles replied. "Picking up some prisoners."

"You sure?" The deputy glanced at a sheet of paper on his desk. "We don't have anyone on the list for you."

Giles took the envelope from his jacket and handed it to the deputy. "I have an order transferring three men."

The deputy glanced at the documents. "Who wants them?"

"U.S. Attorney's office. Judge issued an order this morning."

"I don't think these men are yours. I think we're holding them for someone else." The deputy turned toward the doorway and called in a loud voice, "Hey, Dennis. Take a look at this."

Moments later, a lean, muscular man appeared at the booking desk. The deputy handed Dennis the papers and gestured toward Giles. "He says he's supposed to pick up these guys."

Dennis shuffled through the papers. "Mike Thomas, Jeff Carlisle, and Spencer Adams," he read aloud. "These are the three suspects from that break-in at Liston Cook's office." He glanced in Giles' direction. "These men are city prisoners. We're just housing them." He handed Giles the papers. "I can't give them to you."

"Maybe you better check with someone," Giles said slowly. "They don't usually send me after men that aren't theirs." He gestured with the envelope. "And I have an order signed by a federal judge."

Dennis disappeared down around the corner. Giles took a seat on a metal folding chair and propped it against an empty desk. A few minutes later, an assistant appeared at the deputy's desk. She held a clipboard, which she set on the desktop. "They said to give this to you."

"What is it?"

"Updated prisoner census," she said in a tired voice. "Those three men you were asking about are now federal prisoners. Judge Johnson's office faxed over copies of the indictments and warrants a few minutes ago."

"Have the papers been served?"

"Randall is taking care of that now."

An hour later, the elevator opened and the prisoners appeared in the hallway, handcuffed at the wrist and chained together at the ankles. "Okay, Mr. Giles," the deputy called. "Here're your men."

Giles rose from the chair and crossed the room to the booking desk. The deputy handed him a pen. Giles signed the transfer receipt and gestured toward the prisoners. "Right this way, gentlemen." They followed him down a corridor, through the rear door, and out to the van.

Outside, deputies ringed the parking lot near the loading dock. Armed and ready to react, they waited while the prisoners climbed through the side door of the van and took a seat. When they were in place, Giles leaned through the door and locked their ankle chains through large steel loops that were bolted to the floor. Once they were secure, he backed away and closed the side door. Moments later, he climbed in behind the steering wheel, started the engine, and drove the van away from the building. When he reached the gate at the guardhouse, he paused to wait for traffic, then turned the van to the right, and disappeared.

CHAPTER 47
RHODES

IN THE AFTERNOON, Russo rose from his desk and picked up a large manila envelope. He tucked it under his arm and walked down the hall to the castle entrance. A car was waiting beneath the canopy with the driver seated behind the steering wheel. As Russo approached, a footman opened the rear door of the car and Russo slipped inside. The door closed with a click. The car started forward.

From the castle, they drove south along the coast. Russo stared out the window toward the blue water of the Mediterranean shimmering in the sunlight. Waves lapped gently at the shore and in the distance fishing boats made their way in from a day at sea. But Russo saw none of it. His mind was absorbed in what lay ahead. He had never done anything like Spoleto asked. He had spent his short, young life learning to care and love and nurture, or so he thought. Now he was sent to arrange the end of a life, and from what he had seen and heard since Penalta left, he would be doing more of it in the years that lay ahead. This was not the life he'd envisioned when he took the vow.

Sometime later, the car came to a stop outside a café overlooking the shore. The driver's voice brought Russo back to reality.

"We are here, sir."

Startled by the sound, Russo jerked his head back from the window and smiled nervously. "Thank you." He took the envelope from the seat and slid across to the right. "I'll call you when I'm ready."

"As you wish, sir."

Envelope in hand, Russo pushed open the door and climbed from the car.

*   *   *

From the corner beyond the café, Michael Stadel watched as Russo made his way across the sidewalk and disappeared inside. He pressed a node that dangled from a wire beneath his shirt. "Subject has entered the building."

An answer crackled in the tiny earphone tucked inside his ear. "I have him in sight."

Stadel glanced up the street to see Jacob Dalberg walking toward him. Their eyes met for the briefest of moments, then Dalberg turned to enter the café. Stadel continued on to the next corner and disappeared.

*   *   *

Inside the café, Russo followed a waiter across the room. Javier Roldan was waiting for him at a table near the windows. The waiter pulled a chair from the table and held it while Russo took a seat. Then he unfolded a napkin and spread it across Russo's lap. When he was finished, the waiter appeared with a tray of bread and four plates. He set the bread in the center of the table and set a plate for each of them. The other two he prepared with oil and vinegar. Finally, he picked up a pepper mill and gave it a twist, sprinkling the plates with fresh ground pepper. When all was ready, he gestured to them. "Enjoy. We will serve you shortly."

*   *   *

In the operations center at Beersheba, Oren Cohen pointed to a screen that hung on the wall. "This is a current picture of Roldan?"

"Yes," someone replied. "That was taken last month in Algiers."

"He looks very different now," Cohen mused. "I remember him as a much younger man." He studied the picture a moment longer and remembered their first encounter. Roldan was an agent with Spain's National Intelligence Center. They had been in a bar in Madrid. Both of them were tracking Theodore Spatle, a former Nazi officer. Their work that evening didn't go so well. A waitress had distracted them while Spatle slipped out the back door to an alley. Cohen blamed their failure on Roldan's lack of attention to detail, but he was impressed by his attitude. "We found him once. We shall find him again." And they did.

For a time Cohen kept track of Roldan's career from afar, but then Roldan left the NIC and dropped out of sight. He emerged years later as a freelance operative in the murky world that existed between legitimate intelligence work and surreptitious rendition.

From her console, the operator's voice brought Cohen back to the present. "They are ready." She pointed to a speaker in the corner of the room. Moments later, they listened as a voice spoke from the café.

"I see you brought the file."

Cohen glanced over his shoulder. "Who is this speaking?"

"Javier Roldan," someone whispered.

"We are certain of his identity?"

"Yes. Agents on the scene identified him from the photographs. We are matching his voice now to confirm it."

The conversation in the café continued from the speaker. "It wasn't easy to gather, but I have everything you requested."

Cohen glanced around once more. "This is Russo?"

"Yes," someone answered in a hushed tone. "That's him."

"I wish we had video."

"There wasn't time. This was the best they could do."

Roldan's voice continued. "But you brought photos, documents, records?"

"Yes," Russo assured. "This is his entire history. All that we have on file. I did my best to make copies in a way that are untraceable."

"Untraceable?"

"The computer logs everything."

"This material you are giving me was stored electronically?"

"Yes. Is that a problem?"

"No, I just like to know the details."

"I am giving you everything."

"Relax," Roldan reassured. "It will be fine. People are predictable. They don't change that much. I'm sure I will find him."

"You know how to contact me?"

"Yes."

"Good. I will wait to hear from you."

"We must change the account."

"There was a problem?"

"No. But I do not like to use the same one twice. I will tell you where to send the second payment when I give you an update."

There was a rustling sound from the speaker in the operations center. Then Stadel spoke. "Subject has left the café and is proceeding toward the corner. The car is not in sight. I can move to the alley and check for it."

Cohen glanced at the operator. "Let Russo go."

The operator adjusted the microphone that hung near her chin. "Let the subject go. Stick with Roldan."

"I have him," Dalberg replied. "He came out the back and is walking to his car. He's right in front of me."

"Good," Cohen sighed. "That went as well as we could expect. All we have to do now is follow Roldan, and he will lead us to Barberini."

CHAPTER 48
CHICAGO

KURT MCEWEN SLOUCHED behind the steering wheel of a 1985 Ford pickup and watched out the window. From his spot at the corner of the parking lot outside the Grab-N-Snak convenience store he had a clear view of the road in either direction. Engine idling, left foot on the brake, right foot propped near the gas pedal, he was ready to move at a moment's notice.

In his left ear he had a tiny earphone that was connected by a thin white wire to a radio lying on the seat beside him. With it he listened to the voice of a spotter hiding in the bushes near the Presbyterian church, half a mile to the left.

"You awake?" the spotter asked.

McEwen lifted the radio from the seat, held it near his lips, and keyed the microphone. "I'm awake. Did that guy on the lawnmower see you?"

"No," the spotter scoffed. "I'm fifty yards from him. But he couldn't see me if he wanted to."

"He was closer than that. I saw him looking straight at you."

"Not really. He was just—" The spotter paused, interrupting himself. Then his voice spoke in quick, hoarse bursts. "I think I see the van." There was another pause, then the sound of the spotter's breath, followed by his voice again. "Yeah. It's them. Blue and white van. Get ready."

McEwen put the truck in gear and rose to a sitting position. The spotter's voice continued. "You see them? They're twenty yards to the left."

McEwen looked in that direction. "I got 'em."

"You ready?"

"Nothing to it." McEwen dropped the radio onto the seat and gripped the steering wheel with both hands.

To the left, the blue and white van approached at a steady speed, moving with traffic in the left lane. Through the windshield, McEwen saw the driver, a stocky middle-aged man with graying hair. Directly behind him, but clearly visible, were Mike Thomas and Jeff Carlisle. Spencer Adams sat to the left.

McEwen moved his left foot from the brake. The pickup started forward. As the van drew nearer, he pressed the gas pedal harder. The truck picked up speed. Then he shoved the pedal to the floor. The truck shot from the parking lot, barreled onto the highway, crossed the near lane, and struck the van squarely in the passenger door. McEwen held his foot to the floor and steered the truck to maintain contact with the van, shoving it across the median and into the oncoming lanes on the opposite side. A gray Honda swerved, narrowly avoiding a collision. To the right, a red delivery truck screeched to a halt, just missing the rear bumper of the truck. All the while, McEwen held the pickup's engine wide open.

When they reached the shoulder of the road, McEwen turned the pickup to the left. The nose of the truck slid down the side of the van and tipped it on its side. The pickup rolled to a stop a few feet away.

McEwen threw open the door and climbed out. As he staggered from the truck, a black SUV came to a stop alongside the van. Two men jumped from the passenger seat, crowbars in hand, and pried open the side door of the van. In less than a minute they unlocked the chains from the floor and pulled Adams free. Carlisle and Thomas crawled out after them. McEwen climbed in on the passenger side of the SUV and crawled onto the back row of seats. Carlisle, Thomas and Adams, still dressed in orange jail jumpsuits, got in after him. As the last man closed the door, the SUV sped away.

CHAPTER 49
INDIANAPOLIS

IT WAS MIDMORNING when the bus reached the city. An express could have made it in a few hours but Sisson had been in a hurry to leave and boarded the first thing out of Chicago. That bus was a southbound local. It made stops in every town and village along Highway 31, turning a trip through central and southern Illinois into a nightlong trek.

As they came through the suburbs and drew near downtown, Sisson stared out the window and took in every detail. He'd been to Indianapolis once since working for Sierra and once as a young boy, but the memory of that earlier trip was illusive and every time he tried to bring it to mind it seemed farther away. There was a dog and cotton candy and the smell of engine exhaust. But no matter how hard he tried he could never get any more of it than that.

The driver took his time, easing around first one corner then another, then into a narrow alley, before coming to a stop in a berth behind the station. As soon as the bus lurched to a halt, passengers rose from their seats and filled the aisle. Sisson waited and watched, checking each face, surveying the loading area through the window by his seat, looking for any sign of trouble— a passenger who seemed out of place, someone watching from behind a luggage cart, anything that might let him know if someone was there to spot him.

Finally, as the last passengers stepped to the door, he slipped his arm through the strap of the backpack, rose from his seat, and started toward the front of the bus. The driver stood outside on the pavement a few feet beyond the front tire. He glanced up as Sisson stepped down. Their eyes met and for a moment Sisson thought the man recognized him. Then, just as quickly, the driver turned away.

Sisson made his way through the terminal and stepped out to the sidewalk at the front of the building. A porter leaned against the wall, arms folded. Sisson caught his eye. "Anyplace around here where I can get a room? Cheap."

"Yeah. Up the street." He pointed to the right. "About two blocks. Indiana Hotel."

"Thanks," Sisson nodded, and he turned in that direction.

A few minutes later he found the hotel, a ten-story building from the turn of the century. A sign out front advertised hot running water and a private bathroom for every room. Sisson pushed open the door and stepped into a dusty, cramped lobby. The clerk's counter stood opposite the door. A worn leather chair sat to the right. Behind it was a plastic tree in a plastic container shaped like a vase. Dirt and grime coated them both.

A clerk behind the counter looked up as he entered. "Twenty dollars," he said in a matter-of-fact tone.

"Excuse me?"

"Twenty dollars per night," the clerk repeated. "Cash up front. No refunds if you don't stay all night. Ain't got nothing for rent by the hour."

Sisson reached in his pocket and took out a hundred-dollar bill. As soon as it cleared his pocket the clerk started shaking his head. "No, sir. Uh-uh. Ain't breaking no hundreds for nobody."

"I don't want to break it," Sisson replied and laid the bill on the counter. "I'll pay you up front for five nights."

The clerk looked askance. "No refunds, now. That's the policy."

"No refunds," Sisson repeated. "If I leave early, you get to keep it all. If I stay five nights, we're even."

The man slid his hand over the bill and raked it off the counter. At the same time, he reached with his other hand into a cubbyhole on the wall behind him and took out a preprinted note card. "If you're staying that long, you'll have to register." He put the card on the counter and handed Sisson a pen.

Sisson grasped the pen with his right hand and filled in the blanks on the card. When he finished, he laid the pen aside. The clerk handed him a key. "Top of the stairs to the second floor. Turn right. It's on the left. Front side of the building. Elevator don't work."

"Thanks." Sisson took the key in his hand and started toward the stairs.

"And keep it quiet. My room's on that floor and I like to get a good night's sleep."

Sisson climbed the stairs to the second floor and located the room. He slipped the key in the lock and opened the door. As it swung open he found, to his surprise, the room was spacious and clean. He stepped inside and closed the door.

A single bed sat along the wall to the right with a small dresser next to it. Windows lined the wall opposite the door and beneath them was a table with two chairs. An air-conditioner hung out the window to the left. He found the power switch and turned it on. The motor hummed at first, then the compressor came on. Cold air rushed from the vent.

The bed was neatly made with a blue spread on top. A towel lay folded near the pillow with a washcloth and a bar of soap. He lifted the bedspread and checked the sheet. It was clean, white, and worn only enough to be comfortable. He'd slept in worse for ten times the price.

Sisson slid the backpack from his shoulder and set it on the bed. Then he opened the door to the bathroom and turned on the water for the shower.

CHAPTER 50
TUCSON, ARIZONA

JEREMY BARTLETT STOOD at his usual post, just behind the operator's console, and watched on the screen as images from Chicago played out before them. A camera mounted inside the black SUV provided a live, high-definition video feed. On the screen, the two men from the SUV helped Thomas, Carlisle, and Adams inside. Then they climbed in after them, closed the doors, and drove away. Behind them, in the distance, the blue lights of a police car glared against the afternoon sky.

Bartlett leaned near the operator. "Make certain the police do not follow."

"Yes, sir. Our contact has been notified."

"Is our driver okay?"

"Yes. A little shaken from the impact, but it appears to be nothing serious."

"Good. Have him checked out when they arrive."

"Yes, sir."

Bartlett was joined that day by Dr. Walcott. Trained as a physician, and a specialist in neurology, Walcott was in charge of Sierra's Experimental Operations training program. He glanced in Bartlett's direction with a worried look. "I don't understand," he lamented. "How did Sisson know something was wrong?"

"He was well-trained," Bartlett suggested.

"No. I don't think it was from good training," Walcott replied, shaking his head. "I think he eluded *all* of our training efforts."

"We have to find him." He moved next to Walcott and lowered his voice. "We have to find Sisson and resolve this before anything else happens."

Walcott's eyes were wide. "You want to kill him?"

"It's the only way. I've seen things like this before. It's a tough decision but making it now saves us from even bigger problems later."

"No, no, no," Walcott urged. "Killing him would be a mistake."

"Why?"

"We have to find him so we can study him. His response has revealed an error in our theory. We need to learn what that is so we can avoid it in the future."

"We've been through the training program a thousand times," Bartlett argued. "The program is solid and has produced great results."

"But programs are not people. Each person is different. We had success with a large group, but Sisson is different. If we can find out what makes him different from the group, we can anticipate this result with recruits having similar characteristics. He is a good agent. We need to adjust the model to correct our programmatic error."

"Sisson is the error. Not the program. We need to eliminate our errors in the field. We can't bring them all back here."

"Well," Walcott said with resolve. "Termination of one of my subjects requires my consent, and I do not give it. Find Mr. Sisson and bring him to me." Walcott turned toward the door. "Alive and in good condition."

As he stepped from the command center, Bartlett turned to a desk nearby. He picked up a phone and dialed the number for Sierra's president, Tony Floyd. Moments later, Floyd answered.

"We need to talk."

"Okay," Floyd replied. "I have a few minutes. Start talking."

"Not like this. We need to talk in person."

"Okay, Jeremy. If you think it's necessary. Do we need to have Dr. Walcott present with us?"

"No, sir. I think it would be better if we talked alone. Just the two of us."

"All right. My assistant keeps my calendar. I'll transfer you to her and you can work out a time for us to meet."

CHAPTER 51
ALEXANDRIA, VIRGINIA

AFTER MEETING WITH WILSON and his staff in Detroit, Rutledge returned to Washington, D.C. When he arrived in the office the next morning, he found Brenner and Elizabeth waiting for him. "Bad news from Chicago," Brenner blurted out as Rutledge walked through the door.

"What happened?"

"The three suspects from the Cook break-in escaped."

"How? What happened?"

"No one is sure yet. The Chicago office is working on it. The Marshals. ATF. Everybody has a piece of it. Looks like it might have been an inside job."

"This much we know for certain," Elizabeth interjected. "The U.S. Marshals were moving the three men from the county jail to a federal facility. Somewhere en route a pickup truck collided with the van carrying the suspects. Before anyone could respond, an SUV appeared. According to witnesses, two men from the SUV cut the men loose from their chains and took them."

"Along with the driver of the pickup truck."

"Rutledge!" a voice shouted from upstairs. Everyone turned to look in that direction. Don Harper, the assistant agent in charge, appeared at the top of the stairs. "Why aren't you in Chicago?"

"I just got in from Detroit."

"I want you on a plane now. You need to get back out there and make certain nothing gets missed."

"Sir, I think this is a matter for the Chicago office." Rutledge moved to the bottom of the stairs. "Those men all have lawyers. They have refused to talk. If there's a problem in the Marshal's office, I think we should let them deal with it."

"This is our investigation and I'm not letting someone from Chicago take it over."

"Sir, I don't mean to argue with you, but our case is about something else." Rutledge started up the steps. "I need to—"

"No," Harper snapped. "You need to get on that plane."

By then Rutledge was at the top of the steps. "Sir," he said quietly, "we should talk about this in your office."

"But I—"

"Sir," Rutledge stepped closer and lowered his voice. "Our investigation is about foreign contributions to David McNeil's presidential campaign. We were only interested in Cook because someone from his campaign received that email with the documents. But the documents were about McNeil, not Cook. We should stick to the case we began with."

"You don't think the two are related?"

"Yes, but finding out who took those three men doesn't help us figure out whether Sierra Resources has been influencing David McNeil. We have a good lead on the missing fourth man from the break-in team. He chose to run. I think there's something different about him and if we can find him before anyone else, we might have a chance to get him to talk."

"You have a lead on him?"

"Yes, sir."

"Where do you think he is?"

"I'm not sure where he is right now. But his last address was an apartment here in Alexandria."

"Then why are you standing around here? Get moving!"

"Yes, sir," Rutledge smiled. He turned toward the steps and started downstairs.

"And wipe that stupid grin off your face," Harper called.

At the bottom of the steps Rutledge turned toward Brenner's desk. "Did they send you Sisson's address?"

"Yes. We went over there yesterday."

"Did forensics process the place?"

"Not yet."

Rutledge had a disapproving frown. "Why not?"

"We thought he might return and didn't want to scare him off. We have agents watching it. The place is secure. If anyone goes in, we'll know it."

"I'd like to have a look."

"No problem."

Rutledge glanced in Elizabeth's direction. "Want to ride over there with me?"

"Can't right now. I have a meeting in about thirty minutes." She came from behind her desk and ran her hand over the back of his arm. "That was quite impressive," she smiled. "I've never seen you like that."

"Thanks. Just trying to be an agent." He turned to Brenner. "You got that address?"

"I'll take you," Brenner offered, and he gestured toward the door.

They rode together from the office with Brenner driving and arrived at Sisson's address twenty minutes later. Brenner steered the car to the curb near the end of the block on a quiet residential street. The houses were older two-story structures that had been divided into apartments.

Brenner pointed out the front windshield. "Sisson has a second-floor apartment in the third house on the right. In the next block."

Rutledge glanced out the side window. "I don't see anything out of the ordinary." He nodded to the left. "Is that Sims in the white car?"

"Yeah. Dees is on the next corner in the van."

"Okay, let's go."

Brenner turned the car into the street and drove to the middle of the block. He parked beneath a hickory tree and got out. Rutledge joined him on the sidewalk. They walked together to the front door and went inside.

Beyond the door, a hallway ran down the center of the house. Rooms on either side had been converted into apartments. Brenner took the stairway up to the second floor.

At the landing above, they came to a door marked with the letter C. Brenner pointed to it and drew his pistol from the holster on his hip. Rutledge turned the knob to find the door was locked. Brenner took a key from his pocket and handed it to him. Rutledge unlocked the door and they went inside.

The door opened to a small sitting area with a sofa on the wall to the left. A chair sat at the far end at a right angle to the sofa. Beyond the chair was another door. It was open, and through it Sisson saw a bed with the spread pulled tight and the pillows tucked in place. On the opposite side of the bed was a window with a dresser beneath it.

Brenner nudged the door back with his foot, surveyed the room quickly, then disappeared around the corner. Rutledge wandered to the right toward a small galley kitchen. Moments later Brenner came up behind him. "We're clear," he said, returning the pistol to his holster.

The kitchen counter was clean. A coffee maker sat at one end, beneath the cabinets. A dishcloth hung over the spigot. The sink was empty.

"You sure a man lives here?" Rutledge asked.

"Former Marine. Neatness is probably engrained in his character."

"Something is," Rutledge chuckled. "Don't expect this in my apartment."

"I've seen where you live. That place is like a one-man fraternity house."

Rutledge glanced over his shoulder. "I prefer to think of it as eclectic."

"You prefer to live in a dream world."

"Find anything when you were in here before?"

"Not really. Looked like the place had been wiped clean before he left. I'm not sure there are even any fingerprints in here."

Rutledge backed away from the kitchen and turned toward the sofa.

A table sat beneath the front window, behind the door. A power supply lay on the floor beneath it with a cord that snaked up to the tabletop. Rutledge pointed. "He took the laptop but left the power supply."

"Yeah. I saw that before. Wonder where the printer is."

"Good observation." Rutledge looked beneath the table and saw a trashcan. He stooped over and pulled it out. In it was a single sheet of paper.

Brenner leaned over his shoulder. "What's that?"

Rutledge took out the paper and held it up to see. On it was an airline reservation. The page had been torn in half but the airline information was still legible. He handed it to Brenner. "See if we can find out what that means."

"You want to take it?"

"Did you get a search warrant before you came in here?"

"Yes."

"Okay. Then take it."

"But removing it changes the apartment. A guy as neat as Sisson will spot the difference as soon as he comes in the door. He'll run."

"If Sisson comes anywhere near here, we're going to grab him anyway."

"We have authority to do that?"

"I'm giving you the authority. This is my case. I have the authority to do whatever's necessary to bring it to a conclusion. If he comes around, grab him."

"Okay." Brenner took the page from Rutledge. "Whatever you say."

CHAPTER 52
LOS ANGELES

MEANWHILE, JEREMY BARTLETT boarded a Learjet at a private airstrip outside Phoenix. He settled into the seat and closed his eyes as the plane rose above the Arizona desert. In his mind he reviewed the Cook campaign infiltration— the research and detail that went into planning fifteen simultaneous raids, alternate plans of entry and escape, and then the training at the company's facility in Mexico. They'd prepared for this mission like any other mission— same routine, same standards, same expectations— even if it was on American soil. That something went wrong meant there was a failure with the men, not the program. The men were merely pieces of equipment. They knew that when they signed on. Sisson had failed, like a tractor or a truck that reached its limit. There was nothing more to do but discard him.

Two hours later, the plane landed at the Bob Hope Airport in Burbank. Bartlett rented a car and drove east to the town of Azusa. He found Tony Floyd waiting in a Dodge Durango outside a grocery store off historic Route 66. Bartlett came to a stop near the SUV. Floyd got in on the passenger side of the car.

"Sorry to meet you like this."

"Trouble at the office?"

"Lot of heat coming back off this Cook campaign deal. Didn't want anyone to overhear us talking." He pointed out the windshield. "Turn right up here."

Bartlett did as he was told and followed Floyd's directions to a golf course south of town. They parked near the clubhouse and got out.

"Let's take a walk."

Bartlett followed him down a cart path. "Won't they throw us out?"

"Not if you're with me."

Floyd set a quick pace. Bartlett did his best to keep up. "You think this is more secure than your office."

"It is now." Floyd gestured to an empty tee box and led him out to the fairway.

"Maybe we should upgrade the company security system."

"System's fine. But it can't protect you from nosey office assistants." Floyd shoved his hands in his pockets and strolled at a leisurely pace. "What did you want to talk about?"

"As you already mentioned, we had a problem in Chicago."

"I've done nothing but answer questions about it. Occupied my entire day. I never dreamed Caldwell and the Order could get us in this much trouble."

"Are we in trouble?"

"Most of the calls have been from our own people, worrying about what will happen next. I hope you're not here to give me more bad news."

"I hope so, too."

Floyd shot him a look. "What does *that* mean?"

"We picked up the three men who were arrested. Got them today."

"I heard you had them. How'd you manage that?"

"You don't want to know."

"Where are they?"

"They're safe for now. We're making arrangements to bring them back."

"Safe ... You mean safe from harm, or safe from being found?"

"I really don't think you want to know the details."

"Okay."

"We still have a fourth guy on the loose."

"Right. Sisson."

"You know his name?"

"Walcott called me."

Bartlett felt flush with anger. "I knew he'd try to get around me."

"Technically, he's not getting around you. You oversee operations. He's in charge of development. You're more like peers, with overlapping responsibilities. The two of you really ought to find a way to get along."

"I want to get along, but he has to always be the smartest guy in the room."

"Isn't he usually the smartest guy in the room?"

"Yes, but he doesn't have to always make sure we know it."

"I think I know what you're going to say, but tell me your side."

"Walcott wants to retrieve Sisson and take him back to the facility in Mexico so they can analyze him. Find out what happened, figure out why he failed, and tweak the training process to address it. Sisson signed an agreement when he joined the program. He knew it was experimental and that there could be unforeseen circumstances. I think, given the situation and the level of risk, we should terminate him on sight— assuming we can locate him. Walcott says I can't do that without his consent."

"You know he's right."

"Yes. I understand we must both agree before a termination may occur, but you can overrule him."

"Not this time. We're in too much trouble now to risk having a body to deal with. Besides, Walcott has spent a lot of time on these men. The company has spent a great deal of money developing the chips, the implants, and the software to make it work. If we have a problem, we need to know it now so we can fix it. I mean, we had to change your implant once or twice." He looked over at Bartlett. "By the way, how's that working?"

"Good," Bartlett nodded. "I'm down to three hours of sleep each night with no loss of cognitive function."

"And your body can manage with that?"

"It can with the injections."

"Make sure you monitor it."

"I am." Bartlett turned the conversation back to the issue of Sisson. "Look, I understand the risk of terminating him, but I also understand what will happen if anyone else finds him. He knows way too much to be walking loose on the street."

"Retrieve him. Let Walcott examine him. Might lead to a new breakthrough."

"You're taking responsibility for the consequences?"

"Yes," Floyd nodded. "I'm taking responsibility." He gestured with a sweep of his right hand. "You okay to drive?"

Bartlett looked up, startled to find they were back in front of the clubhouse.

CHAPTER 53
NOWHERE, NEVADA

WALLACE JORDAN SAT IN A PICKUP truck at the bottom of an open-pit copper mine and watched as a giant power shovel scooped up a bucketful of ore-laden earth and dumped it into the hopper of an over-sized earthmover. With tires as tall as a two-story building, the earthmover could hold a five-bedroom house. Still, a single scoop from the shovel filled it to capacity.

The copper mine, located in the Nevada desert, was part of the far-flung empire of Nashua Steel, a company Jordan and his brother, Ted, inherited from their father. It had been their father's dream to create a fully-integrated business— gather the raw materials, process it into useable form, produce an end product, and sell it to consumers. Beginning with the copper mine where Jordan sat that day, their father fulfilled that dream shortly before he died. Now Jordan and his brother were at work on their own dream— returning America to the business-friendly country they were certain the Founders had envisioned. Electing David McNeil was part of their effort to reach that goal.

Jordan glanced across the seat of the pickup to the mine foreman. "What's the latest on how long this seam will last?"

"Geologists aren't sure. At the rate we're going, they think we can keep digging for another thirty years. After that, it's anybody's guess."

Jordan shook his head in amazement. "My dad bought this property forty years ago. The company has been mining it for almost that long. And our children could do the same." He jabbed the end of his index finger against the seat. "All in the same place."

"Pretty amazing."

"Yes, it is."

"I didn't know there was that much copper in the entire world, much less in a single mine."

Jordan's face turned serious. "Has the EPA been back?"

"Not this month."

"Still testing the water?"

"Every day or two."

"What's it test?"

"It's not as bad as it was but still way too much heavy metal. It won't pass an inspection. Those barriers we put up are helping. But there just isn't anyplace for water like that to go. We're in a hole almost half a mile deep. As dry as it has been, I'm surprised there's any water at all."

"Where's it coming from?"

"Still seeping out of that underground stream."

"Can you imagine," Jordan grinned. "In the middle of the desert, half a mile below the surface, and we run into an ancient riverbed."

"That still has water."

"What's the pit look like?"

"Getting pretty full. We'll have to enlarge it or find a way to pump it to the top and do something with it there. Ted suggested trucking it to a treatment plant in Las Vegas."

"Too far," Jordan replied. "Isn't there an abandoned mine out here somewhere?"

"Yeah. Two miles west of us. An old gold mine. It's part of that tract we bought last year."

"How many trucks a day would it take to keep up?"

"Keeping up wouldn't be a problem. We get maybe three or four truckloads a day. We just made the pond too small."

"I'm thinking we pump this stuff to the top. Truck it down to the abandoned mine and dump it in there."

The foreman frowned. "What about the EPA?"

Jordan looked away. "I don't think they'll ever notice."

"We could give it a try. See how it works. Worst case, we dynamite the mine closed and leave it."

"See what you can do." Jordan pointed to the right. "Better take me to the top. I need to get back to the hotel and take care of some things with the office."

When the pickup reached the lip of the mine, Jordan's Blackberry downloaded a dozen text messages. He scrolled through them and came to one from Russo. The message read simply, "Contracts are ready." Jordan felt the muscles in his stomach tighten. Ever since news broke of the trouble at Cook's office, he'd been expecting to receive directions from Spoleto. Now those directions had been sent.

* * *

It was after three in the afternoon when Jordan reached the hotel in Las Vegas. He showered and ordered room service for a late lunch. When he finished eating, he took a laptop from his briefcase, logged on to the Internet, and opened his Google email account. In the draft file he found a message composed by Russo with directions from Spoleto and the Council. "Arrange to meet with Caldwell. Convey our displeasure at the recent developments. Instruct him to arrange for janitorial services at his expense. Be certain the others understand our position. We will expect a report from you on this matter." The tone of the message struck a nerve and brought to mind the old tension that Jordan had sensed when he first agreed to help.

As Jordan's father approached the end of his life, he made a strategic shift in his financial plans in a fruitless attempt to avoid estate taxes. One of those changes involved the transfer of twenty-five percent of the company to their sister. Buying her out proved to be expensive. Paying the resulting taxes created a major business disruption. Already burdened with excessive regulation, Jordan and his brother were forced to leverage the company with debt and sell some of their own assets in order to survive. In the process, they decided to devote their lives to changing the way the federal government treated business. They sought qualified candidates who embraced their conservative ideals and pumped millions of dollars into their campaign coffers. Then, at a Conservative Caucus conference in Savannah, Georgia, they met Henry Caldwell. In a late-night session of drinks and politics, Jordan vented the full measure of his frustration with the government. The following morning, Caldwell took him aside and suggested they talk again, in a more private setting.

Three weeks later, they met at Caldwell's home in Virginia. There, in the quiet of the lush and verdant countryside, Caldwell carefully detailed the work of the Order and its effort to elect just the kind of president Jordan sought. All they needed was money, expertise, and time. On the spot, Jordan agreed to participate. Only later, after it was too late to back out, did he learn of the Order's true agenda— to eliminate Jews from America. The thought of a Nazi-type holocaust made him cringe, and to see it happen in America was even worse, but he was certain business could not remain profitable with a continuation of the current regulatory regime. *Perhaps it will never come to dealing with the Jews. Perhaps we can get the business side of the matter corrected without addressing the other issues.* He hoped so, but if it was necessary in the end, it was a trade-off he was willing to make— for the sake of the family business.

Jordan read the email from Russo once more, then phoned his office and spoke to an assistant. "I need you to check my schedule and book me for the Greenbrier Resort in West Virginia. Make it as soon as possible."

"Yes, sir. Anything else?"

"Call Charlie Meriwether at the EPA. Tell him I want to know a week in advance when his inspectors are coming out to the Santa Croce mine."

"I can tell him that?"

"Just give him the message," Jordan replied. "He'll know what it means."

"Yes, sir."

"And let me know when you've booked me for the Greenbrier. I need to set up a meeting there."

"Yes, sir. Would you like for me to arrange the meeting?"

"Just book me at the Greenbrier. I'll take care of the meeting."

CHAPTER 54
MALIBU, CALIFORNIA

FROM THE MEETING IN AZUSA, Tony Floyd drove back to the coast and made his way to the home of Edgar Logan, CEO of Sierra Resources. Logan's house— a ten-bedroom mansion— stood on a bluff overlooking the Pacific Ocean. As the sun sank below the horizon, the two men stood on the deck behind the house and talked.

"We have a problem."

"That business in Chicago?"

"How did you know?"

"I knew it was us as soon as I saw the news."

"The team in Chicago was only one of several we sent out that night."

"Several?"

"Fifteen, to be exact."

"Spoleto?"

"Galena. And Henry Caldwell."

"The others were successful?"

"They went in and out without being caught."

"But they didn't accomplish the mission."

"No, sir."

"That's a problem."

"Yes, sir. We're addressing it. Dr. Walcott is reviewing the training system and assessing the implant protocol. But there's one more thing."

"One more?"

"One of the men in Chicago bolted."

"Bolted?"

"When the police found the team, he was able to escape undetected."

"He had a chip?"

"Yes."

"Were you able to track him?"

"Part of the way."

"Part? What happened?"

"He found the tracking device and removed it."

"It wasn't just a malfunction? Don't we still have men with the earlier chips and implant system?"

"We do. And he is one of them. We lost contact with him during the mission because of a problem with the chip, but we were able to reestablish the uplink. We followed him awhile, thinking it was him, but—"

"Thinking it was him. Tony, this is starting to sound like a three-ring circus."

"It was a little chaotic."

"So, what happened? Finish the story."

"When we established contact with the chip, it was moving around so quickly we were sure he was in a car and became concerned he was trying to get away. Our men finally located the car and learned it was a taxi. The chip was tucked into the upholstery of the seat."

"Was the driver any help?"

"He told us he let our man out near the bus station. We have men working that area now."

"Check the bus schedules."

"We're doing that."

"You've talked to Dr. Walcott about this one?"

"Yes."

"Can he fix it?"

"I don't know. He wants to try. But first we have to find him."

"What about the other men in that unit?"

"We retrieved them today. They are with us. The command center is arranging for their delivery."

"You think you can find the errant unit?"

"Yes," Floyd nodded. "I think so. Walcott wants to examine him. I think we owe it to Walcott to try."

"Yes, but don't put the entire program at risk."

"Right."

"And, Tony, you realize you're on your own."

"Right."

"Anything happens, you take the hit. Not me. Not the company."

"I understand."

CHAPTER 55
CHICAGO

A BLACK SUV TURNED INTO the perimeter drive outside Midway Airport. It passed through the security checkpoint, made a left turn at the gate, and continued around to the far side of the runway. Minutes later it rolled quietly into a hangar and came to a stop alongside a Learjet that was parked there, door open, stairway extended.

Without word or fanfare, the doors of the SUV opened and two men stepped out. Dressed in gray suits, white shirts, and dark ties, they moved with uncanny precision in movements that seemed rote, planned, almost choreographed. The first man stood facing the plane while the second opened the car's door on the passenger side. They both reached inside and dutifully lifted Spencer Adams from his seat. Adams, now dressed in jeans and a T-shirt, was sedated, which made his body heavy and awkward to manage. The two men struggled to remove him from the SUV. As his body slid out the door, they gripped him beneath the arms and hustled him up the steps into the plane. When he was secured in his seat, they returned to the SUV and repeated the process with Jeff Carlisle and Mike Thomas.

After all three men were in place, they closed the plane's door and retreated to the SUV. The driver steered away from the plane, then came to a stop near the hangar doors. They watched as the plane taxied out to the tarmac and rolled toward the runway. Moments later it lifted into the sky and was gone. As it rose out of sight, the man in the passenger seat took a cell phone from his pocket and typed, "Units are airborne." He scrolled down the contacts list to a telephone number and pressed a button to send the message.

* * *

Four hours later, Juan Ortiz sat behind the steering wheel of a black SUV and watched as the Learjet with Adams, Thomas, and Carlisle aboard descended from the night sky toward a paved airstrip. Located in the rolling hills of northern Mexico, not far from the village of Los Hovos, the strip was long, wide, and smooth, but it had no lights. As the plane neared the ground, landing lights beneath the wings came on and lit up the arid grasslands around the landing strip. Ortiz squinted against the glare while he watched as the plane hung in the air, suspended just above the runway, then gently glided onto the pavement.

The engines whined as the plane slowed, then taxied to the end of the runway and rolled to a stop alongside the SUV. As the plane came to a halt, a stairway extended from a compartment in the fuselage. It lowered slowly to the ground. Ortiz and two others came from the SUV, set the handrails for the steps in place, then pushed open the door and entered the plane.

Two rows down the aisle, they found Adams secured in his seat, looking groggy and disoriented. They unfastened the harness that held him in place, lifted him from the seat, and carried him down the steps to the SUV. When he was seated in back, they returned for the others. Unloading the three men took about twenty minutes.

With Adams, Thomas, and Carlisle now seated in the SUV, Ortiz got in behind the steering wheel and guided the vehicle past the nose of the plane onto a narrow dirt road. As they drove away, he heard the engines on the Learjet roar. He glanced out the window in time to see it streak down the runway and leap into the night.

A few miles down the dirt road, the SUV came to a security fence.

Twelve feet high, it was ringed with concertina wire. A gate across the road was manned by armed guards. One of them looked up as the SUV approached. Ortiz waved at him. The guard pushed open the gate and stepped back to let them pass.

The van rocked to one side as it moved past the fence. Ortiz heard a groan from the back seat. He glanced in the rearview mirror to see Thomas staring at him, eyes open wide but listless and unfocused. At the sight of it, a chill ran down Ortiz's spine.

CHAPTER 56
HARRISBURG, PENNSYLVANIA

SHORTLY BEFORE SUNRISE, Paul picked up Esther from her townhouse and together they made their way out to the Beltway, then turned north. For the next three hours they rode across the Maryland countryside. Near midmorning, they reached the outskirts of Harrisburg.

"Why does he spend so much time up here?"

"Politically, Pennsylvania is really three states. The eastern third, around Philadelphia, is more liberal. The central part of the state is sort of in the middle. But the western part is rural and conservative. More like Alabama than a northeastern state."

"Interesting analysis."

"To stay in the race, Cook needs a big win. Pennsylvania is his best shot. Even if he only comes in second, news reporters will talk about it as a Cook victory and he'll get more media attention for free than he could ever buy."

"What are they doing today?"

"Had a couple of rallies this morning, then a stop at a high school. That's where we're supposed to meet up with them."

"Always seemed like a waste of time, campaigning at a high school."

"Makes for great photographs, then the kids talk to everyone they know about meeting you and seeing you in person. It's a great stop. I always enjoyed working the schools."

Paul turned the corner onto Johnson Street and slowed near the middle of the block. A large two-story brick structure came into view on the right. A sign out front identified it as Joseph E. Mann High School. Paul turned the car from the street. Cars lined both sides of the drive that led past the front of the school, but they found a parking space near the gym. The campaign bus was parked between the building and the football field, putting it in plain sight from the street. The rally on the field was winding down as Paul and Esther stepped from the car.

"Looks like we got here just in time."

"You're sure he'll have time to talk?"

"Yeah."

She glanced in Paul's direction. "What does that mean?"

"That means he needs something, so he'll take the time to listen to us."

"What does he need?"

"I don't know. He didn't say."

From their vantage point near the bus, Paul and Esther watched as Liston Cook concluded his remarks and waded into the crowd. Students and adults gathered around him like a rock star as he slowly moved toward the edge of the field.

"That's an enthusiastic reception for someone who's polling in last place."

"Yeah," Paul nodded. "I think news about the break-in came at a good time."

Esther looked in his direction again. "A conspiracy theorist would be intrigued by that coincidence."

He smiled back at her. "I don't think you'd have to be a conspiracy buff to wonder about it."

A little while later the crowd thinned and Cook emerged from the sea of newfound fans, flanked by half a dozen advisors and trailed by a large following of news reporters and cameramen. He looked up in time to toss a wave in Paul's direction. Moments later they were face-to-face. "Great to see you," he beamed, in full campaign mode. One or two cameramen took pictures while the two men shook hands. Paul introduced Esther, then they followed Cook onto the campaign bus.

Cook led them down the center aisle past tables cluttered with press releases, empty soft drink cans, and a grease-stained pizza box as they made their way to the rear compartment. He opened the door to find three staff members seated there, busily working on their laptops. One of them looked up as he entered. "Sorry. We just needed a quiet place to work."

"And we need the room for a few minutes, guys," Cook replied.

The staffers hurriedly gathered their things, squeezed past Paul and Esther, and scooted out the door. When they were gone, Cook pushed the door closed and pointed to a sofa that sat beneath a window on the right side of the bus. "Have a seat. Need anything? Something to drink?"

"No, we're okay for now." Paul and Esther took a seat on the sofa. Cook sat in a chair across from them. Paul continued. "Thanks for seeing us."

"Always glad to see you." Cook glanced at Esther. "I've heard a lot about you, but I think this is the first time I've actually met you."

"Our paths crossed at a few hearings."

"Oh." His eyes lit up. "Something about cruise missiles for Saudi Arabia."

"Yes," Esther nodded. "I think we were on opposite sides that day."

"Tough issue. You know, I've campaigned hard on a pro-Israel position."

"And that has not gone unnoticed."

"In spite of what I may have said at that hearing, I have always believed we can't have peace in the Middle East without a strong Israel."

"And I agree."

Cook smiled politely and turned to Paul. "So, tell me, what was it you wanted to see me about?"

"The break-in at your office in Chicago."

"I can't imagine why you'd be interested in that, but I'll tell you what

I've told everyone, including the FBI. I don't know anything to tell anyone. The FBI has been calling me every day wanting to set up an interview. I've tried to tell them I don't know anything about it. I wasn't there the weekend it happened and I can't imagine what anyone would want in my office." He gestured to Paul. "You've seen the polling data. I was dead last when that happened."

Paul leaned forward. "Esther has some interesting information she'd like to ask you about."

"Esther?" Cook looked in her direction. "By all means. What do you have?"

"Several days ago, a priest from the Knights of Malta met in Zurich with a representative from the Catholic Church. At that meeting, he outlined activities of the Knights that he claimed were directed toward Jews in America— activities several of my clients have been working for years to uncover. The priest hoped to enlist the help of Catholic authorities in disciplining the Order. He carried with him documents that would substantiate his allegations. Shortly after making his presentation, the priest was murdered. Evidence indicates at least some of the documents were forwarded by email to a man with your campaign."

"Do you know that person's name?"

"Richard Stockton." Cook arched an eyebrow. Esther pressed the point. "You know him?"

"He's in charge of our advance team," Cook said slowly. "And he's dating my niece."

"Has he discussed any of this with you? We think those documents are the reason behind the break-in at your campaign headquarters."

Cook's eyes opened wide. "They were in an office we use for the advance team."

"That would be a good reason for them to choose that office."

"Richard spends most of his time on the road, but he has a space in there." Cook leaned closer. "Listen, I haven't talked to anyone about this, but since you mentioned it, I'll tell you. A few days ago Richard showed me some documents that appeared to indicate David McNeil's campaign was receiving contributions from a foreign source. I didn't keep the documents and I never had them at my office in Chicago, but Richard and I discussed them." Cook paused a moment. "I never thought about that as a reason. I'm certain Christopher Wilson had nothing to do with it, but I never thought about those documents."

"Wilson?" Paul and Esther exchanged a perplexed look. "Why would you think he had something to do with it?"

Cook leaned back in the chair. "You didn't hear?"

"Hear what?"

"One of the men they arrested that night had a scrap of paper with a phone number on it. The number belonged to someone who works in Wilson's campaign."

"Really?"

"It wasn't Wilson." Cook gestured with his hand. "He didn't have anything to do with it."

"You're certain?"

"Wilson isn't worried about me. I'm closest to John Franklin— he needs me out of the race more than the others. If John can reduce our field to just two— him and McNeil— he'll have a shot at the nomination. With me in the race, we split the voters that would otherwise all go to him."

"Interesting."

"Yes," Cook nodded, "but this is even more interesting than that." He picked up a TV remote and turned on a video player. "This is from the surveillance cameras at the building." Paul and Esther turned to watch. Cook pointed to the screen as grainy images appeared. "You'll notice there are four men entering the building through the rear doors."

"I thought they caught three," Paul suggested.

"They did. The fourth one got away."

"No one's talking about four."

"That's because the FBI is sitting on the real story while they investigate."

"Where'd you get this video?"

Cook had a twinkle in his eye. "I still have a few friends."

"Any idea who the fourth man is?"

"No, but I have someone working on it." Cook turned to Paul. "He can track down leads and do all the things detectives do, but what I need most is a friend. Someone I can trust to find out what's going on, without involving the campaign."

Paul nodded thoughtfully. "How many people know you have this video?"

"Other than the person who gave it to me, five now— me, my chief of staff, the detective, and the two of you. No one on my campaign knows anything about this."

"Stockton doesn't know?"

"No. And I don't want him or anyone else to know about it." Cook switched off the television and looked Paul in the eye. "I need to find out what's going on. I need the two of you to help me do that."

"What's the detective's name?"

"Brian Culpepper."

Just then the door to the rear compartment opened and Philip Livingston entered. Cook stood and introduced him. "He's my chief of staff. He'll help you with the details." He turned to Livingston. "They need an address for Culpepper." Cook started toward the door and glanced back at Paul. "I need to see a few more people before we leave. Philip will get you what you need. Might be better if he's your point of contact. He's handling Culpepper already."

"Good."

"Anything you need, Phil will get it for you." Cook looked back one last time. "Good to meet you, Esther." And then he stepped through the doorway and disappeared.

Livingston opened a cabinet beneath the television and took out a leather satchel. "I have the address in here." He reached inside the satchel and found a business card. "Here," he said, handing it to Paul. "You can keep it. I have several more and his information is on my Blackberry. I don't mind telling you, I'm glad for your help. Congressman Cook values your friendship and has a lot of faith in you. This break-in has really bothered him and he's spent a lot of time trying to make sense of it. Having you help will take a lot of that worry away."

"I'm glad to help."

They talked a moment longer, then Paul and Esther excused themselves. When they were gone, Livingston took out his cell phone and sent a text message to Russo.

*   *   *

On the drive back to Washington, Esther reached over to Paul and took his hand. "There's something I didn't tell you before."

"What's that?"

"A friend of mine from the FEC told me they are conducting an investigation of David McNeil's campaign."

"For what?"

"They're looking into whether he has been receiving foreign contributions."

"They have the documents?"

"I don't know. She wouldn't say."

"Why did she tell you?"

"I sent some associates over to their office to ask about records of contributions to his campaign from Sierra Resources. They were surprised I was asking about the very thing they're investigating."

"They have the documents."

"You think so?"

"Yeah," Paul nodded. "I think NSA must have intercepted them when that guy in Zurich sent them to Stockton."

"You think Liston was telling the truth?"

"I want to."

"But?"

"He has documents, but not at his Chicago office. And he never said exactly what those documents were."

"I noticed that. Was he talking about documents from Penalta's files, or just documents in general?"

"And if he has the documents, where are they and why didn't he go public with them?"

"Better yet, why didn't he go to the FEC? If they're as bad as Brody says they are, they would end McNeil's campaign."

"Maybe he did. Or maybe there's more to it than Brody or anyone else realizes."

"What do you mean?"

"I don't know. I just know Liston Cook is a good guy and if he's holding on to documents like that, there must be a good reason."

"Yeah, but what?"

Paul shook his head. "I don't know."

"We need to find out while there's still time to do something about it."

"I'm following Culpepper and the fourth guy on the break-in." Paul pointed. "You track down the documents and the money. Follow the contribution trail."

"That's not easy."

"No, it's not," he smiled. "But it's the kind of thing you like."

"Yes," she grinned. "I do like that kind of work."

CHAPTER 57
WASHINGTON, D.C.

THAT AFTERNOON, RUTLEDGE sat at his desk, still reading the documents attached to the email from Zelman to Stockton, when the phone rang. The call was from Catherine Olsen. "We need to talk."

"Okay. Where?"

"My office. In ten minutes."

Rutledge hung up the phone, grabbed his jacket, and headed downstairs. Ten minutes later, he was standing at the receptionist desk outside Olsen's office. She met him there and escorted him down the hall. "That was fast. Did you run?"

"Not quite." He waited while she opened the door to the conference room. When they were inside, he turned to her. "Okay. What did you want to talk about?"

"We're having trouble getting access to bank records for Sierra Resources."

"Why?"

"We can get candidate records simply by asking, and they disclose a lot of information in the course of reporting. So, we have good records on the candidate side and can ask for clarification of anything we need. But Sierra Resources is a donor, and asking for that is a big deal."

"Why?"

"Because this is America and when a federal agency starts asking about donations to political candidates— especially presidential candidates— everyone gets a little edgy."

"So, what do you want me to do?"

"You're FBI. You can apply for an order under the Patriot Act to get the records without telling Sierra you're doing it."

"You mean a FISA warrant."

"Yes."

"Because it's not public."

"Right."

"Hmm. I don't know which is creepier— having the Federal Election Commission investigating a donor, or the FBI."

"Will you ask?"

"Yeah, I'll ask."

When Rutledge returned to the office, he passed by his desk to the stairs and went up to Don Harper's office. He tapped on the office door and leaned his head around the corner. Harper was seated at his desk. "You got a minute?"

"Only a minute. I have to leave for a meeting."

"I can come back later."

"No. You better see me now. I was hoping for an update on that Cook case."

"Actually, that's what I wanted to see you about." Rutledge stepped from the door and stood near the desk. "The driver of the van turned out to be an imposter. The Chicago office had a little trouble getting access to him, the Marshals didn't want to let anyone else talk to him, but they—"

"That's why I wanted you out there."

"Yes, sir. But they have good people in that office. Matthew Davis is smart, really smart, and Michelle Weaver is as good as they get."

"As an agent."

"Yes, sir. Smart, professional, ahead of me at almost every turn. They interviewed the driver. Turns out he's on the fringe of the Chicago underworld. Friends with a lot of tough guys, but no real record."

"Who was he working for?"

"That's just it. He had the name of a contact, but that's it. The guy paid him in cash, gave him a uniform, told him what to do. So he did it."

"How much did they pay him?"

"Ten thousand dollars. He was supposed to drop the van in Joliet, with the men inside, and walk away. Had his car stashed there and planned to head south right away."

"Did they pay him?"

"In advance."

"And who did he say was his contact?"

"Jonah Baker."

"I assume it's an alias."

"Yes, sir. They met at a café inside The Loop. Chicago is checking for security video and witnesses, but no one expects to find anything."

"Professionals."

"Yes, sir."

"If they're connected to McNeil and his campaign for president, we better find out quick."

"That's the reason I came up here. I talked to a lawyer at the FEC and told her what we were doing."

"You shared our intelligence product with another agency? Without asking me?"

"Well, actually, sir, it was NSA's product. They shared it with us. I only asked the FEC because what we know so far involves a candidate for the presidency and a multimillion-dollar campaign. I thought maybe they had access to information we couldn't get without involving the lawyers."

"Where are you with that?"

"They have information on McNeil but are concerned about asking for donor records. You know, with the campaign and all. They think it might look like they were trying to influence the election."

"And they think it won't look like that if we ask for them?"

"Not if we use a FISA warrant."

"You want me to ask the Foreign Intelligence Surveillance Court to issue an order for the records of a presidential candidate?"

"No, sir. Records for one of his donors."

"Who?"

"Sierra Resources."

Harper sagged back in his chair. "Might be better if we just subpoenaed all the candidates. Do you know anything about Sierra Resources?"

"They're into every black operation we ever authorized, and a few our own agencies don't even know about. Which is why we should do it. If we can get a FISA order, the court won't allow anyone to disclose that they issued it, or the reasons behind it. It will simply order the banking institutions to turn the records over to us, and prohibit them from disclosing that they did it."

"I don't know. This sounds very risky to me."

"Yes, sir. It's risky. But it will be riskier for all of us if we let it slide and McNeil gets elected with foreign interests holding the purse strings."

"I'll think about it." Harper stood. "I have to go now. I'm late." And he brushed past Rutledge as he moved toward the door.

Late that evening, Rutledge was roused from sleep by a call on his cell phone. He answered it and heard Don Harper's voice.

"Okay, Rutledge, I got your warrant. Now we're all standing naked on the street. Make sure no one finds out."

Before Rutledge could respond, Harper ended the call. He rolled onto his back and smiled up at the ceiling. "This is my first FISA warrant. And it's for records about a presidential campaign." He threw back the covers and climbed from bed. There was no point in trying to sleep now. He might as well go to the office.

CHAPTER 58
WASHINGTON, D.C.

THE NEXT MORNING, Paul contacted Brian Culpepper. They met that afternoon at Culpepper's office, a two-room suite in the Wortham Building off I Street. Constructed in 1915, the building had wide hallways with dark wainscoting that reached halfway up the wall. Office doors were made of solid oak with opaque glass panes in the top half. Black lettering on the glass identified the business.

The door to Culpepper's office opened to an area that had once been a secretary's workspace. A dried flower, withered and dead, rested in a small white vase next to a stand holding an IBM Selectric typewriter. Beside it was a desk. The top was covered with stacks of unopened mail. Behind the desk was a table with a fax machine and next to that was a copier. Boxes of plain white paper sat on the floor behind the table.

"Excuse the clutter," Culpepper greeted Paul at the door. "Secretary quit and I haven't had time to hire a new one."

Paul glanced around the room. "How long has she been gone?"

"I don't know," Culpepper shrugged. "Six months. A year." He gestured with a dismissive wave. "Who can tell? Might have been longer than that."

Paul followed him across the room to a doorway that led to a second office almost as cluttered as the first. A coatrack stood by the door. Every hook on it was filled with coats, jackets, and an assortment of book bags and umbrellas. To the right, a green couch leaned against the wall. A file cabinet stood next to it. Papers poked out from the spaces between the drawers and a stack of files lay on top. Directly opposite the door was a huge desk, piled from side to side with still more files, papers, and an assortment of dirty coffee cups and candy wrappers. Behind it was a credenza. Stacks of files, books, and magazines covered the top with only a small space clear around a laptop. Next to the computer was a charging stand with a cell phone resting on it.

Culpepper moved behind the desk and took a seat. He gestured to a chair. "Sit down." Paul took a seat while Culpepper continued. "Philip called me yesterday. Gave me a heads-up that you were going to be working with me on this. I'm glad for the help."

"Liston and I go back a long way. I'm happy to do what I can. Where are you with it?"

"I'm sort of at a dead end." Culpepper leaned back in his chair. "On the night of the break-in, Chicago police arrested three guys in the office. But there was a fourth man that managed to escape. They told you that?"

"Yes," Paul nodded. "I saw a security video that showed four men entering the building."

"I found an eyewitness that saw somebody leave the office building about the time the others were getting arrested. Guy by the name of Derrick Tillman. Got off work that night and was walking home. Passed the depot about the time this all happened. He says he saw a guy climbing down the side of the building."

Paul frowned. "Climbing down the side of the building?"

"Hanging off the downspout, to be exact."

"Did the police talk to him?"

"Not before I got to him." Culpepper reached behind him to the credenza. "And there's this." He picked up an envelope from one of the stacks and took out three photographs. "These were taken from the security camera at a convenience store." He handed the pictures to Paul. "It's down the street a little ways, in the same direction Tillman says he saw the man run after he shimmied down the rainspout."

Paul studied the photos. One of them showed a man approaching the store on the sidewalk. A second gave a full view of his face. The third offered an image from the side. "Think that's our man?"

"Might be. I showed the photos to Tillman. He said it looked like the guy he saw, but he wasn't absolutely certain."

Paul laid the pictures on the desk. "So, how do we find out who this fourth man is?"

"Well, I've done a little work on that question, too." Culpepper leaned forward and rested his elbows on the desktop. "The three guys they arrested all gave false names. Their real names are Mike Thomas, Jeff Carlisle, and Spencer Adams."

"How'd you find that out?"

Culpepper had a satisfied grin. "A friend of a friend works at the Cook County Jail."

"Oh."

"It pays to have friends in all the right places. Janitors, clerks, and busboys are the best. Nobody pays them any attention, but they see everything and know a whole lot more than folks give them credit for. They also have access to about anything you need."

"Like files on prisoners at the jail."

"Exactly."

"What did you find out about those three?"

"They were all Marines. Went through basic training together at Camp Lejeune, then spent time together off and on in the same units. They weren't always together but looks to me like the three of them crossed paths quite a bit while they were in the Corps." He looked across the desk at Paul. "I'm thinking there's a good chance that fourth guy was a Marine, too. And if he was, I'm thinking he went through basic training with the others down in North Carolina."

"Any way to track that down?"

"We could run down to North Carolina and ask around. But they move those guys so much I doubt anyone is still there who would have known them."

"What about service records?"

"Not sure how we'd narrow it down. Hundreds of thousands of records. I suppose we could confine our search to specific years. Maybe look at records on the other three. But I've tried to get records on our three guys. Can't get past the front door with my request."

"I have a friend at the Pentagon," Paul suggested. "He might be able to help."

"Now, that would be great. Somebody on the inside could get us what we need."

"I'll give him a call."

CHAPTER 59
SINAI PENINSULA

A CLOUD OF DUST ENVELOPED the tour bus as it rolled to a stop in the dirt parking lot near the base of Mount Sinai. From his seat by the window Barberini looked out on the barren landscape and smiled. A little way up the mountain, the smooth sandstone walls of Saint Catherine's monastery were visible between the jagged rocks and cliffs. Around him, the busload of tourists chattered, some complaining about the dust, others grousing about the long ride from town. For Barberini, it was like returning home after a long journey.

While still in high school, Barberini had approached the headmaster about his growing interest in the priesthood. His teachers thought it nice that he was devoted to a life of service, but they did not press him for a formal commitment until shortly before graduation. At the end of his final term, he enrolled in seminary. There he learned the story of Saint Catherine's, the oldest existing monastery in continuous use, and during that first year of seminary he purposed in his heart to seek admission. For the next three years he disciplined himself with a regimen of prayer, devotion, and physical abstinence in order to meet what he imagined where the taxing demands of life in such a place. When he completed seminary he applied for admission and was accepted to Saint Catherine's as a candidate. To his amazement, the physical and spiritual rigors of cloistered life were nothing like what he'd anticipated. Meals were served regularly and services were held according to the ritual of the hours, which he'd observed since conversion. For those aspects of life at the monastery he was well prepared. But Barberini was a social person and the demands of solitude were almost more than he could bear. He longed for conversation— endless talk about anything or nothing in particular. The first two years were excruciatingly painful. Then, in what became his final year on the mountain, he was assigned to tend the Room of Skulls.

Confined to only the space enclosed by its ancient walls, Saint Catherine's had little room to bury its dead. In order to accommodate the desire of all monks to be buried within the grounds of the monastery, the remains of the oldest interred there were exhumed to give space for the more recently dead. Removed from the ground, bleached white and dried by the heat of the sand, the bones were placed in a special room where they were tended day and night. That room, known as the Room of Skulls, was set apart from the main buildings and in it, as he watched over the remains of his ancestors in the faith, Barberini found the temptation to speak irresistible. And so began conversations with the dead, that lasted the remainder of his time on the mountain. It was during those conversations among the skulls that he remembered his chance meeting earlier in life with Father Galena, a memory that led him to the Knights of Malta.

And now, at last, he had returned to pick up where he'd left off, if only Abbott Stephen would allow him to remain— and give him back his former job.

The tour group assembled at the far side of the parking lot, but Barberini stepped from the bus and turned to the right, toward the path that led up to Saint Catherine's wall. A tour guide called to him but Barberini ignored her and kept walking. At the opposite side of the lot he stepped onto the path and disappeared behind a boulder. A few minutes later he arrived at the gate. A large brass bell hung from a column to the right with a rope that dangled beneath the clapper. Barberini grabbed the rope and gave it a shake. The bell rang loud and clear. Moments later, a monk appeared, dressed in a white linen alb.

"We are not taking tours today," he said politely.

"I am not here for the tour. Is Abbot Stephen available?"

"Who may I say is calling?"

"Angelo Barberini. Known to him as Philip of Caesarea."

"Ah, you are returning?"

"How is it you know me?"

"He speaks of you almost every day. 'Philip of Caesarea, who talked to the dead.'"

Barberini felt his cheeks glow warm with embarrassment. "Will he see me?"

"Come," the man smiled. "I will take you to him." He pushed open the gate and stepped aside to let Barberini pass. As he glanced over his shoulder he saw the tour guide standing down the path. He waved to her, then turned and started up the walk toward the center of the compound.

CHAPTER 60
DAYTON, OHIO

DAVID MCNEIL STOOD on the court of the Nutter Center, a basketball arena on the campus of Wright State University. He spoke that day, as he had for weeks, to an audience that filled every available seat. His voice resonated clear and strong and though he'd given the same speech hundreds of times, he delivered each line with a freshness that made it seem as though he were speaking to each person individually.

Caldwell stood near the corner of the basketball court at a spot that gave him a clear view of the candidate without blocking the sight lines of the audience. He listened to the rhetoric for a moment and watched the reaction of the crowd.

"We live in a great country," McNeil said with conviction. The audience erupted with applause. "But today that greatness is threatened. Not by foreign forces with planes and ships and men, but by our own complacency— a complacency fostered by a federal government that is bloated with too many employees, and fed with too much taxpayer money issuing too many unwarranted regulations— regulations that intrude on our individual freedoms, which we hold dear and which our ancestors gave their lives to defend."

The crowd went wild in a deafening roar of shouting and clapping. Caldwell backed away and slipped out to the corridor behind the stands.

He made his way to an exit door and stood there in the fresh air, surveying the crowd outside while he listened to the remainder of McNeil's speech.

Beyond the grassy lawn near the building, an overflow crowd, turned away for lack of space, stood two abreast in a line that snaked across the parking lot. They listened patiently to the speech broadcast to them through hastily assembled loudspeakers, hoping all the while for an opportunity to glimpse the candidate as he came from the building.

The event that day, like others at recent campaign stops, had become a spectacle with vendors selling official campaign T-shirts, mugs, and posters alongside others who hawked privately designed McNeil merchandise, including an array of stuffed animals, car tags, posters, and apparel. Caldwell took it all in with a satisfied smile. They'd come a long way since McNeil, a skinny college kid, first showed up at his house. Now they were on the verge of capturing the Republican Party nomination. *And then we'll show them our true power. And the Jews will trouble us no more.*

Just then someone nudged his elbow. Caldwell glanced to his left and saw a young staff volunteer standing at his side. She offered him a small white envelope. "A man told me to give this to you."

Caldwell took it without response and opened the flap. Inside he found a plain white note card with a handwritten message. "Greenbrier. Breakfast. Eight a.m. tomorrow." He returned the card to the envelope and shoved it into his pocket. "Spoleto," he whispered. No doubt he had received word about the trouble in Chicago and now he was sending in the heavy hitters to straighten things out. If they were coming to see him, it meant only one thing. Someone was laying the blame on him and he knew what that meant, too.

CHAPTER 61
MEXICO

INSIDE THE SIERRA FACILITY, Mike Thomas, Jeff Carlisle, and Spencer Adams came from the shower room dressed in hospital gowns. They followed an orderly down the hall and through a set of double doors. Beyond the doors was a large room. Six examination tables with surgical lights mounted on the ceiling above them stood to the left. Cabinets and an array of medical equipment lined the wall behind them. The orderly paused near the center of the room and gestured with his right hand. "Take a seat on the tables, gentlemen." All three did as they were told and sat with their legs dangling over the side.

A little while later, the door opened and Craig Hopkins entered, pushing a stainless steel cart. On top of it was a monitor connected to a computer that sat on a shelf below. Long, thin lead lines ran from the back of the computer and were draped over the top of the monitor. He made his way to the table where Carlisle sat.

"Lie down and roll onto your left side," he ordered. "I need to check your chips." Carlisle dutifully lifted his feet from the floor, stretched the length of his body on the table, and rolled on his side.

Hopkins stepped closer and pulled down the collar of Carlisle's gown, exposing his right shoulder blade. A few inches toward his neck, the dark outline of an implanted electronic chip was visible beneath the skin. Hopkins alternately squeezed it between his fingers and stretched the skin tightly over it, working it closer to the surface, taking care not to break the skin. Then he reached into a tray on the cart for an electrode, peeled off the back, and pressed it in place directly over the chip.

With the electrode affixed to Carlisle's skin, he turned to the cart again for one of the lead lines. He attached it to the electrode and pressed a button on a panel beneath the monitor. The screen flickered, then images appeared, shifting quickly between rows of numbers and the lines of successive grids. Carlisle strained to watch.

"Just downloading some GPS information from your chip," Hopkins explained. "We'll collate it with the coordinates for your assignment to assess unit efficiency, decision processes, and assessments."

A few minutes later, the computer beeped. Hopkins disconnected the line from the electrode and draped it over the cart. "Okay, I need you to lie on your back." Again, Carlisle did as he was told.

When Carlisle was in position, Hopkins reached above his head to an instrument pod attached to the surgical lighting bracket. From the pod he released the arm of a portable scanning unit and swung it into place. Constructed with flat panels held apart just wide enough to pass on either side of Carlisle's head, the unit was capable of providing digital images of the brain with far greater definition and clarity than the best MRI equipment available in the U.S. Hopkins moved the panels into position, then turned to a panel that hung on the wall near the head of the examination table. He pressed a button on the panel, and a screen to the right lit up with images of Carlisle's brain. An electronic implant was visible near the base of his skull.

"Okay," Hopkins said. "I'm going to switch the panels of the scanner to diagnostic mode and connect with the signal from the implant. Hold very still so the machine can read it correctly." Carlisle stared up at the ceiling, arms by his side, and remained motionless. After a few minutes the machine beeped and Hopkins gave a relieved sigh. "That looks good," he said. "I think everything is working well. Are you having any trouble?"

Carlisle nodded. "A little dizziness."

"Frequently?"

"More often than not."

"Is it debilitating? Are you still able to function?"

"I can function, but my efficiency is not so good as it usually is."

Hopkins frowned. "Are you feeling dizzy now?"

"Yes. The whole room is spinning."

"All right," Hopkins said, calmly. "I think the pulse from your implant is too high. We can adjust that without any problem, but you must wait until Dr. Walcott returns."

"How long will that take?"

"That is not for you to know. You are an instrument of the program. You will do as you are told."

CHAPTER 62
INDIANAPOLIS

THE NEXT MORNING, Sisson stood at the window of his room and surveyed the street below. He could see all the way to the bus station and he scanned the crowd, looking for anyone who seemed out of place. After a few minutes, he turned and watched both sides of the street. A vendor stood on the next corner near a newsstand where a man out front sold the morning paper. Down the block, a delivery truck was parked at the curb and a man wheeled boxes from it on a hand truck.

When he found nothing out of the ordinary, Sisson took the backpack from the bed, stepped out to the hallway, and walked downstairs. As he passed the clerk's desk he saw a newspaper in a vending machine out front. Sisson dug three quarters from his pocket, slid them in a slot, and took out a paper. The headlines showed nothing interesting but when he turned it over he saw a photograph that stopped him cold. Below the fold was a picture of a van lying on its side, the sliding door was bent and mangled. Behind the van, a pickup truck sat on the shoulder of the road, front wheels in the ditch, rear bumper high in the air. The headline for the accompanying article read, "Prisoners Escape From Marshal's Van." Sisson didn't have to read further to know what happened. He'd been part of the same procedure three years earlier in Miami. Only then it was a deputy's car carrying a single prisoner and they rammed it with a van.

They should've come up with a new plan. A couple of these and someone will catch on.

That Sierra had sprung its men from custody did not bother him. They had practiced similar maneuvers many times, and everyone knew the company would never leave a soldier— a commercial unit— in jail. It was too risky. One curious snitch, one inquisitive jail nurse and millions of dollars of technology would be lost. And that's what bothered him most. If they were working to take Thomas, Carlisle, and Adams by force from the U.S. Marshals, they were surely working to find and capture him.

He tossed the newspaper in a nearby trashcan and started down the sidewalk. Up ahead, a city bus came to a stop at the corner. He waved his hand to catch the driver's attention and ran in that direction.

For the next three hours Sisson rode the bus and watched from his seat as the city moved past the window. Slowly, the sidewalks and faces faded from view. In their place, he imagined a single face, pressed close to his, and a voice that was hard and stern. *"This is a mission, soldier. You cannot fail. You will not fail."*

Then he was sitting on a park bench. The air was hot and humid. To the left was a statue of a man on horseback. Across the park, through the low-hanging branches of a live oak tree, he could see a church. His hand was beneath the tail of his shirt and he felt his fingers, clammy and sweaty, as they wrapped around the grip of an automatic pistol. With deliberate ease, he drew the pistol from the waistband of his jeans, placed the muzzle against the woman's head, and squeezed the trigger. A silencer on the end of the barrel muffled the report of the blast, but all the same, blood and bone spewed from the side of the woman's head. Then, as if nothing had happened at all, he rose from the bench, strolled across the park, and stepped into a waiting van.

Suddenly the scene shifted and he was in a room, stark white with bright lights that hung from the ceiling. A voice, calm and soothing, spoke from just behind his right shoulder. *"I am going to count to three, and when I do you will no longer remember anything."* But Sisson did not forget and the memory of that day lingered, always in the back of his mind, invading his conscious thought whenever he relaxed and nothing could shut it out.

Brakes on the bus moaned as it came to the next stop. Sisson looked out the window to see the sun was high in the sky. It was noon already, maybe a little later. Out the window he saw a used car lot on the next corner. Almost by instinct he jumped from his seat into the aisle and caught the driver's eye in the rearview mirror. He gestured with his hand for him to wait, and the driver opened the front door. "You finally getting off?"

"Yeah."

"Been by here four times today already."

Sisson ignored him and stepped out to the curb. As the bus pulled away and merged with traffic, Sisson walked up to the car lot. A blue Chevrolet sat in the second row with a sign on the windshield that read, "Great Deal— Only $1995."

A tall, slender man approached from the left. "Make you a great deal on it."

"Does it run?"

"Oh yeah. It runs. Want to take it for a drive?"

"No." Sisson shook his head. "I'll take it."

"Take it?" The man frowned at him.

"Isn't it for sale?"

"Mister, everything I got is for sale."

"Good." Sisson pointed toward the car. "I'll take this one."

The man pointed toward a small white building fifty yards away. "Let's go inside and I'll write it up. You want to finance it?"

"I'll pay cash."

The man glanced over his shoulder with a smile. "That's even better."

CHAPTER 63
WASHINGTON, D.C.

SHORTLY AFTER SHE REACHED the office, Esther received a text message from Brody. "Food court. Art museum." She read it and smiled. "He is so into the spy life. Why doesn't he just call me?"

A few minutes later she left the office and walked over to the National Gallery of Art on Constitution Avenue. Brody was seated at a table near the back wall. She made her way to him and took a seat.

"You know," she began, "they have cameras all over this place. They can see us talking."

"I know."

"Can probably hear our conversation."

Brody shook his head and pointed toward the door. A line of school children formed there. He and Esther watched as the children went through the line, picked up a snack from the counter, then followed their teacher to a row of tables just a few feet away. Soon the sound of their voices rose in a cacophony of chatter and laughter, enveloping Esther and Brody in a cocoon of noise. He leaned closer to her and smiled. "Now we can talk. You met with Liston Cook?"

"Yes."

"What did you find out?"

"He has the documents."

"You saw them?"

"No. But he told us about them."

"Does he think that's why someone broke into his office?"

"He doesn't know why they did it, or who would have wanted the documents. But he knows there was a fourth man. He has a detective looking for him. And he asked Paul to help."

"Stockton showed him the documents?"

"Yes."

"Was Stockton there when you talked?"

"No."

"And Cook didn't tell you anything about the contents of the documents or show them to you?"

"No."

"Interesting."

"I'm not even sure he has copies of the documents. I think Stockton has them. The really strange thing is that he hasn't done anything with them yet."

"I agree," Brody nodded. "Those documents would blow McNeil out of the water." He looked away for a moment, as if thinking, then continued. "Perhaps it's just politics."

"What do you mean?"

"Maybe he thinks that even with McNeil out of the race, he still can't win the nomination and he doesn't want John Franklin to get it."

"Maybe."

"Did you check your sources for contributions to McNeil's campaign?"

"Yes," Esther nodded, "but I don't have anything. Except that the FEC already has an investigation open into Sierra and its support of McNeil's campaign."

Brody arched an eyebrow. "What brought that on?"

"I don't know."

"They told you about an ongoing investigation?"

"I have a friend who works there," Esther replied. "She told me about it because they were wondering why our associates were asking about the very thing they're investigating."

"I assume you didn't tell them."

"I assume you know the answer to that."

"What's the detective's name?"

Esther looked puzzled. "Detective?"

"The one who's working for Liston Cook," Brody explained. "The one Paul's helping."

"Brian Culpepper. Know anything about him?"

"Not much." Brody's eyes darted away. "I think he's been in the business a long time."

"See what you can find out about him."

"Yeah." Brody sounded distracted. "I'll have someone check him out."

CHAPTER 64
MEXICO

WHEN DR. WALCOTT ARRIVED at the facility, he went straight to the examination room. He was eager to learn how the patients had performed and to review the mission with them.

Once again, Thomas, Carlisle, and Adams lay on the tables, arms at their sides, eyes focused on the ceiling above. Lead wires attached to electrodes on their foreheads and necks connected them to individual EEG machines that sat on stands near the wall. A monitor on top of each one showed wavy green lines moving up and down across the screen as the machines monitored brain waves and nerve functions. A paper tape gave a printout of the results. Hopkins stood to one side, hands together at his waist, dutifully awaiting orders.

Walcott made his way slowly up and down the line, checking the printouts from each man, comparing the results, noting the differences. After a few minutes, he turned to face them. "Sit up, gentlemen." All three men dutifully bent at the waist, raising head and torso to a sitting position. "Turn to the side," Walcott continued, "and let your feet dangle over the edge of the tables." Again, all three men turned to the left, dangled their feet from the table, and gripped the edge of it with their hands.

"You all performed as expected and, in spite of the arrest, you did as you were instructed to do. Now," Walcott continued, "I want you to watch this with me." He pointed to a screen at the end of the room. "Let us see what happened and what it may reveal to us that we can use."

Images appeared on the screen, recorded from the van as it arrived at the alley behind Cook's headquarters in Chicago on the night of the break-in. They watched as the mission played out before them— entering through the back door, up the stairway, to the office. When Sisson joined them in the office, Thomas winced. Walcott used a remote to pause the video, then glanced in his direction. "Something went wrong?"

"Incompatible unit," Thomas said in a flat, affectless voice.

"You knew this from the briefing."

"No," Thomas said, shaking his head. "I sensed it."

"In what way?"

"He kept deviating from the plan. Wouldn't follow the script."

"You told him the plan?"

"He received it the same way we all did. From the mobile briefing facility."

"I see." Walcott picked up a writing pad from a counter near the wall and jotted a note, "Sisson running older program. Check for compatibility with latest unit at compliance interface." Then he grabbed the remote and pointed it toward the screen. The video of the mission began again. They watched as Sisson moved to the filing cabinets, his head glanced to the right, then he inched over to the left and disappeared. Once more, Walcott paused the video.

"What should have happened here?"

"We did as we were told," Carlisle replied. "This was a nonlethal mission. If confronted we were to raise our hands and wait."

"Make no statements," Adams offered, "and await our removal by an extraction team."

"Correct," Walcott replied. He glanced in Hopkins' direction. "What is the setting on Adams?"

"It's a little too strong, sir."

"I thought so. We'll adjust it before we finish." Walcott turned back to the others. "Sisson chose not to comply with accepted procedure. Compliance is not an option. It jeopardizes the entire team."

They watched the video to the end, then Walcott moved around the end of the tables and stood near Thomas. "Okay, gentlemen, turn so you face me." All three turned toward him. When they were in position, he stretched his arms wide in either direction. "Raise your arms and extend them their full length." He waited while they complied. "Turn your palms up, tip back your heads, and close your eyes."

When they had complied, he continued. "Now repeat this phrase slowly. 'We serve God and country, to protect and defend.'" The three men repeated the phrase. "Say it again and let the words wash over you. 'We serve God and country, to protect and defend.'" They repeated the phrase. "Washing away all doubt and guilt. All fear and anxiety."

The men continued to repeat the phrase, saying it in unison over and over again. Before long they were in a trance and Walcott moved among them, whispering to each one. "Goodness is overcoming evil. You are making the world a safer place. Others benefit from your work. You have done well."

CHAPTER 65

WEST VIRGINIA

LOCATED IN THE MOUNTAINS of West Virginia, Greenbrier Resort enjoyed a reputation for seclusion and anonymity, which made it a favorite retreat of the wealthy and famous. Wallace Jordan had been there many times. He checked into his room and made arrangements with the dining hall for a private meeting the following day.

The next morning he went downstairs and was ushered to a small dining room where a table was set for two. A few minutes later Caldwell appeared. When they were seated and coffee had been served, Jordan looked across the table. "We have a problem."

"I have all kinds of problems, Wallace. Which one are you talking about?"

"Malta knows about the break-in and they aren't happy about it."

Caldwell sounded indignant. "They aren't happy?"

"No. They aren't."

Caldwell's eyes narrowed. "Our friends on Malta need to stop and think. We didn't dream this operation up on our own. This was the work of the Military Vicariate."

"Execution was your responsibility."

"Right. And if the vaunted Knights of Malta had done their job, none of this would have been necessary."

"How so?"

"We were just to clean up after them. It was their documents we were looking for. They're the ones who let that guy get off the island with them. Him and that Greek."

"I think the extent of what you did was too much for them. And it was your guys who got caught."

"One team." Caldwell gestured with the index finger of his right hand. "A single team. Out of fifteen total. And they were the ones who wanted us to hit all fifteen locations."

"Well," Jordan shrugged, "it was one team too many."

"We planned for that. And made it look like they worked for Wilson."

"That's a problem, too," Jordan replied.

"What?" Caldwell was beside himself. "They have a problem letting the media throw this off on a Democrat?"

"They think the cover story is unbelievable."

"Who cares if it's unbelievable? When we leak this to the press, it'll stick all over Wilson and that's all anyone will remember."

"But Wilson is polling so far ahead, and Cook is so far behind, no one will believe it. The story will be seen for what it is— a cover for something else."

"Then they should have taken care of this before that priest left with the documents. Look, McNeil will win the Republican primary without much trouble. We're ahead of all the Republican candidates. We don't—"

"But," Jordan interrupted, "we don't poll well against any of the Democrats except Jacob Rush."

"I know. That's why we want to run against him. Which is why we put the break-in on Wilson."

"All the same," Jordan reiterated, "Spoleto and the Council were not impressed. They feel like you risked their candidate and all they've worked to achieve. And for not much of a result."

"I've worked hard at this, too, you know. I want the Jews gone as much as anybody. They're ruining the place— them and the Mexicans. But it wasn't our problem we were trying to correct."

"Well, now you have to clean this up."

Caldwell looked over at Jordan. "Are they really upset?"

"Yes," Jordan nodded. "They are serious."

"Are they thinking of finding another candidate?"

"No," Jordan replied. His face was like stone and his eyes bore in on Caldwell. "They're thinking of finding another you."

The sound of those words and the look on Jordan's face sent a chill down Caldwell's spine. He was right— the teams who entered Cook's offices were cleaning up after the Order's mistake— but in the larger picture none of that mattered. They'd failed to execute the mission and now the Order had to clean up after Sierra. If they blamed Caldwell, they wouldn't simply fire him.

"Okay." He cleared his throat. "I'll take care of it."

"Meet with Logan and fix it."

"Logan's in trouble, too?"

"I'm just delivering the message."

CHAPTER 66
WASHINGTON, D.C.

WITH THE INFORMATION he had obtained from Culpepper, Paul contacted Chris Jones, a friend who worked at the Naval Personnel Office in Silver Spring, Maryland. They met at Jones' office.

"What brings you out here?"

"I'm trying to locate someone who was in the Marines."

"Is this business, or are you just looking for a friend?"

"Actually, I'm working on a project for Liston Cook."

"Congressman Cook?"

"Yes."

"Great. We like Congressman Cook. Helped us get funding for our new records system. Sorry to see he didn't run for reelection. Sure wish he'd get the nomination. But I'm certain he won't." He paused a moment and the look on his face turned serious. "Does this have something to do with that break-in at his office?"

"It might."

"Too much like Watergate."

"Yes. It was."

Jones scooted his chair closer to the desk. "Who are you looking for?"

"That's just it. I don't have a name. But I have a unit."

"That's gonna be tough."

"And I have the names of three other guys who were in the unit with him."

"Okay. We can find their unit, but then we have to narrow it down to one person. Any descriptive information?"

"I have a photograph of him."

"I'll say one thing for you," Jones smiled. "You don't make it easy."

"If it was easy, I would have gone to the Army."

Jones grinned. "Let's see what you got."

"I have this one." Paul handed him the photograph from the surveillance video outside the convenience store. "And I have another one that's a little better." He handed him a photo taken from the security camera at the lobby desk. The picture showed a sharp, clear image of a man's face.

"All right," Jones sighed. "Let's begin at the beginning. Give me the names of the men you know."

"Mike Thomas, Jeff Carlisle, and Spencer Adams." Paul handed Jones a page with the information.

Jones turned to a computer on the credenza behind his desk and logged on to a U.S. Navy database. Using Mike Thomas' name, he worked backward to create a list of each unit to which he'd been assigned. Then he searched those units for Spencer Adams and Jeff Carlisle. "Okay," he said, finally. "They served in various units together at different times but I'm seeing only one unit with all three men in it at the same time. That's the training unit at Camp Lejeune."

"Where could we get pictures of that group?"

Jones turned back to the computer. "Let me see what I can find."

Several minutes later, the monitor showed an image of Marine recruits, standing in line outside the barracks— hair cut close and tight, faces lean and taut. Jones pointed to the screen. "Best I can tell, that's your training unit." Paul rose and moved around the desk for a closer look.

From the caption at the bottom of the picture, he located Thomas, Carlisle, and Adams, all in different rows. But standing next to Adams was a slender man with broad shoulders, olive complexion, and dark, piercing eyes. Paul checked it against the photo from the security camera, then scanned the rows of men once more. "I'm not certain," he said. "But I think that's our guy." He tapped the screen with his finger on the man beside Adams. "What do you think?"

Jones took the picture from Paul and leaned back as far as the chair would go. "Sometimes these things are sharper from a distance." He glanced back and forth between the screen and the photo. "The man in the surveillance video is not very tall." He moved closer to the monitor. "So if we eliminate all the tall guys, that takes out Thomas, Carlisle, and just about everyone on the back row."

"Adams is in the middle row."

"Right." Jones looked at the photograph once more. "The man in the video has a square face." He turned back to the screen. "And the guy next to Adams does, too."

"I think it's him."

"I don't see anyone else on here who's close."

"What's his name?"

Jones traced his finger along the caption. "Bill Sisson."

Paul wrote down the name. "Do you have an address for him?"

"That's a problem," Jones grimaced. "Unit photographs like this are public information. Last known address is something different. That's getting into personal information."

"Okay."

Jones turned back to the computer. He exited the photo database and brought up a different screen. With a few keystrokes, he came to a different page. He studied it a moment, then stood. "When he was discharged he gave a forwarding address in Cape May, New Jersey. But that was ten years ago." Jones stood and moved around the end of the desk. "I need some coffee." He shot Paul a knowing look. "You want a cup?"

"Yeah," Paul grinned. "Cream and sugar." He rose from his chair and moved behind the desk. "Make sure it's hot." The page on the monitor showed Sisson's information. Paul took a scrap of paper from the desk and copied the address.

*   *   *

Jones came from his office and walked up the hall to the copier room. A cabinet stood in the corner near the window. On it was a coffee maker. He took two Styrofoam cups from a shelf below and filled them with coffee. When he'd added cream and sugar to the cup for Paul, he took a cell phone from his pocket and typed a text message. "Paul Bryson is asking about fourth man on the team. Gave him information. No current address in the system." When he'd prepared the text, he scrolled down the contacts list for Russo's number. He highlighted it and pressed a button to send the message.

As he picked up the cups to leave, an alert tone rang from his phone indicating a new message had arrived. He checked the screen and saw Russo had replied, "Thank you. Was he alone?" Jones sent a reply, then started from the room.

CHAPTER 67
SARDINIA

NEWSPAPER IN HAND, Josef Sauer crossed the airport lobby and made his way to the security checkpoint. There he took a seat on a bench, opened the newspaper, and leaned back in a relaxed position. Holding the paper by the edges with both hands, he propped his elbows against his chest and stared blankly at the page. Every few moments, he glanced up and quickly surveyed the crowd of arriving passengers.

An hour later, a man appeared near a gate partway down the corridor. He wore gray wool slacks, a white shirt, and tweed jacket. His hair was neatly trimmed and he had no mustache, no tattoos, and no noticeable scars. In his left hand he held a leather briefcase. Walking at a deliberate pace, he made his way past the security station and into the main lobby of the airport. As he went past, Sauer took a cell phone from his pocket and typed a message. "Roldan has arrived." Then he rose from the bench and started across the lobby at a discreet distance.

*   *   *

From the airport, Roldan took a taxi to the Regina Margherita, an elegant hotel near the center of Cagliari, the capital. A few hours later he left his room, returned to the lobby, and stopped at the bellman's stand.

"I was wondering if you could tell me where Saint Sophia Church is located."

"It is all the way out on Via Dei Conversi. Much too far to walk." The bellman moved toward the door. "You must take a taxi." He pushed open the door and stepped out to the curb. A taxi was there already. The bellman turned to look over his shoulder and smiled back at Roldan. "See. Your wish, my command." He opened the rear door of the taxi and gestured for Roldan to enter. Roldan ducked low and slid onto the seat.

On the opposite side of town, the taxi came to a stop at the curb in front of Saint Sophia Church. Roldan paid the driver and stepped out to the curb. He crossed the sidewalk, pushed open the door, and went inside.

The door opened to a foyer with a tile floor and plastered walls. Directly opposite the entrance, a door led into the sanctuary. A picture of a bearded man hung to the right. Roldan assumed he must be a saint, but he did not know the name. Icons ringed the picture and beneath it was a small table with candles and incense. Roldan caught the details of the room in passing and moved in one continuous step from the doorway, across the foyer and into the sanctuary. There he made his way up the aisle toward the front of the church. As he did, a priest appeared from a narrow doorway to the right.

"May I help you?"

"I was looking for Father Hierapolis."

"I am he," Hierapolis replied. "How may I help you?"

"I am trying to locate information about this person." He reached inside the leather satchel for a photograph and showed it to him. "Do you recognize him?"

"Ah," he smiled. "This is Angelo. You know him?"

"Only by reputation. I was wondering if you could help me. His name is Angelo Barberini."

"Yes," Hierapolis nodded. "He grew up here. In this church."

"Have you seen him recently?"

"No. It has been many years. He went away to seminary, came back here briefly, then entered Saint Catherine's."

"Saint Catherine's?"

"The monastery. At Mount Sinai."

"Is he living there now?"

"No. I do not think so. Someone said he was on Malta. With the Knights of Malta." Hierapolis handed him the photo. "But I do not believe it."

"Why?"

"Because he was Orthodox, not Catholic." He said those words with disdain. "No one would leave the church to become a Roman."

"Do you know anyone who might have more information about him?"

"Perhaps," Hierapolis sounded suddenly suspicious. "Why do you ask?"

"I am conducting research on the Knights of Malta and I heard about him from others, that he was a member of the Order. And so I became curious how a member of the Greek Church would enter the Order."

"I can tell you," Hierapolis said, wagging his finger. "You only do it with a sponsor. That is all. You must have a sponsor."

"A sponsor."

"Yes. That is the only way."

"Who was Barberini's sponsor?"

Hierapolis' face twisted in a scowl. "That Galena," he said, spitting out the words as if they left a bitter taste. "It was Galena who seduced Angelo to consider the Order. And it was Galena who opened the way for him to do it."

"Galena was a member?"

"And a Greek himself. Though he rarely admitted it."

"You knew him?"

"Yes. We all knew him."

"How did Penalta know him?"

"Galena came through here some years ago, while Angelo was still in seminary. He celebrated mass all over the island. Lots of people went out to see him. Angelo was here on vacation from school and saw him several times. Far too many times."

"But I thought you said he went to Saint Catherine's."

"He did. And then he joined the Order." Hierapolis looked at Roldan once more. "Are you certain you are here for an honest purpose?"

"I am here conducting research about the Order," Roldan smiled. "You were going to tell me where I could find others who know Barberini."

"North of here," Hierapolis said, pointing with his finger. "Near San Gavino. His parents are dead. He had brothers and sisters but I do not know where they are now. If you ask there, someone can tell you."

* * *

Josef Sauer watched from across the street as Roldan came from the building. He stepped from the curb, hailed a taxi, and got inside. Sauer watched as the cab went past, then turned his car into the street and followed. As they made their way out of town, he took the cell phone from his pocket. Working the keys with his thumb he typed a message while he drove. "Following Roldan north from town." He pressed a button for the contacts list, found the correct number and sent the message.

CHAPTER 68
YALAHA, FLORIDA

MCNEIL GAZED OUT THE WINDOW of the black SUV and let his eyes wander over the fields that lined both sides of the road. Far in the distance, at the opposite end of the straight rows, sugarcane blew in the breeze. Between the road and cane, scores of migrant workers moved up and down rows of tomatoes. Stooped over at the waist, they loaded buckets and hampers, then carried them to a trailer parked in the turn row. When they reached the trailer they handed their baskets and hampers to a foreman. He, in turn, gave them a small round disk, which the workers stuffed in their pockets.

"What's that they're getting?" McNeil pointed out the window. "From the man on the wagon."

Seated next to McNeil was Johnny LaCosta, one of the largest produce brokers in the United States and an avid supporter of the Republican Party. LaCosta glanced out the window. "What do you mean?"

"Right there," McNeil replied, tapping the window with this fingertip. "He just gave that man something. What was it?"

"Oh, that's a chit."

"A chit?"

"Yeah. You know. Like a coin. It's made of brass. They give them one for every basket they pick. That's how they get paid."

"They get paid by the basket, not the hour?"

"Right," LaCosta nodded. "You can't pay them by the hour."

"Why not?"

"Too expensive. And there'd be no incentive for them to work. They'll just lie around and wait for you to pay them." He gave McNeil a knowing smile. "But if you pay them by the basket, what they make depends on how much they pick. Then they work very fast."

"So, the more they pick, the more they make?"

"Yeah," LaCosta nodded. "Something like that."

"That sounds like a good deal."

"Yeah. It sounds like it to the worker, too."

McNeil was puzzled. "What do you mean?"

"That's part of the deal," LaCosta smiled confidently. "It sounds like they can make as much as they want. But they don't make that much, so it works out okay."

McNeil had a confused look. "I'm not sure I follow you."

"There are only so many hours in a day," LaCosta grinned. "Only so much energy in one man's back."

"How much do they make, if you divided it by the hour?"

"Four or five dollars."

"That's less than minimum wage."

"Farm labor isn't subject to the wage and hour law. And they have a lot of children." LaCosta pointed toward the field. "See those young ones out there? They work, too. Their parents are out there somewhere. They all work together. So, they make more that way."

"Hmm," McNeil nodded. "I suppose it's better than living in Mexico."

"For sure."

A caravan followed behind the SUV with vanloads of campaign workers, followed by two buses filled with news reporters and camera crews. The long line blew clouds of red dust into the air. Then, about a mile beyond the tomato fields, they slowed and turned into a compound.

Trailer trucks were parked in the shade of a thick stand of pecans. The dark shade looked cool and inviting, but McNeil noticed the workers moving between the trucks carried pine branches in their hands. "What's that for?" He pointed again out the window. "The branches."

"Yellow flies," LaCosta chuckled. "They use them to swat the flies." He nudged McNeil's elbow and pointed to the right. "This is where the work turns into money."

On the opposite side of the compound were rows of large metal warehouses. Between them, workers unloaded farm wagons piled high with baskets of tomatoes fresh from the field. They carefully poured the tomatoes onto a conveyor belt that carried the tomatoes through a sorting machine. There they were separated by size and weight. Once sorted, they dropped into large vats filled with fresh, clean water where they were rinsed. Another conveyor belt lifted them from the water and eased them onto long rows of packing belts. Workers, mostly women, stood along the belt grabbing tomatoes as they came by and placing them in new cardboard boxes. Young boys carried the full boxes to pallets where they were stacked four rows high, secured with shrink-wrap, and loaded onto a trailer.

LaCosta reached for the door handle. McNeil caught him by the shoulder. "Wait. Let the TV crews get set up first."

"Oh," LaCosta said, sheepishly. "I forgot."

Camera crews and reporters scurried around, jockeying for the best positions. After a few minutes they were all in place and Carter Hewes, McNeil's chief of staff, tapped on the window. McNeil smiled at LaCosta. "Now we can get out." He pushed open the door and came from the car. LaCosta followed, smiling and waving at the crowd. They paused a moment for pictures, then LaCosta led McNeil on a quick tour of the packing lines. They wandered down the rows of conveyor belts, then into the warehouse where they found rows and rows of pallets stacked with boxes of tomatoes, squash, and bell peppers.

"This is quite an operation," McNeil observed.

"Yes," LaCosta beamed proudly. "One of the most successful farming operations in the country. This farm alone supplies fifteen percent of the entire U.S. production of tomatoes."

"What about the workers?"

"All documented. And treated just as any other American worker." LaCosta gestured over his shoulder. "You want to see where they live?"

"Sure," McNeil nodded. "Show me."

With reporters in tow, they walked behind the warehouse to a two-story brick building. LaCosta held the door for McNeil to enter, then led him down a long hallway. On either side were doors with brass numbers on them. "These are the apartments for families," LaCosta explained. He stopped a short distance down the hall and rapped on a door with his knuckle. "We can see inside one if you like."

Before McNeil could respond, the door opened and a young woman appeared. Wearing a freshly laundered blue dress, she wore canvas flats and had a pleasant smile. LaCosta said something to her in Spanish, then gestured for McNeil to enter.

Inside, the apartment was clean and neatly organized. The door opened to a living room with a sofa on the wall to the right. A chair sat opposite it at an angle. A television rested on a cabinet along the back wall. To the left was the kitchen and beyond it a hallway led to a bathroom with bedrooms on either side. It was cool inside and LaCosta gestured with a sweep of his arm. "Air-conditioning, comfortable furniture, and downstairs there is a laundry room where the women can wash and dry the clothes."

McNeil turned to the young woman. "How many children do you have?"

She started to answer but LaCosta cut her off, again speaking to her in Spanish. Then Hewes stepped forward. "Governor, we need to keep moving. We can take some questions when we get outside but we have to get back to Orlando for the event this afternoon."

"Right," McNeil replied tersely. "Have to stay on schedule." He smiled politely to the woman, then turned away and followed Hewes out the door.

Outside the building, McNeil gathered with reporters. He made a brief statement about how agriculture was the bedrock of the American economy and it gave us the ability to pursue all the other things that have led to greatness. Then he took a few perfunctory questions from reporters. When they were finished, he started toward the SUV with LaCosta at his side. As they neared it, Hewes wedged himself between the two. "Mr. LaCosta, I need you to swap places with me."

"Well," LaCosta said, taken aback at the interruption. "I suppose so."

"You can ride in the van with Trent Paine." Hewes turned toward the van and pointed. "He's that guy in the blue blazer right there next to the woman in the red dress. He's expecting you." Hewes opened the door for McNeil, waited for him to get inside, then slid onto the seat beside him.

McNeil frowned. "You were a little abrupt with him, weren't you?"

"We need to keep moving."

"We need his money."

"We'll get his money. He has nowhere else to go." Hewes tapped the driver on the shoulder and gestured with a wave of his hand. The driver put the SUV in gear and they started forward.

McNeil looked away and stared out the window. As they made the turn back toward the road, the left side of the compound came into view. Past the rows of waiting trucks he caught a glimpse of low, single-story shacks just out of sight behind the pecan trees. He leaned forward and gestured over the driver's shoulder. "Go that way."

The driver turned the steering wheel to start in that direction, but Hewes intervened. "We don't have time," he said, his eyes wide and alert. "We need to head back."

"I want to see what's over there."

"We've seen all we can see here today," Hewes replied. "Let's keep moving. We have a major event this afternoon and then a few hours of downtime tonight. Let's not lose it. There's a big day tomorrow in Miami." The driver sat motionless awaiting instructions. Hewes gestured impatiently with his hand and the driver turned the SUV toward the road.

CHAPTER 69
MEXICO

DR. WALCOTT GLANCED UP from his desk to see Tony Floyd standing at the office doorway. "Didn't know you were coming today."

"Thought I'd drop in and talk with you. See what's going on."

"Sure. You're always welcome here. It's just that usually we get advance news of your arrival. Don't you like to partake of the local diversions?"

"Not this time." Floyd came from the door and took a seat in a chair opposite the desk. "Had a visit from Bartlett the other day."

"I assumed he would contact you."

"You two get things worked out?"

"I am not sure about Mr. Bartlett. He thinks too much for one in this … business."

"You mean he doesn't do what you tell him to do, without asking questions."

"If I am to conduct research, I must have a free rein with my subjects."

Floyd gestured over his shoulder. "Let's have a look around while we talk."

"Certainly." Walcott stood. "I'll be happy to give you the tour." He led Floyd from the office and started down the hall. "We are having great success with the latest implants and chips."

"Still using the old ones?"

"Yes. And that was the problem with the team in Chicago. One of the units was operating on an older implant. He was not fully compatible with the others."

"I'm not sure that answers all the questions."

"We'll know more once we get him in and examine him."

"Any progress on the recovery effort?"

"You'll have to discuss that with Mr. Bartlett. He's in charge of that effort."

They passed a door on the right and Floyd pushed it open. "What's in here?"

"I don't think we should go there." Walcott moved to stop him but Floyd ignored him and continued.

The door opened to a windowless room. It had a white tile floor, white walls. Large round fixtures hung from the ceiling and bathed the room in stark white light. Beds lined the walls on both sides and in them were men of every shape and size, some with missing arms and legs. One had no eyes and another twitched so violently the bed shook. In the far corner, a man cowered with his arms over his head, gently rocking himself back and forth.

Floyd gave Walcott a startled look. "What is this?"

"These are the reasons for the advances we've made."

"Failures?"

"Not failures. Potential solutions we were able to eliminate."

At the far end of the room was a second door. Floyd moved toward it with long strides. "And what's back here?" Before Walcott could stop him, Floyd pushed opened the door and found a second room similar to the first, with men equally deformed and grotesque, only these men were of olive complexion. "What the—"

Walcott reached around him and pulled the door closed. "We should talk outside." He gestured with a nod of his head and Floyd backed away. When they were in the hall once more, Walcott steered him outside the building. The sun was hot but they walked in the shade of the structure.

"What did I just see?"

"You asked me to establish the program, and I established the program. We give you regular reports. Don't act like you don't know what's going on."

"Those men were from the Middle East."

"You wanted to know if the implants could exert enough control to permit us to use terrorists to infiltrate terrorist cells. In order to reach a valid conclusion we had to test our theories on people from that region of the world."

"It was a rhetorical question. An inquiry into the feasibility of the project. Not authorization to conduct actual tests."

"We gave you a proposal. You approved the budget."

"I thought you meant—"

Walcott cut him off. "You knew exactly what we meant."

"But what did you do to them? Most of those men hardly know they are alive."

"Whatever we did, I assure you it was to save American lives."

"They can hardly function. Will they ever recover?"

Walcott gave him a dour look. "You know better than to ask such a question."

"Then what will happen to them?"

"Some will be incorporated into the ongoing training program."

"How?"

"We will find a use for them. We use live training already. Perhaps we will add them to the regimen."

"You mean they will be killed."

"Whatever we do to them, they will not remember."

"How did they get that way?"

"Personality modification is a messy business, Mr. Floyd. Some collateral damage could not be avoided."

They walked along in silence until they reached the end of the building. "Well," Floyd said at last. "I suppose if they weren't forced into it."

"They all agreed to participate. And their families were well-compensated for their efforts."

"All right," Floyd sighed. "What about Sisson? Is he going to be a problem?"

"I don't think so."

"Any idea what actually happened? I mean, beyond the implant issues."

"This is not a precise business. There is a margin of error. The technology is not perfect. We must remember that at their basic level, all our units are human and when humans are involved, no matter how much we may alter them with implants, drugs, and training, there is always room for error. Are you worried?"

"I'm a little concerned. This trouble in Chicago is not just about a failed break-in or a botched political campaign. Our business model depends on this technology."

"I am aware of that."

"We pitched this as a counterterrorism measure. Capture terrorists, alter their function, then send them back to infiltrate their own networks."

"And it will do just that."

"But is it ready?"

"Not quite. We need to explore the ramifications a little further."

"What does that mean?"

"Relax." Walcott laid a hand on Floyd's shoulder. "This will work out well for the company. We will locate Mr. Sisson, examine him thoroughly, and adjust to address the issues we discover. This is not a problem. It is an opportunity. But we must find him. He is even more important than the others. They performed as expected. He did not. We will find him and make it work."

CHAPTER 70
CHICAGO

AS SOON AS IT BECAME APPARENT that Sisson was not following predetermined alternative plans, Sierra Resources deployed asset-recovery teams to locate and retrieve him. Using data previously obtained from his tracking chip, they visited every location he'd frequented since arriving in the city. When that proved fruitless, they expanded their search by activating assets already inserted in strategic Chicago agencies. Employees of the city's police, fire, and sanitation departments were alerted, interviewed, and provided with photographs and identifying information for Sisson. Technicians searched the city's communications system and reviewed hours and hours of traffic camera video. Others combed through security tapes obtained from cameras mounted outside government buildings. Additional agents worked with private businesses, cajoling and hacking their way into individual store security systems in an attempt to locate even a glimpse of Sisson.

As part of that effort, Pete Lindale was assigned to Chicago Regional Intelligence Center, a recognized Homeland Security fusion center created to assist in the gathering of domestic intelligence, both from government and private sources. With almost limitless resources, and with links to other fusion centers across the nation, the agency had access to video from airports, bus terminals, and satellites from locations unavailable to local law enforcement. They also had the latest analytical tools.

For the past two days Lindale had been staring at the screen, manually scoping through video while the department's computer ran airport and bus station security tapes through its face-recognition program. Like the FBI's system, only newer and more sophisticated, the program produced amazingly accurate results. Better still, the software was designed to work with video of poor quality.

While he watched images scrolling by on the screen, Lindale's mind wandered back to his home in Colorado. A contract agent with Sierra, he worked full time as an instructor at Colorado Technical College where he taught videography and basic film techniques. He only worked for Sierra when his schedule allowed. The stint in Chicago cost him most of his vacation days for the year, but the pay more than made up the difference.

Suddenly the computer beeped, jerking Lindale back to the moment. A message on the monitor indicated the system had found a match. He pressed a key on the keypad and an image from one of the security tapes appeared on the screen. The picture, taken from the bus station, was sharp but poorly lit. Lindale turned to an analyst seated beside him. "Can you tighten this image and make it a little lighter?"

The analyst scooted over to Lindale's console and, with a few more keystrokes, produced an image that was clear and sharp. On the screen before him was a picture of Bill Sisson. The sight of it made Lindale smile. "That's him," he said, triumphantly." He reached in his pocket for the cell phone and called the command center in Tucson.

*   *   *

Jeremy Bartlett lay on a cot in an office down the hall from the command center. After days of working round-the-clock, exhaustion finally caught up with him. He was sound asleep when a hand shook his foot. "Jeremy," a voice said. "Jeremy," the voice repeated, jarring him awake. "We received a call from Chicago."

Bartlett forced open his eyes and rubbed them with his fingertips. "What time is it?"

"Almost lunch. You've been asleep about four hours."

"Man," he sighed. "I could use forty more."

"Pete Lindale called from Chicago. A security camera caught a shot of Sisson."

Bartlett sat up. "Where was he?"

"The bus station."

"Where was the bus going?"

"We don't know yet. They're downloading data now."

Bartlett threw back the cover and swung his legs over the side of the cot. Fully clothed, his shirt was creased with wrinkles. Specks of lint clung to the legs of his pants. "I look almost as rough as I feel," he groaned.

"We thought you'd want to see the video as soon as it arrived."

"Yeah, let's have a look," and he started toward the door.

In the command center, the video from Chicago was loaded and ready. Bartlett stood near the operator's console and watched as it played on the screen. "That's him," someone offered.

"What about the bus? Can we back it out and get the front of the bus?" The screen went blank, then an image of the bus appeared. "Sharpen that up," Bartlett said. "We need to read the destination in the window above the windshield. Moments later, the word *Indianapolis* came into focus. "Okay, that's where he was headed."

"He could have gotten off anywhere in between."

"Maybe. But for now, we'll focus on Indianapolis." Bartlett leaned over the operator's shoulder. "Send the asset-recovery teams to Indianapolis."

"Yes, sir."

"Who found this video?"

"Pete Lindale."

"Do we know him?"

"Part-timer from Colorado."

"Okay. Send him to the bus station. Find out if they can tell us about the ticket Sisson purchased. If not, get a list of the destinations for every passenger on the bus when it left Chicago." He turned to the room. "Get to work. We know everything there is to know about Sisson. Dig in and find out what connections he has in Indianapolis. If that doesn't work, spread out in concentric circles until we find some connections." He clapped his hands. "We caught a break. Let's make the most of it." Suddenly the room came alive with activity.

CHAPTER 71
ORLANDO

FOLLOWING THE RALLY that afternoon, McNeil and his staff retired to the Grand Bohemian Hotel. An evening with nothing major on the schedule was a rare but welcome moment for the campaign staff. Some spent the time swimming in the hotel pool. Others caught up on sleep. But most spent the time attending to personal details like laundry and phone calls home.

McNeil stood at the window of his hotel room and stared out at the city. The sun was sinking low on the horizon, sending long rays of yellow, red, orange, and purple across the sky. It was a beautiful sight but he hardly noticed. Instead, his mind was occupied with what he'd seen earlier in the day— children at work in the fields picking tomatoes, the shacks he'd glimpsed through the trees— and the sound of LaCosta's voice. *"...if you pay them by the basket ...they work very fast ...they got a lot of children."*

He glanced across the room to the half-eaten salad on the table. *Some kid picked the tomatoes for my salad. That kid should have been in school.*

But what about the building they showed him? With the apartments and air-conditioning. What was that? Just a set-up for the cameras? And why wouldn't Carter let him see the buildings beyond the pecan trees? *I'm the governor of Virginia,* he thought to himself. *And I'm the presumptive Republican presidential nominee. This is my campaign. I can go where I please.*

He turned away from the window, walked to the door, and started down the hall. When he reached the elevator he found a familiar face waiting. "Governor, that was a—"

McNeil pointed to him. "Trent, right?"

"Yes, sir. Trent Paine. I work with the speechwriters."

"Do you have a car?"

"Yes, sir. It's a rental from the airport. A compact. You need to go somewhere? We can get an SUV from the motor pool."

"I don't want an SUV." McNeil gestured with an open palm. "Give me your keys."

Trent took the keys from his pocket and handed them over. Just then the elevator doors opened and they got on with a group from the advance team. They were laughing and joking until they saw McNeil, then they were suddenly quiet. He smiled and nodded politely and did his best to engage them in conversation. When they reached the lobby, Trent leaned close and said in a low voice, "Blue Ford. Parked out front by the sign."

"Thanks." McNeil started toward the door.

It was after nine when McNeil reached Yalaha and almost ten when he arrived at the farm compound. Still, the place was alive with workers processing and packing tomatoes, squash, and bell peppers. Bright lights mounted on poles above the equipment cast a glare across their tired faces as they took the vegetables from the packing belts and placed them in boxes. Small children clung to their mothers' skirts. Young boys stacked the full boxes on pallets. People and machinery moved in every direction.

McNeil parked the car near the trucks and stepped out. But instead of walking toward the packing sheds and warehouses, he threaded his way past the trucks and followed a path through the pecan trees. A few minutes later he discovered the worst sight he'd ever seen.

Beyond the pecan grove were three rows of shacks. Made of plywood and chipboard, they were covered in red dust. Boards along the ground were rotten and a blue tarp was draped over the roof. Near the corner of the building, raw sewage oozed from a pipe into an open ditch that led to a stand of tall green grass a few feet away.

In back there were a dozen portable toilets. Behind them, large wash-tubs sat on the ground, surrounded by puddles of muddy water. A green hose snaked across the bare dirt from the building. Clothes hung from a line strung between the building and one of the portable toilets. And even though it was late, small children wandered aimlessly about. their faces muddy and their bellies distended.

A noise caught his attention and he turned to see a woman stand-ing in the doorway at the end of the building. She was startled by his presence and moved away quickly. Another woman came from one of the portable toilets. She started toward him speaking rapidly in Spanish. "I don't understand," he said, but she didn't stop. He tried again to explain, then remembered a phrase from a high school class. "No comprendo." He hoped he pronounced the word correctly. "No habla Español." She looked puzzled, then the first woman appeared again, this time more brave than before.

"She is trying to tell you that she has papers," the woman said from the doorway.

"Papers?" McNeil turned toward her, a perplexed look on his face. "What kind of papers?"

"Legal papers." The woman stepped from the building and took an ID card from her pocket. "Like this," she said, and she held up the card for him to see.

At the sound of her voice, other women appeared from farther down the building. They walked toward him and produced similar cards, holding them in their hands. "Her card," the woman continued, "is in her purse but she left it in her husband's truck. He has not yet returned from the field and she does not want to get into trouble with you for not having it."

"It's okay," he smiled. "I'm not with the government."

The woman frowned. "You were here today."

"Yes."

"You are the candidate LaCasta told us about."

"He told you about me?"

"He wants to take us all to town so we can vote for you. Promised us the day off if we agreed." She shook her head. "But I don't think that is right. Most of us are not even American citizens. And anyway, we won't be here then. We will be picking oranges."

"Do your children attend—"

Suddenly the women shrank back. McNeil glanced around to see a man who happened to be a worker approaching. "Who are you? What do you want?" Then he stopped and stared. "I know you," he continued, slowly. "You're the man who was here earlier today. McNeil. The candidate."

"Yes," McNeil nodded. "I was here earlier." He gestured with a broad sweep of his arm. "Who are all these people?"

"Workers. They work for the farm."

"Are you going to have them arrested?"

"No." McNeil shook his head. "I'm not going to have anyone arrested. At least not the workers. But why are they living like this? They showed me a nice facility earlier today."

"Yes," the man nodded. "On the other side of the farm. That is for the workers they show to the authorities. It costs them money to process us through the government system. So, they only process enough to convince the authorities that everything is legal. The real work is done by us. And this is how we live."

McNeil glanced back toward the buildings. "Why do you do this?"

"Hard to believe, I know. But this is better than what we have at home."

CHAPTER 72
ORLANDO

CARTER HEWES WAS STANDING with the bellman near the front door when McNeil arrived. Secret Service agents and police officers loitered just inside the lobby. McNeil brought the car to a stop and got out. Hewes stepped toward him. "Where have you been?"

"Why wouldn't you show me those buildings at the farm today?"

"We've been looking everywhere for you."

"You didn't want me to see those buildings. You knew they were back there, didn't you."

"Do you realize the Secret Service was ready to contact the president about you?"

"They weren't worried about me." McNeil looked over at one of the agents. "Bob, were you worried?"

"Not really, sir. But Mr. Hewes insisted we report you as missing. He thought we needed assistance from the FBI."

McNeil held up his cell phone. "Do you know what this is?"

"Don't be ridiculous."

"All you had to do was call me." McNeil shoved the phone in his pocket. "You knew those buildings were back there."

"Yes."

"And you deliberately tried to keep me away from them."

"You had no business back there."

"Why not?"

"We need the pro-business vote."

"And the anti-Castro vote."

"Yes."

"And the anti-Mexican vote."

"Immigration reform."

"That's the send-them-all-back-where-they-came-from vote."

"We need all the right-wing support we can find."

"Well, I don't like what I saw."

"You shouldn't have—"

"I'm the governor of Virginia!" McNeil shouted. "I was elected on a pro-education platform. Over the past eight years we transformed education in our state. And today I saw children who should be in school working in the field instead, picking tomatoes so someone could have them on their salad in Atlanta, and so growers and landowners could ride around in their SUVs and send text messages to each other." He paused and took a breath. "Where's Trent Paine?"

"I'm not sure. I think he's in the lobby."

"I need to give him the keys to the car. It's his rental." McNeil jabbed his finger against Hewes' chest. "And then you and I are going to have a talk about where this campaign is headed." He started toward the door.

"I fired him," Hewes said flatly. "Trent Paine. I fired him."

"For what?"

"For his part in this little charade of yours. We need people on this campaign who can stay on message, and he's not one of them."

McNeil glanced through the front door and saw Trent sitting in the lobby, a suitcase at his feet.

"He's right there. I threw him out of his room."

"No." McNeil came back from the door to stand in front of Hewes. "You don't fire anyone. Because *you're* fired!"

"You aren't firing me," Hewes snickered.

"Yes, I am," McNeil retorted.

"Look," Hewes said, defending himself. "I'm not having a staff member who won't do what he's told."

"Won't do what he's—" McNeil caught himself. A knowing look spread across his face. "You told them not to loan me a car?"

"I told them if you asked, they should send you to see me."

"Why?"

"Listen to me, we can win if we stick to our message. But we can't—"

"What message is that? That God loves America because we're compassionate, caring people? No," he snapped, answering his own question. "You have me out here every day telling the world that our policies have worked to make life better for everyone."

"They have."

"Not for those migrant workers I saw tonight."

"Most of them are illegal. They only come here to soak up government benefits."

"Who told you that?"

"You did."

"Well, I was wrong. They might not be here legally, but they didn't come for the benefits. The ones I saw tonight came to work."

Hewes shook his head with a mocking smile. "I can't believe this."

"Believe what?"

"You're actually considering changing your message."

"Don't you think it's about time?"

"I think if you change your message now, you'll lose."

"But I'll be right. I might lose, but I'll be right."

"I can't do that. I can't run a campaign on that message."

"You won't have to," McNeil reminded. "You're fired."

"Have you talked to Mr. Caldwell?"

"I don't have to talk to anyone." McNeil patted him on the shoulder. "Thank you for your help, Carter. You're fired." He walked inside the hotel lobby. "Trent," he said in a loud voice as he passed the chair where Trent was sitting. "Here are your car keys." Trent rose in time to catch the keys McNeil tossed in his direction. "For now, you're our new interim chief of staff." McNeil kept talking as he walked toward the elevator. "Get to bed. We have a long day tomorrow." He glanced over at the front desk. "Put that man back in his room. He's in charge now."

* * *

Carter Hewes watched as McNeil crossed the lobby, stepped into the elevator, and disappeared. Behind him, Trent Paine retrieved his room key from the front desk and headed upstairs. When they were gone, Hewes took his cell phone from his pocket and sent a text message to Russo. Then he walked across the lobby to the bar. On his third glass of bourbon, Henry Caldwell arrived.

"It can't be that bad," Caldwell said.

Hewes turned the glass up and drained the last drops from the bottom. "He fired me."

"So I heard. How many times does that make?"

"No," Hewes said, shaking his head. "This time he meant it."

"What happened?"

"Little children in the tomato fields," Hewes sighed.

"Instead of being in school?"

Hewes stared down at the glass. "I told you that farm trip was a mistake."

"But we need the votes."

Hewes cut his eyes at him. "I already had LaCosta lined up to bring all those workers to the polls."

"But how were you going to get them registered?"

"That was the easy part. County clerk's an old friend. Hard part is getting the farm to give them time off to go to the polls."

Caldwell ran his hand over his chin as if thinking. "Who'd he put in charge?"

"Trent Paine."

"Hmm. Can't you adjust the message a little to accommodate him? I've known David a long time. He needs a little room. I can get him back."

"I don't think there's any going back on this one."

Hewes gestured to the bartender for one more drink. Caldwell waved him off. "Go up to the room." He took Hewes by the elbow and nudged him from the bar. "Take a shower. Get some sleep."

"No. I'm done."

"Yeah. You're done, all right," Caldwell chuckled. "I've seen you drink and one is your limit." He guided Hewes toward the door. "Let's not do anything rash tonight. Get to sleep. If he hasn't hired you back by the time they leave in the morning, catch a flight back to Richmond and I'll be in touch in a few days."

CHAPTER 73
ISTANBUL, TURKEY

MARIANO KITZIS PUSHED a sweeper's cart through the airport, pausing now and then to wipe a water fountain and empty a trashcan. All the while, he scanned the passengers as they moved up and down the corridor.

Near midmorning a man came from the jet-way at one of the gates as passengers unloaded from a recent arrival. Dressed in gray wool slacks, a white shirt, and tweed jacket, Kitzis identified him immediately as Javier Roldan. He watched Roldan for a moment as he moved past the ticket counter, leather briefcase in hand, and turned toward the main terminal. While Roldan moved away, Kitzis pressed a node clipped to his ear and spoke on his Bluetooth connection. "He has arrived."

* * *

Inside the main terminal building, Eli Revach straightened magazines on the shelves of a newsstand. He moved up and down the kiosk, sorting and shuffling the latest copies of *Novinar*, *Der Spiegel*, and *Anadolu*. With his hands occupied, he surveyed the central lobby. Around him, passengers moved in every direction, some arriving from the street and moving toward the ticket counters, others coming from the corridor to leave the building. He did his best to check each one.

Finally, a man wearing a tweed jacket appeared. Revach worked his way back toward the cash register and picked up a Blackberry phone. He typed a message, "Leaving the building."

*   *   *

In the operations center at Beersheba, Cohen and his analysts received Revach's text message. Cohen paced back and forth across the floor near the back of the room. "What is he doing in Istanbul?" He glanced up, speaking to no one in particular. "If Roldan is following Barberini, why would he visit Turkey? Let's figure this out. We have files on Barberini and Roldan."

Yaron Klarsfeld, seated on the far side of the room, spoke up. "Got it," he called. "Barberini attended Halki seminary."

"Where is that?"

"Princes' Islands. Off the coast of Istanbul."

"That makes sense," someone added. "Russo hired him to find Barberini and that's what he's doing. What did he say? Something about people not changing."

"'People don't change that much,'" Klarsfeld quoted.

"Yeah. So, he's just following the trail."

"But what's the trail?"

The operator pointed to a screen on the wall. Barberini's picture appeared with information about him. "Grew up on Sardinia. Attended seminary at Halki. Served briefly at a parish in Greece, then entered Saint Catherine's Monastery at Mount Sinai."

"Roldan is methodical. Precise. Checking each location."

"Which gives us a head start," a voice said quietly. Everyone turned to see Mara Moss, Cohen's assistant, standing in the corner. She had slipped into the room, unnoticed, and stood watching them as they worked.

The comment caught Cohen by surprise. "Head start? How so?"

"You know Barberini is not on Sardinia. At least, you can assume so, since Roldan didn't find him. And if he's at Halki, we will know it in a short while, when Roldan arrives there. But if Barberini is at Saint Catherine's, you have time to beat Roldan to him."

Cohen's eyes lit up. "Excellent idea." The conversation continued around the room as Cohen strode toward the operator.

"But Roldan doesn't want to simply talk to him. He wants to kill him."

"Do you think Barberini realizes how short his life may be?"

"Not if we get there first."

When Cohen reached the operator, he leaned over her shoulder. "You are sending Gadot?"

"Yes," she replied with a nod. "I have already contacted him."

"Good. Make sure he moves quickly. We need to get to Barberini before Roldan finds him." Cohen turned and looked across the room at Mara. "Good job," he mouthed.

CHAPTER 74
WASHINGTON, D.C.

THE NEXT DAY, Paul met Culpepper at his office. They reviewed the information Paul obtained from Chris Jones.

"Bill Sisson," Culpepper mused. "Interesting name. Looks like he came from Alabama."

"Why do you say that?"

"Going by the Social Security number." Culpepper pointed to the first three numbers. "I don't know if he was born there, but that's where he was living when this number was issued." Culpepper tapped the page with his finger. "But I'm pretty sure this address isn't accurate." He studied Paul's notes a little longer. "It's way out in Rockville."

"But the other information might be helpful," Paul countered. "Social Security number. Service number. Date of birth. That will help narrow down the search."

"Right," Culpepper nodded. "That helps move us forward." He turned to the laptop on the credenza. "There's a website I subscribe to. It has access to a number of databases." He used the mouse to position the cursor on the screen, opened a Web browser, and navigated to the site. "Developed by collections agencies to help track down debtors. Good source of just about anything you want to know on someone. Especially if you know the name."

A page appeared on the screen with a search box. Culpepper entered the information Paul obtained about Sisson. In a moment, the screen changed and the search results appeared. Culpepper traced with his finger while he read. "Here's an address for a Bill Sisson in Alexandria. Came from Cirro Energy in a bill for electrical service." He positioned the cursor over the entry and a text box appeared. "From last month's bill."

"Any way to check the other information? Maybe his Social Security number."

"I'm looking …" Culpepper moved the cursor to a different link. "Yeah," he said finally. "It's the same." He smiled over at Paul. "The numbers match. Good work." Culpepper pressed a key to print the page and turned back to his desk. "You feel like taking a ride to Alexandria?"

"Think he's home?"

"One way to find out." Culpepper took the printed page from the tray on the printer and started toward the door. "Come on. You can drive. I don't like dealing with the traffic."

Thirty minutes later they turned the corner onto a quiet residential street. "I think it's in the next block." Culpepper stared out the window checking house numbers as they rolled slowly along. At the next cross street, he nodded and pointed. "Yeah. It's right up there. Near that tree."

Paul brought the car to a stop at the curb not far from a utility van. Culpepper bounded from the car and led the way up the walk to the front porch. Paul followed close behind. Culpepper moved quickly up the steps and opened the door. Paul hesitated. "Think we ought to knock?"

"Nah. This house has been cut up into apartments." Culpepper pointed to a group of mailboxes hanging from the wall by the door. "Looks like four of them." He stepped inside and Paul followed. Culpepper glanced around quickly, then moved to a staircase that stood to the right. "Must be up here."

On the second floor they came to a door marked with the letter C. Culpepper tried the knob and found it was locked. He took a credit card from his pocket and wedged it into the space between the door and the jamb. "This house is old," he said as he worked the card into position. "Maybe an old trick will work on it."

"Is that legal?"

"You shouldn't ask questions like that." Culpepper slid the card down the door, past the doorknob, and wiggled it into place. Then he pushed open the door. "Good thing he doesn't have a dead bolt." He moved to the left and checked the bedrooms.

Paul held back and remained near the door. Instead of searching frantically, he studied the living room carefully. Along the wall, beneath the window, he found a table with a cord for the power supply. A wastebasket sat near the table leg. When he stooped over to check the basket, he noticed a drawer that slid along the end of the table. He pulled it open and found a notepad, several pencils, and a card from Jimmy John's delivery service. Beneath the notepad was a checkbook. He took it out and flipped through the pages. Four checks had been written on the account, but there was no register. Information printed in the top corner of the checks included Sisson's name and address, along with a telephone number.

Culpepper suddenly appeared and leaned over his shoulder. "Find something?"

"Looks like a checkbook."

"Good. We can run the account numbers." Culpepper pointed. "That looks like a cell phone number on that check."

"I know. I was just about to call it."

"If you call him, you'll just spook him. And he'll throw away the phone."

"Information's no good unless you use it." Paul took a cell phone from his pocket and entered the number. "Besides, he doesn't know who we are, so he has no reason to be afraid to talk to us."

The call went to Sisson's voice mail account. Paul left a message. "Bill, this is Paul Bryson. I'm a lobbyist in Washington. We should talk about Chicago." He added his phone number, then ended the call and turned back to Culpepper. "You find anything interesting?"

"Not much."

"We should probably go before someone finds out we're here."

"What are they gonna do?"

"Call the police."

Culpepper's eyes opened wider. "Yeah. I suppose you're right."

* * *

From the utility van a few spaces up the street, an FBI agent listened to Paul and Culpepper talking in Sisson's apartment. While they looked around, he called Rutledge. "We got two guys in Sisson's apartment."

"Who are they?"

"I'm not sure. I think one of them is Brian Culpepper."

"The private detective?"

"Affirmative."

"Who's with him?"

"I don't know. Clean-cut. Middle-aged. Dressed in a suit. Looks familiar but I don't think I know his name."

"What are they doing?"

"Just looking around."

"Have Tim follow them."

"Check."

"And get me a recording of their conversation. Can you download it to me?"

"I'll send you a link."

"Good."

"And pictures if you have them."

"Right."

By then, Paul and Culpepper were near the car. The agent picked up a camera and crawled to the front of the van. He leaned over the driver's seat and clicked off a dozen pictures as they opened the car doors and got inside. As they drove away, he connected the camera to a USB port on a laptop and copied the photos to the hard drive.

CHAPTER 75
WASHINGTON, D.C.

THAT EVENING, PAUL had dinner with Esther at her townhouse. Afterward, they moved to the sofa for coffee and dessert. "I went to see a friend in Naval Personnel," Paul began.

"What was that about?"

"Trying to locate a name for the fourth man on that break-in team."

"Find anything?"

"His name is Bill Sisson."

"Where does he live?"

"Alexandria."

"Virginia?" Esther was surprised.

"Yes, Culpepper subscribes to a service that lets him search multiple databases. We found an apartment for him over in Alexandria. We went over there."

Esther looked concerned. "You and Culpepper?"

"Yes. Why?"

"Not sure I want you going places with him."

"He's not so bad," Paul shrugged. "A little crass, but effective."

"Effective at what?"

"Getting inside locked apartments."

"That's what I mean! I don't want you breaking into someone else's apartment. What if he'd come in and found you?"

"I don't think he's anywhere around here. Besides, Culpepper opened the door. I just walked in."

"That wouldn't get you very far in court."

"Maybe not."

"Find anything?"

"Found a checkbook with a phone number."

"Did you check out the number?"

"I called the number. Got his voice mail. Left him a message."

"You realize he probably knows everything there is to know about you now."

"Yeah," Paul nodded. "But it seemed like a good idea at the time."

"These are serious people."

"I know."

"They don't play around. This isn't a television game show."

"Esther, I understand."

She leaned against his side. "I'm just worried."

"About what?"

"About you."

"Don't worry about me." He turned toward her and gave her a kiss. "I'll be fine."

* * *

Later that evening, Paul returned home. As he unlocked the front door, a man appeared on the walkway behind him. Tall and lean, he wore a dark gray suit with white shirt and red tie. Even in the dim light, Paul could see his black wingtip shoes were polished to a glossy shine. He was startled by the sudden appearance, but not afraid.

"Paul Bryson?" the man asked.

"Yes, and who are you?"

"Taylor Rutledge. FBI." He held his badge for Paul to see. "We need to talk." He gestured toward the door. "Why don't we go inside where we can talk in private."

Paul pushed open the door and led the way. Rutledge followed and closed the door behind them.

"Okay," Paul said when they were inside. "What did you want to talk about?"

"One of our agents saw you today at Bill Sisson's apartment."

Paul looked puzzled. "The FBI knows about Sisson?"

"Why were you and Culpepper in there?"

The puzzled look on Paul's face gave way to an unsettled squint. "You know Culpepper, too?"

"Breaking and entering is a felony in Virginia. Interfering with an FBI investigation is even worse."

"You know," Paul smiled, "I think someone else had been there before me. I wonder if they had a search warrant?"

Rutledge smiled back. "What do you know about Culpepper?"

"What do I need to know?"

"A lot. Why are you interested in Sisson?"

"Same reason you are."

"Which is?"

"He was the fourth man in the building."

Rutledge looked surprised "How do you know about that?"

"Sources. Stay in this city long enough and you can learn almost anything you want to know."

"Esther Rosenberg and her lawyers have been asking around the FEC. Looking for records about David McNeil and Sierra Resources. Why? Why is she interested in a Republican governor and a defense contractor?" He pointed at Paul. "That would be more in your line of work than hers."

"You'll have to ask her about that."

"I just might do that."

"Look," Paul began in a conciliatory tone. "I don't know what you're after. I'm just trying to figure out whether and why the Order of Malta has any interest in David McNeil's presidential campaign."

"I'd like an answer to that same question."

"So, you want me to tell you what I know, but you don't want to talk to me." Then a look of realization came over Paul. "You guys had access to the emails."

"Maybe."

"And now you're trying to dance around Justice and the FISA Court and—"

"FISA isn't a problem," Rutledge countered.

"Well, if you read the email, then you know why I'm interested."

"Campaign fraud?"

"No, the other part."

Rutledge frowned. "The Jewish conspiracy?"

"The Order of Malta hates the Jews. They've been working for centuries to eliminate them."

"That could never happen," Rutledge scoffed. "Not here. Not in the United States."

"Right," Paul said sarcastically. "And that's what the Germans said about Hitler and the Nazis. They'll never get elected. It'll never happen here. But it did and the world has never been the same since."

CHAPTER 76
LOS ANGELES

THE SUN WAS ALREADY RISING over the mountains when Henry Caldwell's Learjet touched down at the Burbank Airport. A limousine was waiting for him as he came from the terminal. The driver took his bag and placed it in the trunk while Caldwell took the seat in back. The driver closed the trunk and got in behind the steering wheel. Minutes later, they sped from the terminal drive onto the Hollywood Freeway and rode south.

A few minutes later, they turned into the driveway at the Beverly Hills Hotel. The car came to a stop under the canopy at the entrance and a bellman opened the rear door. Caldwell stepped from the car and paused to check his cell phone. The bellman stood nearby. "Will you be checking in, sir?"

"Hold my bag. I'm not sure yet."

"Yes, sir."

The driver took the leather bag from the trunk and handed it to the bellman. Meanwhile, Caldwell located the message on his phone and checked for the location. The bellman came to his side. "Are you trying to locate someone?"

"I'm supposed to meet someone in a bungalow and I was trying to find the message that told me where to go."

"Who are you meeting?"

"Edgar Logan. You know him?"

"Yes, sir." The bellman smiled. "I'll take you to him. We can bring the bag with us so you'll have it if you need it."

"Great." He looked at the driver. "I'll call when I'm ready to leave." Caldwell then followed the bellman into the hotel.

Logan was seated on a sofa when Caldwell arrived. He rose to greet him as the bellman ushered him inside. "I see you made it," he said, gesturing with a wine glass.

"Yes, I made it just fine." He tipped the bellman and waited while he left, then started across the room. "A little early to be drinking, don't you think?"

"I suppose. But the bottle was already open and the glass was on the counter. And it just went from there."

"I'll have a cup of coffee if you have any?"

"Sure." Logan walked into the kitchen. "You want anything in it?"

"I'll fix it." Caldwell joined him at the kitchen counter. "Don't you have a house in Malibu?"

"Yes. You want to see it?"

"We could have met there and saved the expense of this room."

"Bungalow— this is a bungalow."

"This is a four-bedroom house."

Logan set the wine glass on the counter. His voice turned serious. "If you must know, I had my family down last night. They love staying here." He took a cup from the cabinet and poured coffee for them both. "Let's sit over here." He led the way to the kitchen table and took a seat.

"We have to tie this off," Caldwell began.

"We're already doing that. It was part of the plan, in case something went wrong."

"Spoleto isn't happy." Caldwell paused for a sip of coffee. "You can keep this under control?"

"It's under control."

"Ed, you have too many loose ends. You have to clean it up. I know you want to keep your programs moving forward, but this has gone too far. You have to close it down. Before someone finds out."

"Okay," Logan sighed with a sense of resignation. "But I need something."

Caldwell had a troubled frown. "What are you talking about?"

"I got into this on your word alone."

Caldwell didn't like the way that sounded. "You have a problem with that?"

"That's fine. But you're a survivor. A permanent player." Logan gestured with both hands. "Me? I'm just a bit part. Guys like me get hung out to dry on these things all the time."

"You should have thought about that before you took the Order's money to fund your company."

"Well, I'm thinking about it now."

Caldwell set his cup down. "What does that mean?"

"Look," Logan continued, "everyone knows you don't want McNeil to run against Wilson. You would like to run against Rush, but any of the other Democrats will do so as long as it isn't Wilson. So, we go in and do your dirty work for you. Take down the other candidates. Fix it so you can run against whoever it is you want to run against. Then, when your guy is in office, you stop returning my calls. And if someone gets nosey— a reporter or someone over at Justice— or if I make too much of a fuss about being shoved out in the cold, our friends in the Order will get upset and I'm the guy you throw under the bus."

Caldwell propped his elbows on the table. "My word was good enough for you before."

"Yeah," Logan nodded. "I did this thing with Cook's campaign on your word, too, and look what's happened. You're out here meeting with me to say *we* have a problem."

"So, what will it take?"

"I want the candidate all in."

"All in?"

"If your guy wins, we get to keep the no-bid arrangement with the

Pentagon— special programs, training, black ops, rendition, the whole nine yards."

"That won't be a problem. McNeil already has plans to use you."

Logan shook his head. "Not good enough."

"My word on that isn't enough?"

"Not now. Not after all this."

"Then, what?"

"I get a sit-down with the candidate. And he has to ask me."

"Ask you?"

"Yeah. Before we do anything more, he has to ask me."

Caldwell picked up the coffee cup with both hands and sipped from it. "You'll continue with the remainder of our program as we outlined before?"

"Before what?"

"Before our friends got upset."

"Sure," Logan nodded. "As we outlined it— break-ins, smear campaign, document placement, photographs, emails, cyber-attacks, the whole deal."

"Okay." Caldwell took another sip of coffee. "I'll set it up."

CHAPTER 77
INDIANAPOLIS

A LITTLE AFTER TEN that morning, a van turned the corner and came to a stop near the bus station. Mark Ziegler opened the passenger door and stepped out. He waited while the others climbed from the back, then leaned inside and looked over at the driver. "Take the van back to the hotel. Get the center set up in the room."

"Right."

"And make sure everyone is checked in."

As the van pulled away from the curb, Ziegler turned to the men assembled by the van. "Here are the photographs." He passed out pictures of Sisson. "Show them to as many people as possible. Start in the bus station." He pointed. "George will take a team down that way. I'm going up this way." He gestured over his shoulder. "If you find someone who remembers seeing him, get all the information you can and give me a call."

When everyone had a picture, they started toward the bus station. As they moved away, Ziegler caught Ben Warren by the arm. "Come with me." And they walked up the sidewalk to the corner.

Warren looked around. "What's up here?"

"I don't know. I just wanted to step back for a minute and get a feel for the place."

"This isn't the plan we made for this mission."

"It's all right," Ziegler assured him. "As long as there are two of us together, a slight deviation won't hinder our success."

"Is that authorized?"

"Yes. You covered that in your first training session."

"This is my first mission."

"Then you get to see what it's really like." Ziegler tapped him on the shoulder. "Let's cross the street."

They moved up the block to the corner near the hotel. A newsstand stood there and Ziegler approached the attendant. "Ever see this man?" He turned the photograph for him to see. As the man glanced at it, his eyes widened. Then, just as quickly, he shook his head. "No. I don't think so."

"Look again. You might remember him."

"No, I would remember. I don't know him."

Ziegler returned the photograph to his pocket and continued up the sidewalk. Warren walked at his side. "That's how you do it? Ask one or two? Not everyone?"

"The street is a social network, just like any other setting." Ziegler gestured with both hands. "Look around. This is a neighborhood. Not any houses here, but there are people. And where there are people, there are relationships. And where there are relationships, there is order."

"Order?"

"Structure. Everyone has his role. Some are workers. Some are leaders. That man back there. At the newsstand. He's a key figure in this network."

"He sees things."

"Yes. He's an information coordinator. Nothing moves that he doesn't know about. He's seen Sisson. We're getting close."

"How do you know?"

Ziegler tapped his cheek. "I saw it in his eyes. The truth appeared, just for a second. Then he thought better of it and lied."

At the next corner, Ziegler paused, turned back in the direction of the bus station, and scanned the street. "This is the edge."

"Of what?"

"A network."

"A neighborhood?"

"Yes." Ziegler gestured over his shoulder. "Up there, it's different." He pointed toward the station. "Down here, it's the same."

"How?"

Ziegler turned in the opposite direction. "Up here, you have suits, offices, cafés, lunch counters." He turned back toward the bus station. "Down there, street people, transients, prostitutes." His eyes fell on the hotel. "Come on."

"What?" Warren hurried to keep up. "What's the matter?"

"The hotel. The clerk of the hotel is the mayor of this network. He's the guy who can tell us what we want to know."

CHAPTER 78
MIAMI, FLORIDA

BY MIDMORNING, Caldwell was back onboard the Learjet. He flew east and caught up with McNeil working several stops in South Florida. They met in a room at the Four Seasons Hotel.

"You can't fire your chief of staff."

"I already did."

"He's the best in the business."

"He's pushing me to places I don't want to go."

"You need someone to push you. Get you moving in the morning."

"I don't mean physically. I mean with the message. We're riddled with contradictions."

"Like?"

"We're pro-life on abortion, and pro-death on capital punishment. We're pro-life for the unborn, but don't want to help anyone after they're born. The other day I saw children working in the fields. They should have been in school, but instead they're out there picking tomatoes for your salad."

"I understand but—"

"I'm an education governor. I want to be an education president and I'm supposed to be an education candidate. Instead, I'm riding around

Florida with a man who makes certain farm workers can't make enough to send their kids to school instead of to the field."

"Look, we have a situation. We need Carter to help us get through it."

"Situation? What kind of situation?"

"That thing."

"What thing?"

"You don't want to know much about it."

"Liston Cook? That was us?"

"Things got a little out of hand."

"What were we doing in Liston Cook's office?"

"They weren't our people."

"Sierra."

"I know Trent Paine and he's a good guy, but handling this kind of thing is way beyond his ability. It's even more than we can handle on our own."

"What do you mean?"

"We're going to bring in more help than they had planned. I talked to Edgar Logan. We're adding some of their people full time."

"Are you crazy? They're the ones who got us in this mess in the first place. If you bring them into the campaign, we lose all ability to deny we knew about it— which we didn't. At least, I didn't. But if they're working for us, it'll be hard to throw them under the bus."

"We can't throw them under the bus."

"I thought that was the whole deal."

"Not anymore."

"What happened?"

"Spoleto and the others are worried about our latest efforts."

"Right now there's only one person who can link anything to me."

"Yeah," Caldwell smiled. "I know. And if it comes down to it, that's what it will be. But right now we have to clean it up."

"Can't get out, so we find safety by getting in deeper?"

"Something like that."

"Well, I wouldn't be here if it wasn't for you. I'm not throwing you under the bus. So clean it up."

"Only one catch."

"What's that?"

"You have to talk to Edgar Logan."

"Why?"

"He wants you to ask him."

"He wants me to ask?"

"Yes."

"A direct question?"

"More or less."

"What are you two planning to do?"

"You don't want to know about it."

"Okay. When am I meeting him?"

"He'll be out here in a day or two. I'll take care of it."

"All right." McNeil picked up a bottle of water. "Let's talk about our message."

"Not now." Caldwell stood. "After you see Logan. See him. Get him in place, then we can talk about altering the message." He stepped toward the door. "Not much. But some."

CHAPTER 79
WASHINGTON, D.C.

THAT AFTERNOON, Esther went home to the townhouse early and called Brody. "We need to talk."

"Okay. Talk."

"Not like this."

"Where do you want to meet?"

"Pick me up. By the bus stop."

Forty-five minutes later, a gray Honda Accord came to a stop at the corner. Esther was wearing a tattered black dress with a gray sweater and black tennis shoes. Her hair was wrapped with a scarf. Oversized sunglasses were perched on her nose. She held a pink tote stuffed with plastic sacks from the grocery store. When the car came to a stop, she opened the front door and got inside.

Brody grinned. "Now who's into the spy life?"

"Hush," she snapped. "This is important."

"I tell you that every time I see you, and you still make fun of me."

She pointed ahead. "Drive."

Brody pressed the gas pedal. The Honda started forward. "What's so important?"

"You had this car swept?"

"Swept?"

"For listening devices."

"Yes."

"When?"

"This morning."

"They do that every day?"

"At least," Brody frowned. "What's the matter?"

"We went to see Liston Cook. He asked Paul to work with Brian Culpepper to find out why someone wanted in his office."

"Right. We talked about that already."

"Liston had a video that showed a fourth man. Three were arrested, but there was one more."

"Esther," Brody interrupted. "We've been over all this."

"Let me talk." She took a deep breath, then continued. "So, Paul goes to see Culpepper and they get to work looking for this guy. Paul has contacts in lots of places and he figured out the guy's name is Bill Sisson."

"We know that."

"You know that?"

"Yes. We found it out already. I was going to tell you. It would have saved him all that work."

"They got an address for Sisson's apartment and went over there."

"Paul and Culpepper?"

"Yes."

"See, I told you he wanted to get involved. Paul and I should work together."

"No," she snapped. "That's not going to happen."

Brody steered the car to the curb and brought it to a stop. "Esther, listen to me." He turned in the seat to face her. "I didn't kill Ephraim. Cohen didn't kill him. He was killed by Palestinian terrorists."

"*This* killed him!" she shouted. "This right here. This denial that what we do doesn't have direct consequences. We are all in this together. *We* killed Ephraim. We sent him to that meeting alone. We told him we needed the contact." She put her hand to her mouth. "And we are *not* killing Paul."

"What are you talking about?"

"I don't like him breaking into apartments. He's not trained for it. He has no idea who this Culpepper is. He's just doing it because he's friends with Liston Cook and Liston asked him to help."

"So, why are you telling me this?"

"I want you to find out everything there is to know about Brian Culpepper. I asked you about him earlier."

"Okay," he replied slowly. "I can get someone to work him up."

"No." She grabbed Brody's arm. "That's what you told me before. Now, this is what you're going to do. You're going to treat him like a direct threat to the prime minister. You are going to hack your way to the bottom of all that's knowable about him."

"I'm not sure I can do—"

"You do it all the time for people you want to know about. Now you're going to do it for me."

"I can't just—"

"Do it." She grasped the door handle. "Or I will never work for you again." She threw open the door and stepped out to the curb.

CHAPTER 80
WASHINGTON, D.C.

PAUL SPENT THE MORNING working at his office, catching up on issues for other clients that had gone unaddressed. He returned phone calls, responded to email, and prepared for meetings scheduled for the following week.

At noon he took a break and leaned back in his chair. With a moment to relax, his mind turned to Brian Culpepper. He seemed serious about conducting a thorough investigation, but his style was extremely slipshod. Not only was his office cluttered and unkempt, so were his cases. Still, they had gathered more information about Sisson than he had thought they would. Now there was the real possibility they might find him.

But if we know he's out there, Paul thought, *surely others do, too.* It seemed impossible that he and Culpepper, working on their own, could find someone before anyone else, even before the FBI.

He picked up his notes and scanned down the page. When he came to the phone number he'd copied from the check, a shudder ran up his spine. Rutledge was right. He had broken into someone's apartment, and that was a crime. A sinking feeling swept over him as he imagined what would have happened if Sisson had returned while they were there. A sense of violation— of being in another person's home without an invitation— struck deep in his soul.

He pushed aside the guilt and tried to imagine what Sisson would think when he heard the voice mail. *If he even checks his voice mail.* But the mailbox wasn't full, which gave him hope that at least the message would be heard. *And if it is heard, maybe I'll come across as a friendly alternative to whomever else is out there. Sisson is on the run. Surely he doesn't have many friends.*

Paul picked up his cell phone from the desk and scrolled down the screen to Sisson's number. A few seconds later, he reached Sisson's voice mail once more.

*   *   *

Driving west from Indiana, Sisson passed through Quincy, Illinois. On Broadway Street, just past Forty-Eighth, he glanced in the rearview mirror and saw a police car just a few feet from his bumper. Moments later, blue lights atop the car began to flash and the siren chirped. He found a place to stop outside Turner Brothers Garage and steered the car from the road. An officer stepped from the police car and came to Sisson's window.

"Let me see your driver's license and registration, please."

Sisson reached in the glove box and took out an envelope. "I don't have the registration yet. Just bought the car." He handed the officer a copy of the bill of sale.

"I stopped you because you're driving without a license plate."

"Yes, sir. Haven't had time to get one yet."

"Then let me see your driver's license, please."

While in Chicago, Sisson had used an alias. He had a driver's license, credit cards, and other documents under the name of Judson Wells, but those had been used in an effort to create a paper trail that would serve as a firewall to protect his true identity. If Thomas and the others were somehow forced to answer questions about him, they would have given that name as their first response, which meant the police would have it. And they might be searching for him under that name. However, his real name was clean and untarnished. Any check of it would produce nothing but a good report.

"It's in my wallet. On my hip."

The officer took a step back, moving just behind the doorpost, and placed his hand on the grip of his pistol. "Take it out slowly."

Sisson leaned forward, with one hand on the steering wheel, and used his other hand to reach for the wallet. Holding it between his finger and thumb he dangled it in the air as he brought it out. The officer stepped back to the window. Sisson handed him the license.

"Just a minute," the officer said, tersely. And he returned to the patrol car.

Sisson watched in the mirror while the officer checked the license number. While he waited, the cell phone rang. He glanced at the screen for the number, but didn't recognize it. After a couple of rings, the call went to voice mail.

In a few minutes, the officer returned to stand by Sisson's window. "I'm giving you a ticket for driving without a license plate."

"Yes, sir."

The officer tore the citation from his pad and handed it through the window with the license. "If you purchase a tag within the next thirty days, you can show the receipt to the judge and he will dismiss the charge. Otherwise, the fine is one hundred dollars for the first violation."

"Yes, sir."

The officer pointed to a place at the bottom of the citation. "That's the court date right there."

"Yes, sir."

The officer closed his pad and adjusted his hat. "Drive safely."

"Yes, sir."

While the officer walked back to his car, Sisson checked his voice mail. The message was from Paul Bryson. *That's the second time he's called me. How did he get this number?*

* * *

Donna Preston sat at her desk in the Tucson command center, sorting through information forwarded from Indianapolis. As Ziegler suspected, the hotel clerk identified Sisson and provided details of his stay. He'd been there but was already gone by the time the team arrived. The clerk gave them access to Sisson's room, and Sierra technicians processed it thoroughly. They recovered hair and fibers that confirmed Sisson had been there, but the building had no security cameras and there were no records of his stay. Traffic cameras on either corner near the hotel showed him coming and going, and talking to the man at the newsstand, but finding more from the images was a time-consuming task.

In the midst of scrolling through the information, her computer beeped and a dialogue box appeared with a message. "William H. Sisson. NCIS." She followed a link in the box and logged into the National Crime Information System. There she found the record of the traffic stop in Quincy, Illinois.

"Hey," she called out. "We have a hit."

"What is it?"

"This one is current." She scrolled down the record. "Looks like it just happened a few hours ago."

Bartlett came to her desk. "What is it?"

"Bill Sisson." She pointed to the screen. "Stopped by the police in Quincy, Illinois. Driving without a license plate."

"Are you sure it's him?"

She scrolled up to the detailed information. "The number matches. That's his birthdate. And his address in Alexandria, Virginia."

"Listen up," Bartlett said in a loud voice. "We need to get everyone headed toward Quincy, Illinois. And then we need to plot Sisson's route." He turned back to Donna. "Do you know where he was stopped? Which street?"

"Broadway and Forty-eighth."

"All right. We have his location from just a couple of hours ago. He couldn't have driven far. Plot his route. Come up with projections about where he's going from there. Be creative but work fast. We need to get our people into position ahead of him." While others in the room went to work, Bartlett leaned over Donna's shoulder. "Sorry I was a grouch earlier."

"It's okay." She swatted him on the leg. "We're all a little tense."

"Glad you caught that lead."

"I had the site programmed to tell me if they got anything. Did it under all his known aliases, and then I thought about his real name."

"Well, now we have a chance to get ahead of the curve."

"You know…" Donna pointed to the screen once more. "We have all the information on the car. Blue. Chevrolet. Model." She glanced back at Bartlett. "We could do something with that."

"Like what?"

"Report it stolen. Get a warrant. Have the police looking for it. They're already in place. We could get the warrant and get it in the system before our people get in place on the ground. Give us a little extra push."

"That's a great idea. Can you create the documents?"

She switched screens and a certificate of title appeared. "This is what we need."

"That looks official."

"I imported it from an Illinois site."

"Think you can forge a warrant?"

"Give me a few minutes," she smiled.

CHAPTER 81
AQABA, JORDAN

JAVIER ROLDAN OPENED his eyes as the plane touched down. He had been to Jordan many times, but this was his first trip to Aqaba. When they reached the terminal building, he stepped off the plane onto the jet-way. Following the signs, he collected his lone leather suitcase from baggage claim and walked out the front entrance. A friend suggested he stay at the InterContinental Hotel, so he hailed a taxi and rode downtown. He arrived to find his room had a commanding view of the Gulf and the port, but there would be little time to enjoy it.

The following morning, he rose early and dressed in a traditional Bedouin robe. Made of coarse linen, it was white and hung loosely from his shoulders. Next he opened the suitcase and took out a necklace with a small wooden cross on it. He placed it around his neck and positioned the cross in the center of his chest. Finally, he picked up a gray turban from the bed, set it carefully on his head, and started toward the door.

A few blocks from the hotel he boarded a bus filled with tourists, most of them looking like they might be from Western Europe. The bus was bound for Mount Sinai, three hundred kilometers to the south. To get there, they would have to cross into Egypt. Everyone seemed excited at the prospect of standing on Egyptian soil.

At first the trip was easy as the bus cruised down the smooth, wide highway that ran along the coast, but as the road turned inland, the pavement narrowed. The ride became rougher and hotter. By the time they reached the turn onto Saint Catherine's Road, the chatter had died away. Passengers, who earlier had been full of energy and enthusiasm, now stared blankly out the window or rested with their heads propped against the seat.

When the bus finally arrived at Saint Catherine's the tour guide assembled them in the parking lot and began shouting instructions. Roldan, dressed in traditional garb, stood near the back of the crowd. By the time the guide had finished explaining the rules of a visit to the monastery, Roldan had blended in with a cluster of local men.

There was a small village on the northwest side of the monastery wall. Roldan turned away from the tour group and walked in that direction. While the group waited to enter through the tourist gate, Roldan was already at the service entrance in back.

*　*　*

Angelo Barberini sat on a stool inside the charnel house, a few feet from the wire screen that protected the skeletal remains of monks who'd died before. Through the screen he could see the pile of bones and skulls. Hands placed together and resting in his lap, he alternately talked to himself, to the dead whose skulls he could see, and to God, in a seamless conversation.

"I stand in the presence of those who have gone before me, marking the path of obedience that leads to sanctification." He rocked gently back and forth as he spoke, his voice barely above a whisper. "This is the path chosen for me and one which I now accept without reservation. In previous times I did have reservations, but now they all have been resolved."

A voice spoke. "The ones you know of," the voice suggested. "Those are the ones you've resolved."

"Yes," Barberini replied. "I have surrendered them."

"But there may be others that surface from time to time. Rising from depths you have not yet found."

Another voice spoke to his spirit. "Surrender what you know and I will reveal the rest to you. Call on me and I will show you things you have never known."

"Yes, Lord," Barberini replied. "I surrender to you my fascination with a life of ease, the pride of association with the Order, and collusion with its unholy purpose."

"It was not always unholy," the voice in his mind countered.

"But I did not live then and I am accountable for what I know and do now. No matter how painful."

Just then, he felt an object press against the back of his head. "Do not turn around," a voice said from behind. "And believe me, this won't be painful at all."

Suddenly Barberini realized the voice he'd heard was that of a man, and the object he felt was the muzzle of a pistol against his skull. Fear sent a tingle up his spine. Sadness swept over him as the prospect of death collided with the realization that the time he'd spent with the Order had been wasted. He should have stayed right here at Saint Catherine's, in the cloistered life. In the seconds that passed between the moment he felt the pistol and the moment of sadness, he vowed that if he somehow survived what now seemed imminent he would never again travel beyond the monastery's walls.

Then all at once there was a muffled *Pffsst*, followed by the clink of metal as it struck the stone floor. Barberini leapt from the stool and turned to see a man's body crumpled on the floor. A second man stood only a few meters away.

"I assure you," the man said with a pleasant smile. "He didn't feel a thing."

Barberini's mouth fell open and his heart raced. "Who are you?" he gasped.

"I am a friend."

"Bu ... bu ... but what happened?"

The man stooped over and retrieved an empty shell casing from the floor. "You are in grave danger." For the first time, Barberini noticed the automatic pistol in the man's hand. He wiped it clean and tucked it in the waistband of his trousers, then pulled the tail of his shirt over it. "We must leave now."

"Danger?" Barberini was puzzled. "I am here. At Saint Catherine's. What danger do I face? From what? Or whom?"

"Men in powerful places wish to see you dead. I was sent to find you. We have been searching for you since Zurich." The man took Barberini by the elbow. "Come with me. We must leave now."

"I can't leave. This is my home. My work."

"You must come with me."

"Why?"

The man gestured with a nod toward the dead body on the floor. "The Order sent him. He was here to kill you. And when the Order finds out he is dead and you are alive, they will redouble their efforts to locate us both." He gestured with his hand. "Come. I have a car."

Barberini pulled free. "Let me get my things."

"Leave them. We must go now."

"But where are we going?"

"Someplace where you will be safe."

CHAPTER 82
WASHINGTON, D.C.

TAYLOR RUTLEDGE returned from lunch to find a message taped on his chair. "They need you in the conference room. Fourth floor." He read it with a puzzled frown. Elizabeth was seated nearby. He turned to her and gestured with the note, "What's this about?"

"I don't know. Call your friend at the FEC. Maybe she can tell you."

"What?"

"You spend a lot of time with her. Maybe she knows what your messages are about."

"What is wrong with you?" Rutledge stepped over to her desk. "Why are you acting like this?"

"We go out. We have fun. Then I don't hear from you for ... I don't know. What's it been? A week? Maybe two?"

"I've been busy."

"Yeah. With someone else."

"No. With no one else. I've been to Chicago, Detroit. I've spent nights up here trying to figure out what's going on with this case."

"And hours over at the FEC."

"You're jealous."

"Yes," she nodded. "I'm jealous. If you want to go out with her, fine. We didn't make any commitments. Just don't act like everything's okay."

"I'm not going out with anyone." He stepped behind her desk, turned her chair to the side, and gestured with his hand. "I'm going on a trip up to the fourth floor. Would you care to go with me as my date?"

Before he could move, she delivered a backhanded blow with her fist to his stomach. He clutched his abdomen and doubled over in pain and laughter. "You hit me," he guffawed.

"I'm gonna do worse than that if I find out you've been out with her." She nudged his shoulder. "Let's go."

"Go? Go where?"

"You invited me on a date to the fourth floor. Let's go."

They rode the elevator upstairs and made their way down the hall to the conference room. He opened the door for her, then came to an abrupt halt. Standing at the head of the table was Don Harper, the assistant agent in charge of the Counterterrorism Unit. Seated a few feet away was Bert Miller, the special agent in charge of the D.C. office. Rutledge had seen him on numerous occasions but had never been close enough to shake his hand. Next to him was Daryl Driskell, director of the FBI. And seated with his back to the door was Harvey Sessions, the Attorney General. Harper gestured for Rutledge to enter. "I see you finally made it."

"Yes, sir. I didn't realize we were meeting this afternoon."

"We received a report from the accounts and after taking a look at it I thought we should all meet together." He pointed to a chair on the opposite side of the table. "Rutledge, you sit over here. Agent Caffery, we'll get an extra chair for you."

Someone seated farther down the table rose. "She can have mine. I'll get another." He moved down to a door at the opposite end of the room while Elizabeth worked her way to the open seat.

When everyone was in place, Harper began again. "As I was saying, the accountants are ready to tell us what they found." He nodded to a man seated a few chairs away. "This is Bob Landry."

Landry stood. "As you all are aware, pursuant to Agent Harper's request, the U.S. Attorney's office obtained a warrant that allowed us to secure certain financial records regarding Sierra Resources and Governor

McNeil's campaign. Specifically, we received bank account records from Richmond National Bank, Pacific National Bank, CMT Financial, and the American unit of USB. Our team of accountants has spent the past several days going through those records." Rutledge raised his hand, interrupting his train of thought. Landry pointed to him. "Yes, sir, Agent Rutledge. I guess you're the reason we're all here."

"I was wondering, how did you know which records to request?"

"We began with the ones you supplied and went on from there, following the trail as far as it went." Landry nodded to an aide seated in the corner. Lights dimmed and the screen at the opposite end of the room grew brighter. "If you'll look at the screen, we have a diagram of the transactions. They all fit in four patterns."

For the next thirty minutes, Landry walked them through the transaction patterns, all of which originated from a bank in Athens and then passed through multiple foreign accounts before ending up in the PACs Rutledge previously discovered. From there the money moved easily into McNeil's campaign accounts. The transactions involved millions of dollars.

As Landry finished his presentation, Bert Miller stood. "I think we've seen more than enough to convince us that there's a case here. I'm not sure we've gathered enough to actually seek a warrant."

"I agree," Sessions added. "But I think we should get this ready for a grand jury."

"If we do this, we will be shaping a presidential election."

"If we don't, we'll be shaping the nation."

"We have no choice but to pursue this to the end."

"Does anyone know for certain whether McNeil knew about this?"

"We won't know that until we start questioning witnesses and the best way to do that is before a grand jury."

"I agree."

The discussion continued a few minutes longer, then the meeting broke up. As they were moving toward the door, Driskell spoke up. "I don't think I have to say this— we're all responsible members of the federal government— but I'll say it anyway. Don't tell anyone what we talked about here. This is critically sensitive information. I don't want to read any quotes in the *Post* from some unnamed source about what we discussed."

While the others filed from the room, Elizabeth moved near Rutledge. Behind his back, out of sight, she ran her fingers over his back. "Wow," she smiled. "You really were working late."

"I tried to tell you."

"Working late tonight?"

"I don't know. Want to join me?"

"Sure." She squeezed his side, then moved around him and started toward the door. "I'll see you downstairs."

CHAPTER 83
OTTUMWA, IOWA

WHEN THE BREAK-IN at Cook's offices fell apart and Sisson left Chicago, he had been simply trying to get out of town. He took the first bus leaving the station. Once he got to Indianapolis and had time to think, he realized he had to get out of sight, permanently. For that, he had two choices. He could go to New York and disappear among the crowd. Or he could go to Montana and disappear in the vast open spaces. Having lived in the East most of his life, he decided to try Montana. He drove in that direction, keeping off the main highways, and slowly made his way west.

As he drove, his mind began to wander and soon came to the voice mail from Paul. He thought of all his connections in the D.C. area and the people they might know. But none of them took him to a man named Paul Bryson.

On the outskirts of Ottumwa, Iowa, he saw a sign for the public library. The highway turned north onto a bypass that led around the city. Instead of going that way, Sisson turned and followed the library signs through town. In a little while, he arrived at the parking lot outside the library building on Third Street. He brought the car to a stop in an open space and went inside the building to the circulation desk. Jamie Wright, who worked the counter that day, smiled at him as he approached. "May I help you?"

Sisson noted her name from the tag on her jacket. "I was wondering if you have Internet access."

"Certainly. Do you have a library card?"

"No, ma'am. I don't."

"Well, come on. We can work around that." She came from behind the desk and led him across the library to a separate room. Inside were two rows of computers. "This is our computer lab," she said proudly. "We built it with help from Microsoft and the John Whitespunner Foundation." She pointed to a computer near the door. "Try this one." Sisson took a seat and waited while she logged on to the system. "There, you can use the library's card."

"The library has a library card?"

"Yes, for visitors like yourself who don't have a card."

Sisson loaded the Web browser on the screen. Jamie watched a moment, then turned toward the door. "Call me if you need me." And then she was gone.

A simple search of Paul Bryson's name produced several hundred thousand hits. Sisson checked the more promising sites, then found a Wikipedia page for him. From the entry, he learned the basic facts about him and learned that his wife had been killed at the Pentagon during the attacks of 9/11. He checked the references at the bottom of the page and followed several links to news articles about her life, death, and funeral. What he read intrigued Sisson and he wondered whether Paul might be someone who could help him out of his situation, without the need to disappear into the wilderness of Montana. He checked the bus schedule and looked at airlines flying from the region. He was certain an airline would enter his information in a system monitored by the federal government, which meant Jeremy Bartlett and analysts at the Sierra command center would probably have access to it, also. Then he checked the Amtrak site. A train left Ottumwa at six that evening. He glanced at his watch and saw it was three. He had plenty of time to spare and he already knew that the train, like the bus, didn't ask many personal questions.

From the library Sisson rode out to the Stardust Motel on the eastern edge of town. He'd seen the sign for it earlier. He rented a room and parked the car in front, just a few feet from the door. With a T-shirt from the backpack, he wiped down the steering wheel, dash, and side panels of the door. He hadn't opened the rear doors or the trunk and was sure he'd never reached across the seat. Still, he gave the passenger side a wipe to make sure, then went inside for a nap and a shower.

An hour later, he called for a taxi. It arrived fifteen minutes later. Sisson came from the room, set the backpack beside him on the rear seat, and closed his eyes. "Train station," he said without looking up.

"Amtrak?"

"Yes."

"Good way to travel," the driver noted. "Took a trip on the train with my grandson last summer. Actually gave us time to talk."

CHAPTER 84
TEXAS

TWO DAYS LATER, David McNeil appeared at a rally in Austin, then moved on to Houston. His first stop there was a luncheon in the auditorium at Memorial City Medical Center on the west side of the city. The facility was filled beyond capacity with an enthusiastic audience of medical professionals and business executives. Feeding off their energy, McNeil departed from his prepared text to deliver a rousing address on the need for healthcare reform that focused on financial incentives for physicians. Pledges of support from the event topped any he'd received during the campaign swing through Florida.

Outside the hospital complex, he found the streets were jammed with supporters. Traffic was at a standstill. Police and Secret Service agents cordoned off a path from the building to the caravan parked out front, but even then, getting from the building to the car was a slow process. With so many wanting a chance to see and touch him, McNeil took his time working the rope line, shaking hands, signing autographs, hugging supporters.

Twenty minutes later, Trent Paine came to his side and took his elbow. "We need to keep moving, sir. You have another rally in the theater district downtown and a meeting waiting in the SUV. We're running behind schedule already." McNeil shook a few more hands, then reluctantly turned away from the crowd and climbed into the waiting SUV.

Unlike most days, the SUV was empty except for McNeil, the driver, and Edgar Logan. McNeil opened the refrigerator compartment between the seats and took out a bottle of water. "Want one?" he asked, glancing in Logan's direction.

"I'm fine."

"These crowds are getting even bigger. I thought we'd peaked too early in Florida but the crowds here in Houston are even larger."

"They seem glad to see you, too." Logan's tone was polite but reserved.

McNeil swallowed a long drink of water, then placed the cap on the bottle. "Caldwell tells me we have a situation."

"Yes," Logan answered coolly. "Apparently so."

"Think you can fix it?"

"Perhaps."

"That's not much of a commitment. What's it going to take to get this done?"

"Sierra Resources is a sole-source provider to the Pentagon. We have a no-bid arrangement with them. That's helped us develop some unusual programs. But in the course of that we've built out our organization to service those contracts. We have a number of subsidiaries and lots of employees. They've produced interesting and extremely useful programs and technologies. We want to keep the company growing and we're looking for more government work. At the same time, we want to take that technology and adapt it for private-sector applications."

"That shouldn't be a problem." McNeil shrugged.

"Our work is messy at times. We're an easy target when things get politically difficult."

"Caldwell said you were worried you'd get thrown under the bus."

"I'm not part of the lifelong McNeil team."

McNeil glanced in Logan's direction. "I've been doing this for a while, Ed. I understand that elections are never about the issues. They're about timing and intelligence. Staying one step ahead of the opposition. And I assume that's what you and Caldwell were doing in Chicago?"

Logan gave him a knowing look. "I don't know anything about Chicago," he grinned. "Although things would be much easier for you if Wilson were not in this election."

They rode a moment in silence. McNeil turned to look out the window. "Think Sierra Resources could help us with that Wilson problem?"

"We would be delighted."

CHAPTER 85
WASHINGTON, D.C.

THAT AFTERNOON, RUTLEDGE found Susan Dey at her desk on the opposite side of the building. She glanced up as he approached, then opened a desk drawer and took out a file. "You never came back for the results."

"What results?"

"On that bank account you asked about. The one in Greece."

"Oh, I got sidetracked on something else."

She laid the file on her desk. "It belongs to Manos Dianellos. A lawyer with an office on Achilleos Avenue, near the U.S. Embassy."

"Good." Rutledge glanced through her file, then dropped it on the desk. "I was wondering if you could—"

"That's an interesting response." She scooped up the file and returned it to her drawer. "The guys from Justice were really excited about it."

"Justice?"

"Don had me talk to them."

"Why?"

"He said they're taking over now."

"Taking over? When did he say that?"

"This morning. He was looking for you." Rutledge turned away and headed toward the hall. "Hey," Susan called after him. "What did you want?"

"Never mind," he called in reply.

Don Harper was waiting at the stairway when Rutledge returned to his desk. "I've been trying to find you all morning."

"Chasing down some details on Sisson."

"We need to talk about that." Harper put his arm across Rutledge's shoulder and steered him to a vacant office. When they were inside, he closed the door. "You did good work on the case," he began. "You took a situation that seemed like nothing, worked it like a professional, and did a good job."

"But now someone else wants it."

"Justice is taking the lead now."

"Who made that decision?"

"Our boss."

"The director?"

"No. The Attorney General."

"What did the director think?"

"He was inclined to give you more time to tie up some of the loose ends, but ultimately it wasn't his call."

"No one wanted this case."

"No one ever does, in the beginning."

"And then when we work it up and start finding things, everyone wants to take control."

"It's frustrating, I know. But eventually we had to hand it off to the lawyers. They're the ones who make the case in court. We just uncover the evidence."

"I know."

"You did a good job." Harper patted him on the back. "This is a nice office," he continued, glancing around the room. "Has a nice view." He pointed out the window. "You can see all the way ... across the street," he chuckled.

"Yes, sir."

"It's yours if you want it."

Rutledge's eyes opened wide. "Mine?"

"I'll have Facilities move your things." Harper turned toward the door, then paused as he grasped the doorknob. "You really did do a good job."

"Thanks. But, sir?"

"Yes?"

"If it's all the same to you, I'd rather keep my same desk."

Harper frowned. "The one in here is nicer."

"I mean I'd rather sit out there. With Brenner and Caffery."

"They'd jump at the chance to take this office."

"Maybe. But I like working out there. With them."

"Suit yourself," Harper smiled. "Better spend some time getting your notes together. They're convening a special grand jury for this case. They'll need you to testify."

Rutledge returned to his desk and began sorting through his notes. When he first started working on the Cook case, he'd been protective of it and wanted to make sure no one took it away. He'd jealously guarded information and kept the details to himself. Now that the case was no longer his and lawyers from Justice were calling the shots, he found an odd sense of relief and release to move on to other things.

Over the past several weeks he'd accumulated a number of files on his computer and a drawer full of handwritten notes. As he sorted through them, he came to a page with details from his meeting with Paul. Scribbled on a yellow sheet of paper, the notes contained very little detail but in the margin were the words "Jewish conspiracy." He stared at the page and thought about the case.

Paul Bryson was a former congressman and a respected Washington lobbyist. He wasn't a wild-eyed right-wing radical. Yet he was convinced the Order of Malta was secretly working to eliminate the Jews. Just thinking about it now, the notion that such a thing could be true— that an old, traditional organization like the Order would seriously pursue such a plan, now, in this age— seemed ridiculous. But just a few weeks earlier, everyone in the bureau was talking about the possibility that the Order was trying to influence the election, too.

Rutledge dropped his notes in the desk drawer and shoved it closed. He might be out of the case involving McNeil, but that didn't mean he had to stop investigating the Order. As long as he kept a low profile and didn't cause trouble, he could keep working the leads in a different direction. Maybe there was more to the conspiracy theory than he'd believed. He rose from his desk and walked again to the opposite side of the building.

Susan was at a worktable, surrounded by stacks of files. She didn't see him approach. "Where's that file you showed me before?"

She jumped at the sound of his voice. "What are you doing?"

"Didn't mean to startle you. I need that file you showed me before."

She rose from the table and walked toward her desk. "Did the lawyers from Justice get ahold of you?"

"No. Were they looking for me?"

"I think so." She took the file from her desk and handed it to him. "They're scheduling interviews with everyone who worked on the case."

"What did you tell them?"

"That you were here earlier."

"If they ask again, tell them you haven't seen me lately."

"Okay." She leaned against the corner of the desk. "What's this about?"

"Nothing." He gestured with the file. "And don't tell anyone I have this."

"I'm not lying."

"Just don't volunteer it."

Rutledge hurried back to his desk and searched through his notes for Paul Bryson's telephone number. He entered it in his cell phone and placed a call. Paul answered on the third ring.

"We need to talk."

"Okay. Where?"

"Your office. In half an hour."

"I'll be waiting."

*   *   *

Paul was seated at his desk when Rutledge arrived. He gestured to upholstered chairs near the window. "Let's sit over here. We'll be more comfortable." A grin spread across his face. "Am I under investigation now?"

"Not at all." Rutledge took a seat. He had a file in is hand and rested it in his lap. "I wanted to talk to you about something you mentioned the other evening."

"Oh? What's that?"

"The Knights of Malta and the Jews."

"Ahh." Paul arched an eyebrow. "You're finally interested in that?"

Rutledge opened the file. "What do you know about a man named Manos Dianellos?" Mention of the name made Paul's heart jump, but he pushed it aside and maintained his composure. "He's a lawyer in Athens," Rutledge continued, apparently unaware of Paul's reaction. "Has an office ..." He glanced at the file in his lap. "On Achilleos Avenue, near the U.S. Embassy. Does that name mean anything to you?"

"Perhaps." Paul did his best to hide his thoughts. "Why do you ask?"

"He's the owner of an account at a bank in Athens, Greece. The account was used to transfer money between Sierra Resources and several other entities."

"The political action committees?"

"You know about those?"

"A little."

"What can you tell me about Dianellos?"

"I don't think I can tell you anything."

"Why not?"

"I'm a lobbyist, Mr. Rutledge. I have clients."

"Sierra?"

"Yes."

"Okay." Rutledge closed the file. "I was hoping we could talk about your conspiracy ideas, but if you can't, then I'll just put it aside."

"No. Don't put it aside. I can talk about that. I just can't tell you about Dianellos."

"Well, what can you talk about?"

"Do you know Esther Rosenberg?"

"The lawyer?"

"Yeah."

"I know who she is, but I've never met her. She's a little out of my league."

"She's out of my league too, but she loves me anyway." Paul stood and slipped on his jacket. "We should go see her."

"Now?"

"Yes. You have time?"

"I have time, but does she?"

"I think she'll work us in." Paul opened the office door and waited for Rutledge to pass, then followed him into the hall. "What do you know about a book called *The Protocols of the Learned Elders of Zion*?"

"I'm with the Counterterrorism Unit, Mr. Bryson. You can't work in that area without knowing about *The Protocols*. Islamic extremists believe it's absolutely true."

In the hallway, Paul pressed a button for the elevator. "Do you think it's true?"

"It's been proven a hoax by irrefutable evidence."

"Good," Paul smiled. The elevator doors opened. He gestured for Rutledge to enter. "Esther will be glad to hear that. This is going to be fun."

CHAPTER 86
HOUSTON, TEXAS

AFTER AN EARLY-AFTERNOON rally at the Wortham Center, McNeil took a break in a downtown hotel suite. He ate a salad, took a shower, and changed clothes. As he was tucking in his shirt, Henry Caldwell appeared at the door.

"Did you and Edgar Logan have a good meeting?"

"We talked." McNeil fastened his belt. "Actually, I did most of the talking." He gestured toward a chair. "Have a seat." Caldwell dropped onto a chair. McNeil sat opposite him. "I'm a little concerned with bringing on their people."

"They have expertise we need."

"But now it's no longer covert. If they come onboard, and I know it, we lose deniability." McNeil pointed to himself. "I'm the guy who gets thrown under the bus."

"We need them. It's gone too far now. We have to take a more aggressive approach."

"More aggressive?" McNeil scoffed. "Breaking into Liston Cook's office wasn't aggressive enough?"

"With Wilson. Cleaning up the mess in Chicago." Caldwell leaned back in his chair. "There's a rumor going around Washington that the Attorney General is convening a grand jury."

"For what?"

"No one knows," Caldwell shrugged. "Or if they do, they're not talking. But the word is, the Attorney General himself is handling it."

"That's big."

"Yeah."

"That could be us."

"All the more reason to bring on Ed's people. We'll do it in a way that doesn't officially connect them to the campaign."

"Then why the meeting with Logan?"

"So the connection is personal. Between you and him."

"Hmm." McNeil reached to a nearby table for a bottle of water. "You sure you can pull this off?"

"We have to get you elected and to do that, we have to keep Spoleto satisfied."

"That's what this is about?"

"They weren't happy with our strategy."

"*Your* strategy," McNeil corrected.

"Yeah, my strategy."

McNeil's face was somber. "They're not running the government," he said flatly.

Caldwell looked concerned. "What do you mean?"

"After we're in, Spoleto and his Council aren't running the government."

Caldwell wagged his finger in a disapproving manner. "I'm not sure you should talk like that."

"I'm talking to you."

"I know. But not even to me." They sat in silence a moment, then Caldwell smiled. "Look, let's focus on the issues at hand. We'll worry about the rest later." He put both feet on the floor and propped his elbows on his knees. "Logan just wants to continue his present operations. Lucrative contracts. They're making money, his wife and kids are happy, that's all he wants. They've got a lot invested, and the government contracts are a big part of their bottom line."

"They're worried about their investors?"

"They don't really have investors. Sierra Resources and all their other companies are controlled by the Order. They've got a few people involved, but they're just there to make it seem legitimate."

"I don't know."

"Once you're in office, you'll need them to solve the immigration problem. The Pentagon might be reluctant to do all we intend to do, but not Logan."

A frown wrinkled McNeil's forehead. "You really think we're right on the immigration issue?"

"What do you mean?"

"I'm just asking."

"Don't ask."

McNeil stared out the window. He had a faraway look in his eye. "I went back to the farm."

"I know. You told me."

"It's a sham."

"Of course it's a sham. That's how they get past Immigration. Can't make any money if they follow the letter of the law."

"I'm not talking about the farm. I'm talking about the things we say about immigration. It's a sham."

"It's campaign rhetoric. That's all. Words to incite our voter base to get out and vote."

"You don't think we should tell them the truth?"

"I think we should tell them whatever it takes to get you elected."

"We said that LaCosta and the others used legal aliens and operated at a profit."

"Right."

"But the people who are legal are only there for show. The real work is done by illegal workers, who live in shacks behind the trees, with raw sewage at their door, and their kids are in the field instead of in school."

"That isn't our problem."

"It's a problem for the president of the United States. And it'll be a problem for us when the press finds out what's really going on there."

"I'll handle it."

"I don't want you to handle it," McNeil snapped. "You've been handling too much."

"What are you saying?"

"I want to change our message."

"You can't change the message. The entire campaign is built around that message."

"It's someone else's message. Not mine."

"Yeah, well, that someone else is paying the bills."

* * *

Caldwell came from his meeting with McNeil and walked down the hall toward the elevator. As he did, he took his cell phone from his pocket and typed a message. "We may have a message problem." Then he scrolled down the contacts list for Nikki McNeil's number and sent it to her.

When he reached the first floor, his phone beeped. He glanced at the screen and saw a response from Nikki. "He's serious."

Caldwell stopped near the front exit. "We need to talk."

Almost immediately, she responded. "Come to Richmond."

"Make it Atlanta."

"I'll meet you there."

He stepped outside to a waiting car and dropped into the back seat. As the car started forward, he prepared another text message— this one to Russo.

CHAPTER 87
ASHDOD, ISRAEL

UNDER THE COVER OF DARKNESS, Gadot steered the car onto a street near Menachem Garden, a neighborhood on the east side of the city. The car slowed as they rounded a curve, then turned through a gate to the right. As the car entered, the gate swung closed behind them.

The drive led up a low hill to a cluster of buildings. Gadot brought the car to a stop in front of the building on the right.

Barberini, seated on the passenger side, roused from sleep. "Where are we?"

"This is your new home. At least for now."

Barberini looked around. "But where am I?"

"This is the barracks for the military guard that patrols the east side."

"East side of what?"

"Ashdod."

Barberini looked perplexed. "Ashdod? We are in Israel?"

"Yes."

"You didn't tell me we were coming here."

"No. I did not. Do you have a problem with that?"

"I thought we were going someplace safe."

"This is it," Gadot replied. "You are much safer here than anywhere else in the world."

"But what about the Palestinians?"

"They care no less for you than they do the Jews, but they have no vendetta against you, either." Gadot climbed from the car. "Come. We should get inside."

Barberini opened the door and stepped out. "I thought you said this was safe."

"It is safe. But we should not be foolish, either."

Barberini followed him into the building and up the stairs to the second floor. Gadot opened the door and held it while he entered. "This is yours," he said with a sweeping gesture.

The door opened to a small apartment. Directly beyond the door was a sitting area with a sofa, chair, and coffee table. Past it was a kitchen with a table and chairs. To the left, a door opened to a small bedroom with a bathroom at one end.

"It is sparsely furnished, but you will be safe and comfortable."

"How long will I be here?"

"Until we can determine that it is safe to place you elsewhere."

"Can I go outside?"

"You may walk among the buildings, but only in the morning."

Barberini surveyed the room once more. "Well," he sighed, "at least I am alive."

"Yes, and that is a good thing." Gadot turned back to the door. "There is no television here. I will bring you a radio tomorrow."

"What about clothes?"

"I will bring clothes, too. If you need anything before I return, go to the first floor and ask for Yehuda. He will help you. There should be some food in the kitchen for now. Later you can take meals with the men."

Gadot stepped out to the hall and closed the door. When he was gone, Barberini walked into the kitchen. A stove sat in the corner next to a sink with a cabinet above. He opened the cabinet and found a box of tea. Next to it was a container of sugar. Although it was late, he took the kettle from the stove, filled it with water, and put it on to boil.

CHAPTER 88
TUCSON, ARIZONA

AT THE SIERRA COMMAND CENTER an alert tone sounded from the operator's console near the center of the room. A message box appeared on a monitor to her left. "Anyone know were Jeremy is?"

"He's upstairs."

The operator pressed a button on her console and sent a call to his cell phone. In a few minutes Bartlett appeared at the door.

"What do you have?"

"They located Sisson's car. It's at the Stardust Motel in Ottumwa."

He came to the center of the room. "Is he there?"

"No one knows yet." She pointed to the speaker in the corner of the room. "We have audio." She pressed another button on the console. "This is the local police."

A voice came from the speaker. "Charlie, can you see the back of the building?"

"Yeah. I'm there now. Nothing unusual."

"What about the window? Can you see inside?"

"It's the bathroom. I can see the bathroom. Bottle of shampoo on the edge of the tub. Just looks like a bathroom."

Bartlett turned to the operator. "Where's our team?"

"They were downtown about ten minutes ago."

"Did you tell them about this?"

"We just now received the message. You were the first call. I haven't told anyone else."

"Get the team out there to the motel."

Charlie's voice spoke again from the motel. "Gus, are we sure this is the right room?"

"Front desk says this is it. We're checking the car now."

Bartlett glanced across the room to Donna Preston and smiled. If the police checked the registration on the car, they would soon know there was a problem with the information on the warrant.

Gus, the voice from the hotel, broke in. "Charlie, sit tight. SWAT truck is on the way."

"Okay. I'm sittin' tight."

"And those fellas from out of town are coming, too."

"Who are they?"

"I'm not sure. Said something about looking for a guy who broke into some campaign offices in Chicago."

"Yeah, I read about that in the paper. Broke into Liston Cook's office."

"I hear them coming now. We better cool the chatter," Gus warned. "Chief don't like us talking so much."

"Did you check the door to that room to see if it was open?"

"No. Think I should?"

"Might just give the knob a twist to see if it's unlocked."

The operator spoke up. "Our team is right behind the SWAT truck. We're getting their video." She pointed to a screen on the wall. "It's up now."

An image appeared from a camera in the front of the van. It showed a clear view out the front windshield. Ahead of them was a delivery truck that had been painted black and white. A satellite dish was mounted on top and windows in the rear doors had wire-reinforced glass.

Bartlett smiled. "Not much of a SWAT truck."

"I've seen worse," someone replied.

Someone else commented, "It's not the paint on the outside but the men on the inside that matters."

The truck and van turned from the highway into the drive at the motel. Bartlett gestured for silence. On the screen, the blue Chevrolet was visible, sitting in a parking space in front of the entrance to a room. A police car was parked behind it.

As the SWAT truck moved into place, an officer stepped in front of the van. The van came to a stop and the officer moved to the driver's window. "You boys will have to wait here. Chief's orders."

"We were hoping to check out the car and the motel room."

"I'm afraid that won't be possible right now. This is still a live scene. You'll have to wait until this is resolved."

"How long will that take?"

"Can't say right now. The incident is still ongoing." The officer pointed toward the highway. "You can park over there by the front office and wait. Or you can come back later and—"

Just then, the door to the motel room opened and an officer appeared. "It's okay," he shouted. Men from the SWAT truck dressed in full battle gear were already moving toward the building. They came to a halt in the parking lot. Dejected at being called off, their shoulders slumped as they lowered their weapons to their sides.

Images on the screen jumped as the van doors opened and the Sierra team stepped out. The camera moved to a position outside the van and focused on the officer standing near the motel room door. "Ain't nobody in there," he shouted.

The camera started toward the room and the officer stepped out of the way to let them enter. Someone shouted from behind, "Should they go in there? We haven't processed that room yet." But by then the camera was inside the room. Images appeared on the screen as the camera slowly panned from left to right.

After a moment, the image on the screen jumped again and a man wearing a dark blue policeman's uniform came into view. "What are you men doing here?" His voice was gruff and determined.

Someone gave an inaudible answer, then the man in uniform continued. "Well, I'm Chief Culverhouse and I don't care where you're from or why you're here. You can wait outside until my evidence technician processes the room or you can wait in jail." The camera backed out of the room, then went blank.

Bartlett stared up at the screen a moment longer, then looked away. "I guess that's it for the live feed. Play that back and let's have a look at the room." The screen flickered and then an image from the doorway of the room appeared. "Slow it down," Bartlett ordered. Images on the screen moved slowly to show the entire room, from the window to the bed and around to the dresser near the door.

"Back it up and show it again," Bartlett ordered.

When the images reached the bed, he held up his hand. "Hold it right there." The movement stopped, showing the bed and a nightstand next to it with a lamp on top. "Tighten up on the nightstand." A box appeared on the screen around the nightstand, then the image moved closer. "Get it a little tighter," Bartlett added. And the image moved even closer.

"There," he said, pointing. "What's that lying on the nightstand?"

"A spoon?" someone asked.

"No," another replied. "One of those things you stir the coffee with."

"Can you get it any tighter?" As the image moved even closer, the object came into focus. It was blue and yellow and made in a spoon shape with a decorative handle. "It has writing on it," Bartlett suggested. "Can anyone read it?"

"Blue Moon," Donna Preston called. "It says 'Blue Moon Café.'"

"Where's that?"

"Just a minute," she answered. "I'm checking ... It's a café in Chicago. Ninety-ninth Street."

"That's him," Bartlett nodded.

"But we don't know he was at the Blue Moon."

"It's him," Bartlett growled impatiently. "He's playing with us. And we can play right back." He turned to the operator. "Let's get our contact at Rhodes on the line."

CHAPTER 89
ATLANTA, GEORGIA

THE NEXT MORNING, Henry Caldwell and Nikki McNeil met at the Ritz-Carlton Hotel in the Buckhead section of the city. They sat at a table in the corner of her suite and drank coffee while they talked.

"It's late in the game to have message problems," Caldwell said, shaking his head. "I'm worried about David."

"I know. I don't think he ever fully bought the message from the beginning."

"I thought he did. We had long talks about these very topics. Even back when he was in college."

"Yes." She nodded and took a sip of coffee. "I remember him telling me about those sessions. But you have to remember, he was also spending a lot of time with Nelson Hooper, too."

"I forgot about him."

"Not a bad guy, just a different approach."

"Think that's what's bothering him?"

"I don't know. I think it's probably more than that. He learned to articulate the right positions and learned to do a good job with events, but he always had doubts. We used to sit up late at night talking about it. He wanted to know, if Jesus said we should help the poor, why were we saying aid to the poor should be cut off. And why were we saying we were pro-life about babies, but pro-death about criminals."

"Because they're criminals."

"I told him that, too, but he said when we say we're pro-life what we mean is we're anti-abortion and that's what we ought to say. Sort of hard for me to argue with him on that point, so I tried to divert him with the numbers— how many abortions are performed every year."

"Did it work?"

"For a little while, but then the same issue would come back. He was also worried about healthcare."

"Healthcare?"

"For the poor."

"Jesus was talking to people when he said help the poor. We're talking about the government. He never said for the government to do it."

"I know, but he couldn't get past it. Kept saying that our political positions weren't just fiction. They were *our* positions. And if he was really a Christian, how could he have a position on any subject that contradicted what Jesus said."

"I wish you'd told me this sooner."

"I talked to Carter about it. He said not to worry. That he had control of the speechwriters and he would see that the message stayed on point. I didn't talk to you about it because I didn't want it to look like I was interfering with the campaign. And I didn't want you to give up on him. So instead I talked to Morris Wythe and set up the arrangement with him."

"Did it help?"

"Some," she nodded. "He does much better when he sees Morris regularly. Discipleship is important. I always say that whenever I speak to church groups. Keeping that perspective always before you. Keeps your mind focused on what's important."

Caldwell's face lit up. "That's it," he grinned. "That's what we should do."

"What?" Nikki looked surprised. "What did I say?

"Morris Wythe. He was after us to come to his church. Now he wants us to go with him on a tour of churches. We could build a campaign swing through key states, bring Morris with us. Stop at the major churches in the area. Let him lead the show. Build other stops around the church events, but make the churches the focus. Rally the base. Get David a lot of time with Morris."

"I'm not sure it'll work," Nikki frowned skeptically. "But I suppose it's worth a shot."

"I think it's the answer." Caldwell rose from his chair. "We won't try to manipulate the message. We'll keep him saturated in it." He started toward the door, then looked back over his shoulder. "Just don't tell David why we're doing this."

CHAPTER 90
WASHINGTON, D.C.

THAT AFTERNOON, BRODY appeared at Esther's office. An assistant escorted him to a conference room. Esther met him there. "Well," she smiled. "You finally came up here instead of meeting with all the cloak-and-dagger arrangements."

He ignored her comments. "We have Barberini."

She looked puzzled. "Barberini?"

"Penalta's assistant. The one who had the flash drive with the files."

"What did he have to say?"

"I don't know. They are just now beginning to debrief him."

"So, are we finished with my part of this?"

"Not quite."

"What do you mean?"

"I have some information about the man you asked about— Bill Sisson."

"No. I asked about Brian Culpepper. What did you learn about him?"

"Nothing yet." His eyes darted away. "We're still working on it."

She felt manipulated but she was determined to get an answer and pressed the point. "You don't want to talk about him, do you? You just want to dangle the possibility in front of me so I keep doing whatever it is you want."

"We're working on it, Esther. Don't you believe me?"

"I believe you will always do what's in your best interests, what's in Mossad's interest, and leave my concerns until later, if at all."

"We're working on it." He said the words but she could tell his heart wasn't in it. "But listen, Sisson works for Sierra." His tone changed and his eyes were alive. "He's part of their special operations program— assassinations, renditions, all the things the U.S. has condemned and made illegal."

"What's his background?"

"Military. Former Marine."

"So," her tone turned sarcastic, "you had me send Paul to find a Marine— a combat veteran trained to kill with his bare hands. And Paul's never even been in a fistfight."

"He was in a fight before. In the alley. Did you forget?"

She looked away. "Don't remind me."

"I thought he acquitted himself rather well."

She cut her eyes at him. "You weren't with him at the hospital."

"Look, he'll be okay." Brody tried to lighten the mood. "Just tell him not to confront this guy alone."

Esther moved closer. "If you don't get me something on Culpepper by the end of the day," she jabbed him in the chest with her finger, "I'm walking away from this project and never looking back."

Brody turned toward the door. "Just tell him to be careful."

Esther grabbed Brody by the sleeve. "I mean it."

"Okay," he said, shrugging free. "I'll see what they have."

Brody stepped out to the hall and disappeared. Esther took her cell phone from the table and placed a call to Paul. When the call rolled over to voice mail, she sent a text. "Call me."

Then, as she stood there in the conference room, alone and thinking about what Brody said, fear swept over her. Sisson— a former Marine— covert operations. Paul wasn't trained for a fight like this. He wasn't trained at all. He knew how to shepherd a project through Congress, work an idea through the committee process, but not this.

Suddenly images from the past flashed through her mind, of Ephraim and the smile on his face, his lean, muscular body trained and hardened by combat. She banged her fist against the wall. "Why do I choose these men?" She jerked open the door and headed toward the hall. It was late in the day. Paul was probably relaxing at home. If she drove fast, she could be there in half an hour.

CHAPTER 91
WASHINGTON, D.C.

PAUL GOT OUT OF THE CAR and walked up the front steps. After a long day, it was good to finally be home. He opened the door and stepped inside. As he crossed the living room, he tossed his jacket on the sofa and walked to the kitchen. He opened the refrigerator, took out a bottle of Boylan ginger ale, and twisted off the cap. It was dry, sweet, and cold as it slid down his throat.

Just then, the doorbell rang. He walked to the front door and looked through the peephole. On the steps outside was a slender man, about thirty-five years old, with broad shoulders, olive complexion, and dark, piercing eyes. He looked familiar, and then Paul remembered the photographs he'd seen before. *That's Bill Sisson.* He opened the door and stood there, unsure of what to say or do next.

Sisson glanced up without a smile. "You looking for me?"

"Yes." Paul opened the door wider and stepped out of the way. "Come on in. I think we need to talk." Sisson moved quickly inside and Paul closed the door. "I'm having a ginger ale," he said, gesturing with the bottle. "Want one?"

"Sure, haven't had a ginger ale in a long time."

They walked to the kitchen and Paul took a bottle from the

refrigerator, then handed it to him. "Let's sit in the living room. It'll be more comfortable."

Sisson followed him to the sofa and took a seat. Paul sat on a chair. "So," he began. "You got my voice mail."

"Yeah. Why were you calling me?"

"I know you were in Liston Cook's offices. I saw you on the security video."

"Well ..." Sisson looked away. "Mike was supposed to disable that."

"Who sent you?"

Sisson took a drink from the bottle. "Know anything about a company called Sierra Resources?"

"A little." Paul considered whether to say more, then thought better of it and waited for Sisson to continue.

"If you know anything about them, then you don't know very much. Most of what they do isn't publicly available. What they publicize about themselves is a long way from the truth." He took another sip from the bottle and looked over at Paul. "I'm sorry about your wife."

"My wife?"

"You are the Paul Bryson whose wife died at the Pentagon, aren't you?"

"Yes."

"You look like the pictures, only a little older."

"I am a little older."

"If I tell you what I know, you have to agree to help me."

"Help you do what?"

"Get out."

"Get out of what?"

"Sierra Resources."

"Okay," Paul nodded slowly. "I think I can help. What can you tell me?"

For the next ten minutes Sisson gave a quick review of Sierra's operations and the experimental programs they were developing— rendition teams that snatched terror suspects from the streets of foreign countries and political threats from the streets right here in the United States. Assassinations, kidnapping, personality alteration— he touched on every operation the company was pursuing. "So," he said finally, "that's how we came to be in Cook's offices. We were doing some of that stuff for David McNeil's campaign. Shaping the election so he could run against Wilson."

"Wilson's a Democrat. McNeil doesn't have the nomination yet and he was worried about Wilson?"

"He'll win the Republican nomination." Sisson had a knowing smile. "That's already been determined. He and Caldwell are looking to the general election. The whole campaign now is geared toward setting up the fall election. We were just getting our part of it into gear when they heard somebody in Cook's operation had copies of documents about Sierra, the Knights of Malta, and the money. Sent us in to—"

"The money?"

"The Order— the Knights of Malta— has been funding McNeil's campaign. Wire the money in from a bank in Athens. Send it around the world before it gets here. Difficult to trace."

"How did Sierra get tangled up with the Knights of Malta?"

"They started the company. They own it."

"I thought a group in California owned it."

"That's just a front."

Sisson's story didn't quite fit with what Paul had been told but he didn't want to argue. They could straighten out the details later. He did, however, want Culpepper present. "We need to get someone else over here."

"Who?"

"His name is Brian Culpepper. He's an investigator. Liston Cook hired him to figure out who wanted access to his office."

Sisson looked concerned. "Do you know him, personally?"

"Not before this. But I know Liston Cook very well. He and I have been friends a long time. He's a good man."

Sisson moved to the edge of his seat. "Did he hire Culpepper personally?"

"No. I don't think so. I think his chief of staff did."

Sisson set the bottle on the floor. "What's *his* name?"

"Philip Livingston. Why?"

"Sierra has people everywhere." Sisson rose from the sofa and walked to the front window. He pushed aside the curtain and peered out from the side. "There's nothing they can't infiltrate."

"I don't think they have this guy." Paul picked up his cell phone and placed a call. Culpepper answered on the second ring. When he learned that Sisson was at Paul's house, he insisted on joining them.

"I don't like it," Sisson said when Paul hung up from the call. "I didn't come here to see him. I came to see you."

"Why did you come to me?"

"You called." Sisson moved away from the window. "I was going to make a run for it, but then I looked you up."

"Looked me up?"

"On the Internet. Saw what you did in Afghanistan to help defeat the Russians. And then your wife dying on 9/11." He took a seat on the sofa and looked Paul in the eye. "I'm trusting you with my life. The stuff I've told you could get me killed. They're already after me."

"Who?"

"Sierra."

"How do you know?"

"You read about the men they arrested in Chicago?"

"Yes," Paul nodded. "That was strange. The van and the pickup truck."

"That was Sierra."

"Why didn't they get you out, too?"

"Because I didn't follow the plan. I saw a chance to get out and I took it. But they tracked me with the chip."

"The chip?"

"A tracking chip embedded in my shoulder. And that's not the worst of it."

"What do you mean?"

"The implants in my brain."

The words fell with a thud on Paul. He was certain Sisson was crazy and in an instant, images of what might happen next flashed through his mind. He pushed aside the fear and did his best to keep the conversation going. "What kind of implants?"

"You don't believe me," Sisson said with a gesture of his hand. "Nobody does. They put these implants in your brain that help with the personality alteration. Makes you do things no one else is capable of doing. And when you do them, they make you feel like it's okay and then the guilt goes away. Only mine didn't work so well. They tried to change it before, but I managed to put them off and then this mission came up and we had to get ready. Takes a few weeks to get adjusted to a new implant and we didn't have the time. But I saw how the others acted with theirs and I didn't want a new one."

"Where did you—"

The doorbell rang, interrupting their conversation. Sisson jumped to his feet and hurried to the window. Paul started toward the door. "Relax," he said. "This is probably Culpepper." He looked through the peephole. "Yeah. That's him."

Sisson grabbed Paul's arm. "Are you sure that's him?"

"Yes," Paul nodded. "That's him." He shrugged free and reached for the door. Sisson tugged on his arm. Paul glared at him. "What are you doing?"

"Let me check out back."

"He's alone. I can see him standing right out there." The doorbell rang again. "Nothing's going to happen."

"Just wait," Sisson insisted. "Let me check out back."

Paul stood near the door while Sisson walked to the kitchen. He reached for the doorknob to open the door, then Sisson called to him, "We got a problem."

Paul walked to the kitchen and looked out the window. Through the bushes he saw a van parked in the alley behind the house. Four men, crouching low, made their way across the yard toward them.

"I tried to tell you. They have people everywhere." Sisson pushed past Paul. "Your friend Culpepper works for Sierra."

They started back toward the living room, but as they neared the hall the back door flew open and four men rushed inside. Sisson caught the first one with a jab to the jaw. The man's knees buckled and he fell to the floor. A second man grabbed his arm and caught him in a headlock. A third landed a blow to Sisson's stomach that made him gasp for breath. At the same time, a fourth man grabbed Paul, pinning his arms to his side. In less than a minute, both men lay on the floor, hands behind their backs and bound with a zip tie.

Culpepper appeared at the kitchen door. A satisfied grin turned up the corners of his mouth. "You two look rather ridiculous lying down there."

Paul's face turned red with anger. "You were with Sierra all the time."

"Yeah," Culpepper chuckled. "And you were too stupid to notice." He looked over at the others and gestured with his hand. "Get them out of here."

The first two men slipped their arms beneath Sisson's and lifted him from the floor. Paul struggled to stand on his own and looked Culpepper in the eye.

"What?" Culpepper glared. "You want them to cut you loose so you can take a swing at me?" Paul stared at him. Culpepper shook his head. "You should be glad they didn't kill you right here."

Someone opened the back door, then the four men hustled Paul and Sisson down the back steps and across the yard toward the van.

CHAPTER 92
WASHINGTON, D.C.

ESTHER TURNED THE CAR onto the street near Paul's house and pressed the gas pedal. The car picked up speed. *I hope no one backs out in front of me.* Two blocks later, Paul's house came into view. A car was parked at the curb and she was certain the door to the house was open. She lifted her foot from the gas pedal and pressed it hard against the brake. The nose of the car dove as the car came to a stop. If someone was there, she didn't want them to see her. She turned left and drove toward the middle of the block. Halfway to the next corner, she came to the alley and turned right.

Up ahead, a van sat behind Paul's house. Tires on the right side were in the grass. She let the car idle toward it. As she drew nearer, the backyard came into view and she scanned it quickly for any sign of trouble. The hood of the car came even with the front bumper of the van, and from the corner of her eye she saw the back door of the house swing open. She brought the car to a stop and raised herself up in the seat to see over the hood of the van.

Two men hurried toward her, bringing someone with them. Behind them, two more men held Paul. From the look of it, his arms were bound behind his back. She gasped at the sight of it. Then, without thinking of what to do, she pressed her foot against the gas pedal and sped down the alley. At the cross street, she turned left and doubled back, coming around the block toward the end of the alley.

As she came around the corner, the van emerged from the alley and turned in front of her. She turned off the street into a driveway and put the car out of sight. She sat there a moment, waiting for the van to get a head start and rested her hands along the top of the steering wheel. For the first time, she noticed her hands were shaking. Her heart raced and tears formed in her eyes. She choked them back and whispered to herself, "Stay calm." She took a deep breath. "This will work out right if I just stay calm." Beyond the driveway was a child's swing set with a slide mounted to one side. She focused on it and thought of Paul, the twinkle in his eyes when he smiled and the touch of his hand in hers.

"I'm not letting it end like this," she said to herself, this time louder and with determination. She wiped her eyes with her fingertips, put the car in reverse, and backed toward the street. To the left, she saw the van reach the next corner and make the turn. She put the car in gear, pressed her foot on the gas pedal, and started in that direction.

* * *

Inside the van, Sisson and Paul sat side by side opposite the sliding door, their backs to the wall behind the driver. Two men sat between them and the door. As the van made the corner, Sisson scooted his feet up beneath his knees with his heels pressed against the back of his thighs. Without warning, he sprang forward, striking the nearest man with a head butt to the nose. Blood spurted down the man's face and onto his chest. He howled in pain.

Paul, caught off guard by Sisson's move, scrambled to his knees and elbowed his way to the door. He twisted to one side, turned his back to the door, and grasped the handle with his right hand. Though bound at the wrists, he managed to wrap his fingers around it and pressed it tight against his palm. Then he pushed off with a leap toward the back of the van in an attempt to slide the door open. To his surprise, the latch moved and the door slid open, but the movement threw him off balance and he landed facedown on the floor of the van. Desperate to escape, he rolled toward the door, only to feel a hand come over his shoulder as a man who'd been in the passenger seat now climbed in back. He kicked Paul aside with his foot and elbowed Sisson in the face, then grabbed the door handle and pulled the door closed.

At the same time, the other man in back leaned toward Sisson. He held a syringe that was pointed toward Sisson's shoulder. He sank the needle in and depressed the plunger. Within seconds, Sisson's eyes rolled up in his head and he collapsed to the floor. Just as quickly, the man who'd been in the passenger seat produced a second needle and plunged it into Paul's thigh.

* * *

Esther followed the van as it made its way onto the Beltway. She picked up the iPhone from the seat and called Brody. The call rolled over to voice mail, and the van turned onto the Dulles Toll Road. Past the interchange with Sully Road, the van made a right and drove away from the passenger terminal. Near the north end of the runway, it turned left and disappeared inside a hangar. Esther brought the car to a stop and walked toward the building. Before she reached it, a Learjet rolled out of the hangar and turned onto the taxiway. As it passed by she used the iPhone and took a picture of the tail, then she ran back to the car. Her mind raced as she thought of what to do.

A fence lined the apron on either side of the hangar, but near the corner of the building was a gate with a paved driveway. She could ram the gate, drive onto the runway, and stop the plane, which would result in her arrest. It was against the law to breach the security fence and there would be a long interview with the FBI. Or, she could sit and wait— that was the safe thing to do. That's what she did with Ephraim, that's what he wanted her to do— stay out of the way, avoid the risk, let him handle it.

But that's what got him killed. And I'm too old to play it safe now. She put the car in gear, pressed the gas pedal, and shoved it to the floor. The car shot forward toward the fence. She gripped the steering wheel tightly with both hands and held on.

Sparks flew as the car struck the gate. For an instant it seemed to strain against the chain that held it in place, then something broke and pieces flew through the air. She steered the car onto the apron and around to the front of the hangar. Ahead she saw the Learjet, already on the taxiway. Tires on the car squealed as she made the turn onto the pavement and drove in that direction. But before she could reach the plane, a police car appeared in her rearview mirror. Blue lights flashing, it came up behind her. "Stop immediately," a voice from the car's loudspeaker said.

Esther grabbed her cell phone and called Brody. "I'm on the runway at Dulles," she blurted out. "Call somebody. Airport police are about to stop me."

"What are you doing out there?"

"They put Paul on a Learjet. He's in trouble. I'm trying to stop them."

"Esther," Brody replied with unusual calm, "you have to stop."

"Why?"

"The police will treat you as a terrorist threat. They'll start shooting."

"Can't they read my license number and find out who I am?"

"Yes. And they will, right after they shoot you and make you stop. So, stop the car," he said in an even, calm tone. "I'll make a call."

Up ahead, another plane turned onto the taxiway and followed behind the Learjet. There was no hope of reaching it now without dashing onto the main runway. She lifted her foot from the gas pedal and brought the car to a stop. Instantly, she was surrounded by police vehicles.

"This is going to take a while," she said to herself.

CHAPTER 93
VIRGINIA

THE NEXT DAY FOUND MCNEIL and his campaign team back in Florida. Early that morning, under the pretense of discussing an upcoming event, he met Trent Paine in the hotel ballroom. While they talked, McNeil wandered across the room. The security detail followed. McNeil glanced in their direction. "Guys, could you give us a little space?" They lingered near the center of the room while McNeil and Trent moved behind a row of tables toward the service entrance.

In spite of the early hour, hotel staff scurried about moving chairs, tables, and carts of dishes. McNeil worked his way among them and moved closer to the door.

"Give me your car keys," he said, quietly.

"No way," Trent said, shaking his head. "I'm not doing that again."

"Give them to me," McNeil insisted. "I have something I have to do."

Trent took the keys from his pocket. "Caldwell will kill me."

McNeil took the keys in his hand. "I'm going to step out for the day," he said, just above a whisper.

Trent's eyes were wide. "You're going to do what?"

"Relax," McNeil said with a confident tone. "You can handle the schedule."

"But we have meetings," Trent protested. "Donors and supporters who expect to see you."

"I checked. We don't have anything major until this evening. Get Caldwell to stand in for me. I'll be back tonight."

"I haven't seen Caldwell in two days. You can't just run out like this," Trent argued. "What about the press? They'll want to know where you are."

"It'll be okay. You'll think of something." McNeil patted him on the shoulder. "Just tell them I had a scheduling conflict." He glanced warily around the room. Two men came from the service corridor carrying a large table. McNeil stepped back to let them pass. As the table went by, momentarily shielding him from view, he ducked quickly into the hall and was gone.

From the hotel, McNeil drove to the airport and boarded a private plane. Two hours later, he landed in Virginia at the Shenandoah Valley Regional Airport, not far from where he attended college. A rental car was waiting when he arrived. He settled behind the steering wheel and drove south. There were no reporters to hound him and no staff members to pepper him with comments and reminders— just the open road before him and the mountains of Virginia.

Half an hour later, he turned off the interstate and wound through the countryside to Kerrs Creek, a rural community north of Lexington. When he reached the fire station, located in the center of town, he turned left onto Still House Road and drove up the slope of a mountain to the Kerrs Creek Methodist Church. The parking lot was empty except for a pickup truck parked in back. McNeil brought the car to a stop beside it and got out.

The church was a wooden building with plain white siding and a modest steeple on top. Built on a slope, it had a fellowship hall in the basement with two classrooms at one end and a kitchen at the other. McNeil entered the building through the basement door and looked around a moment, then started upstairs.

As he came into the sanctuary, he saw a man down front, kneeling at the altar rail. Dressed in a dark blue suit, he had gray hair and even from a distance his hands looked weathered and worn. He was older now, well past eighty, and a little frail, but McNeil recognized him instantly. He was Nelson Hooper.

Born the son of a Methodist bishop and a Baptist preacher's daughter, Hooper's career as a pastor came early. He preached his first sermon when he was nine years old, conducted his first weeklong revival when he was sixteen, and for as long as he could remember he never wanted to be anything except a minister of the Gospel. With hard work and a uniquely genuine interest in people, he rose through the ranks of the Methodist church and, like his father, became a bishop. On the way to the top, he served eight years as pastor of the Methodist church in Lexington, a few blocks from the campus of Washington and Lee University. He met McNeil, a young student at the time, during his third year at the church, and during a youth retreat that summer McNeil became a Christian. Hooper went on to become bishop and McNeil became governor. When Hooper reached mandatory retirement age, he asked for an appointment to a struggling local church in need of a pastor. Kerrs Creek was the third congregation he'd nurtured back to health.

At the sound of McNeil's footsteps, Hooper turned to look over his shoulder and in a tired voice called out, "Care to join me?"

"I didn't mean to disturb you."

"You're not disturbing me. I heard the car when you drove up." Hooper patted the altar rail with his left hand. "Join me."

McNeil made his way to the altar and knelt. Hooper turned to look at him. McNeil smiled. "Good to see you. It's been a while."

"Where's your campaign?" Hooper replied in a deadpan voice. "With the bus and the band and the news reporters?"

"I ran away for the day."

"You in trouble?"

"No, sir."

"Got a woman pregnant? Isn't that what happens to most politicians these days? Get somebody pregnant, lie about it until the reporters find out, then act as if they 'accept responsibility.'"

"No, sir. It's not that."

Hooper's blue eyes were clear and his gaze intense. "It's not … you know … a man, is it?"

"No," McNeil chuckled. "It's not that, either."

Hooper rolled his hip to one side and slid to a sitting position on the altar cushion. "Then maybe you should tell me what's brought you all the way out here."

McNeil took a seat beside him. "I've worked hard to position myself as the education candidate. And I've done my best to stay faithful to the message— that people should work hard, make good decisions, solve their own problems and not look to the government for help. But I—"

"That's the conservative message," Hooper interrupted.

"Yes. And I've done my—"

"It's a political message," Hooper continued. "Not the Gospel."

"Well … I never thought of it that way, but I guess you're right."

"Don't feel bad. Not many others have seen it that way, either. And don't get me wrong. I understand it's a message that gets Republicans elected. People who think of themselves as Christians hear that message and it sounds good to them— like the good old American way— and they equate that with going to church and being a good person and it sounds to them like if they accept what you're saying and vote for you, they'll be supporting the Gospel. So they vote for you." Hooper shook his head. "But it's not the Gospel."

"Yeah," McNeil nodded. "I see your point."

"Didn't mean to preach to you. Old habit of mine." Hooper looked away. "So, what's happened to your message? Stop working?"

"No. It's working fine for the crowds. They're responding as expected." McNeil had a thin, tight smile. "It's working for them, it's just not working for me anymore."

"Where'd you get this message?"

"College, I think."

"And Henry Caldwell."

"Yes, sir," McNeil nodded again. "Henry has been with me a long time."

"Who else you seeing? Like that, I mean. You got a pastor?"

"Not really a pastor like when I was with you. I guess the person I see most often like that, to talk and pray with, is Morris Wythe."

"Morris Wythe," Hooper scoffed. "He's a salesman, not a pastor."

"What do you mean?"

"He gets a crowd of people together, gives them some good music, whips them up emotionally, then he tells them a version of the message you described, only he wraps a little Scripture around it."

"His church in Nashville is huge. Has his own television network."

"It's nothing but Christian consumerism." Hooper had a dismissive tone. "He sells religious goods and services but he isn't making disciples. And he doesn't pass the test."

McNeil frowned. "What test?"

"There's a parable Jesus used to describe Believers. The ones who make it to heaven are sheep and the ones who don't are goats. And he describes a scene where he separates the sheep from the goats. The sheep go to heaven, the goats go to eternal judgment."

"I remember something about that."

"It's the one where he said to the goats, 'I was sick and you didn't care for me, hungry and you gave me nothing to eat, in prison and you never came to visit me.'"

"Okay."

"Believers were the ones who did those things— cared for the sick, fed the hungry, visited the prisoners. Morris Wythe's message isn't about that. His message is about turning the poor out into the street and letting them fend for themselves. It's about letting the sick die. And filling the prisons with anyone who gets in the way." Hooper wagged his finger. "That's not the Gospel. And if he's been telling you that all this time, it's no wonder you can't see the difference."

"I never thought of it like that."

"Well, think about it. The true Believers care for the sheep. I was sick, in prison, hungry, you cared for me. That's the mark of true Believers. Most people think of that as the Social Gospel and give it a bad name. But Jesus said those who ignore the poor, the sick, the imprisoned, ignore him."

They talked for almost an hour and as they did, McNeil sensed his spirit coming alive in a way he hadn't known in a long time. The heavy sadness he'd felt before— watching the workers on the farm and the children in the field— melted away. Then, all too soon, Hooper glanced at his watch. "It's getting late. The morning's almost gone."

"Yes, it is," McNeil sighed. "I suppose I should get started back."

"Nonsense." Hooper slapped him on the knee. "It's almost lunchtime. Come on." He pushed himself up from the cushion and stood. "Come to the house with me. I'll find something for us to eat."

"I really should head back. They'll be looking for me."

"Nope." Hooper took him by the arm. "You have to eat. Besides, I'm not through talking about this." He guided McNeil toward the door. "We'll take your car. That way, you can drive while I talk."

*   *   *

After lunch with Hooper, McNeil dropped him at the church, then drove toward the airport. As he rode through the Virginia countryside, he called Nikki. Any hope he had of going unnoticed vanished when she answered the phone.

"Where are you?" she shouted.

"Virginia."

"Virginia?" she exclaimed, her voice growing more shrill. "Where in Virginia?"

"Lexington. Well ..." He paused to correct himself. "Almost to Lexington. I went to see Nelson Hooper."

"Nelson Hooper? Do you realize most of the free world is looking for you?"

"Relax," he soothed. "I told Trent before I left. And I had my cell phone. It didn't ring once."

"Trent can't take care of himself, much less a presidential campaign. And your phone didn't ring because there's no service up there in the mountains. Check it now."

He glanced at the screen and saw he'd missed a hundred calls. "Yeah, I see what you mean."

"You blew an entire day with some weak-minded, ineffective, small-town preacher. Are you out of your mind? We are running a national campaign, spending hundreds of millions of dollars trying to win, and you're in some backwoods town spending the day reliving old memories from college."

"It wasn't old memories from college," McNeil countered. "I finally remembered why I was interested in politics in the first place. And let me tell you, we are way off message."

"What do you mean?"

"We're on the opposite side of the Gospel on most of the issues. There isn't a place—"

"Look," she said, cutting him off. "I don't care about the Gospel. This is a political campaign and the only thing I'm interested in is winning. Now, you get back to Florida and stop this nonsense."

*　　*　　*

As Caldwell came through the airport in Orlando, he felt the phone in his pocket vibrate. He took it out and glanced at the screen as he walked down the corridor. A message appeared from Nikki.

"He spent the day with Nelson Hooper in Virginia."

"Why?" he texted back.

"The message is a mess. Get him under control NOW."

Caldwell stepped from the corridor to a chair in an empty gate area. He took a seat and placed a call to Carter Hewes. The call went to voice mail and Caldwell redialed the number. Hewes answered on the second ring. "I wondered how long it would take for you to call."

"Where are you?"

"Los Angeles. Sunny, warm California."

"We need you back here."

"Maybe you should talk to the candidate about that. He fired me. Remember?"

"Well, I'm hiring you back."

"Did you talk to Trent about that?"

"We're going to New York for the morning talk shows. Meet me there."

"When?"

"Just get on a plane now. And call me when you get there."

CHAPTER 94
WASHINGTON, D.C.

TALKING HER WAY OUT of trouble at the airport proved to be an all-night ordeal. Esther didn't reach the office until almost noon. A news reporter was waiting for her when she arrived but she brushed him aside and walked down the hall to her office. There, she logged on to the Internet and went to the FAA website. Using the picture from her iPhone, she entered the number from the tail of the Learjet and learned the plane was owned by AIP Aircraft. She scrolled to the bottom of the page, found a phone number for the FAA and placed a call.

After a frustrating trip through the phone system, she reached Scott Cunningham, a supervisor in the FAA's flight services division. He provided helpful information about the leasing company— they had an office on K Street, just a few blocks away— but when she asked for the destination of the plane, Cunningham refused. "I can't give you that information."

"Why not?"

"We're not allowed."

"Flight plans are filed with the FAA. You're a government agency, which makes the plan a public document. Why can't you tell me?"

"The operator has filed a certification."

"What kind of certification?"

"They say that disclosure of their flight plans poses a security threat."

"Who's the operator?"

"I can't tell you."

"They filed a certification saying they should be exempt from disclosure and you can't tell me who they are?"

"Okay," he sighed. "The aircraft is leased to something called Sierra Resources."

Esther sat up straight in her chair. "And where did the plane go?"

"I can't—"

She slapped her hand on the desk. "Don't tell me what you can't do! Tell me where the plane went."

"Out of the country. But that's all I can—"

"Out of the country where?" she shouted. "Where is it going?"

Cunningham lowered his voice. "Mexico," he said, finally.

Esther switched phone lines and called Brody. She began talking as soon as he answered. "They have Paul."

"This isn't a secure line."

"They grabbed him from his house and put him on a plane to Mexico."

"Esther, I really can't—"

"The plane is owned by a company called AIP Aircraft. It's leased to Sierra Resources." She turned to the laptop on her desk. "I'm emailing information about the plane to you right now. I want to know exactly where that plane went and I need it in the next ten minutes." She ended the call without waiting for a response.

Finally able to catch her breath, Esther leaned back in the chair and closed her eyes. As she relaxed, she noticed a sweaty odor. She leaned forward, lifted the collar of her blouse to her nose and took a sniff. "Whew," she grimaced. "I need a shower." She rose from her chair, picked up her purse, and started toward the hall.

Out front, she noticed the reporter was gone, but when she reached her house he was waiting on the steps for her with a cameraman in tow. "You can't ignore me," he warned as she approached. A light on the camera came on. The reporter shoved a microphone toward her. "I understand you were arrested last night for crashing a gate with your car at Dulles Airport. Why did you do that?"

She placed the key in the lock to open the door. "I have nothing to say."

"The police say you were chasing a plane down the runway."

She looked directly at the camera. "I have nothing to say." Then she pushed open the door and went inside.

As she pushed the door closed, a voice spoke from the opposite side of the room. "They won't go away, you know." Startled by the sound, she let out a gasp and clasped her hand to her chest, then she saw Brody sitting in a chair near the fireplace. "Didn't mean to scare you."

She glared at him. "What did you expect?"

"This is a matter for the FBI, Esther. We can't get involved."

"Can't get involved? You get involved in everything else. What do you mean you can't get involved?"

"We are an agency of the Israeli government."

"No, *you* are. Not me. I'm an American citizen."

"All the more critical. An agency of the Israeli government can't help an American citizen on American soil. It just can't be done."

"Listen to me, Brody. I tried to explain this to you before. I'll try one more time. They have Paul."

"Who has him?"

"Sierra Resources. They came to his house with a van. Snatched him from his own home. Put him on a plane and flew him to Mexico."

"How do you know this?"

"I saw them."

"You were there?"

"I went over there. Saw a car out front. The door was open. I went around back. A van was parked in the alley. About the time I arrived, they came out of the house with Paul and someone else."

"Who was the other person?"

"I don't know, but I need you to find out where that plane went."

"I cannot do that. This is beyond our jurisdiction. The center at Beersheba will not allow it."

"Jurisdiction! You're an Israeli citizen. You don't have jurisdiction for anything. They have Paul. I have to get him back."

"I am sorry. I just can't get involved."

"Fine," she snarled. "I'll do this myself."

CHAPTER 95
MEXICO

SISSON AWAKENED TO FIND he was strapped to a table in an examination room. He'd been there before— the tiled walls with the stark white ceiling and the lights— but he couldn't remember where it was located and he wasn't sure he'd ever known. Snippets of memories flashed in his mind. A plane landing in the desert. An SUV and a ride through the night.

A moment later, a door opened. Footsteps echoed through the room as someone approached. He tried to twist his head around to see but a strap across his forehead held him in place.

"Do not try," a familiar voice warned. "It will only make things worse."

There was a rustling sound, followed by the squeak of a chair, then Dr. Walcott appeared beside him, seated on a stool. "And how are you today, Thirty-one?"

"My name is Bill Sisson."

Walcott had a surprised look. "Who told you that lie?"

"It's not a lie. And no one told me. I remembered it."

"And when did this memory occur?"

"A few months ago."

Walcott leaned out of sight. "You are sure it was a memory?"

"Yes."

There was a clicking sound, and a jolt of electricity shot through Sisson's body. His legs became straight and rigid, his head snapped back, and his teeth clenched tight. After what seemed like forever, the shock subsided and Walcott appeared once again.

"Shall we try that once more? When did this memory occur?"

"About three months ago."

"Three months," Walcott mused. "I need more specific information." He turned to the monitor on a nearby cart and pressed a key on the keyboard. "Tell me about the memory."

"We were in Juarez, looking for Ramon Tijerina. They kicked open a door and we went inside and I remembered my name."

"Where were you? Specifically."

"A house."

"Whose house?"

"I don't know."

"What did you see?"

"A kitchen. With a table and chairs. And the smell of fish cooking on the stove."

"Fish. What kind of fish?"

"I don't know what kind it was. It smelled like fish my mother cooked when we were young. We caught it in the bay. An ice chest full of them, and I remember cleaning them, and she cooked them."

"Which came first— the smell or the memory?"

"The smell."

"Ahh," Walcott nodded. "Now we are getting somewhere."

CHAPTER 96
NEW YORK

THE FOLLOWING DAY, McNeil watched from the back seat of the car as the city moved past. When the motorcade reached Fortieth Street it turned and stopped at the curb across from Bryant Park. The Public Library building stood at one end. A temporary stage was erected near the steps. People jammed the park all the way to Sixth Avenue. McNeil sat in the car and looked out at them.

"Lots of people," he observed.

"The advance team did a great job," Trent replied. "Got all our people out. Bussed in some extras from Hoboken, but we didn't really need them. They chose a great location. We're right in the middle of midtown."

From the car, McNeil saw camera crews gathered near the platform and at strategic locations on either corner. "Looks like we're getting good coverage. I see all the networks. Local stations. Some from New Jersey."

"Yes," Trent agreed. "But we need to get moving. They have a short window and if we hit it just right, we can get you on in every major market in the country. Come on," he opened the door. "Let's go."

McNeil stepped out on the street side of the car and straightened his jacket. The security detail formed around him. Trent came from the opposite side and took him by the elbow. "We're right this way. Everything is set up and waiting. All you have to do is wave to the crowd, walk to the podium, and give the speech. The mayor will introduce you. His name is Lewis Annenberg."

Two steps from the car, the crowd caught sight of them and began chanting, "Da-vid! Da-vid! Da-vid!" McNeil waved to them as he made his way to the sidewalk and into the park. Police and the security team cordoned off a path to the podium and McNeil slowly worked in that direction, shaking hands as he went. When he finally drew near the platform, Mayor Annenberg stepped to the microphone.

"Ladies and gentlemen, let's give a real New York City welcome to the next president of the United States, Governor David McNeil."

Noise from the crowd reached a deafening level as McNeil appeared onstage. He paused there a moment, waving and pointing to people near the front that he thought looked familiar then, after a minute or two more, he stepped to the podium.

"It's great to be in New York City!" The crowd roared its approval. "The world may have other cities, but when they want to see the best humanity has to offer, when they want to see how life should be lived and how a city should operate, they come here to New York." The crowd gave a hearty response.

"And that's why I've come here today. To visit the finest citizens this country has to offer." The crowd was ecstatic. He stepped back a moment and enjoyed the adulation. When they grew quieter, he squared his shoulders and launched into his standard campaign speech about the need for immigration reform. Things went well as he spoke about the need to define the manner in which people immigrate, the strain unregulated immigrants placed on social services, and the need to keep our borders secure from terrorists, but about halfway through that presentation he digressed from the prepared text.

"That's the immigrant side of the issue. They come here illegally, take jobs, and pay no income tax. But there's another side of that problem, and that's the employer's side. One can understand the motivation of a man or woman from Mexico who swims the river or pays an exorbitant price to a courier to get them here. They're just looking for a way to provide for their families. They want the same things for their families that you want for yours. And if you were in their position, you might consider doing exactly what they're doing. But what about the employer who hires them, often paying them at a rate far below minimum wage, and in some cases subjecting illegal immigrants to treatment as harsh as slavery?" The crowd became quiet and still. "That crime— the crime of hiring illegal immigrants at the expense of Americans, taking advantage of them with substandard wages, and subjecting them to slave-like working conditions— that crime is worse than the immigrant who comes here without proper documentation."

For the next fifteen minutes McNeil delivered a scathing rebuke of the nation's business community. Citing facts and statistics, he ticked off a list of business sectors and major corporations— calling them by name— that violated current law. And then he served notice, "When I'm elected president, these practices will stop. We'll end the market for slave labor in this country and those employers who fail or refuse to comply will find themselves in jail. We will no longer be the nation of greed and consumption but of self-sacrifice and justice. Elect me as your president and we're going after the immigration issue, but we're starting at the top where the real crime occurs."

When he concluded, the crowd responded with polite applause, but nothing like the pandemonium that had reigned before. News reporters, however, rushed to get an interview. Unlike past events, McNeil waited for them and spent the next hour at the edge of the platform where he patiently answered their questions. He explained in detail the intricacies of the immigration issue and how starting at the top, with employers, would provide a real and lasting solution.

"This is a departure from your earlier positions," one reporter suggested. "Why the sudden shift?"

"It's not a departure. It's the other half of the issue. And I only talked about immigration today. There's more to most of the issues we face."

"Can we expect similar departures on budget and tax issues?"

"You can expect to hear from my heart. We can no longer be defined by greed, consumption, and waste. We have to once again become a leader in justice and self-sacrifice."

Trent Paine was excited by what he heard, but most of the staff stood by in shock, helplessly watching as the message they'd spent years crafting came unwound.

CHAPTER 97
WASHINGTON, D.C.

AFTER TALKING TO PAUL, Rutledge downloaded a copy of *The Protocols of the Learned Elders of Zion*. He was seated at his desk reading and making notes when Don Harper arrived. Rutledge glanced up as he approached. "Something wrong?" He held a pen in his left hand and twirled it between his fingers while he waited for a response.

"The Attorney General's office called earlier today," Harper began.

Rutledge braced for trouble. "What did they have to say?"

Harper pulled a chair from a nearby desk, brought it over, and took a seat. "They're continuing to prepare the case against McNeil and Sierra Resources, and they like what you did. But because of the political nature of the matter, they think they need to make certain they have everything in order."

Rutledge tossed aside his pen. "They're getting pressure from someone to back off."

"No," Harper shook his head. "So far as I know, no one is suggesting anything to them one way or the other." He folded his arms across his chest. "You interviewed Christopher Wilson and spoke with people from his campaign."

"Right," Rutledge nodded. "They were very cooperative. They don't actually think he had something to do with this, do they?"

"I can't see how they would. But they want you to do the same with McNeil."

Rutledge leaned forward in his seat and his eyes brightened. "They want me to talk to McNeil?"

"They want you to try," Harper smiled. "So that, in the interest of fairness, it looks like you gave him the opportunity to present his side while there was still time to influence the case. Before it goes to trial."

Rutledge slumped back in his chair as quickly deflated as he'd been encouraged. "Is it going to trial?"

"That's the plan. Isn't that what you expected?"

"It's what I wanted." Rutledge looked away. "I'm not sure what I expected."

"Set it up just like you did the others." Harper pushed himself up from the chair. "You make the contact. You determine the time and place."

"You know he'll deny any involvement."

Harper lingered near the desk. "I'm wondering if you'll even get an interview, but you have to give him the opportunity."

"And when I try to pin him down on details of the transactions, he'll say he didn't know anything about it. And he'll deny knowing about the break-in at Liston Cook's offices." Rutledge folded his hands behind his head. "We'll wind up with the campaign manager and the accountants."

"Maybe the chief of staff." Harper turned away. He called over his shoulder as he started up the stairs, "But the case isn't going anywhere without the interview. So set it up."

* * *

Meanwhile, on the island of Rhodes, deep inside the Knights Castle, Spoleto held an iPad and stared at the screen. From a news website he watched a video of McNeil's remarks to the press in New York. Veins in his neck and across his forehead pulsed.

Russo stood to his right. Spoleto looked up at him. "You saw this already?"

"Yes. I checked the site for news, to keep up with developments, and I saw it. I brought it to you as soon as I saw what happened."

"In one speech, he destroyed what we took a lifetime to build. In one speech!" he shouted. "All the planning and maneuvering. And now it is gone."

"Perhaps not."

"What could save us now?"

"Do we have polling results?"

"You sound like a politician."

"I have read the messages. They use polls frequently to test the strength of an event or a speech idea. Have they tested this?"

"They don't need to." Spoleto tossed the iPad onto the desk. "You saw the crowd reaction right there on the video. We are done." Russo picked up the iPad and ran his finger over the screen to make certain it still worked. Spoleto propped an elbow on the armrest and leaned to one side. "Get Wallace Jordan."

Russo opened an email account on the iPad and stood ready to type. "What would you like to say?"

Spoleto glared at him. "You are screening my calls. Now you are screening my remarks?"

"I am prepared to type what you say."

"I don't want to send an email," Spoleto barked. "I want to talk to him. Get him on the phone. I want to talk with him. Now!"

Russo scrolled through his contacts list and found the number, then picked up a landline and placed the call. When he was on the line, Spoleto grabbed the receiver.

"You need to talk to them."

"I tried," Jordan replied. "But they wouldn't listen to me."

"You were supposed to fix this."

"I delivered the message. It was received. But compliance was a problem."

"Then I must make alternative arrangements." Spoleto handed the phone to Russo. When it was safely in the cradle, he leaned back in his chair. "You tried to reach Caldwell earlier?"

"Yes. But he did not respond."

"Very well," Spoleto said, his voice calm and even. "Contact Sierra. Find out when they will be ready."

CHAPTER 98
MEXICO

THE ROOM SPUN AROUND and around as Paul struggled to open his eyes. Dizzy and disoriented, he tried his best to focus on the images before him, but the more he tried the more nauseated he became. His stomach rumbled and a sour taste filled his mouth. He swallowed hard to keep from vomiting and closed his eyes.

Voices around him were clear and crisp and there was the click of heels against a hard surface. He imagined he was lying on a tile floor but when he tried to raise himself up to see, he found his arms were bound at the wrist. His legs were bound at the ankles. He was reclined at an angle— of that he was certain by the pressure of his body against a hard surface— but he had no idea where he was or why he was there.

Footsteps came toward him. A hand took hold of his arm. Something cold pressed against the bare skin of his left shoulder. Then a sharp pain shot down his arm. Someone stood to his right with a hand pressed against the back of his head, tipping him forward. A sharp pain pierced his neck. After a few minutes, the footsteps trailed away and he heard the sound of a door closing. The room fell silent but for the constant beep of a machine. He forced open his eyes once more. Through his disoriented haze, he saw there were electrodes attached to his arms, legs, and chest. Wires ran from them to monitoring equipment that sat on a cart to the right. An IV bag hung on a bracket to the left. Liquid from it dripped into a tube that was attached to the back of his left hand.

The sour taste returned to his mouth. He swallowed hard, closed his eyes, and tried to relax. In his mind he was sitting on the front porch at the farm in Texas. Across the driveway, tall green grass swayed in the breeze. He held a cup of coffee and seated next to him was Esther ... *Esther.* He thought of her and the way her eyes narrowed when she smiled. Remembering her made him smile, too, and he held her image until his sense of consciousness faded away.

Sometime later he awakened in a room, lying on a cot. His arms and legs were unrestrained and the machines were gone, as were the tubes, wires, and electrodes. The room was stark white with lights in the ceiling that cast a brilliant glare. He squinted and looked around to find he was alone. But for the cot, the room was empty. He rolled to a sitting position and glanced down at his arms. Red marks lined his wrists where the straps had been. Beneath his gown, splotches dotted his chest where the electrodes had been attached.

Just then, the door opened and three men rushed in. Dressed in black, they wore masks over their faces and rubber gloves on their hands. They grabbed him by the arms and pulled him from the table. When he resisted, they lifted him at the shoulders just high enough to get his feet off the floor, then carried him from the room. Down the hall they came to a steel door with a bolt across it. One of the men slid the bolt aside and opened the door.

Inside, the room was dark and damp. Water trickled from a spigot to the right. A stainless steel tub sat in the center. Before Paul could move, they grabbed his arms, pinned them behind his back, and secured them with a zip tie around his wrists. Then two of the men picked him up and carried him to the tub. Holding him by the ankles, they lowered him toward the water. As his head went under, he heard the door slam closed. In an instant he was beneath the water and lost in total darkness.

Paul kicked his feet wildly in an attempt to jerk free, but it was futile and only served to more rapidly deplete the oxygen in his lungs. After thirty seconds he'd reached his limit. He was certain death awaited him.

Suddenly he was back at the church in Arlington and he saw the cross on the altar table down front. He remembered thinking of Jesus and how it must have been for him to know he was about to die— the reality of the moment, stripped of all pretension, glamour, and sentiment. Just death and the cold, hard evil of someone bent on ending his life. Jesus faced that moment with more than resolve. He embraced it and found peace in surrendering himself to the will of God, a purpose established long before the Universe.

A voice spoke to him in words so clear they were all but audible. *"When you pass through the waters, I will be with you; and when you pass through the rivers, they will not sweep over you."* Paul recognized it as a verse from the book of Isaiah. He'd memorized it in Sunday school. As a child, it had seemed like a useless exercise— memorizing lines from books of the Bible— but now the words came to him like a promise.

Maybe that's how Jesus did it. Maybe he remembered the promise of why he'd come and he held on to it no matter what. Now Paul faced a similar moment— the stark reality that the men holding him beneath the water meant to kill him. Maybe if he held on to the promise of that verse he could make it through the moment that awaited him.

All of this passed through Paul's mind in an instant, not really as a series of conscious thoughts but as a sense of knowing. He was going to die. He was resolved to that fact. Yet God was with him, and whatever the outcome he was at peace. With confidence that God was in control, he exhaled and took a deep breath, resigned to ending his life then and there.

But at that exact moment, the men holding his ankles snatched him from the water. He came to the surface, choking and coughing as his body desperately attempted to rid his lungs of water and refill them with air.

"You must surrender," a voice said. "This is your hour of decision."

When Paul didn't answer, someone grabbed his ankles, lifted him in the air, and plunged him once more beneath the water. And once again, the process was repeated. He held his breath until it seemed his lungs would burst. At the brink of death, he found peace in the knowledge that whatever happened to him, God awaited him on the other side, and then he exhaled. And each time, at the last possible moment, they snatched him from the water.

After a dozen trips into the tank, a man entered the room carrying a board with straps attached. The board had a support at one end and they positioned it lengthwise over the tub so that the support held the end over the water. Then they lifted Paul from the floor and laid him on the board. Two more men fastened straps around his ankles, legs, and abdomen. Another pulled a strap tight across his forehead. When he was secured, a towel was thrown over his face and he felt his feet rise in the air.

He lay there a moment, wondering what was next, then a trickle of water splashed onto his forehead. The trickle became a torrent and he fought to keep the water from his mouth. He swallowed, gagged, then held his breath. Finally, he relaxed and once again surrendered to the inevitable. He forced himself to think of something else as he waited for death to arrive. An image of Esther appeared and he saw her smile. She was standing at the door of her townhouse and she started toward him, wearing a blue dress with a white collar and high-heeled shoes. It was a dress he'd helped her choose.

Seconds later the straps came off his body and the board slid from beneath him. Someone grabbed his ankles as his head once more plunged beneath the water. This time they left him under a little longer, and as the air escaped from his lungs he felt cold water rush in to fill the void.

He floated, weightless and free, then his feet touched something solid. A bright light appeared before him and he walked toward it. Before long he came to a meadow with flowers and soft grass. A noise came from the right and he turned to see a horse galloping toward him. On its back was a rider dressed in white. There was writing on the rider's chest but Paul couldn't quite make out what it said.

And then the light faded and the meadow grew dark. A voice spoke but he couldn't see from where it came and only heard the words, "You must surrender now. This is your hour of decision."

Suddenly, he was awake again, lying on the cot in the room with the stark white walls and the glaring light from the ceiling. But for the cot on which he lay, the room was empty and his gown was dry. He reached up with his hand and felt his head. His hair was dry, too.

CHAPTER 99
NEW YORK

AFTER THE SPEECH in Bryant Park, McNeil returned to the car. Trent joined him there. "What was that all about?"

"New message."

"The old one was working just fine."

"Not for me."

"Mr. Caldwell isn't going to like it."

"Henry will get over it." He looked across the seat at Trent. "I softened it a little with the comments. You know, told them it was the other half of what we'd talked about earlier."

"I heard. But I don't think that's going to help much."

"We'll see. What do we have next?"

"Two hours ..." Trent glanced at his watch. "Make that one hour at the hotel for lunch. Then we're up to CBS for the Letterman show."

"Great. I love Letterman. What hotel are we in? I might actually eat something today."

"Four Seasons. Up here on Fifty-Seventh Street. Mr. Caldwell wants to see you. I doubt you'll have time to eat."

The car came to a stop at the hotel. McNeil climbed from the car. Trent followed him inside to the elevator and they rode up to the tenth floor. Caldwell was waiting in the room. He glanced at Trent. "Give us a few minutes. I'll call you when we're through."

Trent retreated to the hall and was gone. McNeil made his way to the minibar and took out a can of Coca-Cola. "Got anything to eat?"

"I didn't want you in here to eat," Caldwell shouted. "I wanted you in here to knock some sense into your head."

"Henry," McNeil said coolly, "if you do that, I think you'll have a problem."

"What's that?"

McNeil reached in his pocket and pulled out a small pager. "I hit this panic button and five armed guards will kick down that door. You want to cause a scene like that right now?"

"It couldn't be much worse than the scene you just caused."

"Calm down. I got us more media coverage than we could ever buy. We're on in every major market, and the cable channels have us on a continuous loop."

"They have us on for the wrong reasons." He shoved open the bedroom door. "Get out here," he snapped, and Carter Hewes appeared. Caldwell turned to McNeil. "You still remember Carter, don't you?"

"He's my former chief of staff."

"Your current chief of staff."

"No," McNeil said, shaking his head. "I'm doing just fine without him."

"Just fine at blowing any chance of winning this election."

McNeil looked in Hewes' direction. "Carter, I'm sorry Henry dragged you up here, but you're still fired."

Caldwell leaped toward him. "Have you forgotten our friends on Rhodes?"

"No. I haven't forgotten them. And I've given them everything they asked. But their message is not mine. This one is." He paused to take a drink of Coke. "And not just on immigration but other things."

"Like what?"

"Aid for the poor, healthcare, abortion."

"What about them?"

"We can't just oppose abortion. If we're pro-life, it has to mean pro-life in every respect."

"Are you out of your mind? If you try that, the religious right will abandon you."

"Your money will dry up, too," Hewes added.

"That's right," Caldwell continued. "And worst of all, our friends in the Order will abandon you."

McNeil took an imperious tone. "I thought we were never to mention them by name."

"This is serious."

"I'm serious, too," McNeil responded. He took another sip, then set the can on the table. "Don't you think it odd that the so-called Christian Right embraces our policies— policies of racial extermination that would make Hitler look like an altar boy?"

"They don't think. The Christian Right hasn't had an original thought in years. And if they do, where will they go with it? Are they gonna vote Democrat?"

"That's just it. They look for an attack from the Left, but all the while it comes from the Right." He took a seat on a chair in the corner of the room. "This is the message, Henry. And we're taking it on the road."

"Where?"

"I've agreed to do Morris Wythe's church tour."

"With a message like this?"

"I don't think Morris cares so much about the message as he does about the bottom line. A tour will be good for him and that's all he's interested in."

"Look," Caldwell said, his voice a little calmer, "I've put off three calls from the Order today thinking I could come up here and set you straight. Now, I've got to think about what I have to do for my own good."

"Henry," McNeil said, wryly. "You got me into this. You have to see it to the end."

"What do you mean?"

"There's no way out for either of us except to win."

"Then I think we have no way out." Caldwell pushed open the door and disappeared down the hall.

Hewes looked over at McNeil. "Man, I'll give you this— when you blow up a campaign, you blow it up big." He adjusted the lapels of his jacket and headed toward the door.

McNeil tossed a limp wave in his direction. "See you next time, Carter."

As Hewes disappeared, Trent entered. "What was that about?"

"Nothing important," McNeil smiled. "What's next?"

*   *   *

Shortly after lunch, Taylor Rutledge telephoned Trent Paine about interviewing McNeil. He was noncommittal but agreed to discuss the matter. Rutledge, sensing the need to move quickly, caught a shuttle flight to New York. He caught up with Paine at Grossingers Home Bakery, a few doors from the CBS location where McNeil was taping an appearance. They sat at a table in back and ate a pastry while they talked.

"Okay, you said on the phone you needed to talk. I have five minutes. What did you want to talk about?"

"Not with you," Rutledge said in an exasperated tone. "I need to talk to McNeil."

"About what?"

"I'd rather it was just between me and him."

"I can't let you do that. Not without involving the lawyers."

"You involve the lawyers and this thing will get out of hand."

"If I don't involve them, I'll be on the street."

"I need to talk to him. When can we do it?"

"We're jammed on time. He's in the studio now, and when he gets out of that we have two meetings this evening."

"What about tomorrow?"

"We're off on a church tour with Morris Wythe. But I still have to know the topic. You gotta give me at least that much."

"I need to talk to him. That's all I can say. I can subpoena him, but if I do that, it's in the newspapers."

"Okay," Paine conceded. "You can talk to him. But it'll have to be later in the week."

"That's fine."

"In California."

"What?"

"Take it or leave it. If you meet us out there you could fly back with us and do the interview on the plane. That way I can have the lawyers available and no one will know what's going on."

"All right. But it has to be then. Otherwise, we're filing subpoenas, and whoever wants to know will find out."

"Catch up with us at Word of Life Tabernacle in Los Angeles. I'll get you on the plane." Trent stood. "But right now, I gotta go." He made his way to the door and slipped into the crowd that lined the sidewalk.

CHAPTER 100
HAGERSTOWN, MARYLAND

WHEN BRODY REFUSED TO HELP, Esther took matters into her own hands. Paul was gone. Men from Sierra Resources had taken him. He got in that situation, she reasoned, because he was trying to help his friend Liston Cook. That's how he came to be working with Brian Culpepper and, from the way Paul described him, she was certain Culpepper was involved in whatever had happened. She was counting on Cook to be as honorable a man as Paul believed him to be.

A quick check of Cook's campaign website showed he was traveling in Maryland that day. She drove from the city and caught up with him at Hagerstown. He was seated on the bus when she arrived.

"Esther," he smiled. "I didn't expect to see you. Bring Paul with you?"

She bristled at the question, wondering whether he knew and didn't want to say. "Paul has been working with Brian Culpepper doing what you asked him to do. Trying to find one of the men who broke into your office."

"I was just talking to Brian today. He said they had reached a dead end."

Esther's blood ran cold. What she'd suspected was true. Culpepper was working for Sierra. Now she wondered if Cook knew. She pushed aside the urge to say more and kept talking. "I can't tell you why right now, but I need to find out some information."

"What kind of information?"

She slid a piece of paper across the table toward him. "This is the tail number of an airplane. It took off from Dulles yesterday. I need to know where it went."

"The FAA won't tell you?"

"No," she said, with a shake of her head. "The plane is leased to Sierra Resources. They filed some kind of certificate claiming that release of the information would harm national security."

"Did you ask Paul about this?"

"Paul is … tied up right now." The irony of what she'd said did not escape her, but she kept talking. "That's why I'm here and not him."

"Sierra Resources is one of Paul's clients."

"I know."

"Think you ought to ask him first?"

"Some things are better left unsaid."

"Hmm," he nodded, glancing at the number once more. "I'll make a few calls and see what I can do."

She handed him a business card. "That's my number on the front. Cell phone is on the back. Please call me as soon as you know something." She stood to leave. "And it would be better if you kept this between us."

"Are you sure you know what you're getting into?"

"I know about Sierra," she replied, confidently.

"Not like this," he said with a shake of his head.

She was puzzled. "What do you mean?"

"Rendition, interrogation, assassinations. And not just against terrorists from the Middle East. All those bodies piling up along the Mexican border— they say they're from drug wars among competing cartels, but that's not what's happening. Those dead bodies are the work of Sierra, systematically eliminating the drug trade."

"On their own?"

"No, with taxpayers' money."

"Why don't you say something?"

"In my campaign?"

"Yes."

"I said nothing at all and they broke into my office. What do you think would happen if I started speaking out?"

"So, you know why they came to your office?"

A briefcase sat on the floor beside his feet. He laid it on his lap and opened it. "These came to one of my aides." He took out a stack of papers and handed them to her.

Esther flipped through them and realized they were documents from the email Brody told her about earlier. "The Order," she said, barely above a whisper.

Cook's eyes lit up. "You know about the Order?"

"Yes." She handed the documents to him. "That's why I need the information from you about the tail number of that plane."

"They have tentacles that reach to every aspect of our lives." He glanced around. "Even here, among my own staff."

"Who?"

"As you said, some things are better left unspoken."

Esther turned toward the door. "Well, I have no choice but to keep at it."

"I'll be in touch."

"I really need this quickly."

"I understand."

CHAPTER 101
MEXICO

THOUGH STILL UNPREDICTABLE, Paul's life took on a rhythm—
moments of terror, followed by periods of isolation. Terror and fear came from
repeated water boarding, sustained periods under water that took him to the
point of drowning, and trips to a rack room where he was placed in painfully
stressful positions. And all of it in the harsh glare of lights so bright it made
conscious thought all but impossible. He was forced to endure long periods
without sleep and provided with only a minimal amount of food.

In the course of it all, Paul lost track of time. At first he struggled to orient
himself to the moment when he'd been taken from the house. He attempted
to calculate the time that had elapsed, allowing for the things he remembered— the sensation of flying and a hazy recollection of being carried from
the plane— but the more he tried the more disoriented he became.

Finally he gave in to the rhythm of his circumstances. Instead of reckon-
ing time by hours and days, he reckoned it by the cycles of abuse. He'd endured
fifteen episodes under water in the tank. A dozen times on the water board.
And he'd been to the rack room for five episodes of excruciating pain. The time
in between was less definite, some of it spent in a drug-induced haze, some of
it in fitful sleep. But after his twelfth time in the tub, something changed.

As he came up from the water, a phrase popped into his mind. *"You will
be like a well-watered garden, like a spring whose waters never fail."* He recognized

it immediately. It was a verse from Isaiah, and the thought of it— a verse about water— struck him as ironic, but it reminded him of Scripture and he held the thought in his mind, meditating on it and repeating it over and over as the torture continued.

*   *   *

Down the hall, Dr. Walcott sat in a room lined with monitors and video screens. The screens showed images of each man in the experimental program. Beneath the screen, a monitor displayed data from the implants and tracking chips— basic bodily functions like heart rate, blood pressure, and respiration, along with brain waves, biorhythms, and reactions to sight, sound, and taste. As a result of his interviews with Sisson, the implants were reprogramed to detect and measure reactions to smell.

He turned to Paul's screen and watched as he moved around the room. "This is good," he said, checking the monitor. "This one has been isolated for twelve hours, yet he now shows no adverse reaction. I think we have broken him." He made a note of Paul's condition and ordered less severe treatment.

*   *   *

Paul awakened sometime later to find the harsh lights in the ceiling had now been replaced with the amber glow of incandescent bulbs. He glanced to the right and saw the door to his room was open. Fresh air flowed in from the hall and he heard the sound of footsteps. Moments later, a young man shuffled past. He wore white pants, a white shirt, and a white cap. For shoes he wore canvas high tops and around his waist was a wide black belt with trash bags hanging from each hip. His left arm flopped at his side and when he walked he dragged his left foot.

Paul slid from the cot and walked to the door. He leaned out to watch as the man continued down the hall. To the right, an orderly looked in his direction, then nonchalantly turned away. Paul stepped from the room and hurried down the hall toward the young man. He caught up with him and they walked along together.

"Hello," Paul said with a smile.

"My name is Steven. I pick up the trash. What's your name?"

"I'm Paul." They shook hands. "How long have I been here?"

Steven did not reply but turned into the next room. A trash can sat in the corner and he walked to it. He took a garbage bag from his belt, shook it open, and poured trash from the can into the bag. As he pulled the drawstring tight, he looked over at Paul as if seeing him for the first time. "My name is Steven. I pick up the trash."

At the next room the same scene repeated, only this time, when Steven looked at him, Paul spoke first. "Hey, aren't you Steven?"

"You know my name," Steven smiled.

"I'm Paul."

"You stay in the room."

"Yes."

"No," Steven shook his head. "Men stay in the room."

"It's okay. They left the door open."

"Dr. Walcott told me."

Steven collected the trash from a can in the corner, then walked back to the hall. Paul followed him, glad to have the company of another human. Around the corner they came to a door. Steven pushed it open and sunlight streamed through. Paul glanced outside to see bare dirt, a fence, and the rolling hills beyond.

"You can't come." Steven was serious, his voice stern. "Only I get to go out." He pushed Paul back. "You stay inside."

"Okay. I'll stay inside." He backed away and watched as Steven carried the bags of trash from the building, then the door slammed shut. He turned around to find an orderly standing behind him.

"You should return to your room."

"Yes," Paul nodded and took the orderly by the elbow. "You will show me?" He walked dutifully at the orderly's side, but he silently repeated the scripture he'd heard before. *"You will be like a well-watered garden, like a spring whose waters never fail."*

CHAPTER 102

MICHIGAN

LATER THAT EVENING, the McNeil campaign entourage stopped in Detroit for a rally at the Fox Theatre. It was the last stop before they began the long-delayed tour of churches with Morris Wythe. With the rally going well, Trent Paine slipped away to find Henry Caldwell. He caught up with him outside Cliff Bell's, a restaurant located on Park Avenue not far from the theater.

"We need to talk," Trent began.

Caldwell stepped toward the restaurant entrance. "Not now, kid. I'm going in to meet some people."

"This is important," Trent insisted.

"This is more important."

"No, it's not." Trent took him by the arm.

Caldwell's eyes were wide as he pulled away. "What are you doing?"

Trent grabbed him once more at the elbow and tugged on him. "We have to talk."

Caldwell shrugged free but followed him into the shadows near the street corner. "This better be good."

When they were a safe distance from the door, Trent turned to face him. "I was contacted this afternoon by the FBI."

"About what?"

"They want to interview the governor."

"Interview him?" A frown wrinkled Caldwell's brow. "About what?"

"They wouldn't say."

"Who did you talk to?"

"An agent from the D.C. office named Taylor Rutledge."

"What did you tell him?"

"I tried to put him off but he kept insisting. So I told him if he could get to California he could fly back on the plane with us and talk to the governor then."

Caldwell seemed ready to explode. "You did what?"

Trent put his finger to his lips in a gesture for silence. "It was the only way to put him off," he whispered.

"So you agreed to an interview with the FBI." Caldwell spoke in a hoarse, stage whisper. "Without knowing the topic? And without consulting anyone?" He ran his hands through his hair. "You're more stupid than I thought."

Trent grabbed him by the shoulders. "I'm talking to you now, aren't I?" His voice was loud and angry. "I just talked to him this afternoon. I came to you as soon as I could." He let go of Caldwell's shoulders and took a deep breath. "You haven't exactly made yourself available to me, you know."

Caldwell straightened his jacket. "You should have never agreed to an interview."

"And you shouldn't treat me like an amateur. I saw the agent this afternoon. I tracked you down as soon as I could. If you treated me like you did Carter, I could have told you earlier."

Caldwell looked away, taking a moment to gather his thoughts. "All right. You bought us some time. Gave us something to work with."

"Which is all I was trying to do. So, how do we handle it?"

"We have to get the lawyers involved."

"I agree. Who do we call?"

"I'll take care of it. Just don't let Rutledge near the governor until you hear from me." Caldwell turned away and started back toward the restaurant.

CHAPTER 103
LANSING, MICHIGAN

THE FOLLOWING DAY found McNeil with his wife in yet one more hotel, this time the Radisson located not far from the Michigan State campus. In spite of the grueling day before, McNeil rose early and sat at the table in the room with a cup of coffee. Nikki, still lying in bed, seemed not to notice. As he sat there with a few minutes of peace and quiet, his thoughts turned to Nelson Hooper and the things they had discussed that day. Hooper had worked all his life developing a career, only to find that true satisfaction came from selflessly helping others. *"Not just doing good,"* Hooper had said. *"But doing what Jesus did. Letting him work through me."*

By contrast, McNeil was certain he'd spent his life doing what others wanted. He'd tried to please his father, and when that failed, he'd tried to please Henry. That worked okay, but then Nikki entered his life and he had someone new to please, only she wasn't that easily satisfied. She liked winners and had been attracted to him because she thought he would take her places. They had gone far, but now with the turn in message and the press raising questions, he wasn't sure how she'd react. *Whatever she does,* he thought, *it won't be pleasant.*

An hour later, he was dressed and ready to go. They'd come to Michigan for the first stop on Morris Wythe's mega church tour, dubbed "A Celebration of Faith and Action." They were scheduled for stops in ten

states on their way to the final meeting in California. It was a risky strategy, diverting time, money, and effort from the daily grind to concentrate
on churches, but McNeil was certain the events would energize his base
among the Christian Right.

There was a knock at the door and Trent Paine appeared. "They're
ready downstairs." McNeil stepped to the bedroom for Nikki.

"You look nice." She gave him a cold glare. He smiled and tried again.
"Sleep well last night?"

"Don't talk to me," she snapped. "I saw your notes. You can't say
those things."

"Why not?"

"You'll make me look like a fool."

"How?"

She turned her head away. "Don't do this to me."

Trent held the door while they stepped out into the hall. They walked
together in silence to the elevator and rode down to the lobby.

Following a short drive through town, they arrived at Oak Grove
Community Church, with a congregation of nine thousand people. Wythe's
assistant met them outside the sanctuary and escorted them to a holding
room. McNeil and Trent sat together, reviewing notes for the meeting and
the upcoming schedule. Nikki took a seat on the opposite side of the
room. McNeil glanced in her direction and thought again about the price
they'd both paid for the life they led.

"There's one more thing," Trent added. "Finance says donations fell
off after New York, so we need to come out of this with a good pop."

"You mean we need to raise some money today."

"I *mean* we need to reassure our donor base."

"How do we do that?"

"Stick with the hot-button issues. Immigration reform, cutting taxes,
bringing the federal budget under control."

"The way we used to talk about it," Nikki agreed. "Where's Henry?"

"He had something to take care of," Trent answered. "He won't be
joining us today."

"I was talking to my husband."

"Oh." Trent glanced in McNeil's direction, then rose from his chair. "I think I'll check on things outside."

When they were alone, Nikki looked across the room at McNeil. "Henry's gone, isn't he?"

"Henry is just being Henry. He'll join us in California."

"It's about that speech you gave, isn't it?"

"Whatever Henry is doing today, I'm sure it's in his own best interests."

"And money. How much have donations dropped?"

"The money was always with Wilson."

"The money was with you until you went to see Nelson Hooper."

"Nikki," McNeil said in an exasperated tone, "I'm more alive now than I've ever been."

"You may be alive, but your message is dead. And so is your campaign unless you get back on point."

"Well," he sighed. "We'll see."

In a few minutes Wythe's aide returned and escorted them into the sanctuary. The building was filled to capacity and music, supplied by a ten-piece band, blared at a deafening volume. The congregation stood and applauded as they entered, then joined in a song with the band as Nikki took a seat on the front row. McNeil climbed the steps to the dais and sat beside Wythe.

For the next twenty minutes the congregation and choir sang, followed by a video presentation about the need for renewed emphasis on values and the role the church worldwide played in that effort. Then Danny Ivey, the pastor of the church, introduced Wythe, who introduced McNeil.

The crowd stood and applauded again as McNeil took the podium. There were shouts and whistles and the band played another song, which the audience joined gustily. Finally everyone returned to their seats.

McNeil began as he had at Bryant Park with remarks about immigration and about why we have laws restricting access to the country. He spoke at length about the way the rule of law distinguished America from other nations and the need to secure our borders. "But that's not the end of it for us— for those of us who claim the name of Christ. To whom much is given, much is required and those expectations apply to us in every aspect of our lives. There is no place to which you can retreat and escape the demand of Christ to be Lord of your life— every part of your life, including your attitude about the foreigners who sojourn among us.

"'When a foreigner resides among you in your land, do not mistreat them. The foreigner residing among you must be treated as your native-born. Love them as yourself, for you were foreigners in Egypt. I am the LORD your God.'" McNeil paused a moment. "If you're like me, you didn't even know that was in the Bible. I didn't until the other day. But what does it mean to us, as Believers? It means we have to love them as Christ loved them, and treat them as he treats them. Not as the economists analyze them, and not as conservative political pundits analyze them. And certainly not with racist remarks like 'anchor baby.'"

Then he launched into the second half of the speech he'd given earlier in New York, about how undocumented immigrants come here for the same reasons our ancestors came, how the real problem isn't people who desire freedom and security but those who seek to profit from the immigrant status, and once again he likened the practice of unscrupulous employers to slavery.

Before he reached the conclusion, several members of the congregation left their seats and walked out. One or two shouted at him and were escorted from the building. But for the most part, the congregation simply sat and listened. Soon the silence became louder than the applause that greeted him earlier.

When the service was over, Wythe rushed to McNeil's side. "This is great!" he gushed.

"You think so?"

"Oh my, yes. There were reporters in here. We had them on the back row. And camera crews outside. The cable news stations are playing clips of the service with the protestors right now."

"And that's good?"

"It's free publicity. Everyone's talking about it. We couldn't generate this much publicity with a trillion-dollar campaign."

Nikki came to McNeil's side, interrupting their conversation, and led him across the dais. From the tight little smile on her face, he knew she was angry.

"If you keep this up," she said in a snide tone, "you will lose."

"I don't care about that."

"Well, I care."

"What do you mean?"

"I mean I didn't sign up for this."

"I didn't know you signed up for anything but a life with me."

"Honestly." She rolled her eyes in disgust. "You're as stupid as everyone says. If you do this, then you're on your own."

A frown wrinkled McNeil's brow. "You're leaving?"

"You're finished in politics, David. You're done. And I'm through with you. I married you because you were a winner. Now I don't know what you are and I can't be with someone who isn't in it to win it." Then she let go of his hand, walked down the steps to the sanctuary floor, and up the aisle toward the door.

CHAPTER 104
MEXICO

A BUZZER SOUNDED from the telephone on Dr. Walcott's desk. He picked up the receiver and found Craig Hopkins on the line.

"We are ready," Hopkins announced.

"Very well. I will be there in a moment." Walcott finished the file that lay on his desk, set it aside, and started toward the hall.

A few doors down from his office, he came to the surgical suite. Fully equipped with the latest in technology and medicine, it afforded him the opportunity to plumb the depths of his imagination in devising new ways to alter human function.

In the center of the room, Sisson was strapped in place on a specially designed surgical chair. Surrounded on three sides by the machinery of an Atrion III, computer-assisted surgical robot, only his head and feet were visible from the door. Hopkins stood nearby and Walcott glanced in his direction.

"Are we ready?"

"Yes, sir," Hopkins replied. "Patient is sedated and prepped."

"Good." Walcott nodded.

A monitor and control panel was located to the right of the machine. Walcott took a seat there and logged into the system. On the screen before him was an image of Sisson's brain. A tiny dark sliver appeared near the base of the cortex in the occipital lobe. *There is the implant that is causing all this trouble. But we will soon fix that.*

He rested his hand on a mouse and moved a cursor over the implant, then clicked with the left side of the mouse. Silently a surgical arm glided from the left. In less than a minute, a drill attached to the end of the arm bored through Sisson's scull. The arm withdrew inside the machine, then returned with a slender probe in place of the drill. The probe slid through the hole with ease and moved straight toward the implant, locked onto one end, and slowly extracted it from Sisson's brain.

When the arm was fully retracted, Walcott glanced at Hopkins. "You may load the new one now."

Hopkins placed a new implant in a slot on the side of the surgical machine. Walcott entered a command and the probe arm attached itself to the new device. Then it slowly passed again into Sisson's skull, following the exact path into the cortex, and buried the implant where the other one had been.

After the arm was retracted, the machine moved aside and Walcott stood. He walked to Sisson's side and leaned near his ear. "We will try this for a while. Based on what you told me, I think it might work well for you." Sisson, still sedated, could only moan in response. Walcott patted him on the shoulder. "Many people are watching to see how you perform. I am watching, also. Our lives might very well depend on your performance."

CHAPTER 105
RHODES

RUSSO SAT AT HIS DESK reviewing assignments for the week and preparing correspondence when he received a message on his cell phone. He glanced at the screen and saw it was from Jeremy Bartlett at Sierra Resources. "We can be prepared to move at your direction with a two-day notice." He read the text, then rose from his chair and hurried downstairs.

Spoleto was seated at a table in the courtyard garden, eating lunch, when Russo located him. He took a seat next to him.

"You are out of breath," Spoleto observed. "There is something you wish to tell me?"

"Sierra responded."

"And?"

"They can be ready with two days of notice."

"Very well." Spoleto took a sip of tea. "Notify the Council. We shall meet at once."

Within the hour, the Council gathered around the long conference table in the Hall of Saints. Spoleto stood at the far end of the room. "The time has come when we must act with final authority. McNeil's speech in New York and his recent addresses in the church make it apparent that a threat to the Order now exists."

Father Ottiano, normally quiet and reserved, spoke up. "Must we end the entire project?"

"That is the matter we are here to decide."

"We should terminate Caldwell," Father Molina offered. "He allowed this to happen."

"Caldwell and the candidate," another insisted.

"That would be difficult to manage. There would surely be an investigation."

"We cannot end them all," Father Vignola argued. "There are too many."

"What if we merely stop supporting their efforts?"

"We cannot simply stop our support. The candidate knows too much."

"But who do we use?"

"Sierra," another insisted. "They are ready and prepared."

"They got us into this trouble."

"No. Penalta brought this upon us."

"One of our own."

"But can we trust Sierra?"

"We own Sierra. They will do as we say."

"We must end Sierra, too."

"Not the entire company," Father Sivero interjected. "We can end the experimental phase and say that we only just now discovered it. Even the Jewish media can't attack us for that."

"We have Jobert."

"Jobert botched the Penalta issue that set all this in motion. Use Sierra. They are not perfect but they are prepared. I trust Bartlett more than any of the others we have used in the past."

Ottiano spoke up again. "Shouldn't we refer this to the Military Vicariate?"

"No." Spoleto's eyes met Galena's, then moved quickly around the table. "This is a matter for us now." He rapped his knuckles on the table-top. "And I think we have reached a consensus. We shall contact Sierra and instruct them in accordance with your wishes to end their experimental program at once. And we shall authorize them to take such action as is necessary to contain this matter." Around the table the men nodded in agreement. "You will signify your agreement in the usual manner." In unison, the delegates pushed back their chairs from the table and stood. "Any opposed?" The room fell silent. Spoleto let his gaze roam the table, looking every man in the eye. When he had gone all the way around, he rapped the table with his fist. "So be it."

Then the delegates responded, "In the name of the Father, and of the Son, and of the Holy Spirit. Amen." And with that, the meeting adjourned.

As the men filed from the room, Russo appeared at the door. Spoleto looked in his direction and nodded. Russo retreated to his desk, picked up his cell phone, and typed a message to Jeremy Bartlett.

CHAPTER 106
MEXICO

PAUL LAY ON THE COT in his room and stared blankly up at the ceiling. He remembered a passage from Luke that he'd memorized as a child. *"Fear not, for behold I bring you good tidings of great joy."* He had been eight years old and he'd memorized that verse as part of a church Christmas pageant. Remembering the verse made him think of his childhood and for a moment his mind drifted to East Texas. He saw again the rolling hills near Longview and smelled the fresh-mowed hay. But very quickly he brought his mind back to the verse and focused on the words. "Fear not," he repeated to himself and he thought of what that meant— a life without fear. To explore the topic, he began to think of the things people usually fear. Spiders and snakes came to mind immediately, followed by heights and—

The lock on the door to the room rattled. Then the door opened and an orderly appeared. "They need you in the examination room."

"Which one?"

"The big one at the end of the hall." The orderly gestured with his hand. "Come with me. I'll take you."

Paul rolled off the cot and followed as the orderly led him down the hall to a door on the right. The orderly pushed it open and waited while Paul moved past.

Sisson sat in a chair on the far side of the room, but around him were men whom Paul had never seen before. All of them seemed free to move about but they were constrained by the wires that attached to sensors on their bodies and connected to the row of monitors that stood to the right.

The orderly guided Paul to a chair and placed a series of electrodes on his arms, legs, torso, and head. Then he connected the lead lines similar to the ones that were attached to the others in the room. With them in place, the orderly retreated across the room and disappeared out the door.

A few minutes later the door opened again and Walcott entered. He moved along the row of monitors and checked the details that flashed on the screen. Then he stepped in between the chairs and walked slowly among the men, checking each one. While he walked, he quietly repeated the phrase, "We serve God and country to protect and defend." Others picked it up and soon everyone in the room was chanting it over and over again.

Walcott turned to Hopkins. "I think we have a baseline of their conditions. The implants seem to be functioning as designed. Now let's see what happens when we put it to the test."

Hopkins acknowledged him with a nod and pressed a button on the console of a nearby monitor. Seconds later a door opened on the far side of the room and an orderly appeared, leading five men with him. Steven was among them and he glanced in Paul's direction.

As they moved into place, Walcott walked among them, smiling, touching, positioning each of them exactly as he wanted. He said something to Steven, then moved on to the next man. He, like Steven, walked with a shuffle and held one arm against his side, but he had a blank look in his eyes, and saliva drooled from the corners of his mouth. Walcott placed him to the right, at the end of the line.

After he'd examined each one of them, Walcott crossed the room to a cabinet and took out an automatic pistol. He returned with it in his hand, gave it to Sisson, and said with a smile, "Shoot the man on the right." Then he leaned near Sisson's ear and said in an authoritative tone, "This is not a drill, soldier. I repeat. This is not a drill."

A dull, listless pallor came over Sisson's face. His eyes held a faraway look and it seemed as though he'd fallen into a trance. Without hesitation, he manipulated the slide of the pistol to push a round into the chamber and cock the hammer. Then he raised the pistol to shoulder height, pressed the end of the barrel against the man's head, and squeezed the trigger.

With a loud report, a lead slug exploded through the man's skull, spraying those who stood to the left with a thin red mist and peppering them with chips of bone. Seconds later the man's knees buckled and he crumpled to the floor. Blood oozed from the hole in his head and formed a dark red pool on the floor. His legs shook and his shoulders twitched. Hopkins knelt beside him and pressed a fingertip against an artery in his neck. He glanced up at Walcott and nodded.

Walcott smiled and said in firm and confident voice, "We serve God and country to protect and defend." Sisson, now alert, repeated the phrase. The color returned to his skin and his eyes were once again clear. Others in the room joined in the refrain. Paul did, too, forming the words with his mouth, but in his mind he repeated the Scripture he'd remembered before, *"You will be like a well-watered garden, like a spring whose waters never fail."*

While they continued to chant, Walcott stepped to the monitors and checked their individual responses. He nodded and his eyes narrowed. "The new implant is working much better." He glanced over his shoulder toward Hopkins. "Even better than I expected. They are sensing no stress from the death of that man." He pointed to the screen. "Particularly this one. Look at how low his rhythms have become." He glanced in Paul's direction with a look of pride. "He is adapting quite well."

CHAPTER 107
WASHINGTON, D.C.

ESTHER SAT AT THE KITCHEN TABLE, drinking a cup of coffee. Since the day Paul disappeared, she'd been working night and day, trying to learn where the plane had landed. Her years of practice as an attorney gave her many powerful contacts and she'd called them all, to no avail. Now she sat there staring at the cup in her hand and finally let her mind think of the unthinkable— Paul might already be dead.

The first hours of a kidnapping were the most crucial and he had been gone for days. When she asked Liston Cook for help, she was certain he would respond quickly, but that had not happened. Time was rapidly passing by and with it any hope of finding Paul alive. Perhaps she'd always known it. Crashing the gate and driving onto the runway at Dulles had been an act of desperation. Training and experience told her to wait, observe, and report to those who could craft a decisive, effective response. Instead, she had acted from the heart and in the wake of the trouble that followed she was convinced she'd made a mistake. She was certain she'd known then what she knew now— there was only a slim chance she'd find him alive.

"I should have kept going," she mumbled as she took a sip of coffee. "They might have shot at me, and I might be dead, but Paul would be alive."

As she continued to brood, she thought about Sierra Resources. They had an office on Texas Street and a headquarters in Los Angeles. She could approach them for help. Storm their executive offices unannounced. They might be inclined to respond if she threatened to talk to the press. "I could go to—"

A text message appeared on her cell phone, interrupting her thought. She glanced at the screen, thinking it was one more question from the office, but the number was one she did not recognize. Then she scrolled down and read, "Your plane landed at a site south of Los Hovos, Mexico."

Your plane ... it took a moment for the words to sink in. Then her eyes opened wide as she realized this was a response from Liston Cook. Relief washed over her as she read the message again. Paul was in Mexico. She knew where he was. Then just as quickly despair returned— he was in Mexico.

Esther highlighted the name of the town in the message and tapped it twice with her fingertip on the screen. A map appeared with the location noted by a star. Los Hovos was midway between Hermosillo and the U.S. border. "Northern Mexico," she mumbled. "That's *really* not good." She had few contacts in Mexico and much of the region adjoining the border was controlled by drug lords. Just getting down there would require help.

If she called the State Department and asked them for assistance, they would be a long time in responding and there was a good chance her request would simply get lost in departmental bureaucracy. She could contact friends on Capitol Hill, but she'd already done that in her attempts to locate the plane's destination, and they'd all responded with the same skeptical nonresponse, "We'll see what we can do."

That left Brody. *He makes me so mad. Always wanting me to do something for him but never returning the favor. And I always give in and do whatever he wants anyway. But I have nowhere else to turn.* She pushed back from the table and stood.

The drive to the embassy compound on Reno Road was a short trip. She parked on the street near the entrance and waited while a guard at the gate checked her credentials. She'd been there many times before. The security screening didn't take long. Inside the building, she made her way upstairs and found Brody seated at his desk.

"I need a plane to Mexico," she announced as she entered his office. Even now the words sounded out of place but she was long past caring about that. "This afternoon," she added.

"I'm not a travel agency," Brody replied without looking up from the file in his hand.

She snatched the file away and looked him in the eye. "Brody, I need a plane to Mexico and I need it now. They're holding Paul somewhere near Los Hovos."

"Who told you that?"

"A source."

"Well, did this source also tell you that the region is controlled by drug lords, and that women traveling alone down there are more likely to end up enslaved to a pimp than they are returning home?" He snatched the file back. "There's a State Department order in place. You Americans are prohibited from traveling there."

"I don't care what the State Department says. I'm going there and you're going to help me do it." She tapped the desktop with her finger for emphasis. "A plane at Dulles, on the ground, fueled and ready to go in an hour."

"Impossible."

"It's not impossible," she said firmly. "I've seen you do it many times."

"That was—"

"Just do it," she said, cutting him off.

"Or what?" He leaned back in his chair. "You're going to threaten me again?"

"Just get me the plane, Brody." She started toward the door. "I'm on my way to the airport now."

* * *

An hour later, Walcott ushered Sisson from the room. When they were gone, Hopkins led Steven and the others through a door to the left. At the same time attendants escorted Thomas, Adams, and Carlisle away. A few moments later someone came for Paul and led him into the hall.

Lost in thought about what he'd just seen, Paul was already at the door to his confinement room before he realized he was alone. He glanced around to find the hallway deserted. Instead of returning to his room, he walked to the corner. From there he saw the door where Steven took out the trash. He made his way toward it and gently pushed it open. No alarms sounded. No one came to stop him. So he stepped outside.

The sunlight was a welcome change and he stood there, head back and eyes closed, basking in its warmth against his skin. A breeze blew past and he let it wash over him. The tingle of it against his skin refreshed his mind. Images of Sisson, the pistol, and the dead body on the floor began to fade.

Then a rumbling sound caught his attention and he opened his eyes to see a truck come to a dusty stop fifty yards to the right. Two men climbed from it and entered a building that stood near where they parked. His attention now diverted from the pleasure of the moment, Paul scanned the compound, taking in as much detail as possible.

The building where he was held was the largest. It sat to one side near the fence and ran the length of the compound. Across from it was a row of smaller buildings, all of them constructed of steel with a simple, efficient, commercial appearance. Looking between them, he saw the fence on the opposite side and caught a glimpse of the main gate. Armed guards stood near a small guardhouse, and patrols moved up and down the perimeter.

Beyond the fence, low hills lay parallel to the fence on either side and in the distance higher peaks jutted up from the desert. The sun was sinking to his left. He turned in that direction, trying to orient himself. "That's west, which means ..." He turned slowly to the right to face north. As he did, his eyes fell on Sisson and Walcott strolling across the compound. Paul watched them a moment, then drifted in that direction.

As he drew near, he heard Walcott's voice. From the sound of it, they were having a serious discussion. A Dumpster sat about midway to them. Paul walked toward it and crouched there out of sight. After a moment, he eased to the corner for a look. Sisson and Walcott turned in his direction and their voices grew clearer.

"You must find the building on your own," Walcott explained. "When you get there, climb to the fourth floor and position yourself at a front window."

"You have diagrams?"

"There are no diagrams. You must locate the position for yourself."

"Maps?"

"No maps."

"This is very different from the missions we've done before."

"This one is urgent."

Sisson had a questioning look. "What's the rush?"

"A threat has arisen. It must be terminated as quickly as possible. There is no time for the extensive training we would normally conduct." Walcott rested a hand on Sisson's shoulder. "You are ready. The modifications we have made will serve you well."

"What's the address?"

A helicopter approached and passed overhead, drowning out their voices. When it was gone, Walcott stood just a few feet away. "This is a top-priority assignment. There must be total deniability. You have two days to get to Los Angeles, locate the building, and get into position."

"Very well."

Walcott looked him in the eye. "We serve God and country to protect and defend. This is not a drill, soldier," Walcott said in an even tone. "I repeat. This is not a drill."

Sisson nodded and smiled. The expression on his face, friendly on the surface but with eyes that were coldly emotionless, sent chills up Paul's spine.

*　　*　　*

At Dulles, Esther steered the car past the main terminal and followed the road to a hangar operated by Business Jet Services. She parked in a space near the building and entered through a door near the corner.

A Gulfstream Jet sat inside. The fuselage door was open and the steps were down, but there was no one in sight. She walked over to the plane, climbed the steps, and peeked inside. Brody was seated two rows back. He looked up as she appeared.

"Didn't think I would let you go alone, did you?"

She took a seat beside him, unsure whether to thank him for his generosity or hit him for the frustration he'd caused. "I was counting on you," she whispered.

"I know," he smiled.

An attendant entered the cabin. He closed and latched the door, then took a seat near the front. By the time Esther fastened her seat belt, the plane was rolling forward. Within minutes they lifted off the runway and rose into the night sky.

CHAPTER 108
CALIFORNIA

THE METAL DESK RATTLED as McNeil propped his feet on top. He leaned back in the chair and stared out the window at the parking lot. "What was this before it became our headquarters?"

"A grocery store," Trent replied.

"What happened to it?"

"Got caught in the economic crunch. Went out of business."

"Must have been tough."

"Lots of jobs were lost." Trent took a seat on a folding chair. "But the owners were glad to rent it to us."

"They didn't give it to us?"

"No. We had to pay."

McNeil continued to look out the window but changed the subject. "Is this another one of Caldwell's meetings about our message?"

"No, he's bringing Jack Lea."

McNeil turned to look at him. "The lawyer?"

"Yes. From Chicago."

"Why?"

"Caldwell said he should explain that part to you himself."

Just then McNeil watched as a black SUV came to stop in the parking lot. "Looks like they've arrived."

A few minutes later, the office door opened and Caldwell appeared with Jack Lea close behind. They stepped into the room and closed the door. McNeil, still seated behind the desk, glanced up with a smile. "Jack, good to see you."

"Yes, sir." Lea shook McNeil's hand. "But I'm not so sure you'll be glad when we're finished." He took a seat next to Trent.

McNeil looked over at Caldwell. "Henry, what's this about?"

"A few days ago Trent was approached by an FBI agent who wants to interview you. Naturally, we're not letting that happen without preparation. I had Jack look into it."

"They have documents ..." Lea hesitated and gestured in Trent's direction. "Has he been cleared?"

McNeil smiled over at Trent. "It might be better if you don't hear this part."

"If I'm your chief of staff," Trent protested, "don't I—"

"I'll get you up to speed," McNeil interrupted. "But right now you need deniability and that's what I'm giving you. We'll call you back in a minute."

Trent rose from his chair and walked out of the room. When he was gone, Lea continued. "They have documents from the Order that connects the whole thing. Contributions, the financial trail, everything we don't want them to have."

"How'd they get those?"

"NSA found them in an email to someone in Liston Cook's campaign."

McNeil had a sly grin. "You represented the men who broke into that office."

"We shouldn't discuss that," Caldwell interjected.

"Isn't that a little reckless? Bringing in the same lawyer who handled the Cook thing?" He turned to Lea. "I mean, I like you, Jack, and I trust you. But if the press ever finds out about it, this is going to look like we were involved."

Caldwell looked uneasy, but before he could respond, Lea spoke up.

"We have bigger problems than that. The Attorney General has empaneled a grand jury to investigate."

"So, why did they send Rutledge?"

"Not sure. Apparently the idea to interview came from the Attorney General."

"When he asked for an interview," Caldwell continued, "Trent put him off by suggesting he meet us out here and fly back with you on the plane. We need to figure out how to handle that."

"I don't mind doing it that way," Lea responded. "But we'll have to get him onboard in a way that keeps the press from finding out who he really is."

McNeil picked up a pen from the desk and toyed with it between his fingers. He didn't like what he heard, and having Jack Lea involved left him more than uneasy. Caldwell was up to something, he just didn't know what. After a moment he looked over at Lea. "Perhaps we should delay the interview."

Caldwell folded his arms and leaned back in his chair. Lea seemed unfazed. "That might raise more problems than it solves."

"How so?"

"The Attorney General has empaneled a grand jury to investigate you and Sierra Resources. If the Attorney General wants an indictment, he'll get one."

"Do we have any leverage with him?"

"My office is checking on that, but I don't think so. He's as clean as they get."

"Everyone has a weakness," Caldwell chuckled.

CHAPTER 109

MEXICO

WHEN THE GULFSTREAM LANDED, Esther stepped out on a paved runway. Across the tarmac was a modern terminal building. To the right, large hangars lined the taxiway and a control tower rose above them. "Where are we?"

"Hermosillo," Brody replied.

Anger flared her nostrils. "I told you the plane landed in Los Hovos."

"I know, but there's nothing on the charts there. This is the closest airport."

"Then why did Liston Cook tell me Los Hovos? Did he lie?"

He reached the bottom step from the plane and turned to face her. "Do you think I would come down here without checking the information?"

"So, what about it? What did you find?"

"Apparently there is a private airstrip somewhere outside Los Hovos. But it isn't on any of the charts and no one knows for certain where it is."

"What do we do, then?"

"Only one thing to do," Brody shrugged. "Ride over to Los Hovos and have a look."

An SUV was parked at the edge of the tarmac. Brody got in behind the steering wheel. Esther sat on the passenger side. She glanced in his direction. "Do you know which way to go?"

He opened a compartment in the console and took out a map. "You can navigate." He tossed it toward her. "Don't get us lost."

Four hours later, they arrived in Los Hovos. A dusty, dirty town, it lay alongside Highway 17, a main transportation artery between ports along the Gulf of California and the U.S. border. Brody turned the SUV off the pavement onto a dirt street and came to a stop outside the El Palacio Hotel. Esther looked out at the two-story adobe and brick building. "You sure this place is safe?"

"No. But it's the only hotel in town so it'll have to do."

Brody led the way inside to the clerk's desk. The room was dimly lit but the tiled floor and a ceiling fan made it cool and pleasant. He signed for two rooms and a young woman led them upstairs. Esther took a room with a window that overlooked a courtyard in back. Brody's room was across the hall. The rooms were sparsely furnished with only a bed, dresser, and one chair, but they were spotlessly clean and had private baths.

Though the flight had been long and the drive tiring, they set to work trying to locate Paul and spent the remainder of the day methodically working through the bars, shops, and clubs. Esther showed a picture of Paul and gave the story. "He came down here with a company called Sierra Resources. He's disappeared. I'm trying to find him." Brody asked about the company. "They have a facility near here with a runway. They fly in and out of here frequently. Have you seen it? Have you heard their airplanes? Do you know where the facility is located?"

After a day of questions they were no closer to finding Paul than when they left the airport at Dulles.

*   *   *

Paul spent most of the day confined to his room. No one said why but he was sure it was punishment for wandering outside the building the day before. He lay on the cot and stared up at the ceiling, but instead of thinking about Scripture he occupied his mind trying to figure out what Walcott was discussing with Sisson. Something big, in Los Angeles, in the next two days. But what? And how could he get away to warn anyone? He'd been outside, once. And he'd seen the fence, but there were guards and as far as he could see there was nothing around them but rolling hills covered with grass and brush. *I don't even know where I am.*

He closed his eyes and let his mind drift, which was difficult to do. Since he'd arrived— wherever he was— he'd found it difficult to hold multiple thoughts. Still, he couldn't just sit there and daydream, so he did his best to recount what he'd learned so far.

There had been a break-in at Liston Cook's office. Bill Sisson had escaped. The team that committed the break-in worked for Sierra Resources. He thought for a moment about Edgar Logan and wondered if he knew what had happened. His mind wandered from thought to thought and finally returned to the issue at hand— Sierra Resources and the break-in. Then he remembered what Esther had said about the documents and a link to the Order and—

The lock on the door rattled and the door swung open. Steven appeared and he crossed the room to the corner where the trash can sat. "My name is Steven," he said with a smile. "I pick up the trash."

Paul responded politely, "Having a good day, Steven?"

"I pick up the trash."

Paul sat on the cot and watched while Steven took a trash bag from his belt, shook it open, and emptied the trash can into it. When he turned to leave, Paul noticed the door was left open and then he saw the hall— and a chance to get out. He rose from the cot and walked with Steven into the hall.

Steven took a few steps, then stopped abruptly. "You stay," Steven said in a stern voice.

"I'll help you."

"No." Steven shook his head, but his tone was less strident. "You stay."

"I need a walk."

"You went outside."

"Is that what they told you?"

"You went outside."

"Not today. I'll just walk to the end of the hall, then come back."

Steven started in that direction, glancing back over his shoulder every few steps. Paul followed a few paces behind. At the corner, Steven turned to him and gestured again with his hand. "You stay."

"Okay," Paul smiled. "I'll stay." He pointed toward a spot on the floor. "Right here. I'll stay right here." Steven hesitated, then continued down the hall and trudged through a door. Alone in the hall, Paul seized the opportunity to explore.

Who knows, there might be a way out yet. He turned from the corner and tried the door to his right, but found only a closet. The next door was locked but the one beyond it opened into a break room. A sink sat along the wall opposite the door. On the counter next to it was a microwave oven. He stepped inside and closed the door, then crossed the room to the counter.

In the cabinet beneath the microwave he found a roll of paper towels, dish detergent, and four aerosol cans. He took out the cans and placed them in the microwave. A stack of Styrofoam cups stood to the left. He crammed them in with the cans. *I saw this once in a movie— I think. Maybe it actually works.* He set the power to high and put the timer on thirty minutes. Then he pressed the start button and hurried to the door.

Back in the hall again, he walked quickly to his room and stretched out on the cot. He was lying there when the cans in the microwave exploded. The noise was louder than he expected and there was the sound of breaking glass. He rolled from the cot and walked to the door to see.

Down the hall, smoke drifted into the hall. Someone shouted and there was the sound of coughing, followed by a rush of thick black smoke. The fire alarm sounded with an earsplitting squelch. And then confusion followed as orderlies and attendants scurried in every direction, some trying to see what was wrong, others trying to get out of the way.

In the chaos, Paul came from the room to the hall and intended to slip past the smoke to the door he'd used before, but a woman grabbed his arm and pushed him in the opposite direction. "Get out," she shouted.

"Get out of the building." Paul did as he was told and ran up the hall in the direction she pointed. At the corner near the examination rooms, an orderly appeared with a group in tow. Paul scanned their faces, searching for Sisson, but saw no one he recognized. As they passed by he squeezed in among them. Moments later they reached an exit and he stepped outside.

A drive ran past the building and across it was a storage building. To the right was another building much like the one where he was being held. Through the space between the buildings he could see all the way to the gate about fifty yards away. Suddenly escaping the compound didn't seem so impossible.

While others ran toward the building and scurried about with hoses and extinguishers, Paul drifted farther and farther away until he reached the opposite side of the storage building. Three trucks were parked there and he slipped between, checking through the windows for keys in the ignition. When he found none, he crouched between them and watched, surveying the area for other options.

Smoke billowed into the air, forming a thick cloud that hung above the facility. Then flames burst through the roof. Moments later, waves of heat swept over him. Metal on the roof of the storage building popped and screeched as it expanded.

In a few minutes, three pickup trucks arrived at the gate. The first one had three men in the cab but the other two were crammed with boys who filled the bed. From the look of it, they were locals out for a joyride. Guards at the gate forced them to stop.

Before the trucks could be cleared, a tanker truck appeared, rolling down the road toward the compound, sending a cloud of dust drifting over the grassland. As it drew near the gate the guards became more insistent, shouting at the men in the pickups. It did little good and they were still blocking the way when the tanker arrived. Finally the pickups moved forward and far enough out of the way to permit the tanker to pass. Paul wasn't fluent in Spanish but he could read the markings on the truck and realized it was filled with water.

While the guards were occupied at the gate, Paul came from his hiding spot and made his way in that direction. With the tanker inching past and the pickups adding to the confusion, he crossed the fifty yards to the gate unnoticed. People in the pickups stared at him as he walked by, then burst into laughter as he slipped past the gate and disappeared into the brush.

CHAPTER 110
RHODES

THAT EVENING, SPOLETO came from his office and walked upstairs to his private residence. Russo was waiting as he opened the door. They stepped inside and walked quietly to the kitchen.

A kettle sat on the stove. Russo filled it with water from the tap and put it on to boil. While they waited, Spoleto took down a serving tray and plate. He placed six shortbread cookies on the plate, then set it on the tray. Russo folded a napkin and laid it beside the plate, then rested a spoon on top. Next to the napkin, Spoleto placed a small bowl with cubes of sugar, and beside it a tiny pitcher filled with milk. As they finished with the tray, steam rose from the spout of the kettle. Russo took a teapot from the cabinet, added some loose tea, and poured in the water. Then he picked up the tray and followed Spoleto toward the door.

Spoleto's apartment opened to a wide corridor that led along the north wall of the castle. It was lined with paintings hung in elegant frames. The floor was made of granite tile inlaid with onyx and white marble in an intricate pattern of crosses, snakes, and eagles. Spoleto and Russo paid no attention to any of it as they walked quietly to the corner, then turned left. Fifty feet farther they came to a solid oak door with a latch at one side and a lock above it. Spoleto rapped on the door with his knuckles. A moment later the door opened and Galena appeared. The color drained from his face when he saw them.

"Gentlemen," he said quietly as he stepped back from the door and waited for them to enter. "I was hoping we could meet under more favorable circumstances."

Beyond the door was a small living room. A sofa sat to the right with an end table next to it. Russo set the tray on the table. Spoleto pushed the door closed and locked it. Galena's eyes were wide. "Has it come to this?" His voice trembled. "Is there no other way?"

"I am afraid not," Spoleto replied.

"But I have done my best," Galena implored. "I have done my best."

"And you will be justly rewarded," Spoleto calmly assured him. He moved the cup from the tray and set it on the table. "Perhaps a little tea to calm your nerves."

"Yes," Galena nodded. "A final cup." He turned toward the table.

As Galena reached for the cup, Russo brought a syringe from his pocket. He flicked off the cap that covered the needle, then plunged it into the flesh of Galena's right hip. With the needle buried deep into the muscle, he draped an arm over Galena's shoulder for support and depressed the plunger.

Galena flinched as the contents of the syringe emptied into his body. He groped with an outstretched hand, first for Russo then for Spoleto. He gasped for breath, then leaned forward over Russo's arm and vomited, splattering the contents of his stomach on the floor. Russo held him there momentarily, then eased Galena to the floor.

Russo looked over at Spoleto. "This is how it is done?"

"Yes," Spoleto nodded. "It is tradition." He stooped over and withdrew the syringe from Galena's hip. "It will be reported as a heart attack." The cap lay nearby. He retrieved it from the floor, placed it over the needle, and handed it to Russo.

"What now?"

"By tradition, you are now head of the Military Vicariate. You must finish the task authorized by the Council. I contacted Bartlett and set in motion the first part. Now you must finish it."

"But who should I use?"

"That is for you to decide."

"Then I choose Jobert."

"Very well," Spoleto nodded. "Place the call." He unlocked the door. "And tell Father Ameche we need him."

CHAPTER 111
MEXICO

THAT EVENING, ESTHER and Brody sat at the Café Economico eating a burrito dinner. She gave him a wry smile. "You know what 'economico' means in Spanish?"

"Economical."

"Yeah. But translate it into American slang and you get 'cheap.'" She pointed to the food. "That's what this is. Cheap, filling, and greasy."

"Tastes pretty good to me."

"Oh, it tastes all right. But I'm not sure it'll stay with you very long."

While they ate, an older man approached their table. Tall and slender, he was dressed in blue jeans and a white long-sleeved shirt. Around his waist was a wide leather belt with a silver buckle. He carried a cowboy hat in his hand and wore scuffed leather boots. He took a seat in a chair to the right. "I understand you were asking questions today about an airstrip."

"Yes," Brody replied. "You know something about that?"

"My friend Miguel does odd jobs for work. One day some men came to town. Gabachos with suits and ties. They were looking for help to unload crates from an airplane. We had seen it coming down over the hills earlier. Miguel needed money to support his family and they showed him cash. So he went with them. When I saw him the next day he could barely walk. He had injured his back while working for them. A few days later we saw them again and Miguel told them he was hurt. They didn't like that he approached them about it but they said they would take care of him. I told him not to listen to them but he did anyway and they took him with them. That was the last time I saw my friend Miguel."

"When did this happen?"

"Earlier this year," he shrugged. "Maybe five or six months ago."

"Do you know where the airstrip is located?"

"Yes. I have been there many times looking for him when the planes come."

"You see the planes often?"

"They come sometimes. Then sometimes not."

"Think you could take us to the airstrip?"

"Meet me in front of the hotel tonight. I will show you." He nodded in Esther's direction, then rose from the chair, crossed the room, and disappeared out the door.

Esther looked over at Brody. "How does he know where we're staying?"

"No other hotel in town, remember?" Brody took a bite and swallowed. "Besides, with all the people we've talked to today I imagine the whole town knows everything about us by now."

"Think it's a setup?"

"I think we finally found someone who would talk."

"No. We didn't find him. He found us."

"I know, but I don't think we have a choice. We've been talking to people all day and he's the only one who's even acknowledged that the airstrip exists."

After dinner Esther and Brody sat outside the hotel and watched as the last rays of sunlight disappeared from the western horizon. In its place was a night sky filled with stars. They sat in silence and stared up at the heavens above them.

In a little while a pickup truck came to a stop near the hotel entrance. The passenger door opened and the man they met earlier that evening stepped out. He walked slowly toward them as the truck drove away. Brody stood to meet him. "Are you ready?"

"Yes," the man nodded. "We can go now."

They climbed into the SUV with Brody behind the steering wheel. Esther got in back. The man pointed out the window. "We need to go that way. It is located south of town." Brody turned the SUV in that direction.

In a few minutes they came to a shack that sat near the road. "Slow down," the man said. Then he pointed to the left again. "Turn in here."

Brody glanced into the darkness outside the window. "There's a road out there?"

"Yes, turn left and you will see it." Brody turned the SUV in that direction and watched as the headlights came around to reveal a well-worn dirt road.

A mile down the road, they topped a hill. "This is it," the man said. Brody put his foot on the break and slowed the SUV to an idle. He glanced to the left and right. "Where? I don't see anything."

Esther felt her heart race. Everything she'd learned before told her this was a setup. At any moment the man in front with Brody would turn on them with a pistol and shoot them both. They'd be left to rot in the brush and no one would ever know what happened. These things raced through her mind and she thought once or twice to speak, but she kept quiet and wrapped her fingers around the door handle with a tight grip. She focused her eyes on the man in front, watching for the least sign of trouble.

"Right there, right there!"

Brody brought the SUV to a stop and leaned around, looking. "I don't see anything."

"That is because you do not have eyes for the darkness. Point your lights in that direction."

Brody turned the SUV to the right. The beam of the headlights followed, slicing through the darkness and washing over the desert. Then they came to rest on a smooth strip of pavement. A smile spread across his face. "And there it is," he sighed.

Esther eased her grip on the door handle. "No lights. No control tower. Just a strip of pavement."

"If you have no government regulation to worry about, that's all you need."

The man pointed again. "There are buildings over the next hill. I found them when I came out here looking for Miguel. I think they took him there but I could never find him. It has a fence with guards and I could not get inside."

Brody steered the SUV back to the road and started in that direction. Half a mile farther they began to rise up a hill. "Turn off your lights," the man said.

"I need them to see," Brody protested.

"Trust your eyes. If they see us, they will come looking for us."

Brody pressed the switch and the headlights went out. Darkness enshrouded them and for a moment Esther felt afraid. Then her eyes adjusted to the darkness and she saw the shrubs and bushes near the road come into focus. "Wow! You really can see out here." Brody made no comment and they continued to the top of the hill without incident.

As they reached the crest, the man touched Brody's wrist. "Better stop here," he said. "We can walk now."

Brody steered the SUV to the side of the road and brought it to a stop. Esther climbed from the back seat and met them near the front bumper. When they were all together, they walked up the road to the top of the hill.

As they came to the crest, a fenced compound appeared in the arid swale below. Lit up with bright lights, it stood in stark contrast to the darkness around it. They stared at it a moment, watching the guards at the gate and the patrols along the fence. Then Esther nudged Brody. "Think we could get inside?"

"Impossible," the man replied, not waiting for Brody to answer. "I tried before. There is no way inside except through the gate."

She looked up at Brody. "We could always crash the gate."

"I don't think they would be as kind as the FBI."

"They would kill us," the man offered. "Or worse." He stared down at the scene for a little longer, then turned away. "We should go now."

Esther lingered there alone, staring down at the buildings and wondering if Paul was somewhere inside one of them. And if he was there, what was he doing? Was he safe? Or had he met the end long before now? A lump formed in her throat and she swallowed hard to avoid crying. Then she turned away and followed the others toward the SUV.

* * *

All that afternoon, Paul worked his way slowly forward, mindful of the threat posed by snakes and thorns, but after an hour or two he grew tired and thirsty. He pressed on through the brush, keeping well beyond the road to avoid being seen. As the sun began to wane, he reached the base of a hill. The walk had been exhausting but when he glanced over his shoulder he could still see in the distance the fence of the compound and the buildings beyond it.

A scrub tree stood nearby and he sat down in the late-afternoon shade to rest. He drew his knees up to his chest, folded his arms over them for a pillow, and rested his head. When his eyes opened again, the sun was gone and darkness had descended. Above him, where the sun had been just a short time before, the sky was alive with more stars than he'd ever seen. He stared up at them and tried to capture the image in his memory. The air was cooler and he felt refreshed enough to stand and move forward again.

No longer needing to cloak his movements, Paul cut across toward the road and walked to the crest of the hill. By the light of the stars, he saw an SUV parked on the side of the road. He froze in place and wondered if it was real or merely a figment of his imagination. Carefully he inched closer and ran his fingertips over the door. Convinced that it was really there, he listened for the sound of footsteps. When all he heard was the silence of the night, he grasped the door handle and let his imagination run wild about what might be inside— a bottle of water, a half-eaten sandwich, the keys. For a moment he was unsure whether to risk losing the fantasy by attempting to open it. If he pulled on the handle and the door opened, he would gain a safe place to spend the night. But if it was locked, he would lose even the illusion of happiness. *Only a tired and thirsty man lost in the night thinks such thoughts.* Then he gave the door handle a tug.

Suddenly a hand grabbed his shoulder. Startled by the touch, Paul leaped to one side, hands up to protect his face, ready to fight. "I'm not going back. I'm not and you can't make me!" And then he saw that he was standing face-to-face with Brody. "What are you doing out here?" He reached out with his hand and touched Brody's face. "You are real, aren't you?"

"I was about to ask you the same question."

Esther pushed between them, locked her arms around Paul's neck, and buried her face in his chest. "I can't believe it," she sobbed as all the pent-up frustration now found release in the tears that flowed down her cheeks.

"It's me," he replied, wrapping his arms around her. He pulled her even closer and leaned forward to kiss her. "I'm afraid I don't smell very pleasant," he chuckled.

"You smell like Paul, and that's all that matters to me."

They stood there a moment, locked in an embrace, then Paul glanced over at Brody. "Got anything to drink? I've been wandering out here all day."

"Get in the SUV." Brody started toward the driver's door. "We'll be back at the hotel in a few minutes."

Paul climbed in back with Esther and she rested her head against his shoulder. "I saw them take you."

"I thought that was you."

"You saw me?"

"I saw the car."

"Are you hurt?"

"I don't think so."

"Who was the man they took with you?"

"Bill Sisson. The fourth man in the break-in team."

"They have him now? What did they do to him?"

Paul sat up straight. "They're planning something else." He turned to face her. "In Los Angeles in two days."

"How do you know this?"

"I overheard them talking. Yesterday." He leaned back and closed his eyes. "I think it was yesterday." He ran his fingers over his forehead. "I can't remember."

"So, it was two days from today, or two days from yesterday?"

"Yesterday."

"That makes it tomorrow."

"Word of Life Tabernacle." He sat up straight once more. "That's what they said. Something about the Word of Life Tabernacle."

Brody glanced in the rearview mirror. "I think we should get him to a doctor. He doesn't look well and he's sounding very strange."

"That's what they said," Paul insisted. "Word of Life Tabernacle. Los Angeles. Two days." He squinted and leaned his head back. "Esther? Esther? This is not a drill, soldier. This is not a dr ..."

CHAPTER 112
WASHINGTON, D.C.

PHILIPPE JOBERT WAITED as the plane came to a stop at the gate. When the flight attendant stood to open the fuselage door, he unhooked his seat belt and collected his jacket from the compartment overhead. Then he started up the aisle and into the jet-way.

Moments later he emerged inside the terminal and walked down the corridor. Ahead, standing just beyond the security station, he caught sight of Isabelle Clavier, his girlfriend of fifteen years. When he drew near, he placed his arm around her waist and pulled her close. She kissed him lightly on the lips and smiled. "I have missed you."

"But I was only gone for a few days."

"I know. But the days seem longer now." He released her from his grasp and she took his arm. Together they strolled through the terminal toward the baggage claim area. "Did you remember to bring Corinne a present?"

"What father would forget a gift for his own daughter?"

"One never knows." She nuzzled his neck. "You are a busy man."

"And are you not curious about the gift I brought for you?"

She squeezed his arm. "You are my gift."

"Ahh," he grinned. "Then I should enjoy watching you unwrap that gift."

Baggage in hand, they walked from the terminal and started toward the car. Jobert felt the cell phone vibrating in his pocket. He ignored it and continued across the parking lot. When they reached the car, he opened the door for Isabelle and waited while she took a seat. Then he stepped to the rear bumper and opened the trunk. With the trunk lid shielding her from view, he took the cell phone from his pocket and checked the screen.

A one-word message read, "Assignment." He scrolled past it and found a photograph of a man who appeared to be in his early fifties. Beneath the picture was the name— David McNeil. The sight of it caught him off guard. Over the years he had executed many orders. Some had regarded people of little public significance, others of great renown. But never one of such prominence in the United States.

The car door opened and Isabelle leaned out. "Is there a problem?"

Jobert exited the message and returned the phone to his pocket. "No problem," he smiled. "Just checking the phone." He placed the bag in the trunk, closed the lid, and came around to the driver's side of the car.

As he slid behind the steering wheel, he smiled playfully. "Do we have time for you to unwrap your gift before Corinne gets home from school?"

"If we hurry."

"Then by all means." He started the car. "Let's hurry."

CHAPTER 113
MEXICO

WHEN PAUL REGAINED consciousness he was lying on a bed in a hotel room. Sunlight streamed through a window nearby. A ceiling fan turned slowly overhead. The breeze from it felt cool against his skin. He glanced to the side and saw Esther sitting in a chair. She smiled at him. "You're back with us?"

"Yes, I think so. What happened?"

"You were unconscious."

"For how long?"

"We found you last night."

The door opened and Brody entered. Esther glanced in his direction. "Did you find him?"

"No, and no one seems to remember seeing him."

"Who?" Paul frowned. "Who are you talking about?"

"The man in the SUV with us last night," Esther replied. "After we got back with you he just disappeared. We wanted to ask him a few more questions about the facility."

Paul's eyes opened wide. "What time is it?"

She glanced at her watch. "Almost ten. Why?"

"Did you figure it out?"

"Figure what out?"

"The connection. Sisson and Word of Life Tabernacle."

"No," she said, shaking her head. "We thought you were delirious."

"He's still delirious," Brody quipped.

"It doesn't matter," Paul sighed. "It's probably too late now anyway."

Esther took her iPhone from the dresser and loaded a Google APP, "Word of Life Tabernacle."

"Don't encourage him," Brody said, interrupting.

Esther ignored him. "Go ahead, Paul." She glanced down at him. "What else?"

"Los Angeles. But it's probably already happened. They said two days. I just can't remember which day they were talking about."

"Okay." She stared at the iPhone but her face was alive with interest. "This may be something."

"What?"

"David McNeil is coming there for a rally. Part of Morris Wythe's church campaign tour."

Paul thought for a moment. David McNeil ... Sierra Resources ... Bill Sisson ... the documents that were sent to Liston Cook's *office*. He couldn't make it all fit together but he was certain this was what Walcott was talking about. He looked over at Esther. "That must be it. Whatever they were talking about was big, and I can't see how it gets any bigger at that church than an appearance by Morris Wythe and a Republican presidential candidate."

"You think they're going to hit David McNeil?"

"I don't know. But something is going to happen. What else can it be?"

"They had a big shake-up in McNeil's campaign a few days ago. Fired his chief of staff. Went off message in a speech on immigration, actually reversing his previous position."

"Maybe someone doesn't like it." Paul sat up in bed. "Maybe it's something else. Maybe they're going to hit someone else or something is going to happen that has nothing to do with this. But if Sisson is going to the Word of Life Tabernacle in Los Angeles, it isn't going to be good. He's not trained to hand out bulletins on Sunday morning."

Brody frowned. "What are you doing?"

"I'm getting out of bed."

"For what?"

"To go to Los Angeles."

"You're in no condition to go anywhere."

Esther looked over at Brody. "Can you get us to Los Angeles before morning?"

"Yes."

"Good." She moved Paul's shoes closer to the bed and handed him a pair of pants. "Let's go."

CHAPTER 114
LOS ANGELES

THE FOLLOWING MORNING, with Brody's help, Esther and Paul boarded a Gulfstream Jet with him at the airport in Hermosillo. A little before noon, they landed in Los Angeles and rented a car. Using the navigation app on Esther's iPhone, they located the Word of Life Tabernacle at Fairfax Avenue and Pickford Street. As they drove toward it they encountered increasing traffic as cars and buses jammed the streets.

"We'll never make it like this," Paul lamented.

In the center of the block a car pulled away from the curb and darted ahead of them into traffic. Brody hit the brakes hard to avoid hitting it, then swerved to the right and steered the car into the vacant space. He switched off the engine and opened the door. "Let's go. We can make it if we walk." Paul and Esther climbed out and followed after him.

By the time they arrived, crowds thronged the street in front of the church. Supporters stood on the church side of the street with official McNeil campaign signs that read, "McNeil For President," "Pro Life— For Everyone," and "Capital Punishment Destroys a Life Too."

Across the street, protestors were formed in ranks, waving placards and shouting. The signs read, "Illegal Immigrants are Destroying America," "Cast Off the Anchor Babies" and "An Illegal Stole My Job."

Slogans and insults were hurled back and forth between the groups, but for the most part they kept their distance. Secret Service agents guarded the doors of the church and police snipers, armed and ready, patrolled the rooftops of adjoining buildings. Paul and Esther climbed the steps in an attempt to enter the sanctuary but were stopped by a woman wearing a McNeil button. "Do you have a ticket?" she asked.

"No, but I need to see the governor."

"I'm sorry, but unless you have a ticket, you can't get inside."

"I think something is—"

Esther grabbed his arm, interrupting him, and she smiled at the woman. "Thank you. We'll arrange to see him with an appointment." She led Paul down the steps partway and leaned near him. "Don't say that."

"If I told her why we were here, the Secret Service guys would take us right to him."

"No," Esther corrected. "Those Secret Service guys would take you into custody and haul you down to the Orange County Jail. And an hour from now, after whatever's going to happen has already occurred, they'll come to you and say, 'Now, what was it you were trying to say?' Only then it will be too late."

"So, what do we do?"

"I don't know." She glanced around the crowd. "Do you know anyone with the campaign?"

"No. I don't. I only know—" Through the crowd to the right he caught a glimpse of Taylor Rutledge standing on the far side of the steps. "What's he doing here? That guy," Paul pointed. "Down there. About three steps below us. In front of the lady in the red dress."

"That's Rutledge."

"Yeah. He's a long way from home. Why's he out here?"

"There's a rumor going around Washington that the Attorney

General has convened a grand jury to investigate McNeil. I wonder if he's here about that."

"Maybe he can help us." Paul took Esther by the hand and started in that direction. She said something about no one believing them but her voice was drowned out as the roar of the crowd rose even louder.

Behind them, a long line of black SUVs rolled to a stop in front of the church. Doors opened and David McNeil stepped out. He waved to the crowd, then started toward the steps. A security team fanned out ahead of him, carving a space through the crowd to the church doors. McNeil started in that direction, shaking hands and working the crowd as he slowly made his way up the steps.

As McNeil inched forward, Caldwell came from the far side of the SUV. He walked around the front bumper to the sidewalk, trailing behind McNeil. Suddenly a gunshot echoed through the air. Caldwell clutched at his shoulder. There was a gaping hole in the front of his jacket and blood spewed out, casting a fine red mist over the crowd. Those nearest to him sagged back, then turned and ran, trampling each other to get out of the way. Before they had gone very far, a second shot rang out and Caldwell's head exploded. His body pitched forward, bounced on the concrete, and slid to the curb. Blood oozed out in a puddle.

The crowd, already moving away, broke into a stampede as people raced to escape. Secret Service agents, already on the move after the first shot, lifted McNeil from his feet, shielded him with their bodies, and carried him into the building. Other agents appeared on the steps, armed with automatic rifles, which they held at the ready as they surveyed the buildings across the street in an attempt to find the shooter.

Esther turned to run, but Paul stood still. She tugged at him and shouted, "Let's go or we'll die, too."

"No," he replied calmly, letting his eyes roam from window to window. "This is what they were talking about. Only, I thought it was McNeil they were after."

"Caldwell was the connection," Brody said, suddenly appearing at their side.

Paul glanced at him. "You know that for a fact?"

"Yes. We found that out from our source." Brody looked over at Esther. "And Barberini confirmed it. Caldwell was the link between McNeil and Sierra."

"And Manos Dianellos was the link in Athens for the money."

Brody looked startled. "You know about Athens?"

"I know about ... Wait!" Paul exclaimed, pointing toward the building. "The fourth floor."

"What about it?"

"That's what Walcott said. Go to the fourth floor." Paul concentrated on that level and at the seventh window he saw a shadow. "That's him." He charged down the steps.

"Wait!" Esther shouted. "Don't go in there."

But Paul was already threading his way past the policemen who crowded the scene. When he reached the sidewalk he bolted into the street, maneuvered around a parked car, and rushed inside the building.

Still moving at a run, he made his way across the lobby, searching left and right in a frantic attempt to find Sisson. As he neared the rear exit, he glanced down a hall to the right. Just then, a door burst open and Sisson appeared, carrying a rifle. Paul pivoted in that direction and ran after him. "Wait," he shouted. "It's me. Paul."

Sisson turned to face him and raised the rifle. The barrel was pointed at Paul. He stopped and slowly lifted his hands in the air. Then he remembered the phrase. "We serve God and country," he said between gasps for breath, "to protect and defend."

Sisson's eyes opened wide in a terrified look of realization, as if awakening from a bad dream only to find it was reality. He lowered the rifle, staring blankly at it. Paul crept forward. Sisson looked up, dazed and confused. "What happened?" He threw down the rifle and it rattled on the floor. "Why do I have this?" He pointed to it and shouted, "Why do I have a gun?"

"It's okay." Paul stepped closer. "There are people who can help. I'll help."

"Help me what? I don't even know how I got here."

"It's okay," Paul spoke in a calm voice. "It's okay. It isn't you."

"What are you talking about?"

"It's the implants."

"Implants?" Sisson frowned. "What implants?"

"The ones they put in your brain."

"Are you crazy? Why are you talking like this?"

"I was there with you. Dr. Walcott. Hopkins. The facility in Mexico."

At the mention of those names, Sisson's eyes opened wide. "Stop! Stop! Stop!" he shouted. "You're making me remember." He put his hands to his head. "I don't want to remember."

"It's okay to remember." Paul was beside him now and he put his hand on Sisson's shoulder. Then the sound of footsteps caught his ear and he glanced over his shoulder to check. "But right now we have to move."

"What?"

"We have to go. There's a tracking chip in your shoulder."

"A what?"

"A tracking chip. They know where you are."

"Who knows?"

"Walcott. Sierra Resources. We can take it out. You can be free. But we have to get you to someplace safe first."

There was a sound behind them and four men appeared at the end of the hall. Dressed in dark suits, they were armed with pistols. They pointed them down the hall and one man shouted in a loud voice, "Secret Service. Get on the floor!"

Sisson looked at Paul. "You have no idea who they are. Or who they work for."

"But I know someone who can help. We can trust him."

Sisson shook his head. "I'm not trusting anyone." He backed

down the hall a few steps, then bolted through a door to the right and disappeared.

"Halt!" the agents shouted. But Sisson was already gone.

Paul, still standing in the hall, inched backward with shuffling steps as he struggled to make up his mind. Caught between agents he didn't trust and Sisson who didn't trust him, there was no time to weigh the options, only time to react. The agents came closer, weapons drawn and ready. Whatever he was going to do, it would have to be quick. At the last second, as the agents reached out to grab his arm, Paul darted through the door and followed after Sisson.

CHAPTER 115
LOS ANGELES

ESTHER AND BRODY HAD WATCHED in horror as Paul ran across the street into the building. Esther's heart raced at the thought of losing him yet again, but she was frozen in fear, unable to move. Then Taylor Rutledge appeared at her side. "What is he doing?" he shouted.

"I don't know," Esther cried. "He just took off. I tried to stop him but he kept going."

A group of men, all of them dressed in dark suits and armed with pistols, started toward the building, close on Paul's heels. Rutledge pointed in their direction. "Well, whatever he's doing, I hope he does it before they get there."

"Who are they?"

"Secret Service. Come on." Rutledge led the way down the steps. When they reached the street, Esther felt the cell phone vibrate in her hand. She glanced at the screen and saw the call was from Paul.

"Wait," she shouted and held up the phone. "It's Paul."

Brody and Rutledge stood in the street, waiting, while Esther took the call.

"We're about a dozen blocks away," Paul's voice was tense, the words coming rapidly.

"What are you doing?"

"We're parked in an alley. Find Rutledge. He was standing near the steps before the shooting started. Get him over here. Fast. I have Bill Sisson with me."

"Why?"

"He's the shooter. Find Rutledge and get over here fast."

The call ended and Esther ran to catch up with Rutledge. "Paul has Sisson. They're in an alley about twelve blocks from here."

"Did he tell you where?"

"No, but I can track him from my phone."

Rutledge hesitated a moment, then turned. "Come on. I have a car."

With Brody in tow, they ran to the next corner, then up the street to a parking lot behind the church. Rutledge took a remote from his pocket and pressed it. Lights on a car blinked. They ran toward it and got in. Esther took the passenger seat in front. Brody climbed in back. Rutledge backed the car from the lot. "You got them yet?"

Esther opened a page on her iPhone, then tapped the screen twice. "I'm working on it."

"Work fast." He put the car in gear and turned to her. "Which way?"

"Okay." She tapped the screen once more, then opened it wider with her fingers. "They're on Venice Boulevard."

Rutledge pressed the gas pedal and the car started forward. At the next corner they turned right on Airdrome Street. "This takes us to Venice. Which way?"

"Right. They're in an alley behind Dap Studios."

"That tells me nothing," Rutledge snapped. "I need a street." He slowed the car as they approached Venice Boulevard, then made the turn. Horns blared and tires screeched as they darted into traffic. "Which way? Which way?"

"Left," she shouted as the car shot past a cross street.

"Where?"

"You missed it. Take the next one."

"Where?"

"There." She pointed out the windshield. "Right there." Rutledge turned the car in that direction, narrowly missing oncoming traffic. "Now left again."

"Where?"

"The first left." She pointed again. "There. That alley."

Rutledge braked the car and made the turn at the same time. They bounced into the alley and rolled to a stop behind a white Toyota. Rutledge climbed from the driver's seat and drew a pistol from beneath his jacket. "Wait here." But by then Esther was out of the car. She and Brody followed close behind as they approached the car.

The passenger door opened and Paul, with his hands above his head, stepped cautiously from the car. "He's behind the steering wheel."

"Is he armed?"

"No."

Rutledge moved to the rear bumper. He pointed his pistol through the rear window of the car and aimed it at Sisson's head. "Open the door slowly and come out with your hands up."

"I don't think he can respond," Paul replied.

"Why not?"

"He's in pretty bad shape."

"He's injured?"

"Not physically." Paul stepped back to the passenger door and leaned inside the car. "It's okay," he said with a calm voice. "They can help."

The driver's door swung open and Sisson turned sideways on the seat. He raised his hands in the air. Rutledge returned the pistol to its holster and took a pair of handcuffs from his pocket. With his free hand he helped Sisson from the car, then turned him toward it and slipped the cuffs on his wrists.

"I told him you could help him," Paul began.

"With what?"

"The implants."

"What are you talking about?"

"Sierra Resources."

"What about it?"

"They operate a facility in Mexico where they conduct an experimental program. On humans."

"Well, he'll have a long time to explain it."

"Where are you taking him?"

"Right now to jail. After that, I'm not sure what will happen to him."

"I promised him you would help him."

"I can't promise anything."

"He has a tracking chip."

"What kind of tracking chip?"

"One that tells them where he is at all times. You might start by looking for that."

"Thanks for the tip." Rutledge put Sisson in the back seat of the Chevrolet and closed the door. "You'll have to find your own way back." He opened the driver's door. "I have to get going." He climbed in behind the wheel and backed the car toward the street.

CHAPTER 116
RICHMOND, VIRGINIA

JACK LEA ARRIVED at the governor's mansion to find it surrounded by armed guards. He stopped at the front gate and was cleared into the compound by a Secret Service agent. Inside the house he was escorted to the second floor where McNeil was waiting in his private study. Curtains and shades were drawn. McNeil sat in a chair in the corner, where the angle to the windows made it less likely he could be hit by gunfire. "Sorry to put you through all this," he said.

"No problem."

"We had to meet up here for privacy, but they won't even let me sit at the desk."

"That's all right. We can talk from here."

"Were you out there when Henry was shot?"

"No." Lea shook his head. He took a seat and placed a notepad on his lap. "I ... wasn't even at the church."

"Good. You wouldn't want those images in your head." McNeil closed his eyes and pressed his fingers against them. "I can't get it to stop."

"You want me to call someone who can help? There are psychologists who specialize in trauma."

"I'll be all right," McNeil sighed. He moved his hands from his face and gave a forced smile. "What do we need to talk about?"

"We're meeting them at the FBI building downtown."

"Why can't they just come here?"

"They set the location."

"Are they going to arrest me?"

"No. But you are the target of an investigation. One of the targets."

"How did you find that out?"

"They told me."

"You just asked, and they told you? Just like that?"

"If you're a target of their investigation, and you ask, they're required to tell."

"Oh."

"So, we're going to this meeting as a courtesy to them. They can ask whatever they want. You don't have to answer if the answer would incriminate you. But if you answer, you have to tell the truth."

"What does that mean?" McNeil had a quizzical expression. "Incriminate?"

"If it implies criminal activity."

"I know, but where does one draw the line?"

"I'll help you."

"You'll be there with me?"

"Yes. But I can't answer for you."

Nikki appeared at the door. She was wearing a black dress with high-heeled shoes and a pearl necklace. McNeil turned in her direction. She gave him a warm smile. "I'll be downstairs when you're ready."

Lea caught her eye with a look of concern. "You aren't going with us."

"Yes," she nodded. "I am."

"I don't think that's a good idea." His eyes darted from Nikki to McNeil and back again. He gave the slightest shake of his head. "You should stay here."

She responded with a knowing look. "My husband is the governor of Virginia. I am his wife. The people should see me at his side."

"It'll be fine," McNeil added. "She can sit outside while they question me."

"But if she's there, they can question her."

"I don't mind," Nikki replied. "Let them do whatever they want." She let her eyes focus on Lea. "I'm ready for whatever happens."

Lea and McNeil talked awhile longer, then walked downstairs to the first floor. Secret Service agents met them and escorted them outside. A motorcade was assembled on the driveway with a black SUV in the lead. Behind it was the governor's Cadillac limousine, followed by two more SUVs. Agents led McNeil and Nikki toward the limousine. Lea walked to the SUV directly behind them. When everyone was seated and ready, the motorcade started down the driveway and turned onto the street.

Lea sat in back on the driver's side and as the cars made the turn, he caught a glimpse of Nikki, barely visible through the tinted window. Guilt swept over him as they moved forward and picked up speed. That was his place beside the governor, not hers.

CHAPTER 117
RICHMOND, VIRGINIA

JOBERT STEERED THE CAR from Broad Street into a parking deck opposite the campus of Virginia Commonwealth University. Dented and rusted, the car rattled and smoked as he bounced from the street and up the ramp. Jobert wore jeans and a hooded sweatshirt. With a three-day beard and sunglasses, he was unrecognizable.

On the second level he turned the car into an empty space and took a handkerchief from his pocket. He wiped down the dash and front seat, then the steering wheel and door panel. Satisfied the car was clean, he opened the door and stepped out.

He walked across the deck in an easy, unhurried pace to the railing at the far side. From there he had a clear view of the street below. He glanced to the east in time to see the governor's motorcade two blocks away and headed in his direction. A black SUV led the way with the limousine behind and motorcycles flanking either side. Jobert checked his watch and walked toward the elevator at the corner of the building. As he did, he slid his hand inside the pocket of the hoodie and wrapped it around the cell phone. He felt for a button in the center near the screen. As he approached, the elevator doors opened and a young woman stepped out. She turned and walked toward the opposite side of the building. When she was well back from the Broad Street side, he felt with his fingers for the cell phone and pressed the Send button.

Instantly, an explosion rocked the building and it swayed from side to side. Dust rose in the air and when he turned to look, Jobert saw the façade on the Broad Street side had been torn away.

He continued past the elevator and walked calmly to the stairs. At the bottom, he stepped out to the street and walked to the corner. From there he saw the governor's limousine engulfed in flames. The SUV behind it was stopped and agents were in the street. Some of them tried in vain to reach the car. Others, looking bewildered and confused, surveyed the surrounding buildings. Jobert searched each face for any sign of Jack Lea, but he saw only the blank stares of the agents.

Then a rear window on the SUV lowered. Lea poked his head out and looked around. Jobert waited until Lea looked in his direction and for an instant their eyes met. Then Jobert turned away and walked in the opposite direction. As he did, he placed his hand in his pocket once more and felt for a small remote. About the size of a garage door opener, it had only a single button in the center. With his hand still in his pocket, he pressed the button and listened as a second explosion rocked the street.

CHAPTER 118

WASHINGTON, D.C.

DURING THE WEEK THAT FOLLOWED, Paul sat at home and stared at the television as news shows replayed scenes from Los Angeles and Richmond. With each version, commentators recounted one more time the horrible scene of the gunshots that killed Caldwell and the explosions that ended McNeil's life. And with every show Paul's mind returned again and again to the compound in Mexico and the men he'd seen there. Trapped in an endless cycle of memories, he was immobilized by fear, grief, and depression, unable to work or engage in the normal daily routine.

Esther brought dinner each evening and sat with him on the sofa until late at night. When he talked, she listened, but she avoided giving simple answers and advice. He'd been through a lot, both physically and mentally, and she didn't want to rush him through the recovery process.

For Paul the worst part wasn't reliving the shooting in Los Angeles or even the treatment he'd endured at the Sierra facility. What troubled him most was the memory of Steven and the others like him, helpless victims of Walcott's experiments. Over and over again he saw them shuffling down the hall, drooling, mumbling to themselves, arms dangling, feet dragging. And each time the video on television showed the gunshots that killed Henry Caldwell, he relived the moment Sisson shot the man in the examination room. Again and again he saw the pistol in Sisson's hand with the barrel pressed against the man's head. He heard the shot and saw the fine red mist as it covered the men who stood nearby.

Finally, he could stand it no more. He stuffed a change of clothes in a backpack, left a note on the kitchen counter, and headed to the airport. From Dulles, he flew to Phoenix, Arizona, and rented a car. Brody was right— there was a State Department order regarding travel to northern Mexico, but it was a warning, not a restriction. Paul crossed the border at Agua Prieta without incident and continued down Highway 17.

Shortly before noon he arrived in Los Hovos. South of town he located an unpaved road that matched the description he'd heard Esther and Brody discuss. He turned onto it and drove east from the highway. A few minutes later he passed the landing strip and a little farther came to a hill. At the crest he brought the car to a stop and stared out the windshield. *This is the hill where I found the SUV.* He opened the door and climbed out.

Near the front fender he paused and surveyed the flat grassland that spread before him. In the distance, the compound with its fence and buildings shimmered in the midday sun. Even from the hill he could see the building to the right had been damaged by fire, and it looked as though the main gate was open.

"I suppose I should get help," he mumbled to himself. "But who would I get?" In his heart he knew there was no one to help the men in the compound. No one but him. After a few minutes he returned to the car and got in behind the steering wheel. The car started forward and picked up speed as it rolled down the backside of the hill.

A mile beyond the hill, the road curved to the right. As he rounded it, the compound once again came into view. The gates were open and unmanned but several trucks were parked in the compound. Paul slowed the car as he entered the compound and glanced warily in both directions. Veins in his neck pulsed and he wondered why the place was so deserted and whether he'd made a mistake.

Beyond the gate two storage buildings stood end to end, separated by a passage large enough to drive between them. Through that opening he saw a larger structure that ran the length of the compound. He recognized it as the building where he'd been kept. As he watched, a door to the building opened and a line of men appeared. Disfigured and deformed, they shuffled from the building, some barely able to move. Each one was tied at the wrist with a rope to the man in front. Slowly they made their way to the left, one torturous step at a time. One or two of the faces seemed familiar but he recognized no one until the last man appeared.

"Steven," he whispered. Suddenly the fear and apprehension he'd felt just moments before evaporated. In its place came anger and indignation.

Just then Walcott emerged from the building. He had a pistol in his hand and he gestured with it in Paul's direction, shouting. Seconds later a guard appeared from the corner of the storage building. He was armed with an automatic rifle and pointed it in Paul's direction. Shots rang out and struck the ground, kicking up puffs of dust as they moved closer and closer to the car.

Paul put the car in reverse and shoved down on the gas pedal. He turned sideways in the seat and drove backward with one arm over the seat, looking out the rear window. He steered the car toward the gate, then turned to the right and came around the far end of the compound. As he did, he had a clear view of the men as they walked in a line toward the corner of the fence. A backhoe was parked there next to a large mound of dirt. Guards impatiently herded the men in that direction.

Paul aimed the car for the nearest guard and pressed his foot harder against the gas pedal. The guard raised his rifle and pointed it in Paul's direction. A shot rang out. It struck the rear window and the glass exploded. Paul ducked at the sound of it but recovered and pressed the gas pedal closer to the floor. The guard stood his ground and continued to fire the rifle. Bullets passed through the car, striking the front windshield. All the while, the car moved faster and faster. Too late to move, the guard realized he was in trouble. His eyes were wide as the bumper struck him at the knees and he disappeared from sight. The wheels of the car made a thumping sound as they rolled over him.

Still the line of men continued dutifully toward the corner of the compound. Paul turned the car and brought it back around toward them.

This time he aimed at the guard in front and once again pressed the gas pedal to the floor. The guard stepped aside, calmly raised a rifle to his shoulder, and pointed it at the tires. With little effort, he fired off successive rounds. The car shook violently as the tires exploded.

Paul continued past the line of men and turned the car behind the storage building. He brought it to a stop near a pickup truck and jumped out. In the cab of the truck he found the keys hanging from the ignition. He climbed inside, started the truck, and drove it from behind the building. By then the men were already behind the mound of dirt. Paul steered the truck in that direction.

Behind the mound was a large hole, and the men were spread out along the edge of it. Hands at their sides, they stood still and unmoving, facing the hole. Near the fence were four guards armed with automatic weapons. They raised their weapons to their shoulders and pointed them toward the men.

Paul steered the truck in between the two groups, then spun the steering wheel hard to the left. The rear end of the truck swung around to the left, sending a cloud of dust in the air. He lifted his foot from the gas pedal long enough to let the truck recover, then pressed it to the floor again and drove toward the guards. Wide-eyed, they leaped out of the way as the truck roared toward them.

With no room to stop, the pickup collided with the fence. The force of the crash sent Paul forward. He banged his chin against the steering wheel and flopped backward against the seat, dazed and confused. Though stunned by the collision, he shifted the truck into reverse and backed away, placing the truck between the guards and the men.

When he reached the hole, he tumbled from the cab and shouted, "Get in the truck. Get in the truck." Those who were nimble enough to walk climbed in back, but three struggled to put one foot in front of the other. Seconds ticked by as they slowly made their way toward the truck.

Before they reached it, Walcott appeared from behind the mound of dirt. He held a rifle and he pointed it toward them. "It's too late," he shouted. "You can't help them. They have nothing more to offer anyone."

Only one man remained and he shuffled toward the truck. Steven started toward him to help, and Paul turned to face Walcott. "It doesn't have to end like this."

"Yes, it does," Walcott replied. "I have no choice."

"There's always a choice."

"Not now."

Walcott squeezed off a shot from the rifle. A bullet struck the ground near Steven's feet. Then a second struck his arm. Blood splattered his face and chest. Paul ran to his side and picked him up. "My name is Steven," he said. "I pick up the trash."

Paul carried him to the truck and set him in back with the others. Another shot rang out and struck the fender. Paul helped the last man into the truck, then ran to the cab and climbed in behind the wheel.

Walcott pointed the rifle toward the truck once more and fired a shot. This one struck the driver's door, just below the window, passed through the metal, and lodged in the seat beneath Paul's thigh. His heart pounded as he put the truck in gear.

Meanwhile, the guards gathered themselves from the dirt and ran toward the front gate. As Paul steered the truck in that direction, the guards reached the gate and struggled to move it by hand. The truck bounced across the compound and reached the gate as the men swung it into place, but Paul never lifted his foot.

CHAPTER 119
MEXICO

DUST FLEW IN THE AIR BEHIND the truck as they raced across the grassland. Suddenly a helicopter popped over the hill. Flying low, wash from the prop blew the grass, swirling it from side to side. Behind it was a second and then a third. All of them painted black, with no insignia or numbers. The sight of them filled Paul with fear— were they Sierra's, bringing men to capture them, or were they Mexican authorities come at last to investigate the stories of horror and torture they surely must have heard by now?

As they reached the hill, Paul hesitated and lifted his foot from the gas pedal. The landing strip was on the other side, which meant Sierra could be there in force with well-armed men. *And more helicopters like the ones I just saw.* But a quick review of the situation reminded him the road was the only way out, and that left him no choice but to continue. Maybe, if they were traveling fast, they could blow past whoever was down there and get to the highway first. He pressed the gas pedal. The truck's engine lugged as it started up the grade, then the transmission downshifted and the truck climbed quickly to the top.

From the crest of the hill, the airstrip came into view. A Gulfstream Jet was parked at the end nearest the road. Standing next to it was Taylor Rutledge and beside him was Esther. Tears streamed down Paul's cheeks.

He rested his foot against the gas pedal. The truck idled forward, then picked up speed. When they reached the bottom, he let it coast to a stop near the runway.

Esther was waiting as he climbed from the truck. She wrapped her arms around his waist and squeezed him close. "Don't you ever do this to me again."

"I see you got the note."

She pinched his side. "You should have called me."

"You would have never let me come."

"No, I wouldn't. I'm getting too old for this."

Paul wrapped his arms around her neck and kissed her. As they embraced, Rutledge appeared. "Is this all of them?" he asked, gesturing toward the truck.

"All I could find. And one of them is hurt." Paul pulled away from Esther and walked to the back of the truck. Steven lay there, surrounded by the others. His arm was bloody but he smiled up at them.

"My name is Steven. I pick up the trash."

"It's okay." Paul reached over and tousled his hair. "There are people here who will help you."

Rutledge made a phone call and in a few minutes a helicopter appeared. It landed by the road and collected Steven and the others. When they were gone, Rutledge turned to Paul. "We're making progress with Sisson. He's actually doing well for someone who's been through that kind of trauma."

"You found an implant?"

"Yes. And a tracking chip, just like you said. We're still trying to read the data from them, but Sisson is starting to recover."

"Think he'll ever lead a normal life?"

"The doctors think so. As normal as he had before all of this."

"What about the Order? Still think they don't exist?"

"I'm still working on that one," Rutledge smiled. "But I'm making progress." He turned away and started toward the jet. "Come on," he called. "I'll give you a ride home."

ACKNOWLEDGEMENTS

My deepest gratitude and sincere thanks to Joe Hilley, Lanelle Shaw-Young, Arlen Young, Peter Gloege, Janna Nysewander, and a host of people who had input in making this book happen.

Thank you for the hours and hours of time devoted to making *The Candidate* possible.

AUTHOR'S NOTE

THE FIRST QUESTION an author is often asked is: What prompted you to write this book?

Before answering that question, let me pose three more important questions and their answers:

- *What is the real reason for the ongoing conflict in the Middle East between the Jewish and Muslim populations?*

- *What is the root of that reason?*

- *What is the source of that root?*

Q: *What is the real reason for the ongoing conflict in the Middle East between the Jewish and Muslim populations?*

A: It is important to establish that the conflict in the Middle East has never been about a Palestinian state. It's not about the division of Jerusalem, checkpoints, fences, land or borders. The issue is Israel's right to exist as a nation.

The refusal of the Arab world to accept Israel as a nation is at the heart of the conflict that has raged since May 14, 1948. Until this is acknowledged as the sole barrier to meaningful dialogue, there will never be peace, and in fact the very phrase "peace in the Middle East" becomes an oxymoron.

It is impossible for Israel to negotiate with an entity that refuses to acknowledge the Jewish state's very right to exist. This critical point of contention is ignored by those calling for Israel to capitulate and surrender her defensible borders. Many believe this refusal is nothing more than an honest misunderstanding or raw stubbornness. It is rather a total ignorance of the facts as they apply to the mindset of those urging Israel to give in to her detractors.

The Arab refusal to acknowledge Israel's right to exist as a nation, while at the same time posing as a true partner in seeking the emergence of a peaceful Palestinian state, is, perhaps, the greatest, longest running, and most widely accepted hoax ever perpetrated on a gullible world. The refusal to see this incongruity is remarkable.

Anti-Israeli sentiment has in fact become the new anti-Semitism. It makes Israel the new "collective Jew", and then assaults the individual Jew as an extension of the state.

Q: *What is the root of that reason?*

A: The real reason for the present Middle East conflict has an even more sinister and deeply established root....one that is consistently ignored by the world in spite of the overwhelming and repetitive proof of its existence. This root, expressed in history again and again, is played out everyday around the world. Blind, well-meaning people refuse to believe in its existence today for the same reason they refused to believe in the existence of the ovens and cattle cars of another day: Because it shocks their rational sensibilities. The real root is not merely Israel's right to exist as a *state,* but the right of the Jewish *people* to exist at all.

Peaceful co-existence has never been the goal, nor has the concept of Jews living dispersed in other lands without a country been an option. The real goal has been the very extermination of the Jewish race. This is why

Palestinian children are taught to hate and kill Jews from their first breath and why the Islamic world throws parties in the streets every time Jewish blood is shed. It is why in radical Islamic theology the successful maiming and murdering of Jews represents the highest aspiration many Palestinian mothers have for their children.

Does the world really believe that if the nation of Israel ceased to exist tomorrow, and all the Jews left Israel, and all territorial claims were abandoned by Israel forever, the joy over the shedding of Jewish blood would cease? History screams the answer: NO!

The Grand Mufti and Moslem Brotherhood were complicit in proposing and implementing the Final Solution when there was no Jewish state. The pogroms of Russia were not in response to some argument over deserted land on the East coast of the Mediterranean. The rockets raining down on Jewish homes today from Hezbollah in Lebanon and Hamas in Gaza are not about the soil upon which these homes are built.

The root cause of the Middle East conflict is the refusal to acknowledge the right of the Jewish state to exist, and the right of the Jewish *people* to exist. One is predicated on the other as surely as the dawn is predicated on the turning of the earth.

With this as the ultimate issue, what form will negotiations with Israel's enemies take?

Q: *What is the source of that root?*

A: What is the source of this Jewish hatred? What is the reason for this obvious and sinister racism? The answer to that question is also the answer of why I wrote the series on the *"The Protocols."*

The Protocols of the Learned Elders of Zion originated in France as a diatribe against the French government. It was taken to Russia and plagiarized in pre-revolutionary Russia as one more historical attempt to divert blame from those in power and cast it on the Jewish population. This may be obscure to most of the Gentile population, but every Jew in the world should be aware of its existence. They should be aware of the role it has played and continues to play in the rise and continuation of anti-Jewish sentiment and the hatred of the Jewish people around the world.

First published in Russia in 1903, *The Protocols of the Learned Elders of Zion* was translated into multiple languages, and disseminated internationally in the early part of the twentieth century. Henry Ford funded the printing of 500,000 copies which were distributed throughout the United States in the 1920s.

Adolf Hitler was a major proponent. It was studied, as if factual, in German classrooms after the Nazis came to power in 1933, despite having been exposed as fraudulent years before. In at least one scholar's opinion, the *Protocols of the Learned Elders of Zion* was Hitler's primary justification for initiating the Holocaust — his "warrant for genocide."

The book purports to document the minutes of a late 19th-century meeting of Jewish leaders discussing their goal of global Jewish control by subverting the morals of Gentiles, and by controlling the press and the world's economies. It is still widely available today, often offered as a genuine document, on the Internet and in print, in numerous languages.

Despite being proven a hoax as early as 1921, a large number of Arab and Muslim regimes and leaders have endorsed the protocols as authentic, including Presidents Gamal Abdel Nasser and Anwar Sadat of Egypt, one of the President Arifs of Iraq, King Faisal of Saudi Arabia, and Colonel Muammar al-Gaddafi of Libya. More recent endorsements have been made by the Grand Mufti of Jerusalem, Sheikh Ekrima Sa'id Sabri, and the education ministry of Saudi Arabia.

The 1988 charter of Hamas, a Palestinian Islamist group, states that *The Protocols of the Elders of Zion* embodies the plan of the Zionists:

> *"Today it is Palestine and tomorrow it may be another country or other countries. For Zionist scheming has no end, and after Palestine they will covet expansion from the Nile to the Euphrates. Only when they have completed digesting the area on which they will have laid their hand, they will look forward*

to more expansion, etc. Their scheme has been laid out in the Protocols of the Elders of Zion, *and their present [conduct] is the best proof of what is said there. Leaving the circle of conflict with Israel is a major act of treason and it will bring curses on its perpetrators. 'Who so on that day turns his back to them, unless maneuvering for battle or intent to join a company, he truly has incurred wrath from Allah, and his habitation will be hell, a hapless journey's end.'"*

Former US President Jimmy Carter, wrote a book entitled: *We Can Have Peace in the Holy Land: A Plan that Will Work.* Carter's solution is straightforward; Israel should embrace the Quartet's so-called peace plan. This plan is backed by a group known simply as "The Elders". Carter is one of three appointed as "Elders" to the Middle East. How could he ask the Jewish people to embrace a group known as The Elders?

Mr. Carter's plan is to allow the Quartet to solve the Middle East problem. He calls for "peace-loving organizations" such as Hezbollah and Hamas and states like Iran and Syria to be involved in the negotiating process in order to have peace in the Holy Land.

Carter refers to Jews again and again as "radicals," another word for terrorists. He called Menachem Begin a "radical" and then went on to describe him as the "most notorious terrorist in the region." Of course, he said the British said that, not him. He describes Benjamin Netanyahu as a "key political associate and naysayer" who was strongly opposed to Israel relinquishing control over the Sinai.

It appears that Jimmy Carter is revising history. The Benjamin Netanyahu I know was attending college during the Camp David meetings. In fact, when I recommended him to Begin for a government job, the prime minister did not even know who Benjamin was. I have no idea how Carter was so aware of Benjamin Netanyahu's political ideology; at that time, Benjamin was selling furniture.

The former president writes that Begin agreed to divide Jerusalem. I found that to be astonishing—especially since Mr. Begin had given me a copy of the letter he wrote to Jimmy Carter on September 17, 1978. He wrote:

"Dear Mr. President....On the basis of this law, the government of Israel decreed in July 1967 that Jerusalem is one city indivisible, the capital of the State of Israel."

According to Begin, Jimmy Carter informed him that the U.S. government did not recognize Jerusalem as Israel's capital. Begin told me he responded, "Excuse me sir, but the State of Israel does not recognize your non-recognition."

The former president writes that Prime Minister Menachem Begin agreed to a freeze on building Jewish settlements. Begin told me he had not agreed to a total freeze; he only agreed not to build new settlements for three months, during the negotiations. Carter gives the impression that he and Begin were close friends by saying that Begin and Sadat visited him in Plains to reaffirm the personal commitments each had made to the other.

I found that quite humorous; Mr. Begin told me he had refused to meet with Jimmy Carter when the president traveled to Jerusalem. At that time, he was no longer Prime Minister but was outraged that Carter had misrepresented events that had taken place during their meetings.

Carter viewed Yasser Arafat as a Middle East George Washington. He pens,

"We pursued the concept of non-violent resistance of Hamas leaders and gave them documentation and video presentations on the successful experiences of Mahatma Gandhi, Dr. Martin Luther King, Jr., and others."

Menachem Begin told me of a meeting with Carter during which he gave the president a list of cities in the United States with Bible names, i.e., Shiloh, Hebron and Bethel. He asked Carter, "Could you imagine the governor of Pennsylvania would proclaim that anyone could live in the city of Bethlehem, Pennsylvania, except Jews?" President Carter agreed that such a man, if he did such a thing, would be guilty of racism. Begin replied that he was governor of the state in which the original Bethlehem, and the original

Jericho, and the original Shiloh were located. He asked me, "Did Carter expect me to say that everybody could live in those cities except Jews?"

Why is the peace process so complicated? The Jews have suffered through forty-one years of non-stop attempts. To the Muslim world the answer is simple, Jews are Zionists—and Zionists are devils and must die.

TO SUMMARIZE:

What is the real reason for the ongoing conflict in the Middle East between the Jewish and Muslim populations?
The refusal of the Muslim world to accept Israel's right to exist as a nation.

What is the root of the problem?
The refusal of the Muslim world to accept the right of the Jewish people to exist at all.

What is the source of that root?
A fraudulent, anti-Semitic text purporting to describe a Jewish plan for achieving global domination, written in 1903, proven a hoax in 1921, but promoted around the world to this day by the enemies of Israel and the Jewish people as factual.

So we come back to the original question. Why did I write this book "The Protocols"?

FOR THREE REASONS:

1. It was written in order to expose the lie of *The Protocols of the Learned Elders of Zion* and to reveal the extent to which this lie has led to the ongoing hatred of the Jewish people and the state of Israel by her racist enemies.

2. It was written in fiction form in order to reach beyond an audience of scholars, academics and political pundits to the common man. Most are unaware of the extent to which even their own opinions about modern Israel and the Jewish people have been subtly influenced by the anti-Semitic slurs which ultimately flow from this hate literature.

3. It was written as part of my ongoing, forty-year, non-stop battle, in the United States and around the world, to fight with "the pen rather than the sword" both for the protection of the Jewish people and the guarantee of the right of the state of Israel to exist, within safe and secure borders, free from harassment, persecution, and war.

As a Christian Zionist, a *New York Times* best selling author, and an untiring and relentless friend of the nation of Israel I offer *The Protocols* as one more arrow in the quiver to slay the lies of anti-Semitism and expose the true motivations of her enemies.